From the international reviews of *Diamond Star Halo*:

'A Brontë-esque vibe... Murray's lush prose will put a spring in your step and a smile on your face.' *Independent*

'The style of this irresistible book recalls the lush landscapes and wordscapes of Dylan Thomas... This novel is a delight to read, clever, funny, lush and full of magnificent characters.' *Sydney Morning Herald*

'This is the first laugh-out-loud book of the year.' *Sunday Tribune* (Ireland)

'This beautifully told story is positively dripping with sharply ob-served nostalgia.' *Bella*

'A unique novel... A story with soul.' *Wales on Sunday*

'Life at Rockfarm is always slightly surreal (evening prayers start with Dear God and Otis Redding), which is just one of the many pleasures of this book that is partly about growing up, part family saga and part rock history... Star-studded.' *Herald Sun* (Australia)

'Written with wit and verve. It's not afraid to tackle the darkness on the edge of town ... but mostly it fizzes with a trashy energy of which that glam rock god Ziggy Stardust would have been proud.' *Tribune*

'A wonderful parade of characters sparkle out of this novel along-side a rock'n'roll songlist to die for... This funny, moving, magical, enchanting novel is as good as anything that ever came out of that studio, and I include the harmonies that Freddie Mercury put to-gether there for 'Bohemian Rhapsody'. This is a writer with a real voice, always human, never sentimental, and her zesty writing sparkles like the soundtrack she brings to your consciousness.' *Western Mail* (Cardiff)

'Murray writes affectionately about her eccentric cast of characters. She also handles the music motif well, with David Bowie providing the s...... ansgression.' *Final*

DIAMOND STAR HALO

TIFFANY MURRAY

To my dad, Fritz Fryer

Published by Portobello Books 2010
This paperback edition published 2011

Portobello Books
12 Addison Avenue
London
W11 4QR

A CIP catalogue record is available from the British Library

9 8 7 6 5 4 3 2 1

ISBN 978 1 84627 208 0

Printed and bound in Great Britain by CPI Bookmarque, Croydon

TEQUILA, 'STALLION BOYS'
RECORDED ROCKFARM AUGUST 1977

TRACK LISTING

DUST ROAD BLUES - 5.26   A. Connor / J. Connor

STALLION BOYS - 4.54   J. Connor

SILVER STUDDED NIGHT 5.42   A. Connor / J. Connor / H. Connor /
C. Connor / J. Connor / D. Connor / K. Connor / T. Connor / J. Connor

PRAIRIE GAL - 4.59   A. Connor

KENTUCKY KARTWHEEL - 3.05   A. Connor / J. Connor / H. Connor /
C. Connor / J. Connor / D. Connor / K. Connor / T. Connor / J. Connor

ON MY FAITHFUL KNEES - 4.53   A. Connor / J. Connor / H. Connor /
C. Connor / J. Connor / D. Connor / K. Connor / T. Connor / J. Connor

LITTLE GIRL - 3.32   A. Connor

SILVER BUS BLUES - 4.33   A. Connor / J. Connor

THE BOY'S SONG - 3.19   J. Connor

GOODBYE JENNY - 2.27   A. Connor

PART ONE:

1977

1.

The one thing my family can agree on – and what I can *swear* is true – is that Fred Connor came to us, we, the Llewelyns of Rockfarm, in the parched summer of 1977.

It was a big year for us. It was the beginning of it all.

First the bin men didn't come, and then it was the Queen's Jubilee (though we were Welsh, so that didn't mean much). When my big brother Vincent stole Mum's safety pins to sing along to a different *God Save the Queen*, our Nana Lew said times were shifting. When Elvis Presley, the King of Rock 'n' Roll, died, Nana told us *everything* had shifted.

After Elvis died, Nana said the Evil Eye was out, so she taught me how to give dead legs and snakebites, and how to pray backwards to her Saints in her *capel* made of bones, nestled like a shoulder blade into her hill. After Elvis, my mother stopped worrying about stones falling on her children; my baby sister Molly learned to growl, and Vincent wore Mum's cheese-cloth dress.

After Elvis, we found Fred Connor.

It was a day when the beech leaves were just thinking of colour and change; a day when the warm rain that pounded Rockfarm bubbled and spat. It was a day like any other day when we found Fred Connor wrapped up in a red cloak on one of our guest beds.

This baby was almost breathless; and he was the smallest I'd ever seen. Mum had us kids huddle round that piss-yellow candlewick cover to really take him in, and when she touched Fred's forehead with her cold wedding band, he opened his black eyes. I didn't understand what she meant when she squealed, 'Kids, come look! He's part seal-pup, part bloody Heathcliff.'

I do now.

Of course we all knew where Fred had come from, and it wasn't from the birds and the bees and the shaky knees of our parents: our dad hadn't picked him up, an urchin, one dark and stormy night, and Fred didn't fly half-cocked from Never Never Land, either. No, Fred Connor arrived at our farm weeks before with an American band called Tequila. Though Fred didn't arrive on his own two feet: Fred Connor kind of *floated*.

This is where I'll start then, though the truth is I don't know where to begin because I came out backwards.

'Arse-wise,' Nana Lew calls it; so maybe the story begins with Rockfarm: this home I was born to, this recording studio built by my freckle-handed father on his own Welsh mud.

Rockfarm: a place where rock stars in sunglasses roam, a place where farm cats have toes that run up their legs like pegs on a line.

My Rockfarm.

1

By the time the silver bus turned off the main road that would lead you to the rest of Wales, we were standing in a line in the courtyard. We had walked up the track from Nana's Big House, past her capel, past her glistening fields, because it was time.

Everything, even the crickets and the old bones beneath us, seemed to be waiting.

The courtyard was square. At one end were the stables with our horses, and at the other were the stables Dad had converted into a recording studio: drum solos and playback were our lullabies up here. This was where the bands lived. You see, Rockfarm was a grand farm, and it once belonged to an English Bastard. Now it was just us Llewelyns, and our guests.

A red chicken pecked at a plectrum in the dust at my feet, and I stared at its fleshy crown jiggling with each stab. I thought child-thoughts (you know – those blurry, tasty wisps of things that jump in pictures, fast as the score on a pinball machine).

I was wondering if chickens could swim.

I was wondering if I could eat cowpats.

I was wondering why my dad had a farm if he wasn't a farmer.

He was standing with us, my dad. My dad was conker-eyed. My dad was Ivan Comfort Llewelyn. Nana named him that because she knew her only son would be a comfort to *all* womankind.

'Where is this band from, Ivan?' my mother asked. Mum was balancing my baby sister Molly on a creamy hip. Mum and Molly were twins: dark glossy hair and dairy skin.

Mum glittered. Molly squeaked.

Dad grinned at them. 'They're all the way from America, Dolly love. Somewhere down South.'

'All that way just to come here. Oh, Ivan.'

I felt the flutter between my parents: a warm shiver, like you get stepping into a hot bath.

'And did you hear, Dolly? The eight of them are brothers.'

'No!'

'It's true.'

'That's a lot of feeding.'

Dad laughed. 'You can do it, love – you'll cook up a storm.'

He was right. This was what my mother did. My mother cooked for the rock stars, the bands, and she cooked cleverly. My mum matched taste with sound, and the musicians who recorded here came to depend upon her. In fact, my mother's recipes were encyclopaedic, they were prophetic, and she wrote them all down in a book called *Dolly Llewelyn's Book of Dishes*. You'll know a tune, maybe more, because my mother has fed anthems, classics, and one-hit wonders. Cross my heart and hope to die that without my mother's experiments with saffron and nutmeg, some of our best-loved songs would never have been.

I felt that flutter between my parents again. Our parents fluttered a lot.

In the corner by the real stables, Nana Lew was hosing down the horses. She was done with the praying and the waiting at her capel. She threw the hose into the humbug pattern of her

8

collies, and the dogs bit on the jet of water, barking with pleasure. Ducks jumped and skimmed onto our pea-soup pond, our chickens squawked and scattered, and Nana Lew marched towards us.

It always made me happy, Nana coming closer. She'd be circled with her sea of black and white collies, yipping and yapping and panting with swollen tongues. She'd be a little puffed and oiled with sweat, but her wide thin mouth, and the tombstone teeth she'd got mail-order from America, well, they made me want to smile as wide and as white as her.

'Room for one more?' she asked, because we were standing in that line: first Dad, then Mum holding Molly, then me, then my older brother Vincent. The hem of Vincent's long dress trembled in the hot wind, tickling my leg. Vincent was thirteen and the dress was black satin, probably Nana's.

'What's the band called again?' Mum asked.

'Tequila, love,' said Dad.

'What?'

'*Te-queee-la.*'

'That's a stupid bloody name, Ivan.'

'Had Americans before,' Nana told them. 'Noisy buggers. Some of them go running come the mornings. In their daps. Funny lot.'

I watched my nana and my mother. I listened to the air between them. My mother and grandmother didn't mix. Mum said they didn't *emulsify*.

'Nothing wrong with looking after yourself,' Mum said.

'Hmmm,' Nana sniffed.

'Exciting, isn't it, Mam?' Dad rubbed his hands together and I could hear the hard work in them: he was always working

9

hard at getting Mum and Nana to love each other. Dad shook his red locks while Nana folded her arms across her enormous chest, nudging a palm under each sagging breast.

'Eight brothers is it Ivan?' she said. 'It's a bad number is eight. Seven 'ud be better.'

Mum frowned at her mother-in-law.

'Don't make that face, Dolly. I know my numbers and what they should be. They're bad luck this lot. Bringing it with them.'

'Don't start, Gladys, please.'

'Now girls.' Dad put up a freckled hand. I was the only one of us who was freckle, wax and marmalade like Dad; our red hair didn't grow, it *sprouted*.

'Our Halo sees it,' Nana muttered. 'Just look at her. Fretting.'

'You want the loo, Halo?' Mum asked.

They were both right – something was fizzing in my stomach sure as Nana's nine-day-old stew. I had to put a hand between my legs.

The courtyard was suddenly still. It was anticipation. Beyond the west stone wall our green fields were caught mid-sparkle, bright as light on a dragonfly's back. There, Nana's curly-horned sheep froze, mid-munch. I took a breath of the still quiet.

It was then we heard the bus rumble closer.

'It's them!' Nana growled.

We watched the bus glide under the red-brick arch: it was big, and it was silver.

'Expensive,' Nana Lew said, pointing. 'American.'

It turned, popping gravel. As it did, we waved. We waved hard and we stared at our stretching reflections on its shining silver surface: on the blacked-out windows. We were flag-wavers at a homecoming parade, cheering on the cavalcade, and for a moment we were frozen like that.

The bus shuddered to a stop.

I could feel the heat off it, like it had driven all the way from America. I wiggled on the spot, my stomach burning, and tried to imagine who was inside: what rock star might be puzzled at the sight of a wholesome family, waving. I knew that soon a band would stumble out; soon they'd jump at the whinny of Ziggy and Stardust, our Welsh cobs. Maybe they'd be frightened by the chickens or too stoned to cope with ducks, but by day three they'd be asking to borrow saddles and feeding the pig chocolate.

'It brings out the child in them,' Mum once told us, 'because even to the greatest rock musicians in the world, a lamb is a lamb and a horse is a horse.' It was true, and so I wondered if I could depend upon this band, *Te-quee-la*, to run down to our house to ask where the tack room was, where the horse brushes were kept, and was it wrong to feed the chickens chicken crisps? Maybe it was as inevitable as me coming out arse-wise. Maybe it was as predictable as the shiver that now trembled in my stomach like a frightened hound, telling me that change was on her way.

As the bus hummed and my family drew a collective breath, its silver concertina doors sprung open.

It was a girl who waddled out first. She smiled at us as she held on to the chrome rails, and when she jumped from the last step, dust blew up. I put up a hand and she waved back.

'Hey kiddo,' she said to me.

She stood against the hot metal of the bus, one foot flat on its silver surface and one knee out. She wore a long red dress and I could just see the poke of black cowboy boots beneath the hem. The dress was tight across her tummy, though, and she couldn't close her sheepskin waistcoat. The thing was, her stomach was enormous. This girl looked like the sheep I saw blow up in Nana Lew's field: it blew up and up and groaned, until Dad had to stab it through the belly with an ice pick.

Bloat, our dad said.

I stared and wondered if he'd have to do the same here, then Mum pinched me and whispered how it was rude to stare, that it was a baby in the girl's stomach. But she wasn't much more than a baby herself. I poked out my own tummy and puffed out my cheeks. I stared down, trying to spot my feet. Vincent twitched beside me, electric.

The eight brothers were jumping out, one by one.

Vincent gasped.

Their smell wafted to us: it was cheesecake, smoke, and peanuts. They stretched out the cramp of the bus and we saw these brothers had honey-brown faces and beards of gold that glinted in the setting sun. Eight suddenly seemed a large number as they stood around the girl, protective as wolves on a kill, their blue eyes somehow the same. These brothers were huge.

The most remarkable thing about them, though, was their clothes. They all wore white suits, but these suits were embroidered with pictures as colourful as the pictures in Molly's books. On their lapels were pink and naked girls; on their arms and thighs were great, green cactus trees, silver stars, and big white pills. The stars sparkled and the naked girls seemed to be dancing as the brothers fidgeted. My family, for a small

12

moment, was speechless. One brother turned to gaze out at the courtyard, and I saw a big red cross and a running black horse sewn onto his wide back. I was sure I could hear cantering hooves. These men were wearing stories, and both the brothers and the stories were beautiful.

'This is it, huh?' one brother said.

'Guess so.'

'Man.'

'Where is this, anyways?'

The girl laughed and the eight brothers with beards of gold laughed with her. They all had very good teeth.

'Welcome!' Dad finally said.

'Welcome!' Mum smiled and held out a pale hand. 'I'm Dolly. This is Ivan.' The late sun shone through her cheesecloth dress; Mum didn't care for underwear. I saw a shiver ripple through the men as she moved towards them. They towered above her and they stared.

Most people liked to stare at my mother. Around here they said Dolly Halcyon Palmer-Llewelyn – my mum – was good enough to eat. They said she had cheeks like apples, eyes like chocolate, hair glossy as liquorice sticks, lips plump as cherries: all the old clichés. Even Nana Lew agreed that with a smear of sugared butter her son's choice was good enough to suck. The trouble was, sometimes people bit my mother. Couldn't help it, they said. I watched these brothers in their painted suits very carefully, because Mum had told us about the man in Rhyl who'd nibbled at her fingers in the caravan park until a nip-too-far drew blood. She'd told us about the lady in Lydmouth post office who licked her bare shoulder in the queue. 'Like a horse with a salt block, she was,' Mum said. The thing was, I worried that my mother *let* these people lick and bite her. And because of this, I worried how long she would last. As if she was a cake, a lasagne, a piece of moist quiche, I wondered which one of us would gobble the last slice.

The prettiest brother took a step towards her. 'Abraham Connor, ma'am,' he said. He nodded a little bow, but he didn't bite.

Mum turned to the next.

'Jed Connor.'

'Hale Connor.'

'Caleb Connor, ma'am.'

'Jared Connor.'

'Duke Connor.'

'Knox Connor, ma'am.'

'Trueman Connor, ma'am. Happy to make your acquaintance.'

The men giggled, shy. Then Dad held up a freckled hand as if he was trying to stop something. 'You must be exhausted. Come inside, let's show you the place,' he said.

Ziggy, tied up and wet from Nana's hosing, began her neighing from the stable end of the courtyard, and the girl moved away from the bus. 'Y'all got horses,' she said, as if it were the most natural thing in the world.

'Shall we get you settled? Supper will be on soon.' Mum walked towards the studio and the chalets where the band would sleep. The brothers and my family followed her, without question or pause.

The girl stayed where she was. She held on to her belly with small hands.

'You talk, kiddo?'

I shrugged.

'That your momma?'

I nodded.

'Who's the crazy lady with the dogs?'

'Nana.'

She sniffed hard and stared hard. She had a voice like she was chewing dough and toffee at the same time. 'What they call you?' she asked.

'Halo.'

'Huh?'

'My name is "Halo".' I kicked my left foot behind me and caught it with my left hand. I hopped.

Halo.

It was a funny name but it was mine. I thought of how some called me *Hey-law*, depending on which side of our border I stood, Welsh or English. 'Come over by *yure*, *Hey-law* love.' Or, 'Come here, Halo.' One foot here and one foot there. In and out and shake it all about, oooh! The hokey-cokey! My Nana Lew says border life means you got your fingers in two pies but you don't ever get to eat.

The girl frowned. 'You holy?' A duck splashed onto the pond. 'Believe in the Lord?'

'My nana has a capel. Across the track there, see.' I pointed.

'Must be holy with a name like that.'

I wanted to tell her it was all Mum's idea. For the first two years of my life I was 'Baby', then Mum decided on 'Halo'. 'Diamond Star Halo' to be exact, because she loved Marc Bolan and T.Rex, because I learned to walk to 'Get It On' and Mum said I was dirty sweet and I was her girl.

It was getting dark. Lights flashed on and off in the buildings that squared the courtyard. Dad was giving the brothers the tour.

15

I let my foot go. 'Why do they look the same?' I asked as I watched the band through the big windows.

'They're brothers, dummy.' The girl sighed, just a tiny sigh, and turned towards the stable. 'You ride, kiddo?'

'My horse is called Donny.'

'Cute.'

'Mum said my horse was a crazy little horse so we called him Donny. He's small like me.'

The girl laughed and frowned at the same time. 'Shit,' she said, 'what *is* this place?'

'Rockfarm.'

'Got that right.' Her thumbs rubbed her belly in small circles. She tapped it.

'Are you the singer?' I asked.

'Yeah. Abe and me, we write the songs too.'

'Which one is Abe?'

'Abraham Connor. The handsome-est. The lead. My *husband*.'

'How old are you?'

'None of your business, kid. I'm old enough to be legal,' she laughed. 'In some states, anyways.' She walked towards me, and I saw how young she really was. 'You know, you talk funny. You're cute though. Crazy hair.' She pointed at my soft red sprouts. 'We'll go riding. You sure you ride? You look real young.'

'What's your name?'

'Jenny.' She smiled a freckled smile and her teeth were strong as a horse's.

It was then I did a strange thing: I lurched at her and put both of my hands flat on her drum-tight belly; I don't know why. I felt a jolt like the jolt I got from the electric fence round

16

Nana's sheep. My palms fizzed so much I wondered if this girl was full of nettles.

'Hey!' she cried. Then she grinned, as if people did this to her every day. 'OK, how's about you two get properly introduced? What is it, kiddo, "Halo", right? So Halo, this here's my boy Fred. Fred, this here is Miss Halo, a crazy name for a kid with crazy hair.'

'How do you know that's a boy?'

'Just know.' She blew a kiss to her stomach. 'I always did like the name "Fred". You like it, kiddo?'

'I suppose.'

Jenny pinched my cheek, and waddled off.

In the summer wind, dirt I called mine warmed my bare feet like puppies' tongues. Nana Lew told me there were Roman drains and catacombs in the earth beneath Rockfarm. She said catacombs were corridors piled up with the bones of all the English Bastards that ever were, and she said that meant our underground corridors went on for ever. When she was drunk on her sloe gin or her apple wine she told us that along these passageways of skulls and bones – that weren't *her* ancestors – there was a gateway to hell and good bloody riddance.

Through the lit windows I watched the blown-up girl move through the rehearsal room, and then disappear into my dad's studio.

3

Tequila had been given the tour. Mum and Vincent were serving dinner, and Dad was carrying Molly and me down from the studio. Dad had a funny way of walking, his long legs bowed at each step like fruit-laden branches, but still our dad was strong.

Nana Lew told us that Once Upon a Time she left the farm, went out to her woods, and came back with our dad.

'The wood god had me,' she giggled, and tapped burgundy-chipped nails up to her mail-order teeth, 'and what a fella *he* was.'

She said that the very next day and the day after that and the day after that, she went back to the wood god for more, and that's why our dad – Ivan Comfort Llewelyn – is conker-eyed and every wood you could think of; he's oak and maple and walnut and beech, horse chestnut and fresh pine.

'Just like his father, god-rest-his-woody-soul,' Nana said.

'You shouldn't fill the kids' heads like that, Mam,' Dad told her, 'or mine, neither.'

'Well, maybe he wasn't a wood god, Ivan Comfort, maybe he was just an Irish navvy or a Welsh miner. Who knows?'

'You should, Mam.'

'You're here now aren't you? That's what matters, lad.'

As Dad carried us down under the red-brick arch I watched the lights of the courtyard disappear. Nana had edged Rock-farm with red fuchsias and the night smelled thick and sweet.

We passed Nana's Big House where she lived with her eight collies. She told us, 'if I don't see you through the week, I'll see you through the window,' and she was right. There were five of us but we were crammed into Rockfarm's small gatehouse.

'One girl for each shoulder,' Dad whispered in our ears, 'that's what I've got because I've always charmed the beautiful ladies.'

It was true. Nana Lew said she'd put a charm on him with that red hair. She said it was a charm that could never fail, but I knew the charm was simply that he was Dad: Dad because his legs were oak, Dad because his arms were tigers and his laughs tickled, Dad because his hair jerked like a rooster's crest when he walked. In our letters and postcards now, he's Dear Dad, and he's as Dear as caviar. After all, he was the only man my mother lost her glaze for.

I nestled into the salty crook of his neck, squirreling my hands beneath his shirt and onto his warm skin.

'Your hands are freezing, Halo. Come on, girls, let's get you inside.' And my dad's voice, like any opiate, had me drowsy as Nana's fruit-drunk wasps. I gazed over his shoulder at the summer dusk on our farm.

Nana said none of us were born to farming. Blood-wise, our people were Fairground and the Pit; because our mum was brought up in a caravan that pitched on any wasteland, and Nana Lew was a girl from an endless line of black-faced miners. Nana said it must have been the rhythm of those picks on the coal that had got under my dad's skin so easy, to make him polish up the flagstones where her cows shat; convert the stable blocks into bedrooms and a recording studio, and hang farm machinery from the walls rather than use it. It was here though, the old farm, and when it rained – which was often – you saw it rise to the surface sure as that coal-dust and candyfloss that ran in our veins. Feral kittens drowned then, and red mud, born of clay, coated everything. Animals we didn't own appeared in the rehearsal room, desperate for shelter. There was a wild pony in the studio once. It ate the reel-to-reel. You could smell silage we didn't store and hear the thrum of a thresher on those days, even if that was just my dad trying to tow a lead singer's Rolls-Royce out of the swallowing, gulping mud. I liked the rainy days at Rockfarm best. I'd sit back and watch.

'Bay-*den!*' Molly cried, and something huge bounded towards us in the dark.

'Get down, bloody dog!'

'Bay-*den!*' Molly giggled.

A huge tongue grazed on my neck.

Baden was the Great Dane. A heavy metal band called Howl left Baden with us last summer and it was love at first sight for Molly. Baden slept in the old caravan, and Nana fed him and gave him the name of the man she hated most: Lord Robert Baden-Powell, the hero of Mafeking (though Nana called him Chief Scout Killer and Big English Bastard of the World). Nana said it was a test, naming the dog that. 'Please let me love something with that name, it'll do me good, see!' she pleaded to God or the Devil, or whoever my nana spoke to.

Molly wriggled to be let down. Baden nibbled her toes until she fell on his neck, his tongue plastering her face in thick drool.

'One more for bed, then,' Dad sighed, because no one could fight with Molly.

*

'Does he have to lie there, Moll?'

'Ye*ssss*!'

It had been a battle getting Baden on top of Molly's blankets instead of under them. Now I watched the dog's brown-eye wink as his huge head took up Molly's pillow and she hugged him from behind, her small fingers burrowed into his taupe side, her arm barely reaching his ribs.

'Right then,' Dad said.

We were waiting in our twin beds for our ritual to begin. Dad walked to my record player and picked up the stylus.

Sam Cooke sang his creamy wail, and 'A Change is Gonna Come' began. I watched Dad breathe deep as he sucked in Sam's words about rivers and running and being afraid to die. He kissed my forehead and then Molly's, his lips dry and freckled like mine. Dad paused above the snoring dog and patted his head.

Then my father began.

'When I first saw your mother,' he told us, 'I swallowed my heart.'

I always pictured this part of our bedtime story, whether it was Mum or Dad telling it. Up came Dad's heart – because it had to come up to go down again – until his jaw opened like the knife-cut top of a boiled egg, and there it was, his heart, all pumping and jelly-ish. Then down it went, leaving a heart-shaped lump in his throat. Gulp!

'Why did you swallow your heart, Daddy?' I prompted.

'I was at the Dolls' Fair in Tiger Bay and, boom! There your mother was, on her stall. Candy stripes and the smell of toffee apples, that was your mother all over. Her pitch was called "Shoot the Dictators" because the Palmers had an old-fashioned fairground, even back then. And back then was a time when the world was changing, my nutmeg. And it was the music that was changing us. Elvis Presley. Eddie Cochran. Gene Vincent, all those lads. But your mother was an old-fashioned girl. She loved Pat Boone and she had a little pellet gun in her hand and she was shouting, "Come and shoot the buggers! Get Hitler! Get Mussolini! Right in the puss!" And when I saw her, I swallowed my heart. Simple as that.' Dad yawned.

'What happened next?'

'I paid for three goes, got Hitler, and she ran away with me into the mist.'

'And then?'

He yawned again. 'We built this place.'

Dad was telling us the short version tonight.

'And then?'

'Oh you girls know how it goes.'

'No!' Molly shouted, 'Tell un-ce-pon-a-tyne!'

Dad cleared his throat. 'OK. Once upon a time there was a princess imprisoned in an evil castle of the worst dictators, because these men had taken her from all she loved.'

I could hear the reddish-brown wood in Dad's voice. Polished, it was, polished and warm as a conker held in your palm.

'Who was the princess, Daddy?' I asked, even though I knew.

'That was your mother, Halo. And a charming prince, who was me, a prince with red hair and a Welsh heart, well, he may have been young, but he came and he saved her from that place, see.'

He lay down on my bed and put his hands behind his head, his eyes closing. 'You know what comes next, girls.'

And he was right, I did.

I knew that Nana Lew thought she'd have years and years with her only son before he fell – 'like the great oak he is, boomf!' – and I knew her stomach turned and her legs went to jelly the day he told her – in a letter – that at only fourteen years old he had fallen in love with a girl named Dolly Halcyon Palmer from the Dolls' Fair in Tiger Bay.

The day Mum and Dad met, a queue twisted round the Palmers' candy-stripe tents all the way to Dolly Palmer's pitch, because that summer Dolly Palmer had come into her own.

'I'd grown,' Mum told us, and she'd wink.

'She'd grown into a goddess,' Dad whispered.

'And you, you were just a kid, Ivan.'

Dad went as red as his hair.

They liked to tell the story together, but also apart. They liked to tell the story to one of us, and then all of us. It was because of this that the story came out a little different each time.

– 'There was a crowd around her, something to do with her skin. It was luminous.'

– 'I was all alone, no one to talk to, and then your father comes along.'

– 'And the men in the crowd, well, they kept shooting Hitler after Hitler, Mussolini after Mussolini, and all for her, but she didn't blink an eye.'

– 'And no customers all day, so I started to count the pellets.'

They did agree on one thing, though.

'It was love at first sight.'

'Yes. Love at first sight, it was. He was only fourteen, your dad. He was a baby. And I was almost seventeen, but I only had eyes for him. Funny, isn't it?'

23

Dad told us how he hung around the fairground that night, slept out beneath the flap of a tent with his black leather jacket, the Brylcreem in his hair, and the memory of a Gene Vincent song to keep him warm. He said he vowed he wouldn't leave until he could bring Dolly Palmer home to his mother. As it turned out, my dad wouldn't leave that fair for five years.

'Daddy?' I said. 'Wake up.'

He was snoring along with the dog.

Molly crawled out of her covers. She climbed up onto my bed and punched him in the side. 'Da-dee!'

'Hey!'

'Daddy, wake up, you haven't finished the story,' I told him.

He stretched. 'Oh, you know it, girls.'

'But we want to hear it.'

'Ga!' Molly sat on top of his belly and bounced.

'Moll, OK. OK! So the prince brought the princess back here to his mother's farm, and here they both had a dream. Ow, Molly!'

'What dream, Daddy?' I prompted.

'They dreamt of a farm with no cows, or just four. Moll, lie down!'

'And?'

'A farm with no pigs. Or just one. Ouch!'

'And?'

'A farm with almost no cows, almost no fields of corn or barley or rye or wheat. Ouf!'

I stared up at the swirled ceiling, my body bouncing along with Molly's jumps.

'It was a farm with something much more important, girls.'

'What's more important, Daddy?'

'It was a farm with rock 'n' roll!'

He punched his fist in the air and laughed. Then he was standing, Molly under one arm. He wrestled her back into her bed. 'And after all that building, which took years and years because the prince was poor, at last he and his princess had what they had always dreamed of.'

'What's that, Daddy?'

'The best recording studio in the world.'

I snuggled into my mattress.

'And that first winter, my girls, guess what?'

'Ka-ka!' squealed Molly.

'No. That first winter, bands came from far and wide, your mother cooked up a storm to end all storms and we were *fully booked*. And you know what I did?'

'What, Daddy?' I asked, though I knew – after all, we did this most nights.

'I prayed, my girls. Back under the covers now, Molly, otherwise the dog's out. Right then.' Dad stood at the ends of our beds and lowered his head onto his chest, calm. He put his palms together just under his nose. 'What I did was I gave thanks to those who have come before and helped us.'

'What did you pray, Daddy?'

'You know how it goes, Halo.' He winked at me, took a breath deep as a pastor, and began.

'Cla-rence Pine Top Smith,' he prayed, 'Blind Le-mon Jefferson.'

'Robert Johnson,' I said.

'Good girl. And together: Charley Patton. Ma Rainey. Billie Holiday. Eddie Cochran. Patsy Cline. Sam Cooke. Richie Valens. Jimi Hendrix,' he walked forwards and switched off our bedside

25

lights, 'Mama Cass – come on, Molly.'

'Ca*ssssssss*,' she tried and the dog's ear wiggled.

'Good girl.' Dad brushed our cheeks with the back of his hand. 'Jim Morrison. Janis Joplin. Brian Jones. Otis Redding.' He waved his arms, fingers conducting our mouths to speak the names. 'And who's next, Halo?'

I frowned. Dad's prayer for the rock 'n' roll dead followed no sequential order; it was just the way he remembered it.

'Buddy Holly, ' he prompted.

'Sam Cooke,' I said.

'We've had him, darling,' and Dad ruffled my red hair.

'Otis Redding?'

'And him, sweetheart,' he said, but even then I knew no one could have enough Otis Redding.

'Gene Vincent?' I tried.

'Gram Parsons,' Dad gasped and his head dropped. 'Good night then, girls.'

I loved Dad's prayer. I was too young to know who all those names were; in fact, it's taken me a lifetime to find out. I just loved the way the names sounded, 'Cla-rence Pine Top Smith, Blind Le-mon Jeffer-son.' These were names more bewitching than Sleeping Beauty or Little Red Riding Hood.

And it was because of this list of the illustrious dead that my family knew rock 'n' roll was a dangerous business. Being a rock star *was* as risky as being a fighter pilot or a lion tamer. Rock 'n' roll *did* mean plane crashes and car crashes, gunshots, overdoses, and disappearing-into-thin-air.

Of course there would always be more names for my father's prayer. There would always be a new crop. I didn't know it, but soon there'd be Elvis Presley, Marc Bolan, Sid Vicious. Death

26

was like that. A constant scribbler, Nana called him. In a few precious years there'd be John Lennon, Bob Marley, Marvin Gaye. And when we were more than grown up, there'd be Kurt Cobain, and for a while some even said Fred Connor himself.

It is a prayer without end, you see.

Though back in those fuchsia-scented nights, when my sister Molly didn't know her proper words and loved a big dog more than her own family; when my hair sprouted soft and red from my head, I would listen to my woody dad sing his prayer and then I would smile as he hopped down our stairs and gently closed the front door. I would listen to the crunch of his boots on the gravel as he walked back up through the farm, to the courtyard where his studio stood. And whatever band was there, I would put my hot hands together and I would pray for them. I would pray that none of that rock 'n' roll danger would ever come here to our safe home and hurt them. Of course I knew that it had already touched us – after all, we were a family and we had our secrets; but still, as I lay in my bed and I closed my eyes, I prayed out loud.

'Dear God and Otis Redding, please keep Mummy and Nana Lew, and Molly and Vincent and the horses Ziggy and Stardust and Donny and all the cats and all the dogs and the ducks and the red chickens safe tonight. And Dear God and Otis Redding, please keep my daddy extra safe tonight, and those golden brothers and that girl Jenny and her baby. Amen.'

'Men!' Molly shouted at the night.

An owl hooted back but I was too young to know then that prayers are rarely answered.

27

4

I was back in the courtyard, the morning dark red. Chickens purred, heads buried in their necks; the cock hadn't crowed yet. I flattened my nose against the glass of the door. Inside, the looping corridor that linked each room *seemed* empty, but it was too dark to tell. My nightie slapped against my legs in the wind, harsh as Nana's riding crop, and my bare feet burned on the sharp gravel.

I was here while the rest of Rockfarm slept because of the girl with the blown-up stomach: I wanted to see Jenny. I wanted to check that she was real. Maybe she was just a doll, a little blown-up, blue-veined doll, and I'd dreamt her.

I pressed the handle, the door creaked, and I crept inside. Donny my Shetland whinnied from the stables: a warning.

I walked up the steps to the dining room and Mum's serving kitchen. Plates were clean, the dishes and pots stacked neatly on the counters. That would be Dad and Vincent cleaning, polishing, long into the night, tea towels flipped on their shoulders. I breathed in Vince's Vim and Dad's Fairy Liquid, and I crept along the next corridor to the line of bedrooms.

The air was heavy with growls and the doors were open.

I peeked into the first room, like Goldilocks must have, except here was a bear. His hairy bear-legs were hanging way beyond the pale-pine end of the bed. He hissed and groaned and rumbled, and his bear-head almost rolled off our small pillow. It was a golden brother – Caleb, Jared, Knox, or one of the other strange names, I couldn't tell. A white sheet covered half of him and I thought how his skin was the same colour as the syrup I'd poured onto Mum's French toast yesterday. His red mouth was open, his tongue lolling, and my fingers itched to drop something onto those taste buds: a frog, a chilli pepper, or the tips of my farm-dirty fingers. Instead I leant against the doorframe of his lair and thought that this Tequila-brother looked bigger and more handsome in our small bed than he did standing up by the bus last night. In fact, as I moved along the corridor to the next room and the next brother, and the next – until I'd counted to seven – I realized that they all looked bigger and more beautiful in the red morning light, a light that was catching their golden skin and making it glitter. I listened to each one: close your eyes and you couldn't tell the snores apart. There were seven brother-bears in seven musky bedrooms, and I tiptoed into the eighth room.

But this double bed was empty. There was no Jenny. It was then that I heard the *waa-waa-waa*.

The sound was distant so I ran towards it; back down the corridor, through the dining room, and past the double doors into the bright and cold rehearsal room. It wasn't long before the sound came again; it poured out between the brass hinges of the studio door, sure as soft centres oozed from Nana's posh chocolates. It was a *waa-waa-waa* that made me shiver, and I slap-footed across the linoleum towards it.

I've always thought that my dad's studio smelled of smoke, nylon tights, and mushrooms. Dad said that was on account of the carpet and the Marmite-dark. He said you needed dark in a recording studio because darkness let those old songs lurk, and we all needed what had come before: Dad said you need that to build on.

There was no one at the mixing desk: the place where sliding knobs, like Black Jack sweets, moved up and down; the place where songs were measured and set. The live microphones were on, though, feeding in loud to the control room, and that syrupy sound played on. Black leather sofas lined the walls of this room and I checked for bodies. Not one. I sneaked up to the mixing desk and dragged a chair to the triple-glazed glass. Balancing on it, I stared into the studio itself.

There was the girl, Jenny, pot-bellied and pale. She was sitting on a high stool next to the last golden brother; the one who had to be Abraham Connor, the one Jenny called the handsome-est, the lead: her husband.

She was right, Abraham stood out. His hair looked like Jesus' hair in Nana's illustrated Bible, clean and shimmering, and he seemed delicate, not like his bear-brothers. He was as pretty as a girl.

Abraham was hunched over a guitar that lay flat on his lap, and he was rubbing something silver over it, up and down. The silver was the shape of a werewolf's bullet. It was that that was making the *waa-waa-waa*s. His other hand, brown and long, plucked the strings with silver fingerpicks. This close, the sound was the shimmer above a Guy Fawkes fire. Then the fireworks started as Jenny began to sing.

It was a sad song about a girl who left home, a girl who'd never see her momma again, a girl who walked the dusty lanes somewhere hot, until her feet hurt and she got to the city lights. It was a very sad song, because the girl died. She died to those *waa-waa-waa*s. Jenny's voice cracked on the high parts and right there and then I decided it was the cracks that made it sadder.

Jenny sang Hallelujah, hallelujah, the devil and the deep blue sea, and I wanted to nestle inside that sticky, cracking sound, like a grub.

'And the girl sang, "ohh-ohh, hallelujah
Ha-ha-lelujah,"
The girl-child sang, "Hallelujah"
Cause the old devil won't let her alone.'

I pressed my hot hands against the glass, but the song was over and instead of that flat guitar, Jenny was sitting on her man's lap.

'My little Russian doll,' Abraham whispered into the microphone, he put a brown hand into her chestnut hair, pulling it back from her face and behind her head, tight. He traced a finger from her cheek along her chin and down her clear, white neck, and they started to do the sorts of things grown-ups do.

By the time Jenny looked up I must have been running into the dark control room, then out to the chill rehearsal room, and into the long corridor where the other brother-bears were shaking off their slumber.

I was stuck.

Two brothers had paw-padded to the front door, blocking it off, and the other five were lurching in both directions along the corridor, like golden-haired zombies.

They were naked.

I panicked and ran the only way I could. I rattled past

Vincent and Dad's neat plates, past Mum's serving hatch, to a door off the kitchen that led into the darkness of one of Nana's long, long corridors. This corridor was one that took you the whole square of the courtyard and further: it was the one we were forbidden to walk through alone.

I closed the door behind me and breathed. I could hear the brothers rumbling morning greetings beyond.

'Coffee?' a Jared or a Knox or a Trueman said. 'Where's the goddamn coffee?'

Jumping down the cold stone steps was difficult because it was pitch black. I felt along the damp walls for Nana's wall switches, and once the faint lights came on, I ran.

My bare feet splashed in puddles and slime, and my heart thumped along with my steps. I'd never been this way on my own before. I'd run down here with Nana and a torch, or holding on to Vincent's hand like a little sister should, but never on my own. This was where we played 'dare' and it was a rubbish game because Vince and I always lost. Molly would run in here and giggle into the dark, and we'd have to beg Nana to go and find her. This was a place that Nana said led to the old abattoir, and after that the old catacombs and that gateway to hell. Nana must have been right because it smelled of old rock, red blood, fire, and cobwebs. The electric lights had run out; from here it was going to be pitch black.

I stalled, thinking of running back, but the naked bears were roaring now: I kept on, hands outstretched.

'Nana,' I whispered into the dark. I started to sob.

My toes curled in the slime.

'Na-a-na,' I gasped.

I didn't know whether the creak was behind or in front. I

32

looked up at the vaulted ceiling and saw a shaft of light on the bricks. I wondered what was above me – were there more layers of brick and bone? Or had I really taken that wrong turn into Nana's catacombs, to her gateway to hell, where Dad said she buried her old dogs and her old husbands too?

I was thinking this as a hand grabbed my wrist, a light shone in my face and a voice said, 'I wondered how long you'd take, sunbeam.'

5

Nana sat at her kitchen table. She set her torch down and stared at me. Elvis was singing 'Crying in the Chapel' from the Wurlitzer jukebox that glowed like a luminous boiled sweet from the corner of her vast room. He was grinning down from her walls, too. Her collies were wrapped around each other in front of the Rayburn, a mess of humbugs now, and I pulled out a chair, wiping my salty face on the sleeve of my nightie.

'You get scared in there, sunbeam?'

I shuddered a half-sob and stared up at the brightest Elvis I could find. I shook my head.

There were pictures of Johnny Cash as well as Elvis Presley on Nana's walls, and they seemed to come to life when Nana was in the room. She had twelve huge pictures of Johnny between the two sash windows and she called them *her* stations of *her* cross. Elvis came in bite-size pieces. That was the best way to have him, Nana said. She told us it was Johnny who was the real storyteller, and Elvis, well, he was shine and no whistle, though she loved him. 'Once you're grown, sunbeam,' she'd nudge me, 'you'll know the difference between a boy and a man.' Nana said a singer had to rumble, from their toes to yours; she said a singer had to be like a train coming closer, boom-chikka-boom, like a preacher in the pulpit, like you'd imagine the voice of our Lord himself. And that was her Johnny.

34

'Told you not to ever go in that passageway on your own, sunbeam. Get lost, you will.'

I glanced at the doors off Nana's kitchen: there was the one I'd just come through; then one to the cellar, and the two to a place she called God-Knows-Where.

'I—'

'What if you was in there and no one noticed? You'd be lost for ever, sunbeam.'

I swallowed a big swallow.

'You know how big this old place is – we'd never find you, not even if you screamed.'

Nana was right. Nana's house was big, but its secrets were bigger. Nana told us there were so many stories that belonged to this house, it was hard to tell just one. She said because the stories weren't hers she had to coax them out like you would a wounded and wild animal. Nana said there were ghosts here too, and that come the night it was them as turned her clocks back, hid her keys and stole the creamy bit of her gold top. Nana said that was why she sprinkled red-brick dust on her thresholds. She said the brick dust kept what she didn't want in the house out, and what she did want in. She said she'd learnt all about that down on the bayou, where the oaks grow down instead of up, and where you could hold anything in a jar, even someone's soul, long as you said a few rhymes and screwed the lid down tight enough.

Sometimes my nana spoke in riddles.

'Sugar's what you need,' she told me, and pushed a large Victoria sponge closer. There was plenty to choose from because the kitchen table was patterned with plates of cake. This wasn't unusual; Nana Lew lived on cake. She baked cake and she

35

bought cake and she stuffed the moist mulch of cake into her mouth. Every morning a cake would be cooking behind each door of her Rayburn. She'd open these hatches as if they were windows of an advent calendar. 'Look!' she'd shout. 'A perfect sponge!' like it was all a big surprise.

My Nana Lew had her own 'rules of cake', which were:

1) Eat it
2) Feel better

They were simple to follow.

If you had chicken pox, she'd bake a 'Pox Cake' until your spots crusted over. If you broke a bone, it was 'Broken Cake'. My nana believed in cures. Many summers ago, when she cooked 'Grief Cake' for Mum, Nana told us it would all get better once she cooked and cooked and made her kitchen groan with mouldy triangles of cloying, black sponge.

I blew on my sweet tea and bit a corner of a fruit scone.

'Sunbeam, you going to tell me why you're snooping around the studio this time of the morning? You know what your dad would say.'

I slouched and she nudged a plate of cream horns. 'What's bothering you, love?'

'Nothing, Nana.'

'You going to tell your Nana Lew why you was watching that girl last night like she was honey, then? Saw you when she got off that silver bus. Something about her, is it?'

Nana said I had 'the eye'. I had no idea what this meant, but I did know it made my mother crazy. When Nana said things like that, Mum called her a mad old witch and the hell that lay in the catacombs beneath us would break loose; Dad would go off in the tractor and sit out in Beggars Field under the fat oak until the storm at home passed.

I sipped more tea and made a note not to mention this to my mother.

'Well, something's not right. I can feel it.' She put a plate of purple, green and yellow cupcakes in front of me (Nana liked food colouring; she said it made things *unexpected*).

'It's that babby,' she suddenly said.

'In her tummy?'

'What other babby you see, sunbeam?'

I stuffed a green cupcake in my mouth. 'Duh-ho.'

Nana Lew grinned, teeth bright. 'Hmmm—' She tapped them. 'She'll have him here. You mark my words.'

'"Him"?'

'The babby.'

'How do you know it's a "him", Nana?'

'Could see it. Last night. It's the way the girl stands.'

'It's true! She told me its name is going to be Fred. She told me last night, so it is a boy, it is, Nana!'

'Hmmm.' She stood, ignoring me. She went to her larder and took out a bottle. I knew it was one of her tonics, and this wasn't a tonic like Mum's gin and tonic, it was a tonic with crushed things from Nana's garden in it. She poured two glasses and I winced. Nana's tonics were foul. 'Brings out the liver,' she'd say, but I didn't want my liver brought out anywhere for anyone.

'Drink this,' she told me.

Dad always told us Nana's pills and potions were pointless and dangerous (apart from the goose grease or dragging you backwards through a blackberry bush when you had a cough). 'Try not to drink them, Halo,' he said. 'One day she'll poison us all. She won't mean it but the mad old girl will do us all in, see.'

I took the glass. 'What's it for, Nana?'

'Something that'll make *her* come a-knocking. The American girl. Think you'd like that, sunbeam?'

I nodded. 'Do I have to drink it, Nana?'

'Reckon so.' She smiled and I smiled back.

If Nana believed in cures she also believed in curses, and her teas and tonics came with words like SASSAFRAS and SARSAPARILLA (which sounded like a witches' chant to me; sassafras-sassafras-sarsa-parilla). Come the summers she'd have me out in the garden picking for her special teas, while she knelt beside me and told me the most gorgeous lies.

'I gave little Judy a tea just like this. Had some sarsaparilla in it, mind.'

I would snap and pick next to her. 'Judy who, Nana?'

'Garland, little Judy Garland. It did wonders for her. Better than them pills they had her on, see. And that Richard Burton wouldn't sound as booming, as *resonant* without my tea. His eyes wouldn't sparkle green like that without my tonics, see.'

Nana said there were plants in her garden that could cure whoever you wanted and kill however you wanted: nicely; badly; unspeakably. Nana said her plants could send you off to the land of nod or make you sweat blood in your bed for days, so just you watch out.

People would visit. They'd sit in her kitchen, and she'd have them drink down her tea while they cried. Then they'd sit in her parlour and she'd talk to their dead. Nana called these people her Paying Johnnies. They trusted my nana to put everything

38

right. She was famous for it. There were times when Nana Lew scared me; there are times when she still does.

She was staring at me, her small eyes eager. 'You know, you're a good girl, my little sunbeam. You're special, and you're Nana's girl, aren't you?'

I smiled. I knew my Nana Lew loved me best, but I loved her back, so we were equal.

She drank her tonic with a shake of her head, then she pressed one stub-finger into a groove of her table and closed her eyes. 'I swear by this tonic that if that girl has her baby right here, he'll be right. Anywhere else and I can't help her, see.'

'On the table, Nana?'

'On this very table, love.'

I giggled.

'You mark my words. I've made a pledge now. I swear by the meals and births and funerals been had on this here table, Halo. By the meals, births, and funerals. I swear. Yes, that's life in three words, my girl. Meals. Births. Funerals.'

Nana tapped her porcelain teeth then swayed, thick, strong and bow-legged, towards me. She grabbed my hand and, palm out, spat on it. Wet crumbs of cake floated in the spit. She was pulling me up and pressing my fingers deep into the grooves of her beloved oak table before I could wipe the spit away.

'See these, Halo? These marks here are the cuts and the hacks and the lines of dying.'

Her watery bosoms pushed themselves flat against my back.

'You feel across here by this old stain, pet. It's black now, but once it were rust red. That was life, that one. That was your daddy coming into the world, see.' She paused. 'But this black one over here by the lemon drizzle, well, that one is death. And it wasn't ever red, always black. Go on now, Halo, let your fingers rest in these life and death lines.'

It felt like my arm was being pulled from its socket.

'Yes, you'll soon feel it all well up through your own prints, my girl. Because there's some of them have the ghost of your print here. Some of them as do and some of them as don't.'

She dipped the index finger of her free hand in the top of a nearby cream swirl, popped her finger in her mouth and sucked like a milk-starved puppy. Something spat from the Belfast sink and I forgot the feeling of watery bosoms, of currants and bitter tonic curdling in my stomach.

'What's that, Nana?'

She loosened her scullery-maid grip and looked up at the sink. 'Shellfish.'

'What?'

'Clams, maybe. Big buggers in any case.'

'Why?'

'Ask your mother, pet. She had them come, last night. For her cooking.'

Another arc of clear water jetted up and across the kitchen.

I was released from Nana's firm hand as the jukebox played more Elvis; it was 'Long Black Limousine'.

'Can't get away from Elvis today!' Nana cried, and she grabbed a cushion from her chair to kneel down before her biggest picture of Johnny Cash, her arms out like a bird flying. Nana spoke fast: 'I pray to thee, Big John, I pray to the spirits of Big Paul Robeson and Big Louis Prima, keep the boy safe. Keep the boy safe because boys can never be wolves, they can never roam free. Think of the other boys we lost. Boys that can

40

never be replaced. Boys that can never come back. They all need looking after, Big John. They need looking out for and that's what I'm asking you today. Dear Big John, set your own troubles aside and look to the boy.' My grandmother started to mumble and I knew that I was forgotten.

I backed into her cold and vast hall; cobwebs caught in the back of your throat here. Sun cut through the stained-glass windows, brightening up a stocky John the Baptist in wolfskins and making more colours on her red and black Victorian tiles. The portraits of the English Bastards through history stared down at me, *horrified*, their lips curled in disgust.

It was strange how my nana had become queen of this house. It was strange that my nana had been queen of it since 1919.

Nana was thirteen in 1919, if you care to believe her.

She said she married young and she married well, a Welsh scullery maid to an old squire. It was Nana who called that first husband 'The English Bastard'. He didn't last long, but Nana did, and she ended up with this place. That's the way she tells it, anyway. After all, it was Nana who said that the battle lines you are born with could be redrawn with the rustle and the lift of a red petticoat. 'Listen, loves,' she whispered, 'what they steal and what you give, well, they slip and slide on a border, see, easy as silk,' and she'd lift her skirt to the knee, until we saw a frill of rustling red beneath. I think it was that red petticoat that made my brother Vincent what he is today; but that's another story.

The simple truth was, maybe my Nana Lew was a witch, even at thirteen.

I crossed myself and I gave a wink to the English Bastards that lined her landing. Then I skipped outside to the sun and ran to the lawn. I wanted to stand among Nana's white croquet hoops, her blue-throated peacocks, and her shadows.

The hot summer air was sharp as a knife as I winked at Nana's fifteen sash windows, gazing out, shutters open in surprise. I gasped at her granite blocks because they sparkled like widow's jewels in the sun. I giggled at the rain-worn gargoyles crouching on her gutters, twitching, chattering, and ready to pounce. Nana's Big House was so big it made you gasp – *every* time.

I ran past the gate's stone pillars, past the old white caravan on bricks. I glanced back at those gargoyles patrolling the roof. They were still twitching and chattering, and I wondered what sort of spell held this place in check; what kind of riddle my small grandmother had uttered to make this place hers.

I heard the capel's bell. That would be Nana. My nana had her Big House, her capel, her dogs, her Land Rover, and her own religion. My Nana Lew was a woman of independent means and she was getting ready, though for what I didn't know.

A woodpecker shot out from her plum trees, ready to ride the wind, easy as a seal in water, and right there and then I remembered to pray backwards, just like my independent nana had taught me. I mouthed, 'Nema reve dna reve rof.' I was innocent as any little girl in any fairy tale, and as Nana's bright peacocks wailed mournfully from the lawn, I skipped down the track to my parents' house.

6

Our house was so different from Nana's: it was small and it looked like the gingerbread house from Hansel and Gretel. Nana said that was Victorian Gothic, but Mum said it was cramped.

Right now boys of different sizes but all in green stood on our porch. They were pushing each other, jostling. They wore shorts. One knocked on our door. I crouched by the gate, behind Mum's cluster of raspberry bushes.

'You ask!'

'No, you ask, Cole, you're the smallest.'

'So?'

I knew who they were. Every summer scouts camped on the river Morrow's edge once the shifting banks turned dry. Small, green water voles in their shorts, they swam in the low, black water and lit smoking campfires. When the heavy evenings came, Vincent and I would stick our heads out of the roof window and listen to them sing their weird songs. 'Ging Gang Goolie' would strain through Rockfarm's hum of grasshopper and electric guitar, and it would give me the willies. Then one morning each year these green boys would make the trek up from the river to our house, just because the word 'F-A-R-M' hung from our gate (it hangs there today, off its hinges and eaten by rust). Of course these scouts never got what they wanted, although sometimes they got more.

43

This was their first visit of the summer: these were fresh scouts, a new batch.

My mother opened the door. I watched a ripple, silvery-green like light on a mallard's crown, shudder through the scouts.

Mum was wearing a little camisole with thin straps – one was hanging off her creamy shoulder – and below she wore Dad's white Fruit of the Loom Y-fronts. As she lifted an arm against the door frame, the camisole pulled up, showing her belly to her waist. She smiled, and that green shudder rolled back through the troop like a tide.

'Can I help?' Mum asked.

A scout coughed while another jiggled from foot to foot like he needed to wee.

'Well?' said Mum.

'Milk,' a tall one said. 'Milk.'

'What?'

'Milk.'

Her eyes moved over them, lingering, grazing their small boy-heads. My mother loved boys; she missed boys. The scouts shivered that collective green shiver again, and I noticed the tall one was staring directly at my mother's breasts. I wondered if he'd say 'milk' again.

'Hold on, boys,' she told them, and disappeared.

Alone, the scouts were silent, still, all the jostling gone. They seemed dazed as electrocuted chickens before the chop.

Maybe it was my mother who was the witch.

She was back, shaking a shiny bottle of silver top. The effort had given her colour, her mouth was parted, and the scouts stared some more, their own mouths opening, closing, like landed fish.

44

'There you go then, boys.' She held the bottle out to them.

'But that's not *real* milk,' a small one said.

'No,' another barked at the pint.

'Haven't you got any real stuff, missus?'

'From a cow, like?'

'Oh, you wouldn't like the milk from our cows,' she told them. 'It's green.'

The scouts murmured, back to their jiggling, but Mum was right: our milk *was* green. We only had four cows, and I could see them now from my raspberry bush, lurching across Beggars' Field, their back legs straddled round full-to-the-teat udders. Our cows were Guernseys and Nana had named them 'John', 'Paul', 'George' and 'Ringo', and she fed them seaweed from the Gower. That's what made their milk green. Nana would climb into her old Land Rover late on a Friday, head and daisy hat just above the wheel, and come back in the early hours of Saturday stinking of the briny sea, her seats filled with kelp-black tentacles. 'Makes it salty but sweet,' she told us, 'the best butter, the greenest milk,' and she'd smack her lips like butter pats.

We'd all grown up on green milk. Vince said that was why we were so weird.

'Got any fags, missus?' a scout yelped.

Mum laughed. 'Sorry, boys! That's it!' And she thrust the cold bottle of milk at them and closed the door.

A raspberry thorn caught my nightie as I waited for the scouts to shuffle past. I watched them kick stones down our track. By the time they reached the main road they were running, shouting and punching each other, their boy-ness fully restored.

*

45

'Halo. Mothers Pride. Lurpak. Thick cut marmalade. Eat your crusts, now.' Dad was precise in the kitchen because he was obsessed with toast. Toast was my dad's thing. I kicked my dirty feet under the table.

'Molly, white middle, butter only.'

'Da!'

'Vince. Peanut butter and jam on yours.'

'But, Dad.'

'You need your energy, lad.'

Vincent tightened his already-tight dressing gown, black hair falling on his creamy cheeks. Vincent was named after Gene Vincent, sexy Gene with his blue cap and his Be-Bop-A-Lula, though our Vincent had ended up soft and wide, and like Molly he had our mum's face.

'So where have you been, Miss Halo?'

'Nowhere, Dad.'

'Why are your feet filthy then?'

I kicked them faster against my chair.

'Nutmeg, you haven't been bothering our guests?'

'Did you see their suits, Ivan?' Mum murmured.

We all turned to her. She was sitting on the sofa gluing a hem because Mum didn't sew. The bricks that jutted out from Dad's half-knocked-down wall framed her.

The half-knocked-down wall had happened one morning. Dad said he couldn't stand it when Mum was cooking in the kitchen and he was in the living room by the fire, so one day we woke to the sound of lump-hammer thuds and bricks falling. I remember thinking Chicken Licken was right and the sky really was falling on our heads, but then I found Mum sitting on our narrow stairs, a hot piece of buttery toast in her hand. She was laughing.

'Ivan's doing some decorating, baby,' she told me. 'He's going out to get a girder in a minute. It's so funny, he said the house could *fall down!*' Puffs of cement dust pulsed like jellyfish into our hall and she laughed again. 'Well, he loves me, he does. At least he loves me.'

I remember thinking that even if the house did fall down, it was nice to see Mum laugh.

Dad was swooping on us. 'Eat up.'

Mum didn't eat but she liked to watch breakfast. She said it pleased her, she said it made her see that we could all do without her if needs must. Of course she was fooling herself if she thought toast could fill *her* gap.

'The suits, Ivan,' she said, dipping the brush in the Copydex pot.

'Molly, eat up, I won't say it again.'

'Ivan *Comfort.*'

Dad looked up; we all did.

'The band. Their suits last night.'

'Yes, love, they were amazing, weren't they?'

'Abraham told me they came from California, from Los Angeles.'

'I thought they were country lads? From the South somewhere.'

'No, the suits, silly. The suits come from Los Angeles. Some old guy makes them. Sews, embroiders all that himself. An old Russian guy, Abraham said.'

'Yes, I know, love.'

'Oh well, they seem nice.'

'It was nice of them to dress up for you, Dolly.'

'They were very handsome, weren't they? All eight boys.'

Dad stopped spreading butter.

'I mean, they were stunning really.' Mum closed the hem and pressed.

'You think so?'

'Oh, yes. Startling, they were.'

I looked up at my dad and he seemed sad. He stared at Mum as she picked glue from her hands

'Of course that girl,' she sighed. 'That girl looks like she's about to drop, poor little thing. She couldn't be any age. No age at all.' Mum was biting her lip. 'I hope they're gone before *that* happens anyway.' She looked up and caught us staring. We were like those scouts, our mouths opening, closing, like landed fish.

'What?' she asked. Then suddenly she giggled and that sent a shiver rippling through us. Vince let his fingers sit in the peanut butter jar and Molly stared at Mum with her toasty mouth open, crumbs captured in drool hanging from her soft chin.

'What?' Mum said again. She shook her head at us, then picked up a dress from the pile and went back to gluing. 'I've got to go to the Cash and Carry later, Ivan,' she mumbled. 'There's a shellfish delivery, too.'

'Nana's got that,' I told them all, breaking the spell. 'Nana said there are big buggers in her sink. They spit.'

'Halo,' Dad laughed, but Mum was drifting off.

I got down from the table. 'Mummy?'

'Hmmm?'

'Can I go and see if Jenny's up?'

'Jenny?'

'The girl who came last night.'

I knelt in front of her: I was trying to glimpse the nub that

48

poked down like a tiny stalactite – plump as a fingertip – between Mum's two front teeth. Red as raspberry jelly meant happy and pale as blanched asparagus meant sad. In between was marbled, like raw steak, and that was always good enough for me.

'Oh, the *girl*.' Mum stretched her bare arms up above her head and I saw her pretty belly button. No stretch marks – the full-fat cream in her had seen to that. 'She won't be awake yet, baby. Wait a while. You can go up later when I need helping. You're helping your Mummy cook, remember? And don't hassle, baby. They don't want little kids bothering them, see.' Mum leant over the arm of the sofa and flicked the switch of her turntable. She dropped the stylus herself, impatient. Neil Young sang 'The Needle and the Damage Done' and she sat back, took out her tobacco tin and rolled a joint.

She looked up at me. 'After all, Halo, they're here to work. They *are* musicians.'

Our mum – Dolly Halcyon Llewelyn, née Palmer – liked to lie on countertops and kitchen tables. It was how she thought about food.

'It's like she's dead and laid out,' Nana would mutter whenever she found her daughter-in-law prostrate on any kitchen table, surrounded by a medley of ingredients, maybe a ham hock, a bunch of carrots and a bag of artichokes.

Mum said it was the way she decided what to cook. She said the food 'spoke' to her like this. Some people called our mum a hippie.

'Do you know yet, Mummy?' I asked. I bent a leg behind me and jumped on the spot.

We were in the Big House. It was the only place big enough for Mum's experiments. Nana's cake had been cleared and Mum was lying on the huge kitchen table, staring up at Nana's gravy-coloured ceiling. Her arms were crossed on her chest while the sea trout, herbs, bouillon, two tins of black treacle and one of golden syrup, a meat joint, and eight lemons stood around her. I followed Nana's collies as they circled my mother. Molly sat beneath the table on the slate floor, shelling peas and spraying them across the room.

'Let me think,' Mum said as Napoleon, the biggest collie, snapped at the joint.

Molly growled and he backed off.

'I think they need something to clear their palates, girls. I think they need something to let them start afresh.' Mum sniffed her elegant fingers. 'Hmmm. I'll marinate the sea trout – they can have it raw, like, with ginger and radish.'

'That's good, Mummy.' I circled, pushing the dogs away.

'But they'll also need something of home, something of comfort. Something familiar, something they know.'

I counted the doors off Nana's huge kitchen: the one to the cellar, the two to a place she called God-Knows-Where, and the one to Nana's secret passageway. My belly jumped.

'What are they called again, Halo?'

'Sorry Mummy?'

'The band.'

I stared at the door and I thought of the gold-skinned brothers. '*Tee-qee-la.*'

'Tequila. Oh yeah. It's still a bloody silly name.' It was strange how our mum forgot things; at least she tried to.

I watched her bare foot tap the still air.

'And they're all the way from America. All the way from America,' she said again, but it was to herself.

Mum sat up, sudden, firm. A lemon bounced onto the slate floor, and her black and glossy hair shook. 'Bibles and flags,' she muttered, and jumped off. 'Elvis Presley. The Band.' The dogs scattered. 'Pork. Salt, sticky and sweet.' She grabbed a cloth and marched over to her silver oven because once my mother came round, she came round fast. 'The Band and "The Night They Drove Old Dixie Down". Elvis and "American Trilogy". Sticky, sweet sounds, see. Gram Parsons,' she muttered.

'Geeee!' Molly cried.

'*Te-qui-la*,' Mum said, as if she were tasting, chewing on the word. 'It really is a stupid bloody name, girls,' and she snatched up a tin of golden syrup.

The sticky pork was crackling in the oven and Mum stood over the sea trout.

'You watch me, Halo, while I fillet.'

She was expert; pink flesh cut away from silver skin as her hands darted. She laughed and somewhere crystal chinked. I watched as she reached for the pestle and mortar and the herbs and spices I didn't know the names of.

'Stop daydreaming, love. Work the lemon into the fish. Yes, with your hands.'

I pressed juice into the cold and bouncy flesh.

'Girls, do you want me to tell you a story?' Mum asked.

'Ga!' My sister sprayed more peas across the big room and hit her head on the table. Molly didn't cry. Tough as old boots that kiddie, Nana said, and it was true.

'What story do you want to hear?' Mum trilled, and I watched the nub between her teeth flush red.

'Hay-o!' Molly yelled.

'You want the story of our Halo, Moll?'

Us Llewelyns knew The Story of Me, and we knew that The Story of Me was Molly's favourite. Mum beat the herbs with the pestle, her breasts wobbling at the top. 'You know how it goes, Moll.'

'Ga!'

'OK then. Where was Halo born?'

I cringed, fishy.

'Studcho!' the under-the-table voice cried.

'That's it. Halo came into the world in Dad's studio, just like you, Molly, just like Vincent, and—' Mum stopped; she shook her head like a collie in a new collar. 'But you know the difference between Halo and you, don't you, Moll?'

My sister crawled out from under the table, grinning her few teeth. 'Ha-yo die!'

'Yes. That's it. Halo *nearly died*. And because of Halo, *I nearly died*, too.' Mum put the pestle to her throat, drawing it across.

'Yey!' Molly squealed.

I stared at the bells that drooped like old men's ears from a board on Nana's kitchen wall. I prayed for one of them to ring. I prayed for the story to stop.

'So that night, Molly, your Nana had used up her prayers, her curses, and the goose grease from the larder, and we all thought it was hopeless. We all thought Halo here would never come.'

Mum pressed down into heady garlic.

'She was stuck, see. Stuck and nearly dying while I was nearly dying too. Your dad was in a terrible state. Rang the

52

ambulance, he did. Then suddenly she appeared. *Backwards. Bum-first. Arse-wise*, your Nana Lew says. Halo came out the wrong way around. Didn't you, baby?'

I nodded.

'And then she popped out so hard and fierce, and with so much of your nana's goose fat on her, that when Daddy tried to hold her, he couldn't. Slippery, weren't you, love?'

I nodded again. The tops of Mum's cheeks were rosy, like a doll; she was even more beautiful when effort was painted on her face.

'So Halo goes and slips out of your father's hands, and she falls. But because we're up in the studio, see, behind Dad's drum kit, Halo just bounces on the snare drum, then she's hitting against the cymbals! We all thought we'd never get a hold, but you know what, Moll?'

'Dah!' Molly had used a chair and a dog and now she was sitting on the table squeezing butter through her fingers, just like she squeezed earthworms.

'It was that bounce on the drums that saved her, because the cord was wrapped round her neck, see.'

Molly laughed, butter smears on her face.

'Yes, and that's when she went from a blue like cornflowers to a purple like good beef, and then she yelled her lungs out.' Mum wiped her brow, slowing: our mum only had so much in her.

'After that the ambulance comes and they whisk me off to stop me dying and they take her into an incubator to stop her being, well, funny in the head. Starved of oxygen, she was. Your daddy calls it the beautiful music of a breech birth; it was a miracle.' Mum sighed. 'That's what he calls the night Halo came into the world. A miracle.'

She dropped the pestle.

'But I just call it *lucky*. We were in the hospital for two weeks after that. Awful place. Never go back there, I won't. So when you came, Molly, you were a good girl. You were easy.'

'Gaaa!'

Mum walked over to Nana's jukebox. She pressed in the white buttons, her tongue between her teeth. 'So Halo, baby, what does that make you?'

It was a good thing I knew my cues.

'It makes me a born drummer, Mummy.'

As the jukebox clicked and whirred I could see Mum's cow-blankness was coming: her face was draining of colour and her plump lips were blanching, too.

'Good. And what do you call someone who hangs around with musicians, Molly?' Mum asked.

'Pok!'

'The answer is "a drummer".' Mum laughed a quiet laugh. 'And what do you call a drummer with half a brain, girls?'

We shrugged.

'Gifted.'

These jokes were never funny. I think it was because Mum didn't put her heart into them. Mum didn't understand jokes because she didn't understand timing; Mum did what she wanted when she wanted. Luckily, whatever my mother wanted and whenever she wanted it was always enough for us.

The needle crackled on the old 45, and Elvis sang 'Are You Lonesome Tonight?'. Mum sat down at the kitchen table and opened her tobacco tin. She rolled one of her cigarettes, her eyes closing.

This happened to my mother.

Dad explained it to us once; he said it was like shutters coming down because of What Happened. I thought it was more like the guillotine falling, and bam! I had to put just the tips of my small fingers out to stop it, before it fell and cut off my mum's head.

Nana Lew said we had to be rough on a fairground girl like Dolly Halcyon Palmer and if kisses didn't work, Dad had to play 'War Pigs' by Black Sabbath, or put a battery on her tongue. Or pinch her. Nana said her daughter-in-law was a beautiful pup you thought was dead and it wasn't until you rubbed and rubbed it, even punched it and then popped it in the bottom door of the Rayburn, that it squeaked and mewled with signs of life.

Mum had pills from the doctor she didn't take, and then sometimes she took too many.

'Mummy!'

'Hmmm?'

'Don't stop, Mummy!'

'Hayo! Tell Hayo!' Molly yelled from the table top.

'Oh yes.' She tried to focus on us. It was hard. 'And what did we call her, Molly?'

'Hayo!'

'That's right. Halo. Diamond Star Halo Llewelyn, because she learned to walk to "Get It On". Because she's dirty sweet and she's my girl.'

I let Mum sigh as my buttery sister laughed. I let Mum light her special cigarette, and the room puffed with her sweet smoke. I was never sure if I liked The Story of Me. Nana said it was a knife-edge tale and I was lucky my mother didn't hold it against me. After all, I had nearly killed her. The strange thing was, I was sure I remembered the cymbals and the drum: the cold and shimmering metal that crashed me into the scream that cleared my lungs, the somersault on the tight snare that helped unwind the thick cord wrapped twice around my neck and turning me blue. I was sure I remembered my first gulp of the studio's smoky air. Nana says that sort of remembering is a gift, and a curse, so it's Nana who still asks me, 'Do you really remember, Halo love? Are you sure? Because what came first, pet? The chicken or the egg, eh? Is it really that night you remember, or do you just remember the *story* you've been told?'

Maybe she's right; maybe I just remember the stories. After all, the stories aren't what *really* happened. They can't be. Not at all.

Like our mum.

Our mother was born in a drawer. At least that's what she told us. Nana Lew says even with the family my mother had, this is impossible. '*Found* she was, Halo. She was found in a drawer.'

It was a blacked-out night, the bombs were falling on Swansea and Mum was just a few hours old. She was swaddled tight, red and quiet in the bottom drawer of a tall mahogany chest, of Room 213, The Halcyon Hotel, Angel Road. It was an establishment cheap on the pocket as well as the eye. Mum told us she didn't really remember.

'There's nothing, apart from a strange love of whistling and small, dark places. I know it wasn't exactly normal, kids, being left like that, but it wasn't unusual. Not unusual at all. It was the war, after all. People loved faster then.'

Like my Nana Lew said, my mum wasn't born *in* the drawer, but the someone who'd brought her into the world and then left her in Room 213 was a someone she'd never meet again. This was because a woman by the name of Minny Palmer found Mum, and Minny Palmer was a woman who would never let her go.

I suppose back then many Welsh girls had their bellies filled by the war and a dazzle-mouthed GI; I suppose countless babies were found in your fleapit hotels on pitch-dark nights as the bombs whistled down outside. Mum calls herself lucky: lucky she was found by hands so small and kind, lucky that the threat of namelessness (or worse, a Doreen, a Phyllis, a Myfanwy) was taken away by this second mother, Minny Palmer, who called the little baby 'Doll'. 'Dolly Halcyon Palmer', who, by sixteen, was big enough and girl enough to man the Shoot the Dictators stall at the Dolls' Fair in Tiger Bay, and make her own pennies.

Mum has a catch of the Bay in her words still, and a catch of Wapping too, where she spent her winters. Half cockney, half Welsh – but maybe neither – my mum has a voice that has come out strange. My mother who whispers 'Salsify!' before she drops into sleep, my mother who is only lit by Dad and the burners of her cooker, my mother who won't put a foot inside her mother-in-law's capel, my mother who stares out at our rocky fields and growls.

I don't think Mum minds the fact of the drawer: a practical Welsh manger, she calls it. In fact, if you take a look in our house you'll know she doesn't. In her bedroom, in the living room and in the hall, tall chests, long sideboards and home-made cupboards are lined up against the Anaglypta-papered walls. They all have countless drawers, and each drawer, big or tiny, has neat brass handles with a plate above. Inside the plates are labels, marked with my mother's neat writing. They run all the way from 'Aerosols' and 'Arseholes' (that drawer is filled with the handwritten name or the photograph of the offending 'arsehole') to 'Zips' and 'Zebras (Toy)'.

Our house is filled with drawers.

'It's because she's hopeful,' Nana Lew tells us. 'She opens all those drawers from time to time just hoping to find her boy, just hoping to find *him* again, poor lamb.'

7

Two days later Jenny was standing on our porch, sun in her horse-brown eyes and the end of her pigtail in her mouth. She wore clogs and a short, strapless sunflower dress that hugged her stomach.

'Hey, kiddo,' she said. 'Wanna come riding?'

'Of course she does,' Mum answered for me. Mum had opened the door to Jenny while I stood behind her at hip height. Mum bit at a loose nail and stared at Jenny. Jenny chewed on her hair.

They bit and chewed at each other, like cows on cud.

'Jenny, are you sure *you* should be riding a horse?' my mother asked.

Jenny smiled with her big front teeth. 'I can ride real good.'

'I'm sure you can, it's just—' Mum nodded at Jenny's stomach, '—I don't like...'

'What you got cooking for us, ma'am?'

'I haven't decided yet. Jenny, I think you—'

'Y'always cook?' Jenny's chin pushed out, determined.

'Not always.'

'What else you do?'

'A lot of things.'

'You ride?'

'Not *always*.'

Mum stared at Jenny's big baby-stomach. Two Red Admirals fluttered around Jenny's head, fighting, and finally Mum shrugged, resigned. 'Have fun,' she told us, and with a final stab at care she shook her head.

Jenny walked up the track towards the stables. I skipped behind.

'She is real pretty,' Jenny muttered, 'but she's *old*.'

'Nana's old, not Mum.'

'She ain't as young as me, kiddo.'

In the moist heat of the stable we pulled leather girths tight on our barrel-bellied horses. Jenny had Stardust, the darkest Welsh cob, and I had Donny the Shetland. Tequila were filling the courtyard with the 'dum-dum, dum-dum, dum-dum' of a bass guitar trying to find its rhythm.

'Do you have a horse at home?' I asked.

Jenny snorted. 'Do *I* have a horse? Sweet thing, I was born a horse.'

I pondered this. If Jenny was born a horse, how did she turn into a girl? Was it in one fell swoop? One day she woke up human? Or did she have the horsey bit hidden in that big belly of hers? But which bits? Hooves? Fetlocks? I felt dizzy and grabbed hold of Donny's hairy side.

Jenny tugged the bridle and led Stardust out into the court-yard, his metal shoes sliding on old cobbles.

'These ponies spook easy, kiddo?'

Donny bared his sugar-bad teeth at me.

Jenny kicked off her clogs and stood up on the mounting block. 'You gonna help me here, kid?'

Stardust was wide muscle. Jenny really did need all the help she could get; maybe she needed all the help in the world. I skipped out, Donny lagging behind me, and locked my small hands for Jenny's bare foot. As she pulled and I pushed, her dress caught in my open mouth and it tasted of caramel and smoke. Jenny was about as heavy as a girl could be.

She laced her fingers through Stardust's rough mane. 'This here horse sure is sweet, man. Sweet as Jesus.'

I decided Jenny had a funny ha-ha voice, loose and loud around the lips. I went up on my tiptoes on the mounting block. 'Where are you from, Jenny?'

'America.'

'Where-in-America?'

'Wyoming, where the cowboys come from, where prairie colts are wired.'

'Are they electric?'

'What, kiddo?'

'Nothing. How long does it take to get there, Jenny?'

'It's about as far as you can get, I guess.'

Stardust whinnied, shaking his head.

'Are you all from there?'

'Nope, the band are southern boys, South Carolina.'

I looked up at her. 'My mummy says you're young to have a baby.'

Jenny laughed. 'What does she know? Old coot.'

'What does your mummy think?'

'C'mon kid, let's ride.'

Our unmatched horses hot-stepped out of the courtyard and I noticed Jenny's feet weren't in the stirrups. Her feet were pushed, heel first, into Stardust's sides, her toes splayed like a monkey's.

She looked down at Donny and me from her height. 'I feel like I'm home!' she told us.

61

It was odd, playing with a stranger. I only played with my sister and my nana. It was odd, playing with a singer. The singers and the bands didn't play with us kids. They'd pat us on the heads, maybe write a song about us, get us in for a rousing chorus, but they wouldn't *play*.

I giggled along with Donny's staccato trots while Jenny laughed like a child on a beach. She rode like the devil too, but she didn't jump. 'Abe told me "no", kiddo,' she shouted through her hair. 'I mean, I ain't ever gonna fall off, but I do what my man tells me.' She pulled Stardust into a stop and lay back on his rump; her arms hung down his sides like the holy cross on a donkey.

I listened to the field buzz.

'Stupid, ain't it?' she finally said, staring up at the few puffs of thin clouds.

I didn't know what was stupid but Jenny scratched a tight breast then grabbed hold of the reins and hoisted herself up. Stardust shook his head and grunted. She started to speak, but before I could hear her words, a quick canter swallowed them.

I bounced with Donny's stabbing trot, my teeth rattled and I tried to catch up.

Jenny and I lay on our backs in the boggy grass, the horses munching chickweed and clover around us. This close, Jenny smelled of maple syrup and fruity sweat. She tore at daisies and lifted them up into the sun.

'Where in the hell are we, anyways?' she asked.

'This is Beggars' Field and that's Beggars' Hill because Nana says we're all beggars round here.'

'No, kid, *here*,' she thumped the earth, 'where in the hell are we in England?'

I stared down at the tops of her blue-veined breasts. 'We're not in England.'

'Huh?'

'This is Wales.' I sat up and pointed across to the other side of the small road. 'England's over there.'

'We ain't *in* England?'

'No. But it's not far.'

'Shit.' Jenny threw the daisies. 'I've done and told everyone I'm living in England. Where the Stones are. The Beatles. Where Hendrix came.'

'We've got cows named after the Beatles. John, Paul, George and Ringo. I like George the best. She's the prettiest.'

She giggled. 'You're crazy, kiddo.'

I noticed that Jenny had freckles on her eyelids, just like me. She turned her head, a hand shielding the sun. 'It's "Halo", right?'

'Yes.'

'Ain't calling you that.' She pulled at the long grass and stuck a blade in her mouth. 'I'll call you "Haley" like Bill Haley and his Comets and "Rock Around The Clock".' She picked at more green blades, examined them, then put one between her thumbs and blew out a high-pitched squeal. I jumped. Later, I found that Jenny had a habit of tearing up grass and carrying it around in her pockets; she said you never knew when you might need a good handful of fresh, green grass. She said it was those dry years on the prairies made her do it.

'"Ha-ley"?'

'Yes?'

'Shush – just trying it out. "Ha-ley"?' Jenny shifted on the ground until she was finally on her side; sweat beaded her brow and lip. 'Ha-ley? You like boys?'

I thought of Vincent, who'd plucked his eyebrows yesterday. He looked surprised, and ill. 'Not really.'

'Tell the truth. Your momma ever say "Always tell the God's-honest"?'

I thought of Jenny's band, Tequila. I thought of the golden brothers with their golden skin in our small beds.

'One day you'll love boys.' Jenny took a deep breath, and as the green clover softened beneath us, she sang, slow and sweet.

> 'They come from the prairie,
> Oh them colts they sure are wired,
> While the whining tall grass sings wild licks,
> like a steel guitar on fire.
>
> Stallion-boys kick like whiskey,
> They'll squeal like a woman, too,
> Them boys need it a-all so bad
> They can't see for blue.'

Jenny scratched her thigh like she needed it. She took a breath and sang some more.

> 'Stallion boys are in town tonight
> Stallion boys, they're gonna drink down and fight…'

She gasped. 'It's hard to goddamned sing with this.' She slapped her belly. 'Touch it. Go on, kid.'

I wrinkled my nose. Jenny was a balloon filled with water that kicked. Her skin bubbled like the tops of Nana Lew's cakes in the top of her Rayburn. I sat up straight and I poked her. Then I pressed down on Jenny's belly with both hands, hard as I could. All she did was laugh, then burp.

'Hey, that tickles!'

I pressed again and suddenly I wanted to lie on her with all my weight – which wasn't much then – and feel those inside-belly kicks, kicking into me.

I clambered on.

'Hey! Scoot! Scoot off-a me, girl. Ha!'

I was lying on top of her, arms and legs off the ground. This time she burped *and* farted.

'He's kicking, kiddo. You woke him.'

I could feel her belly ripple beneath me like it was filled with eels. I let my head rest on her pillow-like chest.

'When is he coming out, Jenny?'

'Fred? Oh, I figure, soon.'

'Will he be born at my house?'

'No. We'll be long gone, kiddo. Hey, your momma's had three, like my momma, right? She had them right here, your poppa said. At home.'

I slid off. I wondered if I should tell Jenny it was four. My mum had had four babies. She had four children. Now it was just three: Molly and Vince and me.

'How old are you *really*, Jenny?' I asked instead.

'Well.' Jenny pulled a cigarette from her dress pocket and struck a match. 'Thing is, my momma said I was born old. And there ain't no need to frown like that, kid – if you born old, you born old, and that's me. Momma said she never could hold me.

I was already gone, like I knew it all before I tried it. Yes, sir-ee. She said I was an old spirit who cheated on God and came back too soon. Momma was crazy like that. Like *your* grandma over in that big old house, she's crazy too, right?' Jenny giggled and puffed. 'Even Abraham thought I was older than I was. When I told him the truth, he cried like a darned baby. Never seen a grown man cry, not without drink. He didn't like it, me so young. But it's OK because I'm older now. I'm just the right age for everything. Ha!'

'But back then, see, my Abe wouldn't touch me for the longest time and that all done but killed me, so I told him, 'Listen, I'm still me and you's still you, Abe, so make me old, honey. Just make me old.' We been together two years now, and though we're married now and got the baby, it'll all be different when my birthday comes around, kiddo. I would have walked this here earth for a whole seventeen years then. And that's old enough, kiddo, old enough for anyone. My momma had three of us, time she was eighteen. So I'm working on it.'

Jenny threw the cigarette into the clover and scissored her arms over her face. The skin on her arms was translucent, not creamy like Mum's. I wanted to stroke her. Red Admirals rose and fell like bright colouring books, opening and closing above her. Jenny was snoring. I nestled down close to her and thought how she smelled of milk already.

'Can you come over and play with me every day, Jenny?'

She swatted a hand out like I was a fly. 'I ain't hanging out with no *kids*, kiddo.'

'Pu-leese.'

'I'm a grown woman. Got my man to think of. We got work to do here.'

'What about a picnic? We can go to the woods. Pu-leese?'

I put my face to the side of her belly. I tried very hard to see it through her dress. Whatever was cooking in there thrilled me. I had been too young to notice Molly in Mum, and anyway this one was different. This one rippled and farted and burped and made my hands hot. I wanted to speak to it and tell it everything.

Right there and then in the mossy field I prayed a prayer (backwards) just like Nana had taught me.

'Baby-A-Want-I
Baby-A-Want-I
Baby-A-Want-I.'

I whispered this twenty-one times, as crows purred like wildcats around us – my chorus of witches – and my nana's blackthorn and hawthorn bushes circled us with their claws.

'Baby-A-Want-I,' I said out loud, 'Baby-A-Want-I. *This* One.'

'What you say, kiddo?'

8

Jenny Connor, a singer with an American rock band called
Tequila, was officially my friend.

'Your friend's here, Halo,' Vince would shout.

'Your friend's out on the porch,' Dad would tell me.

I went riding with Jenny and she'd baby me in the fields.
Practice, she called it, as she cradled me against her belly like
some doll. She soothed as I cried, patting my curls. She'd lose
patience fast.

'Ah, quit it,' she'd snap, 'you ain't no goddamn baby.'

We went down to the river with Baden, and while I swam (or
gripped handfuls of Baden's thick neck as he did), Jenny would
float in the weak summer current, her white belly poking up
above the surface like an island. Jenny was so swollen I was
afraid she might pop or float away. Afterwards, still wet and
weedy, we'd lie on the bank and she'd tell me all about cowboys;
she'd sing about them too in her sweet and croaky voice. *Stallion boys, they're in town tonight, those stallion boys, they're
gonna drink and fight*, she'd sing, and I thought how wonderful
it was having a best friend: a best friend in the world, ever.

In one way, though, Jenny *was* like my mother. That was
because one day she would be happy and yee-hawing in the
fields, and the next day she was blank: glassy eyed and gone.
Abraham would have to tell me to come back later. He said they
had work to do.

But on Jenny's good days we'd take the horses out; we'd ride and she'd teach me the words to 'Dusty Skies' and 'Home on the Range' and 'I Want to be a Cowboy's Sweetheart'.

On one of those hot August days I sat on the fifteenth step of Nana's wide staircase and looked up at her curling balustrade. It was maple and it creaked for its own pleasure. Nana said in her scullery-maid days she had dreamed of polishing this glorious wood; but a scullery was a scullery. Now she didn't have time for it.

I was waiting. I wasn't allowed beyond this fifteenth step, not until my hips and my chest grew, not until *things happened* to me. I didn't move, but it wasn't because I was an obedient child: I simply couldn't. Vince said our grandmother had buried something beneath this step to stop us kids – an old dried baby cat, he said. I looked up at the gilt-framed paintings of Bastards-past. Their fierce eyes glared at me, their noses turned. Beneath them were Nana's family photographs – framed images of black-faced miners with eyes bright as diamonds, and hard-faced women standing by garden gates. I smelled coal and carbolic.

'Breaker. Breaker. 1-9. FoxyRed calling. FoxyRed. Breaker, breaker,' Nana said. The buzz-fizz of her CB radio tuned in and out like a blast of wind on incoming fog. Nana was a CB enthusiast. Nana was FoxyRed.

'Breaker, breaker' – hiss-fizz-click – 'your prayers are needed, sons and daughters. Breaker, breaker. FoxyRed calling. Anyone got their ears on? 1-9.'

'Hey, FoxyRed, 10-4!' – click-hiss-fizz – 'what's your 20?'

Nana had made contact.

'Rockfarm. Here at Rockfarm. 1-9. FoxyRed,' she told them.

'Country Joe, FoxyRed, got your 20.'

Click-buzz-fizz.

From the very top of Nana's house, old chains held a great brass light in place. It was patterned with dragons, so neatly drawn in metal and gilt that I could see each lock of backbone, each push of their ribs as they quietly breathed the fire that lit the hall. Nana said this light had been there since before the Bastard's time. In Nana's scullery-maid days she said these dragons breathed a blue, gassy fire, but now her very own Ivan Comfort had wired them up and poked 60-watt bulbs in their narrow, dragony mouths. I listened to their muffled breath.

The oak front door creaked and I heard the slap of big feet, the rustle of a plastic bag. 'Vin-cent?' I tried, because you never knew in Nana's house.

Vince walked in with his head down, his big, square chin to his chest and his white arms floppy at his sides like boiled bratwurst. Dad said Vince hadn't grown into himself yet. He said Vincent was a small boy inside a big body, but one day the two would meet. It was like Vince was the Hulk without getting angry or green.

'Vince?'

He looked up, slow as a camel. Vincent's eyes were Mum's: black, beautiful and fathomless. He had plucked his eyebrows to nothing now. I'd heard Mum saying thirteen was a most difficult age.

'What are you doing, Vince?'

'I could ask you the same.'

'I'm waiting for Nana. I'm going on a picnic with Jenny.'

'You'd better ask Mum.' Vincent stared up at the portraits of the Bastards. 'It's hot,' he said. 'I'm going to play the piano.'

'That's nice.'

For a moment Vincent looked at me and he almost smiled. Then he was gone into Nana's parlour.

Johnny Cash's 'Folsom Prison Blues' boom-chikka-boomed from Nana's bedroom. I supposed her Breaker-Breaker-Foxy-Red prayers were all called out, called in. Nana had been doing a lot of praying lately; in fact, it was ever since Tequila arrived that she'd come down from her capel most mornings, filmed with sweat.

Nana's collies thundered down the stairs and past me. She was standing on the landing in a thin nightie. She coughed as Vincent began his scales. The tick-tock of a metronome joined the tick-tock of the grandmother clock and the boom-chikka-boom of Johnny Cash, each swing of each pendulum, each chug of the musical train rippling the waters of the Big House.

'What do you want today then, Halo? You want a scrap of tongue?'

'Something for my picnic.'

'It's a picnic you're having then? And who's invited?'

'Jenny.'

'And who else?'

'Just Jenny.'

'Hmmm.'

Instead of rifling through her cupboards or cutting a wedge of bread, Nana sighed; she smelled of vinegar, and that was the smell of worry.

'Why are you sad today, Nana?'

She sucked her big teeth. 'Never you mind, sunbeam, never you mind.'

'Are your friends coming to make you better?'

'Who's that?'

'Your friends on the radio.'

She pinched my cheek. 'They will, sunbeam, they will. Now, you want something for your picnic?'

'Yes please.'

She pointed at the kitchen table, laden with cake.

'Help yourself.'

I had hoped for ham and cheese sandwiches, even egg.

'No,' she mumbled to herself, 'it can't be, it can't happen.'

'It's only a picnic, Nana.'

'No!'

But she wasn't looking at me any more; she was staring at the pictures of Elvis and Johnny above her jukebox. 'I'll get them all here and we'll pray, we'll pray as hard as nails, we will.' She marched to the Rayburn, slammed a copper pan down on a hotplate and threw the gluey contents of three jars into it. I pushed through the warm wall of collies towards her.

'Is that for me, Nana?'

'No,' she said, flat, 'it's something to stop something bad happening, sunbeam. It's something to make someone stay. Can't eat it. Have to bury it. Out there in the garden.'

'To make who stay, Nana?'

'Can't tell you.'

'Mum and Dad haven't gone anywhere. Vincent's in your parlour and Molly's *somewhere*.'

'Don't tell tales.' Nana froze. She was murmuring, not making much sense. I noticed how her thin nightie was stuck to her hot back.

'Here we are, sunbeam.' She picked up a plate of rock cakes

72

and dropped them in a Co-op bag. 'You have these. For your picnic.' Nana clapped her hands together. 'Now, out you go, sunbeam, enjoy the day before it dies! Come on now.' She shooed me and went back to her muttering. 'The bad will soon come. Ominous. That's the word. French it is. *Om-in-ooos.*'

She nodded out the window. 'Outside's green and heavy with it, sunbeam. *Ominooos,*' and she did more than sigh, she moaned a little. 'Stay. Stay. Stay, boy, stay,' she muttered over her pan as her troop of collies howled like white-faced gibbons around her, teeth bared.

Vincent was playing 'Oh! You Pretty Things' in the parlour, because Vincent loved David Bowie. Vincent worshipped David Bowie and Tippi Hedren, and no one else. He said they were chameleons that dressed smart and he liked their thin faces. He said his favourite film was *Marnie* and his favourite song was 'Life on Mars?'. Vince was a boy set in his ways. I shivered in the big hall and pushed the big front door. The sunlight startled me: it was so dark in Nana's house, particularly today.

As I cantered up the gravel track with the bag of rock cakes, my hands hoofing the air, strong as Champion the Wonder Horse, I looked out for Nana's heavy green.

And there it was.

It was a high summer green and it sprouted from our verges as heavy as the dirty wool that hung from my grandmother's sheep.

It was hot.

I galloped under the red-brick arch into the courtyard, and neighed.

Nana was right, it was ominous.

Om-in-ooos.

*

Jenny was crouching near the duck pond. She wore a red velvet cape and she was quiet; it was one of her blank days. I knelt beside her at the edge of the green water, and she smelled of smoke and dark treacle. She was drooling like Molly did when she was a gurgling baby. Jenny rocked back and forth and I held on to the red cape in case she fell in.

'Can you come for a picnic, Jenny?' I whispered.

Jenny's dirty fingers picked at her dirty bare feet. Her fingers and her feet were swollen: in fact, all of Jenny was swollen, so swollen I didn't lie on her now because she *could* pop. I didn't like Fred the baby so much any more. The baby had made Jenny blow up, watery; the baby oozed from her.

A bass guitar thum-thum-thummed across the courtyard, then Abe's voice yelled out.

> 'Little girl, let your hair down
> Little girl, dance for me
> Little girl, when it comes to night time
> Little girl, set me free!'

A heavy guitar whipped round his screeching voice. Tequila had changed their sound.

I reached for Jenny's hand and pulled. 'Are you coming?'

Her eyes were as glassy as the eyes of the dead kittens Molly found in the stables the month before.

'Come on, it's not far,' I told her, 'it's not far to the wood.'

I slipped my small hand onto Jenny's bare knee. It felt hard, crusty as the knee of a floor-crawling toddler. I reached for her softer hand and pulled, and smooth as pouring gravy, she stood.

When we got to the garden gate, I made her wait as I picked up my small rucksack, packed tight with two sheets, baler twine, my *Beano* comics, and a damp box of matches, because years of Boy Scouts camping in our fields had taught me something.

9

Truth is a hard thing to remember. It's even harder to tell.
Nana says if you tell the truth it can only ever be a story. I now
know that there are stories within stories, and in telling one,
another slips out. You can't help it.

That day in Beggars' Wood I was very young and skintight,
my muscles small as wound-up mice. I was as powerful as I
wanted to be. That day I was innocent enough to put ribbons in
my hair, and wicked enough to burn them later.

I'm still not sure how it all happened, because it started in a
wood: a wood that was as bright and safe as a drawing-room
fire, a wood that was as dark and delicious as a fairy tale.

After all, people get lost in woods.

Later, Fred and I would make Nana Lew's wood our own; he'd
lie in the fern and ask me: Was it here, Lo-Lo?

– What did she say, Lo-Lo?

– What did her voice sound like? Did it sound like mine?

– What was she wearing?

– How on earth could you lose my mother, Lo-Lo?

I try and tell him about Jenny's red cape ('Are you for real?'
he says). I try and tell him the sort of gold those buttercups
made on her throat. I try and tell him the glassy eyes . I try and
tell him the mumbling words, the giggles, and the sound of her
voice when she sang about her stallion boys: but all in all it
doesn't add up to much. It's hard to have to tell Fred his own

mother. Particularly when she is just a girl who's a blur on a record cover: a girl who still sings for us but a girl whose face has got mashed up, messed up, with every freckled American girl I've glimpsed since.

Is she a young Joni Mitchell? Is she Elizabeth Walton, or the sassier Erin Walton?

– 'Goodnight Elizabeth, Goodnaght Erin!'

Is she Jodie Foster in *Bugsy Malone* or Jodie Foster in *Taxi Driver*?

Jenny: the cheeky, hung-lipped girl who talked through her teeth with a wisecrack. On her quiet days Jenny was little Sissy Spacek, squeaking and whispering through freckled, hooded eyes.

I can never decide, because truth and memory have little in common, and truth and What Really Happened have little say in a wood – a place where my nana can lie down in the leaves and let the wood god get her, even if he is just an Irishman working the tarmac on the M40.

So a wood is a place where people disappear – though they haven't really disappeared; they are just deer or trees and much happier now thank you. There's history in a wood, too. There's stratum, there's topsoil and heartland, and too much of it, because the past, the present and the future all meld into one misremembered tale in a wood. A tale with a series of turns and twists so sharp in the path, not even breadcrumbs can help.

I try to tell Fred about his mother, but it's never enough.

Yet that day *was* lemon-hot, birds *did* gasp from the oaks, and me and the Jenny I think I remember *did* build our den. At least, I built it while she sat against a trunk and watched.

'Where have you dragged me, kiddo? What is this goddarned place?'

'It's a secret,' I told her, a finger to my lips, but she was muttering, playing with the split ends of her pigtails.

'Abe leaving me alone so long. Ain't my fault. Right, kiddo?' She wiped her mouth, mumbling now. 'I been a good girl. Just this one time. It's nothing. Hey, kiddo, what we gonna *do* here?'

I tied a line of baler twine between two close beech trunks and took out a white linen sheet. I had to stand on a tree root to pull the sheet over. This was going to be our tent. I tugged the white sides out and laid stones on top of the tight sheet edges. Dad had taught me this. He said waterproofs and zips and groundsheets were for sissies.

'There's lots to do,' I told her. 'We could build a den with sticks, too. My daddy taught me how to cut the bracken and use it for the walls. But I don't have a knife. We could play hide-and-seek. We could play horses. Black Beauty. Cowboys and Indians. We could sing "Stallion Boys".'

She closed her eyes. 'Come find me then, little girl.' Her voice waved in and out like the sounds on Nana's CB radio.

Jenny didn't play the hiding part of hide-and-seek; in fact, she didn't move from that tree trunk. I watched her swollen chest rise and fall, and I breathed along with her. She pulled the red cape around her and then locked her hands over her vast belly. She said, 'Fire, I want a fire, kiddo. I'm so cold. So cold.'

It wasn't hard. I made it with the red-headed matches and the yellowed pages of my *Beano*s, while Jenny lay against the stretch-marked trunk, opening and closing her drooling mouth like a parched man in a desert. My little hands gathered dry, copper bracken from underneath the new green fans, and I poked my fire with a stick. I put stones around it because Dad said you can never be too careful, not after last summer when rivers went underground and the whole of Wales and a bit of England got burnt. Scorching is scorching and the ground has a memory for it, Dad said.

I had picked the perfect spot. Every drop of coolness was here beneath the oak and beech trees because over there – past the barbed-wire fence where Mum's old horse Crazy Love had once snagged his belly – the cold breath of a forest blew in. You could hear the creaks of the tall pines: the rush of wind through them that sometimes sounded like the ocean.

Jenny agreed. 'This is perfect, kiddo,' she whispered and rolled away from the tree trunk and onto husks of old bluebells. I watched shadows from the beech leaves play on Jenny's face like dropping pennies and I knew that Nana Lew was right and this wood was a church if you bothered to look.

I bashed down ferns with my fists and sat down next to my friend.

'It's just *purr-fect*, kiddo,' she sighed, and even though she was right, I knew that there was another side to this coin, to the pennies that danced on Jenny's eyes.

Perhaps it was down to that cold breath of forest, because things had always spilled over from that darker place into Nana's wood. Like the black skinned deer that jumped the fence, bringing in their musk and their hooves like chiselled coal. There were no tight borders here and it wasn't *all* bright light and bluebirds singing. There was darkness and dark fairy tales; there were knolls here and that's where the trolls lived, *trolls in their knolls*, Nana said. There were burial mounds of bracken that hid ankle-biting badgers. There were wild boar and woodcutters; there were wolves and black bears; and one thing I was certain of, because it was lying here in front of me; there was a girl who slept beneath the trees in a red velvet cape.

I stared at Jenny. She was on her side, snoring. Her big white breasts pushed a flush of blood up into her cheeks and she looked better for it. I put my hand into a small box of Frosties and crammed sugary flakes in my mouth.

'Wa-up, Je-he,' I told her.

'Hmmmm.'

She shielded her eyes. The bluebell husks cracked beneath her. 'What in the hell are we doing, kiddo?'

'Camping.'

'What?'

'We're camping. We're making a den.'

'You're crazy,' she said. 'You drag me here?'

'Do you want a Coke a Cola?' I held a red can out and she shot up – as much as an over-pregnant girl can – and ran behind a beech trunk. I heard her retching and I put my fingers in my ears.

She didn't stop for the longest time, so I hummed and thought about the services my grandmother held not far from here. It was at the lip of the quarry. Nana would stand on top of a great flat stone and talk to the wood like it was talking right back to her. 'Great God the Almighty!' she'd shout at it. 'Listen! Listen!' Then she'd bend over and press play on her cassette player. It was usually Cash or Presley singing the Gospel Greats.

'Ahhm gonna
Lay down my soul,
In the bosom of

80

A-bra-ham,
Oh baby,
A-bra-ham,
Oh baby,
A-bra-ham.'

My grandmother did this in the summer for her flock, for the people she called her Paying Johnnies, the people who visited her at odd times – in the middle of the night, at Sunday lunchtime – the people who believed my grandmother did something and they were willing to put their hands in their pockets for it. So when Nana had a summer sermon, the Paying Johnnies would come out with black Bibles and prayer cushions for the damp. They'd come with flasks and corned-beef sandwiches for the comfort. Sometimes a band from the studio would follow my Nana here too, and afterwards they'd go back and record songs like 'Sermon in the Forest' or 'Layline in the Woods'.

I pulled my waxy fingers from my ears. Jenny wasn't retching any more: she was leaning up against the trunk, her face white again. She held her stomach tight, as if it was trying to crawl away.

'You got a wipe?' she gasped.

I nodded and handed her the roll of lavatory paper. 'Are you having your baby?' I asked.

'Don't be dumb. You see a baby coming out of me? Shit.' She spat on the ground. 'Talk to me, kiddo.'

'What about?'

'Anything, just talk.' Jenny staggered towards the tent, then she fell to her knees and crawled in; the sides puffed out as she settled. 'Talk to me, girl,' she groaned.

I didn't know what to say. I stared at ropes of bramble, dotted with blackberries, still too red and hard for tasting.

'Please, kid.' Her voice cracked and it sounded like she was crying. I thought about goose grease, drums and how to birth a baby. 'Haley, please,' she moaned. 'You're my friend, right?'

'Yes.'

'Then help me. Tell me a story.'

I tried to think.

'OK, you want me to start? Right, you gotta answer a question—'

I heard her breath, sharp through her teeth.

'What's the first music you heard, kiddo? *Tell me.*'

I looked up at the discs of beech leaves. I didn't know: my mother's reedy voice like wind through bamboo stalks? Cass Elliot singing 'Dream a Little Dream of Me'? Dad miming to Sam Cooke's wail in 'A Change is Gonna Come'? They're the snapshots of music I remember. Perhaps the first song I truly heard was Nana Lew's breathy timbre telling me, 'Rock a bye baby on the treetop, when the wind blows the cradle will rock, when the bough breaks the cradle will fall, and down will come baby, cradle and all,' because that was just the way the world was, Nana said. It was a world of crashing babies and breaking boughs, and my nana wet-whispered these words right into my ear.

It was a warning to have my wits about me.

'Kiddo, the first music I heard was church. Ahhh!'

My skin fizzed with panic. I felt greasy as citrus peel. 'Shall I get my mummy?'

'No!'

'My nana—'

82

'Tell me a fucking story, kiddo. Please.'

I looked down at the wood floor where young green hazelnuts had dropped, still jacketed and frilly as anemones. They were so young I could crack them with my back baby teeth and they'd taste fresh as milk. I pushed my fingers into the chilled ground.

'We-we w-went to London,' I stammered, because I wanted to cry. 'And Mummy says Vincent hasn't been the same since.'

I stared up at the green-green leaves.

'We went all together in the old car that smelled of fish and it was me, Mummy, Daddy, Vincent and Robert because Molly wasn't born yet.'

And that was the way it worked: before Molly there was Robert and after Molly there was no Robert.

I glanced at the white-sheet tent; the top of Jenny's head was sticking out of one end, pockets of sun playing in her amber hair. She was coughing, her face red, so at least she had colour back.

'And it was so brilliant, Jenny. Because me, Mummy, Daddy, Vincent and Robert, we went up to London and it took ages because Daddy's old car still had ladders on the roof and they whistled all the way. London's a very long way away.'

Blackbirds scratched at the ground.

'And Robert was a big boy and he walked into the concert with Mummy and Vincent, and I was on Daddy's shoulders and we all had tickets to watch David Bowie be a person called Ziggy Stardust and that's why Mummy says Vincent hasn't been the same since.'

I closed my eyes and I saw the fogged-up Morris Minor, Robert singing 'Lilly the Pink' and me as young as Molly. I was nestled between my two brothers. We had different haircuts and different jumpers then: stocky fringes were heavy on our foreheads, bright wool stripes crossed our chests, and our jeans flared.

I lay back in the dead bluebells of my grandmother's wood and I tried to get a better look.

The year 1973 wasn't that long ago, but in 1973 I was a much littler girl, potty-trained and in love with the biggest of my brothers, my brother Robert. In 1973 a man called David Bowie was Ziggy Stardust for one last time and he made lots of women and lots of men cry: lots of girls and lots of boys, too. And Vince hasn't been the same since.

10

'Mum, tell Halo not to lean on me. She's leaning, Mum.'

'Give her here, I don't mind, Vince,' Robert laughed.

It was Robert who first called Vincent 'Vince'. Robert said things were *groovy*. He said they were *cool*.

In 1973, Robert was ten and that's where he ended: always my big brother, but always a ten-year-old boy.

Robert had two girlfriends at school. He had one for the mornings and one for the afternoons. Robert received Valentine cards. He'd leave them on the kitchen table, unopened. Robert had tight brown muscles I nestled into. Nana says Robert was the spirit of our father on the inside, and the beauty of our mother on the outside. She says that because of what happened, our Robert will always be perfect and he will always be young.

'But she's *leaning*,' said Vincent.

'Leave her alone, Vince, she's only a baby.'

'But she is, Rob, she's *touching*. I don't like it. Mummy! She's touching. Rob, make her stop!'

Touching Vincent was forbidden; blowing on Vincent was forbidden. He was funny about germs, particularly ones that lived in the air, on your fingers, and on your head.

'Getheroffme!'

At mealtimes Robert would blow on Vincent's food and Vincent would push the little blown-on bit right to the edge of the plate. If we went over to Nana Lew's, Vincent would cry and lock himself in the bathroom with the Fairy Liquid, until any memory of the collies' tongues was wiped away. Vincent was a little better now. He had his plastic bag of cleaning fluids. He had gloves and a comb and keys to lock his doors to the germs.

'Getheroffme!'

I felt the stab from Vincent's elbow push me into Robert. I cried out.

'You're OK, Halo, don't be silly. It's only Vince.' Robert tickled me under the chin because he knew I was faking. 'My little La-La girl.'

My heart melted and I giggled because I couldn't talk that much. Robert wiped the hot-car sweat from my forehead. I pressed my face into the side of his T-shirt that smelled of straw and boy, and girlfriends.

'How long is it to go?' Robert asked.

'Hmmm?' said Mum.

'I said how long is it to go, Mum?'

She sighed. 'How long is it to go, Ivan?'

'How long is a piece of string, Rob?' Dad told him.

'Yeshowlongisittogoooo?' Vincent wailed.

'Just settle down, please.' Dad shook his head; his hair was brighter and his voice was firmer then. 'Settle down, all of you. Sing a song, for godsakes.'

So we sang 'Lily the Pink'. Or rather I gabbled while the rest of my family used proper words.

'Lilly the PinkaPinkaPink!'

I looked up from the hum of Robert's chest to watch smooth lorry wheels spin past.

We have Polaroids of that day: there's Robert and Vincent holding hands in a lay-by and Vincent looking small; Robert outside a petrol station near Newport in a brown T-shirt that says **Humble Pie** in yellow letters; Robert holding me like a child holds a fat cat. Robert's black hair is long, feathered around his face like David Cassidy's. His flares are ironed and tidy.

Mum's fingers have browned these photos round their edges. She keeps them under her bed in a cardboard box.

When we got to London, we ran through a place called Hammersmith because we were late. We were always late. I jiggled as Dad piggybacked me through the underpass. I heard chanting girls' voices crying, 'David! David! David!'

For most of that concert I slept against Mum's hip or on Dad's shoulders. Robert was forced to hold Vincent's hand all night. Bright lights flashed and when I woke up David Bowie – who was Ziggy Stardust – was standing at the front of the stage in a woolly multi-coloured suit, with one leg bare. Ziggy Stardust smelled of pear drops and sweet white wine, and his one bare leg was thick and hairy. Ziggy had gold lips.

From Dad's shoulder I saw Rob and Vincent: suddenly two small boys too short to see the stage. They disappeared into the crush of the crowd, and I cried out. No one could hear me, the noise was too loud and sharp and bright.

And then there was just the high buzz in my ears on the way home because for all my remembering, that's all I remember of that.

'Well, he's done now,' Dad said as the ladders on the roof rack whistled.

'He'll be someone else though, love. Bound to. He's too young to retire. Love to cook for him, I would.' Mum yawned. 'You enjoyed it, kids? Your first gig?'

I was awake between my brothers. Robert's breath smelled of milk and spinach and beer. Vincent looked stunned as he stared at the white lines in the road.

'Yes, Mummy, it was brilliant,' Robert said, because even if Robert was a little man with brown muscles and ten-year-old lip fuzz, Robert still called his mum 'Mummy'.

As we turned onto the Severn Bridge, Robert told me that that concert would always be the best concert ever, 'because it was my first, Halo. My first proper gig. It'll always be better than anything else.' I nestled into my brother's strong body, but I didn't realize he was right. We rattled over the bridge, its cables whistling along with the ladders on the roof rack, and Vincent began to cry. When Dad asked him why, he said he was crying because Ziggy Stardust was gone for ever and he loved Ziggy Stardust more than anything else in the whole world.

'There'll be others,' Dad said, 'don't worry now Vince, David Bowie'll be someone else soon, you mark my words.'

But Vincent couldn't stop. He was hysterical and he cried all the way home.

Nana Lew tells me things just *happen* and life is made up of accidents like Robert's. There's nothing you can do to stop them. She says some of these accidents are for a reason.

'Look at Johnny Cash,' she says. 'Think he'd be where he is today without what happened to his brother? The wood saw that cut that poor brother down, well, it gave something to Johnny, whether he wanted it or not. And then there's Elvis, his twin going like that, just a few hours old. But our little Elvis lived. They leave something behind, these Beloveds, these ones that are taken from us, and the gaps they leave are gifts, and those gifts are for those that remain, if you have the balls to see, my girl. Look at me. All my big brothers were taken from me. Three lovely big brothers I had, then the Great War snatches them, but they left me with a gift now, didn't they? What you think Robert left you?'

I try and think. I try and remember.

It's Mum's hands and nails I remember most: her nails that I'm sure have never healed. They still split when she skins onions. It was because she wouldn't go down without a scrap; it was because she fought with the rocks and the stones.

After Mum came back from the hospital and told us that no one could help Robert any more, she walked out into the night. Mum went out to Nana's graveyard and she fought.

That night I lay against my grandmother's vinegary bosom on the brown couch in her parlour, and I listened to the old pickup's wheels spinning in the graveyard as Nana whispered, 'Let her, let her,' into my toddler-ear.

'Let her, Halo love; if she gets to morning it'll cure her some.'

Dad and Vincent were upstairs in Nana's bed, floored by my grandmother's sleeping draught. None of us could bear to go back to our house. With my baby-blinks I spied Robert's green jumper on the back of Nana's armchair.

There are no gravestones in Nana Lew's churchyard because that night my mother cleared them. She cleared the ones telling us 'Here Lieth', and the ones saying 'For God and Country'. That night as Nana Lew held me close we listened to the pickup wheel spin in the capel's boggy ground. We heard the angry engine flood into silence once or twice, but Mum was scrapping; my mum wasn't going down without a fight, and she soon started it up again. She had patience. Tenacity. Grief.

The thing was, Mum was up there roping the thick and heavy gravestones; she was lassoing the marble 'Here Lieths' like baby calves in a rodeo ring. My mother was a cowgirl. She was pulling them out like the rotten teeth they were.

Months later, when she could talk, when she could hobble down from her bedroom without falling, she told us that that was the saddest thing; those bloody gravestones had been so hard to pull up, where just a single day earlier one had come away easy as over-boiled meat from the bone: and all to crush a boy who was hiding.

'Ridiculous,' she spat.

I was there when Robert died. Vincent was too. We were playing like brothers and a sister should, all three of us up at the capel going at hide-and-seek behind the headstones.

Robert had told us it was a baby-game and he was too old for hide-and-seek. He wanted to play Commandos, Action Man. He wanted to play Shooting. He said he had Some Fags to Smoke and Some Girls to Kiss, but Vincent wanted hide-and-seek.

So hide-and-seek it was.

I was playing my own nameless game which involved running around the same gravestone, barking, and then poking Napoleon – Nana's oldest collie – in the eye. Napoleon was my patient protector. Round and around, bark, poke, and yelp. Round and around, bark, poke, and yelp, until my brain was a fusion of an old dog's pain and my pleasure.

It was because of this that I didn't hear Vincent's screams right away. It took me a while to toddle over to my brothers, my chubby legs unsure at the joints. By the time I reached them, Napoleon the collie was howling along with Vincent.

Vincent's hands were between his legs; there was a dark patch where he'd wet himself. I wobbled as close to his noise as I could get and I saw what he was screaming at.

The top of the tallest and thickest headstone had fallen. Whether it belonged to an English Bastard or a Llewelyn, I didn't know. It was as if a lightning bolt had cracked the granite halfway up the rain-faded words. I smelled the freshness where it had broken in two: where it had split, pitched, and crashed down.

Black was spreading through the couch grass, and Robert's head and shoulders were beneath the fractured part of the stone. He must have been lying there, hiding. Perhaps he leant too close, perhaps he pushed against it and that ancient split had finally quivered and dropped. His legs and arms seemed fine, though they jerked like cartoon arms and legs. I wondered if soon he would get up; his head flat as a pancake until he shook it – gobble-gobble-gobble – and it rose up again like sponge cake. Later, I heard Nana Lew say Robert wouldn't have felt a thing, the blow was so sure, but to me, wobbling on a grave mound, it looked like a very bad boo-boo. I puffed out my cheeks and stared at the black that still poured out of my brother and mixed with that coarse grass.

I think about that black blood even now. It was as if his body had been dead all day, as if his blood had long congealed from bright red to black. Perhaps Robert's body had died before his Shreddies, before his kick-about and hide-and-seek; perhaps it had taken our Robert – the Robert-inside-the-body – all day to do all the things he wanted to do, before he could catch up and die too.

I stood on that grave mound and barked at the thick headstone. I wanted to find the hole where Robert was bleeding from, screw in Dad's bicycle pump, and pump him back up again. I barked and I barked and Vincent screamed and he screamed until Dad came.

I barked for a long time after that.

Vincent screamed, too.

Blackbirds shrieked beneath the Ribena-coloured bramble stalks and crows purred from the warty oaks above.

'I had a big brother called Robert,' I whispered up into the leaf shadows.

I could never understand how one day I would be older than Robert, but at the same time he would always be my big brother. Robert who smelled of bubblegum and mints; Robert who was as hard and as soft as toffee, you just had to know how to warm him; Robert, a boy who dreamed of sailing all the seas in the world until he simply dropped off.

Jenny was quiet beneath the tent.

I nestled into the ground, closed my eyes against the setting dappled sun, and sucked my thumb.

Nana Lew called that sucking a terrible habit: 'You'll suck that thumb away sure as a cough drop, my sunbeam. Then the Scissorman'll come and chop-chop-chop it off and where will you be? Stumps, that's where. And the fresh blood'll come dripping!' She'd hold up her own thumbs to me then, bent and white, knuckle up and the rest hidden. 'There see, he had me, too. The wood god had me, and the Scissorman had me, and they're both fierce fellas, sunbeam. They both had me, they had me good,' and my sturdy Nana would chuckle.

11

Maybe it was my fault. Did I dilly-dally like Prissy in *Gone with the Wind*? You know the girl, the squeaky-voiced girl who trills and sings as Atlanta burns. Prissy, who kicks against the white picket fence as Miss Melly is huffing and puffing her Southern Belle self to oblivion, and getting weaker as her weak-as-a-kitten baby comes into a changed world.

Was I as dilly-dallying as that?

I did run. I remember the whips of nettles. I was running so fast they couldn't sting.

Nana's song ran through my head as I leapt over tree roots and my skin tore on bramble.

> 'I'm going to
> lay down my soul
> in the bo-som of
> A-bra-ham,
> Oh baby,
> A-bra-ham,
> Oh, baby.'

But all I was thinking was, Jenny's gone.

It was as simple as that. I woke up. Jenny was gone. It sounded like a Johnny Cash song.

'Well I woke up this morning
Put my head inside your door
But you weren't there to greet me,
And I'm in trouble now fur sure.'

At first I thought she was hiding. I thought it was hide-and-seek. I crawled inside the sheet-tent to check because I knew what hide-and-seek could do. Moths bashed against the sides in the fading light, but Jenny wasn't there. I tried the trees around us because I knew I'd see the bulge of her stomach sticking out from behind a trunk. But as I ran, as the wood path twisted and turned, I lost my way. I prayed for breadcrumbs to lead me home, and all of a sudden I knew that Jenny had vanished.

Into thin air.

Into a wardrobe.

Into the wood god's clutches.

Up a beanstalk.

Under a gravestone.

The Scissorman had got her.

Branches hit me in the face and a dip packed with dead leaves left me sinking.

I gasped, 'Jenny!' My short legs tried to run on the spot; like Tom, like Jerry, going nowhere in the dank stink of leaves.

'Jenny! Mummy! Na-na!'

A robin spat his song from a hazelnut sapling. In the dusk light I saw a tiny wren twittering from branch to branch, never still. Nana Lew had three gold farthings, a wren on each. 'This is precious money,' Nana said, so she tied them up in a bag and buried them in her freezer. 'It's what my three brother-Beloveds saved up during their war service. Three gold farthings. Cost them their lifetimes, my pet, and it was all left to me. Most precious inheritance I have, isn't it?'

The knots on the trunks round me swirled and grew into the faces of wolves, the faces of woodcutters and grannies, but all I wanted was *my* Little Red Riding Hood; all I wanted was Jenny in her red cape. I whimpered, because after all I was only a little girl and I was lost in a wood. I cried. I cried the way I should have when that thick, tall gravestone fell on Robert. I cried until snot and salt filmed my cheeks and a newborn gasping left me calm.

Nanaaaaaaaaa, I wailed, and then I stretched out my arms and gathered the crisp summer-dried leaves to me. Insects were burrowing, crawling about me, but it didn't matter. It was a bed: a hollow. I wasn't going to find Jenny. The wood god had got her and it was all my fault.

I shivered a breath and tried to think of a lie; a lie that would get me out of this: a lie that would work.

Seeing your house from the outside, rooms lit up warm in the dark, you feel like a thief. I lay on my stomach between two croquet hoops at the edge of Nana's lawn. The big cedar towered above me, a giant lurching in the wind.

The thing was, voices peppered the lawn sure as the nesting peacocks.

'How did it happen?' one voice was saying.

'Nobody knows, love.'

'It's like that President Kennedy, it is. It's like the man on the moon. We'll always remember tonight. Won't we Stan? We'll remember where we was when we heard. Oh Stan, love, don't.'

I heard the muffle of a grown man crying, but I couldn't see much.

'I'll remember tonight. I always will. You test me, Stan, you test me later. It's like the world's ending.'

My stomach lurched because I knew they were talking about Jenny.

Nana's outside lights flickered on, and I saw how many people there were. A group of Teddy boys stood by a round pillar. They had greasy quiffs and those funny shoes like sponge cakes. The crying Stan was closest to me, near a white croquet hoop and an angry peacock; the woman holding him had big bouffant hair. She patted his back as he sobbed. Cars and silver-shiny motorbikes blocked my nana's driveway. People were muttering beneath the Big House's sash windows in ringed groups: kicking gravel, smoking.

A woman in a tight pencil skirt cried out, 'It can't be, it can't be true, Mary!'

But it was true. Jenny was gone. My legs smarted from the touch of nettle and bramble. I was still trying to think of the perfect lie.

She made me.

She got us lost.

She's older than me. By a million. She told me to, Miss.

Jenny had lots of friends and they had all come specially for her, maybe from the prairies, from Wyoming. Jenny was a popular girl.

Through the bay windows, wide as the hull of a ship, I saw my Nana Lew in her parlour, talking to someone. It was Nellie, Nana's best friend. Nellie stood by Vincent's piano and she had big hair, like Dusty Springfield. It was a wig, and Nana was pushing different wigs onto her own head, trying them out. At last she chose a black one done up in a Dusty beehive too.

My grandmother disappeared for a moment, and then she was marching out of the front door into the porch light: she looked stately in that wig. I could smell her, even from this distance: Nana was cake and cloves, incense and talc, vinegar and fish paste. I saw her light a big candle that flared up, and then the rest of the crowd lit candles from this, one by sobbing one. For a moment I wondered if this was a search party because they started to walk out through the gates, the trail of their yellow candle flames like dogs' eyes in the dark.

They were climbing our hill and walking around the back of

the Big House under Nana's fruit trees; they were walking to her capel.

Breaker-Breaker-FoxyRed-10-4.

10-4, FoxyRed, what's your 20?

Your prayers are needed, sons and daughters. 1-9. Rockfarm. Here at Rockfarm.

Three motorbikes – with handles like big horns – bubbled and spat past me. The riders mounted the grass verge and I saw their silver exhaust pipes rumble like factory chimneys. The riders had beards and they still wore sunglasses in the night. A spit away from me two girls were holding hands. They looked exactly the same except one was thin and one was fat. They had the same bouffant black do, with a white bow at the crown. Their powder-white faces were smeared with black eyeliner and tears, and they wore matching white minidresses with plastic, white knee-high boots. The fat one's legs bulged from the top of her boots and I heard her nylons chafe as she jigged on the spot.

'Oh, Mand, I can't. I can't do it, Mand,' she said.

'You got to, love, you got to pay your respects.'

'I'm scared.'

'I'm here, I'm here, precious. He don't want to see you cry. Think of the nipper, the little un.'

'Poor mite.' The fat one sniffed up her snot and wiped it on her white chenille sleeve. 'We got to be strong for her, haven't we, Mand? Got to.'

'Yeah.'

'Gwil said we should have a disco. Down the Shire Hall. A disco and a collection for that little kiddie, like.'

The thin one pulled her fat twin closer. 'Don't be sad,' she said.

'Yeah,' the fat one shuddered, 'he's in a better place now, isn't he? He'll be singing with the angels and with his mam and his little brother. They're all together now, singing, isn't it?'

Both girls burst into fresh tears.

'That you down there, Halo girl?'

I turned to the voice behind me, and stared up at the bright end of a cigarette.

'What you doing there out on the ground?'

I wondered how the Devil knew my name because it had to be the Devil burning red like that in the dark. Then I smelled stamp glue and Basildon Bond and I knew it wasn't Satan, it was Rhysie the postman: the man who delivered more than post to my Nana Lew.

'Catch your death down there you will, love.' The tip of his fag glowed as he sucked and leant forward. 'Dear, dear me, up you come. A little bab like you shouldn't be out so late.'

He stood me on unsteady legs and hugged me. His body was warm through his crisp and white sorting-office shirt. This was what my grandmother felt, then: this warmth, this smell of tobacco and brown envelopes, of Brylcreem and rubber bands. As he lifted me up I buried my face in Rhysie's neck, heavy with sweat and blackheads.

'You coming, Halo?'

'Where?'

'Find your nana.'

'Is it starting?'

'Soon, pet. They're all going up the capel. Look.'

I tried to move my lips, I tried to ask him: is this all for Jenny? But the words wouldn't come.

Rhysie's steel-capped boots cracked on Nana's gravel as he carried me into the house.

It was warm in the Big House hall. Rhysie put me down in a chair.

'You wait here and speak to your nana when she's done. She's in the parlour. I've got to get up to the capel. There's crowds. Bye, pet.'

I waved as he winked from the front door, then I heard Nana's voice.

'Speak up, lovely,' she was saying.

I tiptoed to the half-open parlour door and peeked through a crack. Nana was kneeling over her chaise longue; over something that lay there. She still wore that big black beehive wig and I watched her arm moving up and down, stroking the something. I saw feet under a blue blanket, twitching.

'Now give it here, love. Give it to me. Good girl. You don't need that stuff now. Sweet tea's what you need, best thing for it because you got to be a good girl, right? For the babba's sake. No more of that. Cake's what you'll have. My special tea and cake. Get all that bad stuff out of you.'

I moved to the threshold, opening the door a little. Nana's velvet drapes, her carpet and the thick tablecloth were all deep and red and warm as blood. My chilblains ached with it.

'You have a rest now,' Nana Lew said to the lump on the chaise longue. 'Don't you worry about all that outside. You've got Nellie here, haven't she, Nellie?'

'She has that,' a voice from the corner said. I couldn't see, but we all knew Nellie sure as we knew our own hands and feet. Nellie had looked after us all.

'You've got Nellie so there's nothing to fret about, and I'll be back in a moment or two. Get you my special tea.' Nana Lew strained up, knees clicking. 'You're right as rain. It ent yet, but soon. The babby ent coming yet, but tonight, tomorrow, maybe longer, and if you don't want no doctor – there, lovely, I know you don't – don't fret because you got your Nana Lew here and Nellie and we've birthed oh, so many babies, so be a good girl, eh? You got to rest now.'

The feet beneath the blanket jerked up and down. 'Yes ma'am,' the other end said.

I swallowed my breath and ran into the kitchen.

I skidded across the floor and under Nana's big oak table because I didn't know how it had happened, but however it had and however Jenny had been saved, it wasn't down to me, so it was still *all my fault*.

Nana Lew whistled and I heard the thunder of her collies down the stairs. Nana clickety-clacked into the kitchen and banged a few doors of the Rayburn, letting out the golden smell of her rising sponge.

'You can come out, sunbeam.'

I froze.

'Must be chilled to the bone. Come on.'

'I'm not here,' I said and Nana laughed.

'You are foolish sometimes, Halo, you know that, don't you?'

'Nana?' My voice was light with fear.

'Yes.'

'Is that Jenny in there?'

'Why shouldn't it be Jenny? She says she lost you in the wood. She said she went for a Jimmy Riddle in the fern and when she got back, you'd gone. That was hours back. Where you been? You get lost out there, sunbeam?'

Bang: the bang of Nana's cakes onto the counter, and how

could soft sponge make so much noise?

'I wasn't lost. She was.'

'Well she's been fretting about you ever since. Came down here to wait for you then had a turn.' Nana sucked air in fast. 'She wouldn't have the doctor, she was mad for a while. Though she's fine now. It'll happen soon, but soon ent now, is it? I've got my flock to attend to, and she's got Nellie and the doctor on the end of the telephone,' Nana was talking to herself now, 'she'll be right as rain, it's the babby we should pray for. Foolish, foolish girl.'

'I'm sorry, Nana,' I gasped.

'Not you, love, her. Her in there not looking after herself or that babba. Her doing bad things. But I'll cure her. I will.'

I stared up at the swirls of wood knots underneath Nana's table and I had an awful thought. 'Nana?'

'Yes, pet.'

'Nana, are you sure that *that's* Jenny?'

'Who do you think it is?'

I didn't know: a wood sprite, a fairy, a shape-shifter, a zombie or a ghost, because I'd left Jenny to die in the wood and I didn't know what *that* thing beneath the blanket in the parlour was.

'That's her, sunbeam, don't you fret. Though she's got bigger problems than getting lost in the woods.'

'Why, Nana?'

'Told you, she had a turn. Should be in hospital, should be' – she muttered the rest.

'Why doesn't she go to the hospital?'

'Why doesn't she indeed? Here.' I heard her knees click as she pushed a plate of cake and a saucer of tea between the chairs. 'Don't make me bend down again, Halo love, my old self won't take it tonight.'

I took the plate. 'Thank you, Nana.'

'You're welcome, pet.'

I chewed, hungry as a fledgling. 'Who is everybody?' I mumbled through cake.

'Funny question.'

'All those people outside, they're going up to the capel. Why, Nana?'

She sighed. 'Sunbeam, I got bad news.' Nana's voice cracked. 'Halo, I'm afraid the boy died.'

I stuck my head out. 'But Nana you said she was fine. You said the doctor—'

'He's past doctors now.'

I dropped the half-eaten sponge, and as the corners of my eyes spurted tears I heard my grandmother's thoughts click loud as her knees.

'Sunbeam! It ent him, love, not the babby. Don't be silly. The babby'll be fine, God willing. No, the boy is *him*.' Nana pointed at a picture on her wall, her shoulders deflated.

'Who?' I asked.

'*Elvis*—'

'Your Elvis, Nana?'

'Yes, pet.'

'But he's not a boy.'

'He is to some, darling. He *was* to some.'

'What happened, Nana?'

She sighed and cut into her sponge with the greasy carving knife. 'Now there's the million-pound question, my pet, there it is. I'd say he died of too much. The lad just had too much.' She fingered the tea towel of Tupelo she'd tin-tacked above the Rayburn.

'Nana, are Jenny and Fred going to be OK then?'

She looked down at me, golden crumbs of cake round her mouth. 'Fred, is it? Is that the babba's name? Yes, I reckon they'll be all right. They will be, long as that girl listens to me and to Nellie. Don't you worry about them.' Nana wiped her face. 'You come with me now, sunbeam. Everyone's waiting. You missed all the drama tonight, and it's not over yet. Your Nana Lew's got to get ready.'

I crawled out and put my arms up, and stocky Nana Lew lifted me. I heard her grunt as her black beehive wig shifted. My legs dug into her soft sides and she walked through the hall, her collies a black and white train behind her.

'Should I go and see Jenny?' I whispered.

'No, pet, let her sleep. She needs her strength. Could be a baby in this house soon.'

My legs tightened around my grandmother and quivered.

My nana was strong as an ox, or as strong as a postman at Christmas. As she walked up to her capel through the August night, the crowds made way.

'Evening, Mrs Meredith,' she said.

'Mrs Lew.'

'How are you, Gwen?'

'Ticking on, ticking on, Glad.'

'Sad news, eh, Mr Williams?'

'Yes, sad news, Glad.'

'Very sad, Mrs Lew.'

'Nice to see you here.'

'Sad day, Mrs L. Sad day.'

'That it is.'

'We heard about it on the CB.'

My grandmother nodded and winked at each face as we passed and I saw that all these people were waiting for her to put them back together. My nana was used to that, after all, she'd done *that* with all of us.

As she carried me through the crowd, they seemed to brighten, smile. Nana Lew was their Breaker-Breaker. She was their Come-in, FoxyRed, FoxyRed. Come-in.

The capel was packed. I sat on Rhysie's shoulders at the back as Nana made her way to the pulpit. I watched the congregation: some were crying, out of control, some simply stared into space, while others gazed at the capel's ceiling and walls, their mouths open.

The thing was, my nana's capel was made of bones, or least it was decorated with them. These bones belonged to the monks who had lived here. Nana explained it to me, she said once upon a time these men had decided to waste not want not and decorate the walls and ceiling of their church with their very own bones. And so, above us, skulls were framed by thigh bones, while Nana's pulpit looked like a tower from hell, tibias and fibulas jutting out from step to step. Nana said it was a great leveller, gazing up into those eyeless skulls, at those gum-less teeth, not to mention the words on the stained-glass window above the altar that told us, 'Here lie our bones, awaiting yours…'

It was a word to the wise, said Nana.

Rhysie held my ankles, I breathed in bone dust and I saw my mother. I had to fight the urge to leap off his shoulders and run to her in the first pew. It was the first time she'd crossed this threshold since the night she pulled up those headstones: it was the first time since Robert. Dad sat on one side of her and Vincent on the other, their arms over her shoulders. I started to wiggle until Rhysie looked up and asked if I wanted the little girls' room.

There was murmuring, and from my height I saw the crowns of eight golden heads walk in. The Connor brothers moved sure and direct to the altar as if it had always been their stage. The room went quiet.

Sadness made the brothers more beautiful. Their blue eyes seemed bigger, darker, and their beards glistened. Strain heightened the muscles in their arms; the sinews on their brown necks stood out like steel strings. Abraham, Jenny's husband, stood in front of his brothers and I felt the congregation gasp. He looped a rainbow-coloured strap round him and tuned his guitar.

Ding-ding-ding-ding

A vein throbbed in a perfect line down his honey-coloured forehead. I thought of Jenny at the Big House with Nellie, maybe having her baby. Maybe it wasn't now, but it would be soon. Abraham turned his fierce eyes to his brothers and nodded.

'A-one, a-two, a-three—'

They sang so perfectly that I saw Vincent tilt his head like a dog. He left Mum and Dad and moved forward as the harmonies of the brothers netted him.

They sang Elvis's 'Don't'. And I felt the ground shiver. Abe's voice cracked and I watched his face get wet. It shone. Don't. Don't. Don't. Don't.

Mum's head fell onto my father's shoulder. The skulls cried down on me from their eyeless sockets, and I felt Rhysie shudder beneath my thighs.

I closed my eyes, tired now. I let my body rest on Rhysie's head. There was the echo of Abraham's crystal voice in the bone-dust air, then silence. I prayed for Jenny to be well, for her baby to be well, and then I heard my nana clear her throat.

'Dearly Beloved,' she began. 'Yes, Dearly Beloved, for that's what you are tonight, see. Beloved in grief. Beloved in sorrow. Dearly Beloved.' She paused. 'The boy came to us poor, brought up the best way a boy can be, and the boy brought us music. Maybe not his, but he brought it all the same. And the boy went to the place of the sun where our own Beloved Mr Johnny Cash did go, and at this place the boy found his voice. And in this voice we did find ourselves. Isn't that right, Loved Ones?

'Now sometimes roofs and bricks of bones make sense. Tonight they do. I know you boys and girls come here in this darkness for a reason and I'm glad my capel here can go some way to cure you. I'm glad that I, your Mrs Lew, your Gladys, your Nana, can go some way to cure you. But you, yes you, Billy Pritchard, and you, Sadie Lewis, and you, Jacob Evans, and you, the Connor brothers from America, all of you sitting here, I say to you now that you've got to be strong. A boy died today but that don't mean he's gone. For what is gone is only just the man, the flesh and the blood like this old arm here, this old strong forearm of mine. It's just this that's gone, see, and the rest, the spirit, the soul, whatever you out there want to call them, they are with us still and for ever, just as long as we listen to this boy sing.

'And as long as we hear "Hound Dog", as long as we hear "Blue Suede Shoes", so long as we cry our hearts out to that "Long Black Limousine", the boy will be with us always.

Because whoever disappears from our midst is never gone. Hear me now. Hear me.

'So you think yourselves lucky, young fellas, young lasses – you nod now – because there are those not so lucky, those that were killed, taken, before they could hear his voice, or see our Elvis move like the Devil himself. And who knows? He may come back, he may be screaming and bawling in some new bundle of life now. He may be given another chance. Because I tell you now, my kindred, I tell you that something is moving, something is changing, and it's coming this way. Take heed.

'Now bow your heads and join with me in a prayer. Join me in a prayer for our New Beloved tonight, our Beloved who will join those others. And then your Nana Lew'll bed you down and give you comfort.

'My son there, Ivan Comfort, you join in with me, and the rest of you, you'll all get it after a while. Ivan, begin with the boy, begin with the last to go. This is our prayer here at Rockfarm. Now listen.

'Elvis Aaron Presley...'

13

Jenny knew her way around the control room: that was for sure. She knew which buttons and levers to slide and press. She even knew where the light switch was.

'Ain't right in here, kiddo. Without them, I mean.' Jenny hugged herself the way grown-ups do when they're lonely. Jenny could hug herself now: her stomach was almost gone.

The baby was the smallest baby I'd seen, and I wondered why Jenny's belly had been so big. The baby shook with little-baby shivers, and it had a high-pitched but quiet cry. It sounded like Jenny blowing on those grass blades between her thumbs, yet at the same time it was the tiniest of sounds. The baby cried all the time.

'Hmmm, hmmmm. Hmmmm, hmmmm,' it whittled the air like a knife on a stick. 'Hmmm, hmmmm, hmmmm,' the baby said.

'There now, sweet thing,' my mum soothed, 'there, there.'

We weren't allowed near the baby. Nana said it was ill, and though it wasn't doctor-ill, it didn't need our germs and dirty fingers. Jenny didn't want the hospital, and Mum agreed. The baby *was* a boy and the baby *was* called Fred. Fred was two weeks old and Elvis was two weeks dead, though Nana didn't like to talk about that. The baby lived in Nana's house and she fed it with *her* Formula. Nana said warm baths and wrapping it tight would bring its voice out and clear out those lungs, so

Jenny let her. Nana said little bird-sips of her special tea would help the baby and Jenny too; we just had to be patient.

Jenny and I stood in the studio. I remembered how Mum used to drag us up here, and no matter who was recording – big names, small names, not-yet-discovered names – the singer would always stop mid-song, the lead guitarist mid-lead, and they'd wait while we stood around them in this small room, and Mum gave her speech.

'Now, children,' she'd tell us, 'what do we have in here?' She would lift her arms, her breasts rising, and the men would gasp; one or two would have to sit like she'd gasped the breath out of them.

'Children, what we have is a Fender Telecaster, a Strat and a Precision bass. And here are two Marshall stacks, a Fender Rhodes keyboard, a Hammond organ, and in the cupboard are your father's drum kits – a Ludwig red sparkle and a Premier – while right here above your heads are some lovely, lovely Neumann mics. Aren't they sweet? Go on, say something. Vince? Halo? Molly?' But we'd just stare, voiceless, and that was Mum's task carried out. She'd nod at whatever band it was, and march us out. I often wondered how long those rock stars stayed like that: stunned and crouching on the studio floor.

Right now the studio smelled of the Connor brothers: it was a heavy sweetness mixed with clean skin, peanuts, and smoke.

Jenny touched Abraham's National guitar. She touched the cold metal mics and the skin of the snare drums. She sighed. Abraham and his brothers were in London for two whole days. They'd left Jenny to look after Fred, and so Jenny had left the new baby with Mum. 'Your momma likes him,' Jenny said, 'and who wouldn't?'

Jenny was spending the day with me.

She touched the cradles where the acoustic guitars sat. 'You know what, kid?'

'What, Jenny?'

'Well, when those boys get back, kiddo, you and me, we're gonna have to say goodbye. I mean, we're all done here. It all came at the same time, right?' She laughed to herself. 'All the tracks done and me a momma. Can't get used to being a momma, it's crazy, right?' She laughed again, one of her open-mouthed yee-haw laughs.

I sat on the ground, back up against a Marshall amp, and crossed my legs. I played with the toy rings on my fingers. I didn't want to think of saying goodbye.

'Aw, kid, don't be sad. I'll write.'

I shrugged.

'Hey, are we gonna waste this day or are we gonna sing some-thing, kiddo? The boys are gone so we can have fun, right?'

I crossed my arms into my chest and Jenny knelt down in front of me; she could move better now.

'Go on, kiddo.'

'I can't sing.'

'Why in the hell not?'

Jenny grabbed a pair of marshmallow headphones and put them over my ears. 'Come on, Haley, one last bit of fun. You stand over there. Go on. I'm a momma now, I got to grab the fun where I can. Right?' She giggled, kissed me on the cheek and skipped out of the studio. I saw the light over the mixing desk flash on.

'You gotta sing, kid.' Her voice was suddenly loud inside my head. I jerked up and saw her talking into the control-room

111

microphone; all that way away and I could hear her. I climbed up on a black stool and talked into a microphone.

'I can't sing, really Jenny,' I said. 'Mummy said I'm going to be a drummer.'

'How so?'

'That's just what my mummy says.'

'Then drum.'

I looked at the kit behind me and wondered which brother played it.

'Come on, quit whining, kiddo, and sing me a tune.'

I sang. 'Hum-pety Dum-pety sat on a wall. Hum-pety Dum-pety had a great fall. All the King's horses and all the King's men, couldn't put Hum-pety together again.'

Jenny laughed. 'OK, kid, so you're a drummer! That's cool.'

That afternoon we laughed a lot. I said all the rude words Vincent and Nana had ever taught me into the microphone.

'Hey, you know I'm recording this, right?' Jenny said. 'You wash your mouth out now!' Then she came into the studio and said ruder words. She told me I had to cover my ears, because sometimes a girl was just too goddamn young.

There was a conversation too, captured for ever on silky tape:

'Hey kiddo, what's hanging?'

'This is Diamond Star Halo Llewelyn-from-Wales asking Jenny-from-America some things.'

'OK, shoot, kiddo.'

'Hello, Jenny. Jenny, what is your favourite film?'

'Movie, right? What's yours?'

'Um, I don't know. *Dr Doolittle*. I like the big snail.'

'Mine's *Night of the Living Dead*, it's about flesh eating zombies! Rahhhhhhhh!'

And we giggled. You can hear us crash into the drums, the cymbals, because Jenny was chasing me around the room.

Jenny was a zombie.

'Rahhhhh!' she said.

'You're not really, you're not really!' I said, and then I stopped, because she got me and she was eating me up.

You'll probably know the song that Jenny sang that day. She'd figured it all out in her bed that morning, she told me. She couldn't write music, not like Abraham, not properly on the page, but she knew the way things should sound. 'Like a coyote should sound like a coyote,' she reasoned.

Jenny sat me in the big black chair in the control room. She put two cushions beneath me so I could see over the mixing desk and she told me to press two buttons. That was the first time I'd felt grown up: hiked up on those cushions, my legs dangling in my dungarees. I pressed while Jenny stood in the studio and sang about a boy, a fresh young boy who was born far away from home. A boy who was nearly lost, a boy who would grow up to be the greatest thing. I've always liked the chorus best. As Fred says, the rest is too much to live up to, too much expectation.

'Hey, my little boy, don't you worry, don't you cry,
    About tonight, tonight, tonight.
'Cos your mama, she's gonna shake those stars
        down for you,
    Tonight, tonight, tonight.

Hey, my little man,
Don't break your woman down.

113

Tonight, tonight, tonight.
'Cos she'll, she'll find a way for you to smile,
She'll make you smile, tonight, tonight,
Tonight.

'Cos you're gonna sing those stars right down,
Tonight, tonight, tonight,
You're gonna make every woman cry,
Tonight, tonight,
Tonight.'

Jenny smiled as she sang this, and when Dad came in with two cups of hot, sweet tea and a plate of Jaffa Cakes I smiled too.

'How's my boy, Mr Ivan?' Jenny asked him.

'Dolly's with him,' Dad said, and he looked a bit angry. I'd rarely seen him like that. Dad looked creased. Not that Jenny noticed: she was itching for something else.

'I guess we're done here, Mr Ivan.'

'Aww!' I moaned.

'Time for bed, nutmeg,' Dad told me.

'Hey, don't freak out. Meet me here in the morning, kid.'

I stood at the studio door and smiled an orange-chocolate smile.

'And we'll finish the song real good. We'll get it all down and it'll be my gift to you. That a deal, kid? I'd like to give you something before we scoot.'

'Yes.'

'You tell Miss Dolly and Miss Gladys I'll be down soon to my boy. That OK, Mr Ivan?'

Dad nodded, a quick nod.

'Jenny?' I said, bouncing on the spot, Jaffa Cake sugar pulsing through me. 'Jenny, do you know what my nana says?'

'What does she say, kiddo?'

'She says, "If I don't see you through the week I'll see you through the window."'

Jenny laughed, flashing her teeth like a healthy mare. 'All right, kiddo. See you through the window.'

The next morning Mum and Dad shook their heads at me from the kitchen table because I was standing by the front door, already dressed and pressing warm toast into my open mouth.

'Got ants in your pants?' Mum asked.

'She wants to go and mess about with Jenny Connor.'

Mum smiled but Dad didn't.

'Oh, let her, Ivan.'

'That girl won't be awake yet. And I bet Mam has been up with that baby all night, too—'

'Ivan, please. He's a baby. A beautiful baby.'

Dad shoved his knife in the marmalade jar. 'It's about time Abraham and Jenny Connor took their beautiful baby back home.'

Mum looked at him, confused. 'The baby is fine, Ivan, we don't mind the baby.'

Dad let his knife drop. 'That girl should be looking after her own. The band's done what they came here to do.'

'Please.'

'They should be gone. They're trouble, Doll.' Dad stood up. He walked to the wood burner and kicked it.

'Ivan *Comfort*.' I watched Mum's hands; they began to shake.

115

They did that sometimes, when her cow-blankness didn't work. They did that on Robert's birthday, on his anniversary. They did that when she cut too many onions, too.

'I don't want to hear it, Dolly.' Dad's voice was gravel.

'Hear what?'

'What's in your head.'

'Ivan—'

'You need to let them go. You need to let *him* go.'

'I'm not keeping them or *him* here.' Mum's voice was suddenly hard. It was odd to hear.

'Dolly, you aren't thinking straight.'

'Don't tell me what to think, Ivan. Don't you dare.'

I watched her. Mum couldn't keep that hardness up. The shake was in her arms, her neck, and in her voice now. 'Ivan, I—'

Dad turned. 'Dolly. Oh, Dolly, I'm sorry.'

'Ivan—'

He ran to her and knelt in front of her. He grasped all he could of her. She looked so small all of a sudden. She fell forwards, into his arms. 'Doll,' Dad whispered. 'There now.'

'Help me.'

'Shh. There now, my Dolly.'

I watched Dad's hands, his strong oak-arms wrap tight around my mother. They moved over her, as if he was checking she was all still there.

'There now,' he kept saying, 'there now.'

Her shaking subsided, his moving arms calmed, and I bolted out of the door into the morning sun. I ran as fast as I could, far from my mother's trembling: I ran up the track and to the studio.

*

Habit is a strange thing, but it's never strange until it's broken. Then you see it for what it is: reasonless, fathomless. I mean, why do you chew your nails? Why do you count up to ten and tap your toothbrush three times on the side of the sink each night, just in case?

In case of what?

Who knows? It is habit, after all.

When I walked into the dark control room and couldn't find Jenny, it was habit that told me where to wait, so I crept along the mushroom-corridor that led to the studio and I slipped in. I knew where I was going. I was going to the place I knew.

When I was very small, I'd take my baby naps beneath the drums. Nana said it was because of the way I came into this world, bouncing on Dad's drum kit like that. I liked to crawl under the stool and curl up in front of the big bass drum. Sometimes I'd trace the strange letters scrawled across its skin (although from my side 'L-u-d-w-i-g' became 'g-i-w-d-u-L'). I'd stroke the fur-clad beater and stare up at the shimmer of cymbals before I rolled up and slept. I'd been trodden on, lying here. Drummers didn't like finding a kid at their feet. 'Jesus Christ!' they'd yell.

I pushed the drum stool out of the way and tucked myself in between it and the cold chrome pedals. I was bigger now and I had to nestle closer to the bass drum to fit. I stared through the skin, but there was nothing written on this one.

Dad was right; Jenny wouldn't be up for ages.

It was like staring through the corrugated plastic roofs of Dad's sheds: I could just make out Tequila's guitars, upright and waiting. I saw the blurred squares of black amps and I saw a mound on the carpet to the side of them.

I decided that the mound was red. I decided it looked like a magician's trick, as if a big 'Ta-dah!' was underneath. I'd have to pull that off and, maybe, beneath would be a huddle of white rabbits blinking in the light, or a bunch of bright silk flowers.

Because I was bored, because I was waiting, I snaked out of my hiding place. The pedal on the bass drum gave a heavy 'duff' and the cymbals shimmered. I picked up a nipple-ended drumstick, and I walked over to the red mound.

I knelt down at the side of it and I sniffed.

It smelled of patchouli oil. It had hair and it was strange that a mound should have hair.

'Hello?' I whispered. I poked it with the drumstick. 'Hello?' I poked and then I put my hand on it and pushed.

It was heavy. Solid. I sat back, and that was when I realized this mound was covered by Jenny's red cloak. It was then I realized that that was Jenny's hair.

I leaned forward, picked up the side of the cape and took a peek underneath.

I know I shouldn't have.

Jenny's face was at an angle, neck bent and cheek to the floor. Her face was the wrong colour; it was purple, a birthmark purple. There were little un-popped bubbles around her mouth: bubbles that didn't move, bubbles that looked like they'd been there for the longest time.

Jenny's eyes were open and they had dust on the surface of them.

She was in such a strange position. She was kneeling but her top half had flopped down and over her thighs, her bare arms bent at her sides beneath the cape. There was something like a dart sticking out of one arm and her colour there was that mottled purple again.

'Jenny?' I said. I poked her cheek; it was solid and cold. 'Jenny, are you doing pretend?'

I stared at the bubbles on her lips – her lips that were mushed into a sleeping pose, though her eyes were open-awake.

I stared at the tiny bubbles.

Then one of them popped.

It couldn't have made a noise, but that 'pop' made me jump up. It made me run out of the studio, through the control room, and into the rehearsal room, slapping my hands against doors as I cried out. I sprinted to the outside air. I ran across the courtyard, scattering ducks and chickens, and under the brick arch, down the track to our house. I didn't stop until I was standing next to Dad's side of the bed. Dad pulled the quilt up to his bare shoulders and told me to go downstairs. He told me he and Mummy were talking. Mum lay back on the pillow next to him and smiled.

'But she's got bubbles, Daddy.'

'What?'

'There's bubbles.'

'What are you talking about, love?' Mum's hair was ruffled.

'Jenny. She's up in the studio and she's got bubbles.'

'Nutmeg, calm down.'

'You have to go and see, Daddy. Get the bubbles off.'

'OK, pet, OK. Calm down.'

He did, of course, go and see, and that's when it all began.

I sometimes wonder; what did Jenny say to Fred that night, before she left him with my nana and walked up to the studio on her own? What were her last words to her baby as she

119

nestled him in her freckled arms?

'See you later, kiddo'? Or, 'Night, night, sleep tight, mind the bed bugs don't bite'?

How about, 'Hey my little boy, don't you worry, don't you cry, 'cos your mama, she's gonna shake those stars down for you, tonight'?

That is what I tell Fred in any case.

The afternoon the ambulance came for Jenny, it rained. It rained so hard the back field flooded, and Nana said, 'Why'd they bring an ambulance when that girl's past such things?'

Dad came in late, that evening. He didn't make toast; he didn't run upstairs to my mother's face. He just stood, dripping on newspaper she'd laid down for him in our small kitchen. Dad took off his boots and wiped the mud from his face with kitchen paper. My father didn't speak for two days after that.

Nana said it was his sadness.

It was Mum who told us it was anger.

After that everything went too fast. I remember staying with Molly and Vincent in Nana's house while the grown-ups did the things that grown-ups had to do. I remember people I had never met before asking me questions about finding Jenny. Nana said they were policemen and policewomen. I remember our own sort of funeral for her. Then finally the brothers left, and it was Mum who found Fred.

That morning she ran down to our house, yelling, 'He left him! He's ours!'

Dad and Nana were out.

So it's true that the day we found him we all knew where Fred had come from: that it wasn't from the birds and the bees and the shaky knees of our parents; no one picked him up, an urchin, one dark and stormy night, and Fred didn't fly half-cocked from Never Never Land. The morning my mother found Fred wrapped up in a red cloak on one of our guest beds, we clearly knew who had left him and at the very same moment we knew he was ours. That was when Mum had us huddle round that piss-yellow candlewick bedcover to really take him in. That was when she touched Fred's forehead with her cold wedding band and the baby opened his black eyes. That was when she cried, 'Kids, come look! He's part seal-pup, part bloody Heathcliff!'

Vincent put his hands between his legs: Vince my older brother, Vince who keeps the best secrets till last.

Molly said, 'Go way ba-ba, dunt like you.'

I moved in closer.

Did I tell you there was a note? Well, notes, really.

Childish scribble. Capitals mixed with lower case, the sort of thing that drives me wild today.

'Love me,' one said, though it was ♥✳★ *LOvE mE* ♥♥★. This was pinned to the red velvet cape.

There was a golden urn on the bedside table. There was a note beneath that too. 'Bury me,' it said, though it was ♥✳★ *bUrY mE* ♥♥★.

The final note was on the pillow of the made bed. It said, ♥✳★ *FoRgiVe Me, tEll HiM WhO I aM, AbRahAm* ♥♥★

That morning our mother ignored the golden urn of Jenny's ashes, even with the sun screaming on its surface, and she carried Fred out of that musty room and down our farm track in folds of red. Without flinching, she climbed the stairs of our gatehouse and put the new baby in The Room We Didn't Speak Of. The room with 'R-O-B-E-R-T' still carved into the white paint of the door.

She did that straight off, like she'd been waiting.

She didn't move anything out; the unused, folded T-shirts; the boy's dusty daps and Marvel comics; the LPs in alphabetical order – they all stayed where they were. She just plonked our other, ready-made baby brother onto the single bed.

The Llewelyns' day had begun.

When Dad came home, he let Mum speak and didn't say a word. He looked at Mum for a long time and then he reassembled Molly's cot. Of course he didn't know it, but there was a gluey feel to our mouths that day and it was hard to keep anything down. Now I believe that that was the heavy and sticky presence of a new love.

Nana said it was a jigsaw puzzle and Fred was one of those pieces you have to press in because it's all you have left and there's a gap; so even if you have to take the scissors to it and snip it into shape, it has to do. 'But it makes a pretty picture anyway, don't it, sunbeam?' she said to me. 'Cut off a few of those scrag-ends and it'll soon fit.'

And I suppose Fred did.

'Lo-Lo,' he'd whisper to me once he could speak, 'Lo-Lo,' because that was what he had chosen to call me.

'Fred love Lo-Lo. Lo-Lo love Fred,' and he'd chew his soft feet and drift off to sleep.

GOODBYE JENNY

Good-bye, Jenny D/A/D///
Goodbye little child of time D/A/D///
The sweetest song-bird's purest soul D/D+/G///
Your spirit was so hard to find E///A///

Good-bye, Jenny D/A/D///
Goodbye sweetest child of mine D/A/D///
My little blackbird-Jenny girl D/D+/G///
Hope you make it to the other side A/A7/D///
My little blackbird-Jenny girl D/D+/G///
I'll see you on the other side A/A7/D///

PART TWO:

1988

1

I was done with exams when Mum stood in my bedroom and closed the door like she had something difficult to say.

'You have to stop him, Halo.'

She leant against my brass bedstead and played with the gold charms that hung from her wrist. She twisted the shire horse and the top hat until I was sure they'd snap. The fairground had risen to her surface, fierce as hot oil, these past few years. Our mum would yell out, 'Tuppence a go!' from Nana Lew's cooker.

'But he just climbs in with me, Mum.' I pulled the laces on my running shoes. 'And anyway, how do you stop Fred?'

She sighed and jangled. 'Don't encourage him, baby, that's all I'm saying. He is growing. I mean, he's *grown*. What is he now?'

'Eleven. Fred is eleven, Mum.'

She glanced round my room, skittish, as if someone was hiding behind the wardrobe, under the bed. I wondered if my mother was a little afraid of my youngest brother.

'Just tell him you need your privacy, Halo. Can't you put a lock on your door? You *are* a girl, after all.' Her pretty eyes fluttered around my thin hips, my long boy's waist: I could tell she wasn't sure. Mum's eyes settled on my flat chest, so different to hers. The only things that had grown on me were my legs and the hair on my head. Vince said I was a colt with a mane that corkscrewed crazily, but I often thought, 'Is this it?' when I felt my body. I was hard to the touch but I dreamt of softness. I was long and straight, but I dreamt of curves. I visited Nana's capel on Sunday nights and, face flat on the bony floor, arms out like Jesus on his cross – because I'd seen Audrey Hepburn do that in *The Nun's Story* – I prayed for bosoms. I prayed backwards, but still I prayed for bosoms like my grandmother's: bosoms that could carve channels through any sea. Molly was only thirteen and things had happened for *her*. She moved over to Nana's Big House the day they did, and now she had her own bedroom *and* she wore Dr White's once a month. I hadn't had so much as a round hip or a period. I'd been to the doctor, the specialist, who told me to 'stop running, eat red meat and wait'.

I looked up at the exam timetables that dressed my walls. I hadn't bothered to take them down because I liked to be reminded of that hold I had over time: the hour for biology, the half-hour for maths, and whole evenings for *Women in Love* and *Hamlet*. For a moment, breastless and boyish, I cursed human biology.

'The thing is, Halo,' Mum continued, 'he is your little brother and you're a girl and he's a boy and well—' Mum was struggling. 'Well, the thing is, Fred isn't a baby any more.'

There it was: our eyes met. Truth does that. Bam! Right in the puss. *Fred isn't a baby any more.* At times I knew my family had doubts about whether Fred was, or ever had been, *a child*.

Mum was right. Fred – my little milk-smelling brother – had dark patches under his arms, and hair *down there*. When Fred stretched and yawned there was downy black above the line of his belt. 'Clocking on early,' Nana Lew called it, as if puberty was a job. Last month he'd locked me in the bathroom with him and asked me what I thought.

I couldn't speak.

128

'You have to stop him sleeping in here with you, Halo.' Mum rattled my bedstead, 'He's got his own room, you know.'

I shrugged and stretched a hamstring because Fred sleeping in my bed was the way things were. Since he could crawl out of his cot and lift my blankets, Fred Connor was simply there beside me because Fred liked me best. Sometimes he pulled the sheet over our heads, lit a torch and said, 'Read me this, Lo-Lo.' Sometimes he made a tent of my single sheet and asked me to take him away to magic places; sometimes he sang to me.

Mum nodded out the window at Beggars' Hill. 'You're going up there to meet him, aren't you, love?'

'Yup.'

'Then you have to tell him,' she whispered. 'House rule, Halo. From tonight.'

I looked at my mother. Face on.

Dolly Halcyon Palmer-Llewelyn was still good enough to eat. Her cheeks were still apples, her eyes dark chocolate, and her lips plump as cherries. There was something though: a little grey under the eyes, lines thin as gossamer where she had smiled. Dad said that just made things better.

Mum pressed her nose against the windowpane. 'Have you seen anything yet, Halo?'

I shook my head.

'Maybe they've forgotten this year? Maybe they won't come?'

'I doubt it, Mum.'

'If they come, Halo, we'll escape, we'll go out for a drive. What about the Gower? It's lovely this time of year. You tell Fred that. We'll go, in the pickup.' She turned from the window and stared up at the posters on my walls. I preferred runners to rock stars, and up there were Abebe Bikila, Jesse Owens, and Flo-Jo.

'I'll tell him, Mum. I'll try.' I watched that nub that poked down like a tiny fingertip between her two front teeth: it was so hard to tell nowadays.

I slipped past my mother and ran down the narrow stairs.

'From tonight, Halo. He sleeps in his own bed. I'm serious!'

I heard her slump onto my mattress with a groan as I stretched my coltish limbs at the foot of our stairs. I knew it was going to be impossible to keep Fred to his own bed; the impossibility was carved onto my bones with a pin. I looked at Mum's framed photos – the photos she'd gathered of the rock stars that had left us – Marc Bolan, Elvis Presley, Ian Curtis, John Lennon, Bob Marley; they were there, along with Jenny Connor. Mum had lost her heart a little over the last eleven years. 'Music. It's a dangerous business,' she'd tell us, mimicking our father.

I skipped out of our front door into the September warmth; I skipped to our garden gate – after all, I was almost seventeen. The great-great-something grand-chicks of Nana's peacocks wailed from her lawn, still mournful, and I ran down our gravel track to the main road. The road where you could turn left to England. Across it was our Beggars' Hill.

I was in a hurry: I had to get to Fred before they did.

2

When Fred and I were smaller, Mum called Beggars' Hill our Penistone Crag. We never knew what she meant.

Of course I do now. *Wuthering Heights* is my favourite book.

I skipped the rungs of the cattle grid, climbed the gate, and took a breath because Beggars' Hill was steep. Beggars' Hill was the sort of hill where accidents happened; where the wrong footing could have you crash down into spiked machinery, neatly hidden in the hedgerow. It was a hill where you could ride a fast sledge as if all your worries were gone, until you slammed into the fat oak on the left. I'd carried Fred up this hill when he was too toddly to manage; it was the hill he walked up himself when he got those postcards from Abraham, the ones that said:

Hey Kid,
In Pittsburgh for the show. Looks like we're bigger than Elvis. Keep up the good work and respect your elders,
Your Pa,
Abe Connor.

These were the postcards that said nothing at all. Still, Fred tied Abe's postcards up with a black shoelace and wrapped them in Jenny's red velvet cloak that he kept under his bed.

I ran: it was the only time my flat body made sense. I could outrun my family, any of them. I could run away and not come back, if I chose to. I'd go running among the hard hill farms that circled us. The old men up there – the ones that talked in a high-pitched part-Welsh, part-English; the ones that sat at their wood burners, rubbing the matted backs of their collies and sparing just a tickle of a thought for their worn-out, dead wives – well, they'd shake their heads at me and tell me how if I had a husband there'd be no need for such a waste of energy, for such foolishness.

I took a breath and waved because there he was, Fred – at least the dot of him right at the top.

I grabbed at couch grass and pulled myself up.

Before I get there, I feel it's only fair I warn you about my little brother. If you like, do as I do and focus on his dark eyebrows just above those double lashes of his, because Fred's eyes will unnerve you for good. In the sunlight his black irises can shift to violet; in winter they go a grey-green indoors. Quite simply, Fred is too beautiful. He doesn't particularly look like Abraham. He doesn't particularly look like Jenny, although his laugh, mouth wide and open, reminds me of her yee-haw.

Fred Connor looks like his own person and that person is a knockout.

As I climbed I thought of the people who had already swooned for my brother. I thought of the girls, the boys, the women, the men, the dogs. I thought of the friends, the teachers – at his old school, at his new school – the postmistresses, the postmasters, the singers, bass players, drummers, piano players, guitar players, guitar players' girlfriends, the wives, the groupies. I thought of the waitresses, lollipop ladies, dinner ladies. I thought of my mother. I thought of me. We were all putty in the palm of Fred's hand, and as Mum pointed out, what a beautiful hand it was. Nana joked – you're a heart-breaker, my lad! Though Fred broke hearts in the messiest way: ventricles and veins pulled out and mauled; kisses in the straw and nothing more.

I gulped for breath.

'Lo-Lo, Lo-Lo! Up here!' he yelled.

Our dad's Guild guitar was beside him and I thought of the tips of Fred's fingers; last time he held my hand they were hard as heels from practice. Hard as heels and as slippery as an eel, that's that lad all over, Nana said.

'Hey, Lo-Lo.'

'Hey.'

I panted and sat beside him on the damp grass. I focused on my breath. I tried to focus because Fred was shirtless. He was golden brown like his dad and his uncles, and his muscles were tight from helping my dad with the bales.

'Have you seen anything yet?' he asked and scratched under his arm.

'Nu-uh,' I shook my head.

Fred began rolling the tobacco he kept in a silver tin. He lit the roll-up and pretended to inhale.

'Fred, put it out, you'll get sick.'

'No I won't.'

'I'm not cleaning it up this time.'

'You don't have to. We're up a hill.'

'So.'

'So' – he took another pretend-puff – 'I'll throw up on the grass. Anyway, I've got to get used to it, Lo-Lo.'

'Why?'

'It's cool.'

'No it's not. You're too young.'

'Lo-Lo, I'm old enough for *anything*.'

'Fred—'

'You're such a fuddy-duddy.'

'And what are you?'

'*I'm* Fred.'

He looked at me straight and sure as a fighting cock. I shivered a little. Fred was right: he was old enough for anything. Fred was eleven but these were Fred-years. Fred was a boy who wrote 'Live Hard, Die Young' on his pencil case. He spent part of the year here with us, and part of the year in New York with Abraham, so maybe that was it: Fred had doubled up. Maybe deep down he was twenty-two. I stared at his black, spiked hair. This summer Fred had become a punk. It was eleven years too late, but he told me he was catching up. 'I was only just born then, Lo. Nineteen seventy-seven was *my* year and I was just born! Can you believe it?' So Fred took Vince's hair gel and wore Mum's kohl. He spat and listened to her Patti Smith records. He made Nana tell him about the night the Sex Pistols came to Caerphilly. Fred played Vince's vinyl *Never Mind the Bollocks*, and the last time Vince was home he sewed zips on Fred's black trousers and razor-bladed holes in them. He called his little brother a chameleon and kissed his perfect spikes.

'Where's Dad, Lo-Lo?' Fred liked to keep tabs on the family. He always had.

'In the studio.'

'Mum?'

'At home.'

'Nana?'

'In the Big House.'

'Molly?'

'Dunno. And before you ask, Vince is on his way down from London, you know that.' Over the years Vincent had become 'Vince' to us all.

'I suppose.'

I looked down at the farm: at our house, at Nana's Big House, at her capel, at the wide courtyard where the bands stayed and our horses whinnied. Not much had changed.

'What's up, Lo-Lo?'

I turned and tried focusing on his eyebrows.

'Tell me, Lo.'

I shrugged. 'It's nothing.'

'No it's not.'

'OK, it's Mum.'

Fred ruffled. After all, he wanted our mother's attention as much as we all did. 'What about Mum?'

Mum. Our mum. His mum.

'Lo-Lo, *tell*.' He threw his cigarette into the wind and stood up. Fred was tall; Fred had had his growth spurts at nine. He was looking down at me and grinning.

'What?'

He shrugged and then he leapt on me. I was almost used to this: Fred pinning me down. He pushed me flat onto my back because Fred was strong. He fastened my arms above my head and pressed his knees into my sides. I watched the hair under his arms and gave up.

'Tell me, Lo!'

His face was inches above mine. He began to drool. I could smell his familiar scent of oranges and musk.

'Tell.'

'All right!' I looked him in the eyes, a mistake. 'She said you have to stick to your own bed. She said you're not to crawl in with me any more.'

He freed a hand to put a finger to my lips. He was trying to smudge one of my freckles off. I looked down and saw a clover leaf squashed flat to his tight and brown belly skin. Fred climbed off me. 'OK,' he said.

I stayed where I was: I felt winded. My bones hurt. It was *OK*.

'Here.' Fred held out a postcard. I took it and held it up to the sky. On the front was a coloured photo of a house called 'Graceland'. I turned it over.

Fred, (it said)
We'll all be thinking of her together.
Catch you in the holidays, kid.
Abraham

'They'll be here soon. I know they will.' He snatched the postcard back. 'Lo-Lo?'

'Hmmm.'

'I have a question.'

'What?'

'Lo-Lo, do you think we mate for life?'

'What are you talking about?'

'I don't mean like *doing it* for ever, Lo. I mean choosing a mate for life, like the dolphins and the whales. Do we do that?'

It was just like Fred, using words beyond his years: 'mate', like he was a vet, a zookeeper, a breeder of cats.

'I mean, once we fall in love—' Fred stretched his arms up

136

and lay back next to me in the grass '—is that it?'

I chewed a frizz of my red hair and I thought of Mum and Dad. I thought of Cathy and Heathcliff. I thought of Jane and Edward Fairfax Rochester, Elizabeth and Darcy, Anne Elliot and Captain Wentworth: the library van had been kind to me over the years.

I thought of me.

'Maybe,' I shrugged. 'I don't know, Fred, it's a stupid question.'

'No it's not. It's the most important question, Lo, the most important one ever. I think we'd like to mate for life, in here, and here,' he tapped his head and then his heart because, like our dad, Fred was sentimental. 'But really we can't. We can't be with one person for ever and ever, can we? Just one. What do you think, Lo-Lo? You *are* older than me.'

I sat up. 'So?'

'You must have thought about *it*. At least *thought* about it, Lo-Lo? I know you haven't done anything else.'

I blushed, redder than usual.

He turned onto his side, his head in the palm of his hand. Coquettish. Fred grinned, and then he winked. 'Or have you done it, Lo-Lo?' He let his voice purr. 'If you have, what's it like? I bet Vince has done it, he's miles older than us.'

I hid my hands up the sleeves of the green army jacket I'd taken from Dad. It smelled of Dad and I brought it up to my face. I felt the bounce in my crazy hair.

'Lo-Lo?'

'What?'

'Haven't you got to first base?'

I hated it when Fred tried American. It meant he was different to us. It meant he left us to spend months with his *real* dad.

Fred would come back to us ready for school but smelling of hot dogs, his pockets filled with magic sachets of a powder called Kool-Aid. Fred would come back saying 'boner' and 'trash'. Fred had another life of backstage passes and Tequila's groupies. Fred got up to God knows what.

A crow bounced on a cowpat and gagged up its song like a cat flushing fur balls. Fred's eyes were buzzing around me, dark, fathomless – like a shark. He yawned and I stared at his little white teeth.

'Lo-Lo?'

'Yes.'

'When you do it, will you tell me?'

'Do what?'

'Sex.'

I shivered. 'I'm never doing it.' I crossed my hot legs.

'You'd do it with the person you fancied.'

'I don't fancy anyone.'

'You'd do it with a person you *loved*.' Fred pulled out a matchbox and lit another cigarette. 'Anyway, when I do it *all*, you'll be the first person I tell.'

'I don't want telling. You're too young. Who do *you* fancy anyway?'

'I've got loads of girlfriends.'

'Well good for you.'

Fred grinned. 'You'll want me to tell you all about it, Lo-Lo. I know you will.' He threw the cigarette away again, and the wind carried it along, sparking it redder. 'And when *you* do it, you can tell me. After all, Lo, you *are* my sister.'

Fred was a weasel. He'd turn and twist and wrap himself around you – then he'd bite. He picked up Nana's binoculars and scanned the road. 'Have you seen them yet?'

'No,' I mumbled.

He stood up. 'Come on, Lo-Lo. I'm going down. It's the anniversary. *Her* anniversary, and they'll be here soon.'

He picked up *my* father's guitar and slipped his T-shirt back on, and I watched him run full pelt down Nana's hill. He jumped like a springer spaniel in a field of wheat, the guitar held above his head.

'Come on!' he yelled.

You roll for the longest time down Beggars' Hill. You roll for as long as Alice took to fall down that rabbit hole. Thistles graze your face, then there's a cowpat under your head, a mushy pillow, and the clouds and ground are rushing to meet each other with a loud hum.

I had tried to run after Fred, but too tall and too skinny, I'd tripped over my own legs, lost my footing, and now I was rolling.

Wind pushed out of my chest. It hurt. I gasped until my body finally stopped on flat ground.

The sky was spinning and I felt Fred's hands finger the hair from my face. I felt the weight of him on top of me again. 'You hurt, Lo-Lo?'

I couldn't focus.

'You've got a bit of blood.'

I felt a wet touch on my lips.

'There.'

I felt him cop a feel of my breasts-that-weren't-there.

'There.'

I felt a little poke of tongue. This wasn't the first time Fred had kissed me.

*

That first time, Fred was eight years old.

We were sitting on the floor by the telly watching Morrissey sing 'The Boy with the Thorn in His Side' on *Top of the Pops*. Morrissey was all arms, hands, and a lily-white neck. Morrissey stretched up and Morrissey had 'BAD' written on his throat. That was when Fred leant across and pressed his open mouth against mine.

Mum was standing in our kitchen, whisking cream and brandy and singing along because she thought The Smiths were clever. I remember how Fred pulled away and wiped his mouth on the back of his hand like he'd just eaten. He turned back to the telly and sang along, his voice babyish, too young for what he had just done.

A week after that Fred had us playing Commandos among the bales of hay in the barn, cocking our fingers and firing. It was me and Fred versus Vincent and Molly. As Molly crawled into the bale tunnel and Vincent cried 'Truce!' Fred pushed me over, climbed on top of me, and kissed me. This time, though, it was different. This time, he meant it. He meant it so much I fainted in that straw, and when I came to, all I saw were stars and Vincent's big moon face telling me to wake up.

After that I would sit close to Fred – knees just touching – but he didn't pounce again. I had the guts to ask him why, just once, and he laughed in my face.

'Don't be silly Lo-Lo, you're my big sister aren't you?' he said.

3

Brother. Sister. These were strong words.

For the longest time Fred was a baby in our house, not a brother. He was the strange cuckoo in our nest and we fed him, lovingly, but he was never a brother.

One night when I was still young enough to be lifted, Nana and Mum sat me on his changing table. I lay down on it inhaling Fred's oranges and musk – the scent he left like a marking polecat – and I stared at him, asleep in Molly's crib. I listened to his watery breathing.

'It's like he comes from the sea,' Nana said, 'like he's one of those selkie folks, you know the ones, Halo' – of course I didn't – 'we had them further up the coast. Pembroke. They was seals in the sea and human on the land. They'd dive in that salty brine and soon as their hands touched that water, Allie-kazam! – them hands would turn to flippers. And soon as their noses sniffed that seaweed, Allie-kazoo! – they'd be hairy, twitching snouts.' Nana's salt-and-pepper perm shook then, and her own nose twitched. 'So they'd pop into the water a human, and they'd pop out a seal, and those folks, Halo, you remember' – though I didn't – 'you remember how you had to steal their skins to make them stay, because they'd break your heart with their beauty, they would. Only way to keep them on dry land was to take their seal hides, otherwise they'd get drawn back into that water. It was too strong a calling. Yes, they'd break hearts with their beauty, them selkies would—' Nana cut off and turned to Mum, mouth open, eyebrows up. 'Hmmmm,' was all she said, like it was the beginning of a thought or a song.

When I was little enough not to know any better and Fred was old enough to sit up in the bath, I poured cooking salt in his water. But his hands didn't Allie-kazam! turn into flippers, and his nose didn't Allie-kazoo! grow into a hairy, twitching snout. He didn't pop into the water a human and pop out a seal, but he was well on the way to breaking my heart. Fred may not have been an animal but my love for him was. It was born in my fingers the first night I touched Jenny's huge stomach and now it crouched in my chest, thick-furred and feral. It would twitch from a quiet dormouse to a Scottish wildcat at the drop of a hat, screeching and scratching at my insides.

As a toddler, Fred didn't learn by example, he did everything on his own. One day he was sitting in his full nappy, his leg muscles loose, and the next he was wobbling up the track. Mum would run up and down our hedgerows crying, 'Fred Llewelyn!' because she'd rubbed her nose into the folds of his skin long enough to claim him, and because he had a habit of crawling into the sharp hawthorn and getting stuck. She usually found Fred in the studio, beneath the mixing desk or curled up on the black leather sofa.

'Someone must've carried him. Halo?'

'I didn't, Mummy, honest.'

'Vincent?'

'No.'

'Molly?'

Molly frowned; she was only five, but Molly resisted Fred. 'Out, baybee,' she'd say. 'Go away, Fed. Dunlikeyou.'

At three, Fred hadn't said a word. Nana Lew gave him drinks that could turn your stomach inside out, never mind your voice box, but Fred rarely *tried* a noise. Fred sighed, he smiled, he opened his mouth wide in a silent laugh, he sucked breath in sharp when something hurt or astonished him, but bar the watery breathing, there was little else. Nana said, *deaf and dumb, get him checked*, but Fred started at the sound of a guitar and Mum wouldn't have doctors.

Then one morning Dad made toast and Vincent pressed the big silver stop, rewind and play buttons on our new VHS video recorder (the one Nana bought because she wanted to be the first). Vincent was watching the video to 'Ashes to Ashes' and the clanging synthesizer was making us all tremble over our breakfast. Vincent said it was historic. Nana laughed and told us it was just that young boy, David Bowie, dressed as a clown in front of a JCB. Vincent shuffled closer to the telly screen, close enough to have Nana yelling, 'You'd make a better door than a window, son!' and he sang along with David; he sang about Major Tom being a junkie and by then we knew what that was. Suddenly Fred coughed like he was cleaning out cobwebs, butterflies, dust, and 'the old taste of the sea', Nana said later; suddenly Fred said, 'Play gain!'

'Vin-cen. Music. Play gain!' Fred shouted as the synthesizers finished with 'wa-ah, wa-ha, wa-ah, wa-ha, waaaaaa-waaaa-waaaa-waaa'.

After that, words came out like water: water from a burst pipe, Nana said. 'Can't we plug him up, Dolly?' she asked. I think Fred had been saving words up. *Fender*, he said, *Major Tom, pony Stardust, Mummy beautiful, slide glitter, Fred want spaghetti hoops, Ince and Olly and Fred.*

And me, I was *Lo-Lo*. At the start, everyone said Lo-Lo was all he could manage.

Lo-Lo. Lo-Lo. Lo-Lo.

Lo-Lo do that for Fred. Lo-Lo get that for Fred.

And it stuck like a bluebottle in a cobweb. When we played doctors and nurses, Fred put a packet of digestives up to my heart and listened. I felt my blood pump madly as he said, 'Lo-Lo, Lo-Lo, Lo-Lo' in time with my pulse. I was 'Lo-Lo' because he couldn't manage the 'Ha', but I think Lo-Lo was what Fred had decided on. He wanted to call me Lo-Lo, so Lo-Lo I was.

I still am.

Before the talking and the walking, it was Nana who was the first to ask, 'Is there something wrong with the kiddie, Doll?'

'Like what, Gladys?' Mum snapped.

'Maybe it touched him.'

'What touched him?'

'That bad stuff.' Nana tapped the side of her head. 'What his Mam was up to. Maybe it touched him up here.'

'He's *fine*.'

'He still sounds funny to me.' Nana clucked. 'You hear from the father, Dolly?'

'You know we do, Gladys.'

'And all that's sorted now?'

'You know it is.'

'And all that's legal now, is it, and you get your cheques?'

'Gladys!'

I didn't know what *all that* was, so that night I sneaked out onto our dusky porch. I remember listening to the quiet side of our house: to the crickets and toads rubbing legs and larynxes. I remember trying to count the stars, as my mother and grand-

144

mother's voices rose and fell into the night.

I did know *all that* was something to do with the postcards Fred received. Fred didn't get private letters; Abraham's postcards were for us all to see. As Fred grew they plopped through our letter box with a photograph of a city on the front. 'Detroit', 'Los Angeles', 'Rome', 'Munich', 'New York'.

Hey Kid!
How are you doing?!
Here's the city we're in!
Your Poppa's working!
See you kid!
Abraham

I thought they were like shouts; shouts across the sea.

My dad would read Abraham's words to Fred and I would sit on the landing and listen. My dad even tried Abraham's American voice when he read them: he thought that was only right. And over time, Abraham was losing his shout.

Hey Kid, (Dad read)
Got your pictures. You look like our grandpa round the
eyes. Your hair's real dark, not like me and your momma.
We're doing the tour. Had the idea to do it on the train.
Travel all over Amtrak-style. A crazy ride. Eat your
greens, kid. Be good. I told them you got to stay there
until you're good and ready. It's better this way.
Family's all it takes and family's those that love you.
Your Father
Abe Connor

145

Then one day Mum and Dad signed some papers from Abraham and Fred had a family over here and a family over there and *all that* was done with. Though in the end I suppose *all that* became unimportant because Fred simply was. So Fred's growth spurts cluttered our houses: our gardens were littered with snapped catapults, torn-off plasters, and the rusting stabilizers he unscrewed from his bike. We kept these trophies. Nana had Fred's milk teeth in a jar by the tea caddy and she rattled them for good luck. When Mum trimmed his hair she laid the cuttings flat in the books she would never read. When Fred grew out of his shoes, she sneaked them under her bed until she had a pile of worn plimsolls, sandals and boots. His sweet wrappers, his butter-square wrappers, his cracked plectrums, his scribbles and the class pictures he bothered to bring home – Mum would fold these away.

So yes: Brother, Mother, Father, Son, Sister; these were strong words. The truth was, Fred wasn't our brother because we were a family already: Mum, Dad, Nana Lew, Vince, Molly and Me. Another truth was that Fred was a little bit like each of us, and nothing like us at all, and yet another truth was that it was Molly, the youngest of us, who finally allowed Fred to be a brother.

It was a hot day in May. Fred was already seven and we walked into town. Molly carried a hockey stick she wanted felted in the sports shop. She lagged behind us, picking ragged robin and cowslips, pretty in a Laura Ashley dress, a black Alice band, and suede Kicker boots. Molly was a whisker off ten and she looked thirteen; I was almost thirteen and I looked ten. Fred walked those two miles into town in wellington boots too big

146

for him. Rubber shuddered on the tarmac all the way there and I didn't know his feet were raw; I didn't know his heels were bleeding until he gasped when I pulled those boots off later that night. Vince walked tall and wide past the ryegrass verge, all in black, and we marched in a line up the main road into town, saying nothing. We flicked our wrists at nettles and kicked at the goosegrass that clung to us, trying to claw us back home, safe.

The cobbled high street was hot, and we each had a yellow plastic bag with one thin vinyl record inside swinging against our legs. Fred had bought David Bowie's *Low*, because he liked the orange picture on the front; Molly had Wham's 'Freedom', and we all had pasties in white paper that burnt our hands and our mouths. We were sitting on different levels of a plinth that became the statue of a king called Henry.

Vince had cut off his Boy George braids and now he had a Morrissey short back and sides. It didn't suit him much; you could see the rolls of fat on his neck, but he still wore Nana's diamante earrings and her pillar-box red on his nails and lips. Fred had some of that too, just the fingernails, and I thought my brothers looked handsome with their black hair and their dark eyes and their red nails: I thought they looked like real brothers.

Shoppers stared and old men sucked their false teeth at us as they passed, because we were the weirdos from that farm-that-wasn't-a-farm: that Rockfarm.

We were with Gram: the boy from the record shop, Vinyl Heaven. We'd spent the morning at his Dad's place, flipping through albums and posters, trying on stud belts and badges. I loved Vinyl Heaven. You had to walk down outside stone steps to get there and its walls were black; it smelled of joss sticks, new leather and plastic, and it was *our* place. We'd been coming for years after school, with half a bag of Mr Furneyhough's pear drops in our pockets, ready to finger through vinyl.

I watched Gram nibble the sides of a pasty. Gram Rueben Philips was almost as beautiful as Fred. He was dressed in black, down to the black ribbons and leather bracelets on his wrists. Gram was my age but he went to the posh boys' school.

He smiled at me.

Fred was snapping at his pasty until his eyes watered. Molly stared at hers because Molly hated oil in her dinner. It was strange how Molly and I had never looked like sisters; of course, she was Mum, dark and edible, and I was Dad, freckled and red. Molly was pretty with that black Alice band; even her Laura Ashley dress and her suede Kicker boots oozed Molly-charm.

'I saw The Smiths,' Gram told us. 'Last Tuesday. Gloucester Leisure Centre. Johnny Marr's a god.'

'Morrissey is beautiful,' Vince said. Vince was off to France grape-picking for the summer. Vince was done with school as we knew it; he told me he'd found a new sort of freedom, and I wondered what.

Vince slid his new record out of the plastic bag and stared at the cover. It was a single with a black-and-white photograph of a lady with big bouffant blonde hair, standing in the middle of a dirty, muddy street. There were long lines of houses on each side of her, blocking her in. The lady looked a bit like Dusty Springfield with her hair dolled up like that, but she was fat and miserable. Vince passed it down to me.

'Wipe your hands first, Halo.'

I stared at the woman's face. She was hard, I knew that. She was harder than anyone round here; she was as hard as we were soft. She was harder than the hill farmers that circled us, harder even than the matted coats of their collie dogs. The woman was wearing a white winter coat and pointy black boots, and 'The Smiths' was written in the top right-hand corner of the sleeve. The song was 'Heaven Knows I'm Miserable Now'.

My legs wrapped around themselves and I wanted to laugh.

As I handed the single back to Vince the sun went out. I shivered, then looked up to see too many boys standing around us.

Spit landed near my shoe.

'You them weirdos from up the studios?' a boy asked. He spat again and the spit was green and I wondered how boys did that. Consumption, Nana would say.

'Look at that one, Dean,' another boy said, 'he's got nail varnish on, he has. The queer.'

I looked up at Vince, who scrunched up his pasty bag and nodded for us to go.

'You ain't going nowhere. You queer.'

'That little kid's got nail varnish too, Dean. That little un there, they're both homos.'

Fred cracked a knuckle.

'That one's from the record shop, they're weirdos, too.'

Gram flushed pink, but didn't move.

Then Molly, my little sister, piped up.

'Sod off, Dean Turley.'

We all stared at her.

'Yes you, sod off. I know you and I know your sister. And your mum sleeps with your bloody uncle. So piss off.'

Molly stood up.

149

'Come on Vince, come on Gram. Fred, you and Halo too. We don't need to listen to this from these bloody *twats*.'

I watched Dean's mouth open.

Vince got up. Vince, my eighteen-year-old, sixteen-stone brother who towered over those boys. Then we all stood and they backed off.

'Yes,' said Molly, 'and the next time I see any of your family, Dean, I'll tell them what a horrible little bully you are. Even if they are all in *prison*.' She parted the blob of boys and walked through them with her newly felted hockey stick.

We followed her down the high street.

Only Molly spoke.

'I think he got the colours just right,' she said, holding out the red-and-yellow top of her stick. 'Don't you, Gram?'

Molly and I were different in so many ways, but that day in May I decided that Molly, my baby sister, was a lot like the land here and she was like the woman on The Smiths cover: our Molly was hard.

Vince skimmed the furthest. It was in the wrist, he said. Fred preferred to chuck big rocks, held in two hands, at the skin of the river.

We walked across it on jutting stones and watched tiddlers dart.

'Don't get your record wet, Fred, give it here.'

'It's not a record, Lo-Lo, it's an album,' he said, wobbling on a green rock.

Molly shared out her cold pasty. Gram sat close to her while Fred practised imaginary shots with her hockey stick.

Gram took out a cigarette.

'I don't like cigarettes,' Molly sniffed.

'OK,' and Gram lobbed the yellow-tipped thing into the river.

'Don't do that – a swan will eat that and die,' she told him.

'Sorry.'

'That's not good enough.'

'I said sorry.'

'Go and get it.'

'The current's taken it now.'

'There's no current there.'

'It's dangerous.'

'Oh, *boys*,' and Molly marched off, following the river round the bend and back towards the town.

'Is she always like that?' Gram asked.

'Always,' the rest of us said in unison.

I chewed on a grass blade and lay back against the dry bank. I thought of the scouts who camped here each summer, the ones who still wandered up our track each summer singing 'Ging Gang Goolie' and asking for milk. I watched Fred; the small muscles in his arms tensed as he stood on the bank and took hockey shots at rabbit shit. Vince and Gram were talking, serious-faced, Gram trying to be older, as old as Vince, and as strange.

It was Fred who was the first to look up. Fred had hearing like a bat. Vince and Gram didn't notice; the trickle of the river or the rumble of their conversation muffled other sounds. Suddenly Fred was gone, the hockey stick in the air.

Then *I* heard the sound, a scream, and I recognized it.

Sprinting was something that suited me. I'd started running at junior school and now at the comp I loved cross country. Sprinting was something I was good at and I brought my arms

151

up like pistons – palms flat, fingers together; elbows into the body and straight. I leapt over the stones at the river's edge. That day I was Zola Budd: barefoot, flat as a pancake and puffing up the dirt of my homeland. I steamed past Fred within seconds. I was following my sister's path along the river bend.

They were up in the field by the fat oak. I saw four boys. I also saw Molly's Alice band on the ground in front of me, brown with mud, and I knew she'd be furious about that.

I heard that sound again.

I jumped up the bank.

'Lo-Lo, wait!' Fred cried.

I ran, like open scissors, I ran and I ran across that field until I rounded the oak, and before the four boys had the chance to look up, I slammed right into the body of Dean Turley: Dean Turley, who was kneeling over my sister, my sister with her Laura Ashley dress up over her head and a flash of torn white knickers.

I slammed into Dean and I winded us both.

It's odd, being winded. It's like being sick in your lungs. You gasp and fill up, but it's just the wrong thing to do because all you can hear is the noise of a punctured tyre.

'You bitch,' I heard. Then Dean was up, and he was kicking me in the side. 'You bitch.'

Molly was right. Dean wasn't blessed with imagination.

I groaned. His face was red and he was pulling up his trousers. I saw black hair there, and a thin, pink dick.

'Get her lads, get the fucking ginger bitch.'

The other boys didn't move. I laughed.

'She's mad,' one said.

'They all are up there, Dean – come on, you've had enough.'

152

'I'm gunna fucking teach them all.'

'Yeah, leave them, Dean, that one's only a kiddie.' The biggest boy was pointing at Molly, who hadn't moved. She was still lying flat, the dress covering her face, her big knickers ripped on one side from the hip down.

'Molly,' I said, 'your dress is up.'

She pulled it down, obedient, but still she didn't move. She just stared up into the warty oak branches.

'She's a kid, Dean,' the big boy repeated.

'So what?'

Another boy was staring at something beyond the tree. He was staring like it was something interesting. He didn't shout, 'Watch out!' or, 'Leg it, lads!' He just stared, half a smile on his face.

That was when Fred raced around the tree in his big wellies. He saw Molly lying there, then me. And with the speed of someone closer to the ground, he jumped over my little sister, ran in front of Dean, and swung Molly's hockey stick all the way from the ground and up. It was a well-practised swing that landed right in Dean Turley's face.

It's funny how bone crunches, how teeth crack. No matter how much you want a person to hurt, that sound doesn't seem quite right. Blood sprayed first, teeth followed. One arced up and landed with a tiny white plop in the gliding river.

'Fuck off my sisters!' Fred yelled, and as Dean fell to his knees, Fred took a step back to swing again.

I still think that if Molly and I hadn't both landed on Fred – her prising the hockey stick from his hand and me sitting on top of him and holding him down by the wrists – he would have killed Dean Turley. Fred thrashed and spat and kicked me with

153

his legs, but I wouldn't let him go. Dean was moaning, crawling through the grass, spitting out teeth and blood. Molly walked over to him with her hockey stick and – calmly, without Fred's wildness – took a measured hockey swing right between his legs.

Dean didn't have the breath to scream; he hissed.

Molly spoke. 'If you even look at me again, Dean Turley, I will tell everyone you tried to rape a ten-year-old. Then I'll get my grandmother to kill you. She's good at that, she can do it with a few drops in your drink, a bit of chalk on your doorstep, you'll see.'

With a goodbye passing shot, Molly aimed again, and as Vince and Gram rounded the tree, they were just in time to watch the largest boy pick Dean Turley off the ground like a baby.

'Sorry,' was all that the big boy said, and he turned back towards the town, carrying Dean home.

We didn't walk back for the longest time and we didn't say much when we did. Molly told us that Dean hadn't got that far. She said check if you want, he didn't actually do it to me, he didn't rape me and I know what that is, I'm reading *To Kill a Mockingbird* aren't I?

Vince said, so that makes it all right does it?

That night, once Gram called his dad, and our mum had made up a bed in Vince's room for him, we all crammed into the bathroom. Vince sat on the closed loo, fully dressed, while the rest of us kept our undies on and crawled into the soapy bath water together: Fred at the front, then Molly, then me, then Gram behind me – it didn't seem to matter any more.

'Do you think the police will come?' Fred asked from the taps.

'No,' Vince said first. 'No, definitely not.'

'Why?'

Vince sniffed through his thin nostrils, his hands crossed over one another, palm to palm, his arms out straight like his legs. He was sweaty in his black jumper. 'Well,' he told us in his best clipped voice, 'that git Dean Turley would never admit to being beaten up by a kid, two girls and two queers. Now would he?'

I saw our reflections in the mirror on the back of the bathroom door, crammed into the big bath, and we all looked a little stunned – confused children, shampoo frothing in our hair. After all, Vince was so much older; I'd never truly realized that. In a month my big brother would be gone, finding his other sort of freedom and picking grapes in that big black jumper under the South of France sun. I rubbed the shampoo into Molly's hair and twanged the strap of the training bra she refused to take off.

They take a lot of training, Molly said.

That was our last day with the Vince we knew, if he let us know him at all. But it was our first day with a new little brother, a brother who would protect us, kill for us if he had to.

Molly kept to the farm after that, and she didn't pick up her hockey stick again even though Fred washed the blood from it. Fred took to practising his punches on the bags of grain in the barn; he said that with Vince gone it was time for him to grow up, for his sisters' sake at least.

And me? Well, I'm still the best cross-country runner in the county, as if anyone bothered to ask.

4

My head was still spinning: from rolling down the hill *and* from my brother's kiss. Ten minutes, fifteen minutes had passed, and I was dazed. I sat picking Beggars' Hill thistles from my hands and face. Fred walked over to the hedge and looked out at the road.

'Come on Lo-Lo,' he hissed, 'they're here!'

I crouched then staggered over to him. I saw that 'they' were three girls and two boys who carried a guitar case, tent poles, and a crate of drink. 'They' were about to turn up our drive.

'Hippies,' Fred said and he climbed the gate.

'Wait!' I whispered, because it was my job to keep an eye on him, today of all days.

I heard the intruders laugh and I dashed over the road as Fred slunk behind them, deep in the shadow of the hedge. They turned past Nana's Big House, into her orchard, because they knew where to go. It was like finding Jim Morrison's grave in Père Lachaise Cemetery; there were maps. It was because of Jenny that hippies sauntered up our drive on a certain day each September, with guitars, tents and cheap wine. It was because Jenny Connor died here at Rockfarm that they'd sit in Nana's graveyard, light coloured candles and sing her songs.

Fred darted away from them, under the red-brick arch and into the courtyard.

'Fred, where are you going *now*?' I sprinted after him and the ducks around the pond scattered and skimmed.

Middle-of-the-night guitar solos still blasted out from this place, shaking our houses past midnight and waking the horses and pigs; my father still told us these were the best lullabies.

'Fred, wait!'

'I'm going to get the girls, Lo.'

'Don't get *them*!'

He jumped the steps and disappeared into the long rehearsal room.

'The girls will help us, Lo-Lo,' he shouted back to me, 'the girls will get rid of the bloody hippies!'

It wasn't that I didn't like the girls. The girls had been coming to Rockfarm since they were babies with their mum and their dad and their uncles, because their mum and their dad and their uncles were a band called The O'Boyles and they made wafty, shivery music. The girls were triplets and they were called SHOVE-ON, NEEEVE and A FREAK. They were fifteen now and they said they came from a place in Dublin called DUNLEEERY where old men jumped naked into the sea from a place called Forty Foot. One summer the triplets wrote their names in the dust of our yard, and SHOVE-ON became SIO-BHAN, and NEEEEVE was NIAMH. A FREAK was AIFRIC.

'They're better names than your one,' Aifric told me.

'They're not.'

'Oh yeah? "Halo"? What kind of fecking name is that?'

Aifric loved to swear and when she did the freckles on her nose creased. 'Yeah, and that's not all. "Diamond Star Halo". *You're* the fecking freak.'

I didn't like it when the triplets made fun of me, but I did love it that they could say 'feck', which sounded just like 'fuck', right in front of their mum, their dad and their uncles.

'Get off me, ye fecker!' Siobhan would yell at Fred, and their mum carried on shelling peas. Her name was NOOO-LA, which the triplets spelled 'NUALA' in the dust.

Though Niamh, Siobhan and Aifric were triplets, they weren't identical. They had red hair like me, but different faces, and this summer my favourite, Niamh, had an earring in her ear *and* her nose because she loved a singer called Sinead O'Connor.

I followed Fred through the rehearsal room and soon the studio's thick black door was sucking shut behind me. I slipped into the control room, my back against the cold wall. The smell of mushrooms and smoke was here and the black sofas were full of Irish uncles. Nuala and another uncle were at the mixing desk.

I still got a fizz of excitement in the recording studio. I smiled in the dark and felt a hand on mine. Fred pinched me.

'Can I tell them to stop?' he whispered.

'Shh!'

'That's it,' Nuala said, 'now we need the chorus again.'

'Ah, Mammy!' Niamh's voice was amplified into the control room. I walked forward and saw her through the glass.

The triplets were at their microphones, ready to play. Niamh had a penny whistle, while Aifric sat at her harp. Siobhan had the end of a violin – which she called a fiddle – resting on her breast. The triplets had great breasts, though Siobhan's were the biggest. She'd grown hers first and she liked to show them off. Last year Fred said Siobhan had breasts like bubbles.

Fred and I had learnt most things from the triplets. They told us that in Ireland, willies were called messages but they were also called mickeys. They said that messages were also what your mammy sent you down the shops for, though your mickey was always your mickey and that was that. The triplets had me as confused as Nana Lew did when it came to boys and girls and sex.

Then there was the torch.

That was two years ago.

That lazy and hot afternoon I was on the sofa reading *My Guy* and Molly was tut-tutting from the kitchen, pulling down her skirt.

'What's going on, Moll?' I was asking this because the triplets had locked themselves in the bathroom with Fred, and Molly had just escaped.

Molly straightened her blouse and stuck her nose in the air. '*They've* got a torch, Halo.'

I tried to read the photo-story about kissing. 'A what?'

'A *torch*. They make you take your clothes off and they tell you to stand like a dog does, and they look up you.'

I let *My Guy* drop. 'They look up you?'

'They told me they wanted to "look up my hole". They've got Fred now.'

'Your "hole"?'

Molly sniffed as if someone had farted.

'But Moll, Fred doesn't have a hole.'

'He does.'

'What?'

'Have-a-hole, Halo. I've seen.'

'But he's a boy. Where does he have a hole?'

'Up his bottom.'

It took a moment for me to run to the avocado door of our downstairs bathroom. I slapped it. 'Fred, come out, this instant.'

'Go-way, Lo-Lo!' he giggled.

I hit the door again. 'Fred, come-out-*now*.'

'Feck off, we're seeing up his hole!' Aifric cried.

'Leave him alone, he's only a baby!'

'No he's not! He's nine.'

There were more giggles.

'Fred!'

'Go-way Lo-Lo! Or they won't let me see their holes!'

Of course now the triplets had forgotten about torches and holes. Now boys were 'a ride', 'a stud', and they were 'grand'. They still practised on Fred though. Two days ago all four of them came down from the barn with cloudy eyes and red chapped lips. When I saw Fred's black hair tied up in tufts with the triplets' coloured scrunchies, something in the pit of my stomach growled.

I pressed my nose against the cold studio glass. I considered that violin at Siobhan's breast. I wouldn't have minded being that thin warmed wood, perched on her magnificent bosom.

'Get a move on, Niamh,' Aifric said into her microphone.

'Shut up.'

'Shut up yourself.'

'Get on with it, Niamh.' Siobhan tapped the end of her fiddle bow on her other breast.

The triplets looked daggers at one another.

'All riiiigh—'

Uncle Tommy played with the buttons at the mixing desk and the playback came. Niamh had sung it already but what they wanted was layers on layers on layers on layers (when in truth all Niamh wanted to do was to yell like Sinead O'Connor). Siobhan tapped out a rhythm on the same breast and then the fiddle went under her chin. Aifric was swaying backwards and forwards in the chair in front of the harp. Finally Niamh let the penny whistle drop and cocked her head to one side; she closed her eyes and she sang.

> 'When the cold morning comes,
> I-osa, I-osa,
> I'll hold you my love,
> Come closer, come closer,
> When one love leaves me,
> For war love, for war.
> The cold beach I'll walk, sir
> I'll walk, sir, I'll walk.
> Until you return. Back to me, sir. To me, sir,
> From the cold country beyond—'

She sang, eyes closed, a different Niamh. She sang about patience and faith and how one day he'll come back while the girl paces up and down on the sand. I watched Siobhan and Aifric and they were different too. Transported, Nana would say. Like the spirit had them.

Niamh captured the last note, and then there was silence. The girls opened their eyes.

'Are we fecking done now?' Niamh asked.

'So what do you mean, the hippies are in the graveyard, Fred? Is that some kind of fecking code?' We were standing inside the stables, the smell of straw and horse shit sweet as toffee. Niamh had one of Fred's roll-ups in her mouth.

'Are they old hippies, like?' Siobhan asked.

Fred was staring at her breasts.

'No, they're young,' I told them. 'Different people come every year.'

'Why?'

A horse scraped a metal shoe against the concrete floor.

'Today's the anniversary. It's when Jenny Connor died.' I nodded at Fred and he obliged by staring at each triplet with big seal eyes.

'Ah, you poor thing, Fred.'

'Ah, Fred, we didn't know it was today like.'

'Come here to me, pet.' Siobhan opened her arms and Fred walked in. He buried himself there, nudging his face down like a dog in a bowl of food. All Siobhan could do was put her arms round him and shrug.

'Ye poor wee fecker,' she said, but there was nothing poor or wee about Fred.

'So what does he want us to do?' Niamh asked me.

'I don't know yet.'

'Does he want us to get rid of them, like?'

I nodded.

Siobhan giggled as Fred made fart noises between her breasts. 'Fred! Stop!' she laughed.

Fred stepped out, his cheeks flushed. 'Don't worry, I've got it all planned,' he told us.

'Shouldn't we wait for Molly and Vince?' I asked.

'No.'

'Why?'

'They know when to be here. They know what they have to do.'

'What do you mean?'

'You'll see,' and he winked.

5

Of course Jenny was bigger now than she ever was the summer she came to us. Nana told me death can do that; make you bigger than you were in real life.

'Look at that Rudolph Valentino,' Nana said, 'look at that James Dean.'

And because Jenny was big, her band, Tequila, was big. Abraham and his seven brothers were rock stars, and Tequila still sang Jenny's songs. Fred told me when he saw them at Madison Square Garden the band projected an old film of his mother, singing. He said his mum was a hundred feet high and looked young enough to be his sister. He said his dad and his uncles sang along with her, and the crowd lit lighters. He said a woman next to him started to cry and right then and there he knew that *he* couldn't.

'I mean, I never met her, Halo,' he said, 'I don't know who she is, and she doesn't look much older than you. Why would I cry?'

Fred was like that.

I followed him and the triplets as they ducked under a laden apple tree. Fred was telling us to get down, to slide on the grass and edge forward on our elbows.

'Why?' Niamh asked.

'Shh!'

'This is stupid – what are you going to do, Fred?'

The hippies had pitched what looked like a tepee by the old

yew in the capel grounds. We sank further into the grass and watched as they drank from bottles. I heard the first chords of 'Stallion Boys'. When I was small I thought it was about wild mustangs playing out on the prairies Jenny would tell me about. Since, I've learned it's about a whole lot more.

'*Stallion boys kick like whiskey, they squeal like a woman too,*' the intruders sang, and Fred forgot his stealth tactics, sprang up and stormed through the high grass. The hippies didn't notice us slip through the kissing gate, they didn't even hear Siobhan giggle as Fred clicked the latch of Nana's capel. We walked inside.

It was dark and musty. Particles danced in the light.

Niamh shivered next to me. 'I hate it in here,' she said.

Siobhan nodded. 'Me too.'

'Yeah,' said Aifric.

The triplets crossed themselves, one knee dipping in a bounced curtsey. I copied, stiff, and Fred ran towards the two big black speakers that were standing at the altar: he had definitely had help.

'Jesus,' said Niamh. 'Fred, what are you planning? What are we meant to be doing? You know we fecking hate it in here.'

'Niamh!' Aifric squeaked.

'OK, OK.' Niamh crossed herself and bounced. 'Fred, can't we just go out there and tell those people to feck off?'

'Niamh!'

'Sorry.' She bounced and crossed herself again. 'Fred, tell us why we're here.'

'This is where we've set it up.'

'Set what up?'

'*Everything.*'

'Who's "we"?' I asked.

'What's "everything"?' Aifric had her hands on her hips.

Fred was too busy opening a small latticed window to answer. It looked as fragile and brittle as the skulls of the monks above us. A late-summer wind swirled the bony dust around and we coughed.

'I've just got to get this set up,' he whispered, 'then I can scare the living daylights out of those fucking bastards.'

'Fred!'

'Fred!'

'Fred!'

'Fred!' I joined in with the triplets and our snappy girl-voices came back at us like little slaps in the dry capel.

'Are you lot going to help me or what?' Fred swooped down off the pew; the red at the top of his cheeks made him look like Andy Pandy. 'Well, are you?' He was using his seal eyes again.

'OK,' Siobhan sighed.

'You promise? Cross your hearts and hope to die?'

The triplets frowned.

'Cross your hearts and hope to die?' Fred repeated.

They nodded.

'Right, so now we wait.'

'For what?' I asked.

'For dark.'

'I'm not fecking waiting in here in the fecking dark,' said Niamh, bouncing and crossing herself twice.

'Me neither.'

'Me neither.'

'Me neither, Fred,' I told him.

'Well you all have to because you promised. And a promise is a promise, especially in here. This is a holy place. It is and that's that.' Fred stomped off to the font; he sat on the floor with his back to us. I watched as his shoulders shook.

We knew he'd got us. Later it was Niamh who said, 'We had to stay, didn't we? I mean, how could we leave that poor boy in that place with all that death?'

We were standing on the pew beneath the window, listening to the unwanted visitors out on the grass. The wine had worked and they'd been crying and kissing for a while now. Each time we heard a sob, Niamh stuck her fingers down her throat.

'I can't believe she's here,' a girl was saying. 'I mean, she's really beneath me? *The* Jenny Connor? Right now?'

'She's growing in the grass,' one of the men said.

'She's all around us,' another joined in.

'What a bunch of fecking tossers,' Siobhan whispered.

The tops of Fred's cheeks were redder now.

Of course I knew it wasn't true. Jenny Connor wasn't beneath them. I remember Jenny's funeral, and it wasn't here. That day was wet and I wore dungarees in red cord and socks with rings of stripes to Jenny's funeral. That day we stood at the other end of Nana's garden (through the orchard and round the back of the English Bastard's huge greenhouse) and that's where Jenny is, or the tiniest part of her, at least. The rest of her, well, I have no idea.

The morning of the funeral I sat dangling my legs over the edge of my bed in white knickers and a white vest. Somehow I knew I couldn't be sad for Jenny because I was sad already. A black-bird was pecking at the glass of my window in the rain and

Mum was shouting goodbye from the hall, telling us they'd all be back from the crematorium soon. She yelled that it would all be all right, Nellie was staying with us, and later we'd go to Nana Lew's for black cake. Dad peeped the horn and I heard Mum sigh before the door slammed.

I watched the blackbird and I worried about not having a black dress. Nana said it didn't matter. She said Jenny was a girl of colours so in colours we should go. That's why I pulled out a bottom drawer and chose my bright red dungarees and my socks with their rings of different-coloured stripes. I knew I'd have to pull up my trouser legs to show the socks off.

When my parents came back from the crematorium, we stood on our porch under umbrellas, and I saw the blackbird again. He was hopping mad, and stabbing our chrome boot scraper with his yellow beak.

'It's because it sees itself,' Vince murmured. 'It sees itself and it thinks that that's an enemy. He's defending his territory, see.' Vince let his head drop and his black hair fell in his face.

I tugged Dad's sleeve. 'Is Jenny's mummy coming?'

'No, nutmeg, no.'

'Does Jenny's mummy know what happened?'

'Yes.'

'And she's not coming?'

'No.'

'Why?' I started to cry and Dad had to kneel in front of me and hold my shoulders. 'Not everyone's mummy loves them as much as your mummy loves you, nutmeg.' I didn't believe this but I let Dad take my hand.

Rain spat as we walked across the track to Nana's. Vincent held my mother's hand and Molly skipped on her own. Baden the Great Dane was loose, chasing the peacocks and peahens on the lawn. We walked up Nana's drive, skirting the shrieking birds. The air buzzed and smelled of a boozy rot, because the apple trees had dropped their fruit early and clusters of wasps sucked. At Nana's big front door I stopped and asked Dad where Jenny was.

'God has her, sugar lump.'

'What's God going to do with her?'

'Look after her.'

'But Jenny can look after herself, she told me.'

Dad shrugged; he was best at that.

'Will Jenny sing for God?'

'Of course, nutmeg.'

'Will she sing him her song about the stallion boys?'

'I expect.'

'He'd like that, God. Because she's very good at singing.'

Dad opened Nana's garden gate and I walked through. 'I hope there are horses in heaven, Daddy.'

'I bet there are.'

'Jenny won't like God without horses.'

'Right, nutmeg.'

'Will she come and visit us?'

'What?'

'Come down and see us, I mean?'

'No, Halo. She won't.'

That grey afternoon I remember staring at the eight Tequila brothers. They seemed smaller without Jenny: as if her size had made them so big. They wore those same beautiful suits: the ones sewn with stories in coloured thread and jewels, the ones where blonde-haired girls and horses ran beneath cactus trees

169

and red crosses, the ones where big white pills floated next to golden stars. Their white suits were almost blue in the rain though, and mud had drawn a tideline up their flared trousers; the brothers had splashes of dried mud on their faces, too. Nana told me they'd been pacing our fields all night, up and down. 'I watched them from my window, sunbeam. I reckon it was a sort of a wake and a penance too. They were walking the little girl's spirit out, walking it out and setting it free.'

Abraham's eyes were so red they matched my dungarees, and his brothers held on to parts of him as we all stood in a circle outside Nana's kitchen door. While his brothers held him, Abraham held Fred. I worried that he was holding him too tight, in all those blankets.

'Where's Jenny?' I asked, too loud.

There wasn't a grave because there wasn't a coffin. Jenny was ash and one of the brothers was holding a golden jar. Mum and Dad had gripped at a similar one when they brought Robert back from his funeral.

Nana walked out from the kitchen; she wore a red dress and a red shawl edged with a black fringe. She wore red lipstick. I pulled my trouser legs up to show my striped socks and she winked. Then Nana sucked through her teeth and cleared her throat. The rain got harder.

'This is the most difficult of days,' she said out loud. 'A girl has been lost.'

The brothers, who looked more and more like the same person to me, shook themselves like golden dogs.

'Spirit of Death!' Nana cried. 'I talk to you here!'

Nana couldn't help a little drama.

'Spirit of Death! Bring this child back home! Why do you

have it rain? Is the girl so bad you want to wash her tracks from this earth? Let the sun shine down on her path, oh Spirit, let the sun shine down on her path!' Nana, arms out, gazed up at the sky like she was willing it to talk back. She sank a little in the rain-bubbled grass, water spilling over her red high-heel shoes. Nana turned to Abraham. 'You ready, boy?'

Abraham nodded. He walked over to Mum and gave Fred to her. Then he turned back to the brother with the golden urn and he took it. Abraham was sobbing and the urn shook along with his sobs. He took off the lid and dipped his hand in.

'She's warm,' he told us, and he scooped up just a little of Jenny. I watched grey puff out in the wind. Then the grey ash went black with rain.

Abraham began to sing.

'Good-bye, Jenny
Goodbye little child of time
The sweetest song-bird's purest soul
Your spirit was so hard to find.

Goodbye, Jenny
Goodbye sweetest child of mine
My little blackbird-Jenny girl
Hope you make it to the other side
My little blackbird-Jenny girl
I'll see you on the other side.'

Spitting rain blew into Abraham's open mouth, but I couldn't see Jenny in what he was singing: not the girl I'd made friends with that summer. Not the yee-hawing Jenny who had the

171

dirtiest fingernails, the biggest freckles and the meanest laugh. Above us all a blackbird, maybe the one I'd seen all morning, settled in the wind by the back-door porch.

So you see, those intruders with the guitar out on Nana's capel grounds had it wrong: Jenny Connor wasn't beneath them. A little of Jenny Connor was lost in the molehills of my nana's lawn, but most of Jenny Connor was still in that golden urn Abraham left behind and Dad had hidden somewhere.

Dad had hidden it because we were all still waiting, waiting to know where Jenny should go.

When you're outside playing – laughing, hiding and screaming – darkness creeps up on you, like sleep. When you wait for dark, it takes an age. The hippies had sung *all* of Jenny's songs. We had sat through eight 'Stallion Boys' and four renditions of 'Little Girl' and 'Dust Road Blues'. Fred passed around a bottle of R Whites lemonade. I swallowed sugar-thick gulps, and then I heard a voice: it was coming from Fred's pocket. He took out a toy walkie-talkie and shook it.

'Starman receiving,' he said.

'Lady Stardust here. All clear,' the voice in the walkie-talkie replied. It was Vince.

'Fred, what's going on?' I asked, 'why is Vince—?'

'Lo-Lo, you get the switches over there. Girls, you follow me. It's time.' Fred's eyes were violet in the pearly darkness.

He dived behind the back pew. He trailed cable, while we flicked switches at his command. Bulbs hanging from the monks' toothy jaws blinked and the capel tripped into light. Fred plugged in sockets and pressed buttons and levers on a machine at the altar. It looked like a lighting board or tiny mixing desk and it had big reels of tape that he spun, backwards, forwards. I ran to the window to see sudden colours flash from fairy lights strung along the roof and gutters of the capel. The intruders pointed up at the lights. They were smiling. Then Fred pressed a button, and that was when I heard another voice.

It wasn't Vincent, it was Jenny Connor, loud and clear.

My stomach twitched.

'Hey kiddo, what's hanging?' Jenny said.

I watched the lit branches of the yew tree shiver.

'You OK, kiddo?' The words echoed into the night, loud and with all of Jenny's twang.

It was then I heard a child's voice; it took me a while to recognize that it was me.

'This is Diamond Star Halo Llewelyn-from-Wales asking Jenny-from-America some things,' my child-voice said.

'OK, shoot, kiddo.'

I remembered the day Jenny recorded this up in the studio. I remembered because it was the last day Jenny lived. Sometimes it was nice to think that she lived it with me. I wondered how Fred had found it, and I realized Dad must have squirreled it away. Poor Dad, he had to hide so much –under beds and in forgotten pantries – to protect us all.

I listened to the baby-me and Jenny play again and again. We were on a loop.

'Hello, Jenny. Jenny, what is your favourite film?' my voice said.

'Movie, right? What's yours?'

'Um, I don't know. *Dr Doolittle*. I like the big snail.'

'Mine's *Night of the Living Dead*, it's about flesh eating zombies! Rahhhhhhhh!'

Fred was holding a microphone, and up on his tiptoes, like a hungry pup, he took a deep breath and then he yelled into it. 'Rahhhhhhhh!'

The old glass in the windowpanes shook and the triplets held onto bits of one another.

'Rahhhhhhhh!' said Jenny.

'Rahhhhhhhh!' Fred said.

I was dazzled. The fairy lights flashed, and I swear to God there was smoke out there in the capel grounds.

'Rahhhhhhhh!' Jenny said again and again.

Then I saw something move.

Something was floating up from that sudden mist. It swayed as it travelled in the air past the yew tree. As it moved closer I saw it was a cloak: Jenny's red cloak, the cloak we found Fred wrapped up in the day his father left him here. Now it was lit up each side by bright white beams.

'Rahhhhhhhh!' Jenny said on the tape.

The hippies stood in the flashing fairy lights, but they weren't laughing now. The three girls and the two boys were backing away, as if a bear was attacking, slow step by slow step.

'Rahhhhhhhh!' Fred screamed, and they rounded on their stuff, cramming it into rucksacks.

'Rahhhhhhhh!'

The biggest of them, a man, fell on his guitar: it smashed.

'Rahhhhhhhh!' said Jenny.

The red cape was so close I saw it shudder above them in the misty wind. Then I heard another voice. This time it was a boy's voice and it was shouting into the night, 'Go away! Go away! Leave my mother alone! Leave my mother alone!'

That was when we all joined in – me, Aifric and Siobhan –

174

and we ran to the capel door. We stood there and yelled, 'Get out! Out! Out!' Niamh jumped up to the open capel window and she screamed at the hippies in Irish: she made it sound dangerous, a witch's curse.

The intruders were still grabbing at their belongings, and that was when the final touch of Fred's masterpiece came bounding out into the foggy, fairy-lit graveyard: it was Baden.

Baden was old – Nana reckoned on fourteen, and she said big bones didn't last, not even in the earth. Baden lived for another two years after that night, but that night was his finest.

Baden bounded out of the blackening mist, our own Cŵn Annwn; our own hound from the bowels of the earth, teeth sharp as the Devil's. Baden bounded out from behind the yew and he landed on the hippies' blanket; they screamed. His eyes were green in the flashing beams of light, and he howled.

We all froze. Niamh was quiet at the window and Fred put down the microphone. It was, after all, over-egging an already rich pudding. We simply walked out of the church together, leant against the porch, and watched the dog. Maybe it was the exertion caused by all that howling, but Baden crouched on the intruders' blanket; he was readying himself.

His big taupe and grey paws trampled the abandoned plates and bottles. Paw to blanket, Baden stomped round and around – whimpering now – in the effort to relieve himself. When it finally came, Baden shat like an old man, his legs shaking with effort.

It stank. Poor Baden.

We pinched our noses at the capel door and Jenny's fans fled. In the still-flashing fairy light I saw Fred speaking into his walkie-talkie.

'Starman calling. Plan B a success. Invaders dispersed. Pulley back in. Over.'

The walkie-talkie fizzled. 'Lady Stardust receiving. Roger that. Now come in and have some supper, Fred. It's over. Over.'

'Thanks, Vince.'

The lights, the smoke machine and the cloak on pulleys, they had all been down to Vincent, my theatrically talented big brother.

It took time for Fred to move. He was watching Jenny's cloak blow in the wind. I watched it too, and I wondered if Jenny would have laughed at her prankster son, her vengeful son. I saw Fred's wishful-thinking face in those fairy lights, and I wondered if he thought, just for a moment, that he'd brought his mother, Jenny Connor, back from the dead: our very own little Victor Frankenstein.

But Fred wasn't one to waste time on thoughts or wishes, and he wasn't a truly spiteful child. The next morning Fred Connor packed up the intruders' tent and the rug with the big circle of turd on it, and he chucked them into a bin liner and left them at the bottom of our drive with a note.

PISS OFF (it said)
From Fred Connor

6

I lay alone in my bed because Fred had stood by my mother's command – he always did – and tonight he slept in his own bed. Of course he wasn't there now, and he wasn't there because I had heard him, Dad, and Vince creep out.

I'd opened my window when I heard their voices. I'd listened to them out on the porch.

'Did you find it, Dad?' Fred asked, because he'd never been able to call our dad anything else.

'Yes. You sure you want to do this tonight, son?' Dad said, because he liked to call Fred this.

'Tonight is the only night, Dad. It's been eleven years.'

'True, son, true.'

'Where was it?' Vince asked.

'Under one your nana's brass beds over in the Big House, so many bloody bedrooms that woman's got. Here, you take it, Fred.'

They were quiet for a moment.

'She's so small, Dad.'

'Yup.'

'Dusty, too.'

'Are you OK?'

'Yeah, Vince. I'm fine.'

'Well. You ready?' Dad asked.

'Definitely.'

I heard them walk away, and Dad coughed. Then the Land Rover revved and they drove away.

Later, much later, Vince told me they started on Beggars' Hill. Dad drove the Land Rover up the ragged track, and Vince said they had had to turn their backs on Fred, out of politeness, because the boy was crying so much. Vince said it was hard to fight the urge to hug him, to kiss him; to make it all better. Vince was right when he said that would be the last thing Fred would want. What Fred wanted that night was to put his mother to rest at last. And so finally Dad found the golden urn of Jenny's ashes and Fred tipped a little of Jenny into the night. Vince said Fred tried to sing 'Stallion Boys', but it was hard, so they'd all joined in. Then they drove back down to the farm and circled the tracks. Fred let little handfuls of Jenny go: in our grass verges, in our blackthorn hedges, the hedges our Nana had laid around Rockfarm as a young bride. Vince told me Fred said he wanted his first mother to be everywhere here at Rockfarm, wherever he walked, so he had left pinches of her in the studio; in the control room, under the mixing desk, beneath a black Marshall amp. He'd even sprinkled her into the microphones, like precious dust.

I asked Vince why Fred didn't take me that night. After all, I knew Jenny better than anyone in my family.

Vince said, 'Well, maybe that's exactly why, Halo. Maybe that's the reason.'

7

The O'Boyles were having a party and the O'Boyles's parties at Rockfarm were legendary. Dad said people went missing among the hill farms above us for days, though they always came back in a good mood.

I lay in my bed and stared up at my poster of Flo-Jo. I'd watched the Seoul Olympics, and when Greg Louganis hit his head on a diving board, Vince rang me up and cried. He told me London was a hard place for a country girl like him. He told me he would live and die a virgin, and I told him to join the club. Now I could hear Vince next door, singing along to Suzanne Vega's 'The Queen and the Soldier', and it was a nice sound to hear: it was great to have my big brother back. I knew that Vince would be sitting at his dressing table, plucking and drawing his face on: Vince would stay long enough for Nana to feed him up, and then he'd drive away moaning about a month on Slimfast.

I thought of how, when Vince was a kid, he'd collect shiny things: whistles and medals mostly. Then Nana gave him a metal detector with headphones and he spent days circling Beggars' Field, Beggars' Hill, the courtyard, her peacocks and peahens: all for his gold, his treasure. He never found it, but he carried a plastic bag with him wherever he went. In those days his room smelled of Brasso and soil. I thought of how he'd play David Bowie's 'Life on Mars?' every morning and Dad would leave toast outside his door. 'How about a different tune, Vincey?' Dad would ask and knock. Nana said Vince was firm about his tastes; Molly said he was just *bizarre*.

I stood on our tiny landing. 'Can I come in, Vince?'

'Leave me alone.'

'What are you going to wear tonight?'

'Never you mind.'

'Please.'

Vince had spent the afternoon in the bathroom, and now we had no hot water and the house smelled of liquid wax.

'Enter,' Vince told me in his best croak.

I pushed the door.

When Vince was away his room was lifeless, dark. I'd often creep in because I missed him. I'd open his oak wardrobe and try on his frocks, but it was never the same. I'd shiver and creep out then, an oversized dress left like a skin on the floor. It was my brother's actual presence that transformed this room; within minutes crêpe de Chine scarves, lights that blinked in red, green and white, and strings of aquamarine beads would hang from curtain rails and light fittings. Mum said Vince Llewelyn had the heart of Blanche DuBois.

Vince still had my mother's face and it was beautiful, though he remained an ungainly boy in a big man's body.

He was at his dressing table, his hair scraped back and in a thin brown net. I stepped over opened magazines and record sleeves; I walked through the debris of clothes pulled from cases, into a smell of Chanel No. 5 and smoky bacon crisps. I made a jump for it, onto his little single bed.

I watched my big brother at work. He wore a kimono and it

180

hung loose at his sides. I thought it smelled of old ladies: old *Japanese* ladies.

'What are you wearing to the party, Vince?'

'Halo, I don't know yet.'

I knew this was a lie. Vince always knew. Vince planned.

'I thought something bright,' he told me, though *bright* wasn't a surprise. 'And what about you, my dear sister? The usual baggy black jeans and T-shirt?'

I made a face.

'I don't know, Halo. God gives you all that and what do you do with it?'

'All what?'

'Halo, you haven't got an inch of fat on you.'

'Yeah, I know *that*.' I looked down at my flat chest.

'You should be grateful. I'm the one with our nana's bloody genes. The wide, the fat, and the Welsh.'

'Well whose genes have I got, a bloody stick insect's?'

'You, my dear, are a throwback.'

'Oh, thanks a lot.'

'To the Irishman from the M40. Nana's *wood god*. Our imaginary grandfather no less.'

We both laughed.

'You know, Halo, you're like a marvellous chestnut colt. Or a filly, I forget which is which. Anyway, you're all legs and mane. Superb.'

'Oh shut up!'

'I'm serious.'

I turned onto my back and stared up at the shadows his twinkling lights made on the ceiling. I didn't realize how much effort Vincent put into everything. I let the warmth of the

181

room, of my brother, pour over me as he added another layer to his face.

'Vince?'

'Hmmm?'

'Who do you think Fred will end up looking like? Jenny or Abraham?'

He put down his kohl pencil. 'Fred,' he said like he was savouring the word. 'Fred is the most beautiful of us all, darling. He will and he does look utterly and totally himself.'

'I know.'

'Yes,' Vince picked up a huge brush and powdered his face, 'I know you know.'

'Vince?'

'Hmm?'

'The other night—'

'What about it?'

'When you went up on the hill with Fred and Dad, what happened?'

'How do you know that?'

'Heard you.'

'Well never you mind.'

'Don't be coy, Vincent.'

'Men's stuff, Halo.'

'Tell me.'

'I'll tell you one day, my love.'

I curled up on Vince's single bed and I wondered how he had always fitted in this tiny space.

It was true that Vince was a strange child, even Nana Lew admitted that. He was born up in the studio like the rest of us, four years before me, and though he was a big baby he did

Mum no harm. Soon he was a big boy who came home from school with black eyes and split lips. Then he came home from school with a rucksack of Walker's smoky bacon crisps and closed his bedroom door on us all. Now Vince was a big man who couldn't settle. He was a big brother who went away but always came back, because Vince never put a step wrong. He sent Mum flowers on the days she needed them most. Nana received Turkish delight whenever she had a new set of teeth. And I'd get a regular talking to, a sort-your-life-out-Halo-it's-time-to-grow-up-now, because Vince has a habit of putting us right. He does now and he did then: he puts us right and forgets about himself, that's our Vince.

He locked the door and let me take coughing puffs of his joint. He said I'd need it.

Vince changed the record – he would always prefer vinyl – and 'Life on Mars?' played, just for me. I felt sleepy, and as I sat in his chair – my back to the mirror – Vince plucked hard. It was a makeover long due, he told me: an industrial effort. I closed my smarting eyes to the sharp smell of foundation, the soft brush of powder, the waxy coat of lipstick and the cool strokes of eyeliner, as Vince attacked my face. When I looked up, bleary-eyed, I had a headache. My face felt heavy and Vince was standing over me with an Elnett can. He was a half-done geisha in a girdle, with the end of a hairbrush held between his teeth.

'Ner-ey don,' he said, and tugged a little more on my corkscrews of hair.

He chose the dress. It was turquoise, Chinese, with little buttons that ran from one shoulder and across the chest. Vince safety-pinned it tight.

'I would never have got myself into this one, Halo. It's yours.'
He took a step back, arms folded across his corseted chest.
'Why, Miss Halo, you are just bee-oo-tiful.' Vince laughed. 'I'm
serious, you're a model, sis.' He bit his lip then clapped his
hands. 'And now, my dear, I must finish myself. Go on, chop-
chop.'

Vince shooed me out of his room. I could barely walk, the
dress was so rigid. I fell onto my bed, unable to move my face. It
felt like it had been plunged into a bowl of wallpaper paste and
now I was letting it dry. I stared at the sprinters who were con-
stantly running round and round my walls.

I went to sleep.

8

I woke to music Niamh would call a fierce diddle-e-die-do. I knew our house was empty, that was apart from the squat shadow perching on my bed like a goblin.

'Wonder'd how long you'd take.'

'Why didn't you wake me up, Nana?'

'Need your beauty sleep.'

'Oh, cheers.'

I listened to her shuck-shuck breathing. 'Don't rub your face, girl, you'll take all our Vince's good work off.'

I switched on my bedside light and watched Nana refold her arms, a palm under each breast.

She had hardly changed. She still baked too many cakes and collected collies like Wedgwood. Paying Johnnies would sit in her kitchen and drink down her special tea because Nana still concocted tonics that could cure and kill.

The O'Boyles' fiddles went up a notch. Cars raced up our gravel drive towards the courtyard.

'It's almost midnight, sunbeam. You need to get yourself to the party.'

'I don't want to go.' I touched my hard, caked face.

'You look beautiful.'

'Don't.'

'You only get one chance you know, sunbeam.'

'One chance for what?'

'Seen it in my tea leaves.'

I sighed.

'Tonight's your night, lovey.'

'Oh, Nana.'

'It's true. And there's a surprise up there waiting for you. Something special. I've seen it, sunbeam. Trust me.'

I smiled because Vince was right, he *had* inherited most of our nana, and as she slipped off my bed and found her balance, I suddenly saw him, older and shrunk. 'Come on now, sunbeam. Not a moment to waste. You got to grab at life, can't lie about and have it waiting for you, you know.'

It was cold. I insisted on wearing wellingtons up to the studio and Nana threaded her arm through mine: she was at least a foot shorter than me now.

'Hurry up, pet.'

I was slow in my tight turquoise dress.

The fat of Nana's arm pushed into my bone, and her thick man-made dress chafed against my skin; our mum said that Nana's dresses were made of material that should be glued to floors.

We walked under the red-brick arch, and the square of the courtyard glowed. The chalets were packed and the O'Boyles had taken over the rehearsal room. Inside they'd set up a stage. That was where the fierce diddle-e-die-do came from. People spilled out of the doors.

I stopped.

'I can't, Nana.'

'You look a peach. Apart from those bloody gumboots. Now get on and get in, girl.'

Music echoed into the night. I thought of the hard hill farms that surrounded us and those old white-haired farmers who right now would be sitting at their wood burners, their collies howling, as below them Rockfarm played.

'You been smoking that funny stuff, Halo?' Nana asked.

'No—'

'Well get in, Cinderella.'

She pushed me from behind. I shuffled up the steps.

It was sticky and sweet and hot inside. The air smelled of cider, dope and hot bodies, and the buzz of talking and laughing moved in waves, hemming me in.

I hated parties.

Vince was leaning up against a wall, his high heels in his hands, his kimono askew; it was easy to spot Vince. Gram from the record shop in town was standing next to him. They'd been good friends since that day, the day of Molly's hockey stick.

It took me a while to spot Molly; she was pouring drinks at a trestle table. Molly wouldn't drink herself, but she liked to provide. Molly had a boyfriend. He was on hand tonight, a well-polished boy from the posh boys' school in town. Molly liked that type and she'd been through a number already. I smiled as she pointed at empty glasses, directing him.

I moved towards Vince and Gram, but the music cut out and an amplified voice said, 'Good evening.'

I stopped.

'Good evening, I'd like to sing a song for you,' the voice said. 'It's a simple song. We've only one song for you tonight so we hope you like it.'

Fred was on the makeshift stage. I went up on tiptoes in my wellies and saw him in a brown T-shirt that said **Tequila**. He was looping the rainbow strap of our dad's acoustic Guild guitar over his head. He tuned it, *ding-ding-ding-ding*.

I pushed forward.

Fred wore black eyeliner, smudged in the right places. He had silver glitter on his cheeks and his eyelids. The most striking thing about him, though, was a pink angora sweater: maybe it was one of Mum's, but it clung to him, strange and perfect, and added ten years to his age. With Abraham's old leather trousers pulled up with Molly's stud belt, Fred made pink look moody.

'You look beautiful!' Mum shouted from the side.

'So do you,' Fred said into the microphone, and winked.

Dad was sitting on a straw bale on the stage. He had a National guitar on his lap and he was gently running his fingers up and down the strings. Niamh, Siobhan and Aifric were on the stage too. They shared one microphone to the left of Dad, and they were all gazing at Fred, transfixed.

They'd been practising together and I'd had no idea; they'd been doing this behind my back.

Fred raised the end of his guitar and told them, 'Ah-one, ah-two, ah-one, two, three, four,' and my dad began to play: he played Abraham's waa-waa-waas on that National guitar, and Fred and the triplets hummed along.

Fred had chosen 'Stallion Boys'. He closed his eyes, pushed out his chin, and he sang it his way.

'*A stallion boy'll steal your whiskey,*' he gasped, '*He'll steal your woman, too—*'

Fred let his black hair fall in his face as his voice crawled out, deeper, slower: croakier than I'd heard it. He wasn't a punk tonight. Fred sang with an American lilt. A country lilt, a blues lilt: it was an everything lilt and the room edged closer.

'Out on god's prairie,
I'm a colt and I sure am wild.
I'll bite, I'll scratch,
I'll make you scream, girls.
I'll lick those steel guitars—'

Dad took over, running that silver steel up and down and picking the whining strings of the National guitar.

'A stallion boy, he'll kick like whiskey,
And he'll squeal like a woman, too,
'Cos the boy needs it all so bad
That boy can't see for blue—'

The triplets 'ooh'ed' and 'ahhh'ed', swaying their arms from hip to hip; but no one took their eyes off Fred. Then the song was over: the last waa-waa-waa echoed in the room. It took a moment of silence before the cheers came.

'Thank you,' Fred told us, his voice small again. He bowed, the triplets crowded him and he was lost in a crush of people.

The low buzz of the room came back.

'Is that really her son?' someone behind me said. 'How old is he anyway?'

'About fifteen I reckon, he's recording here with the Llewelyns. They brought him up, you know.'

'Is it?'

'Yeah. Some say they *stole* him.'

'No—'

'Oh, yes, there's a lot of money, and now they're his guardians, see. Until he's eighteen. His real dad, well, he went off the rails. Left the lad here. That Jenny Connor died in the studio, you know, *just over there*. They didn't find the body for days. Awful it was.'

'No.'

'Yes.'

'They should put up a plaque.'

My brain fizzed. I was considering a crafty kick of my wellington boots, but before I could someone tapped me on the arm.

'Is Fred Connor your brother?' a man's voice asked.

I turned. 'Yes he is and we didn't steal him and we didn't get any bloody money and he's only eleven years old.'

'OK.' The face smiled. 'You're Halo, aren't you?'

'Yes.'

'Jesus.'

I saw the man had Niamh's eyes, but it wasn't Niamh. 'Are you an O'Boyle?'

'I am.'

'Which one?'

He smiled. 'There's enough of us, right? I'm Brendan, the girls' brother – one of them, at least.'

'Brendan O'Boyle?'

'Yup.'

He looked at me and he laughed. He had teeth like Nuala, all neat and small.

'Are you the brother that lives in New York?'

'I am.'

'Fred goes there to see his dad. Whereabouts are you?'

'Avenue B and Seventh. It's a mad building.'

'Why?'

'One toilet down the hall and my bathtub is in my kitchen, and everyone's from Dublin on my floor.'

'Why?'

He smiled. 'Just the way it is. An Irish oasis among the punks and the junkies I suppose.'

'What's the point in that?'

'In what?'

'Living abroad with lots of people from where you come from?'

He laughed. 'A fair point. Do you get out to New York yourself?'

'I've never been anywhere. I like it here.' I bit my lip and I felt him stare. 'What?' I frowned.

'Nothing.'

'*What?*'

'It's just my sister Niamh told me her friend Halo had a mind like a vice and hair like a Celtic princess. She didn't tell me you were a glamour puss too.'

I groaned. 'I'm not. It's my brother, Vince. He did this to me. I look stupid, I know.'

'You look gorgeous. He's done a grand job.' He laughed again. 'Do you want a drink, Halo?'

'All right.'

I followed Brendan O'Boyle's soft shoulders through the crowd. I glanced back at the stage and saw a short man with a ponytail talking to Fred. Brendan grabbed my hand and pulled.

There were grasshoppers outside and cider had made my head bright. I liked Brendan's arms around me. I had shown him the horses and the stables; we'd sat in the tack room and he told me about New York.

I told him about Wales.

'Show me everything in the place will you, Halo? My family goes on and on about Rockfarm but I missed it every time. I went up to Cavan instead. To my granddad and his sawmill. Loved it. Though the truth is I can't sing or play a bloody thing. I'm not much use for the O'Boyles.'

'Are you much older than the triplets?'

'Oh yeah. I'm fecking ancient. A whole five years older.'

'That's old enough.'

We ended up in Nana's polytunnel, in between her rows of rhubarb. The ground was damp.

'Shh!' I said. 'Listen.'

'What?'

'Just listen.'

Brendan put his drink down on the ground, lay back, and closed his eyes. I didn't need to close mine: I could hear it as clear as a walnut cracking in a vice; it was the sound of my Nana's rhubarb growing in the dark. It was a sort of stretch, a popping stretch, a small crackle as stalks reached up and out into the night.

'Can you hear it?'

'Wow,' Brendan said.

'Yes.'

I lay next to him because the cider had also made me fearless, and maybe my grandmother's tea leaves were right. Brendan turned towards me. 'You know, you're beautiful, Halo.'

I frowned in the half-dark.

'You are. And it's not your brother and his make-up.'

He kissed me then, he leant over and part-bit my top lip. He had light stubble and he felt grown-up. The kiss was gentle

192

enough to send a buzz right down my thighs to the soles of my stockinged feet. He leant on his elbow and stared down.

I smiled. 'You're too old for me, Brendan. You said you were ancient.'

'I'm only just twenty.'

'I'm—'

But he didn't let me finish, he curved a long hand behind my neck, and I shivered as he moved and kissed me full on the lips. He glided from one side of my mouth to the other with his tongue, then back again.

It was my first grown-up kiss.

His hand moved down my neck to my collarbone, and along my arm to cradle my rough-skinned elbow.

'I love your wellies,' he whispered in my ear.

'Thanks.'

'I love your hair,' he told my neck as he bit it.

'Thanks.'

'I love your name.'

I couldn't thank him for that one because my breath, let alone my voice, wouldn't come. Brendan was buried in my neck and I felt like a racehorse running on a flat, open beach.

'Rhossili Bay,' I gasped. 'Cefn Sidan, Freshwater.'

'What's that?'

'Barafundle Bay!'

Brendan stopped. 'Are you OK, Halo?'

'Oh yes.'

In the end I had to call him a persistent bastard and he laughed. I don't know why he kept groping for breasts I didn't have and never would. I have no idea why the thought of my

193

long legs in rubber wellies drove him to pant and move his delicate freckled hand down my flat body and in between my thighs.

'Brendan!' I told him.

'What?'

'Stop.'

'Why?'

I thought about it: I was old enough and I liked sprinting on that flat stretch of beach, hooves in the sand, my big horse-heart pounding. 'I'm too young,' I tried.

'You're eighteen. Niamh told me.'

'I'm not, I'm—' But he wasn't listening.

'Don't you like it when I do this?' His soft hand moved slowly, rasping against my tights. I felt those hooves; I was cantering again. 'You like it, don't you? Don't you, Halo?'

Don't get me wrong, I still had my knickers and my thick wool tights on, but Brendan was a good toucher. Maybe it was the thrill of anyone apart from me touching *me* down there. Maybe it was Brendan.

He kissed the air back out of me and I was Red Rum, I was Crazy Love, Mum's old horse, pounding up the fields of Rock-farm, galloping wherever he pleased.

In the end I think we got tired: tired and hungry, so talk took over.

Brendan wore a St Christopher he said his great-grandfather had given him, because when his great-grandfather got to one hundred he told the family he had no need to travel any more. Brendan said that back in the day when his great-grandfather was a young man, he sold tickets across the water to America. He said he sold them from his polished stool at the bar in

McHughes and that he gave every lad and every mother-of-every-lad a St Christopher for the passage. Brendan said his great-grandfather stopped selling tickets and believing for a while – he said he turned to the drink and the horses – after he sold seven tickets for a boat called the *Titanic*. Brendan told me the old man wouldn't speak to the priest for three years, he said he went out on his own little fishing boat into deeper waters than he should with no saint round his neck. Brendan told me his great-grandfather went out and drifted, he went out to see if those poor seven souls wanted revenge on the man from McHughes who had sold them those seven cursed tickets.

But not one of them bit. Not one of them lurched up from the waters to drag him down, and each evening the old man would row back, wet to the bone.

'Because it wasn't his fault,' I said.

'It wasn't how he saw it, Halo.'

'Did he die?'

'Died sitting on that stool in McHughes. He lived to over a hundred, remember? Mum wrote a song about it.'

'I bet it's lovely.'

'It's sad.'

'I bet it's all wafty and shivery and about cold wet men waiting in the misty water in rowboats.'

Brendan laughed.

'But *you* wear the St Christopher, Brendan, and you've travelled to America all right.'

'Yeah.' He shifted, holding me tighter. 'But that was British Airways, Halo. May my mother forgive me.'

For a while we lay there and listened to Nana's rhubarb. We listened to that crazy stretching crack in the moonlight and – if you care to look close enough – we watched the swell of the stalks, streaked with a pink sap that rose up from my grandmother's Welsh soil. We listened to the drips fall from the polytunnel plastic while two tawny owl fledglings fought in the cedar above. My stomach growled and Brendan moaned as I bit his neck, kissed his collarbone, his left nipple.

'Brendan, can I tell you a story?'

'Sure,' he gasped, 'shoot.'

I decided to tell him about Crazy Love, my mother's Arab stallion: Crazy Love who was dead but never truly buried.

I don't know why I chose this story. Perhaps it was like Crazy Love himself, it just came to the surface. I held on to Brendan and I began.

'Once upon a time my mother would ride an Arab stallion called Crazy Love for hours, until they both came back pockmarked with bramble cuts and steaming with sweat. The thing was Crazy Love was a crazy horse. It was said that Crazy Love had kicked a man to death and it was my mum's mum – a lady we call Grandma Min – who'd saved him. Grandma Min bought the horse for too much and tethered him on her fairground, and if it hadn't been for my mother, Dolly, Crazy Love would have bolted. But from the very beginning that horse and Dolly loved one another. They were inseparable. They'd ride for hours, for days, along the wastelands of Tiger Bay. Sometimes they went further. And when my mum married my dad and came here to Rockfarm, Crazy Love came too. In the end, though, Mum said no one could save Crazy Love, he was a law unto himself, and one night he kicked down the stable door and was gone. Three days later, from her bedroom window, Mum heard a terrible noise, and she looked out to see him lying

196

in her garden, half his belly hanging out.

'She ran out to him.

'She said she lifted his big head and held it in her lap. She kissed him and wiped the froth of white foam from his silky neck. The thing was, Crazy Love had got himself caught on the barbed-wire deer fence, just at the edge of the forest. And though the fence wasn't high, somehow Crazy Love had mis-judged it. Mum told us love was like that. Love got it wrong, so very, very wrong sometimes.

'She also told us she walked quietly to Nana Lew's house. She said she found the horse gun Nana called Kindness – the thing that looked like a bicycle pump to me – and my mother walked back across our track while Crazy Love squealed that awful horse-squeal. As soon as he saw her, though, he calmed. Once again my mother knelt at his head but this time she aimed and she fired. Though just before she did, she said Crazy Love's black eyes looked at her and he smiled. She said she was killing him with Kindness and he smiled at her, because love is like that. Love is Crazy. Love is forgiving. Love has to be put out of its misery.

'It was Dad who buried the big horse behind the chalets – he had his digger on the job for a day – but Crazy Love didn't end there. Dad had chosen the wrong place and when it rained Crazy Love rose to the surface like heavy cream. So Dad moved the grave, but the same thing happened: year after year after year. We've now buried Crazy Love more times than I can rem-ember, and we're used to him reappearing when the rains come – a little scabbier than last time – though still our mother's crazy stallion. Mum says love is like that, especially Crazy Love: it can kick you to death, misjudge what it sees, kill itself;

197

but still it will rise to the surface, no matter how deep you bury it. Crazy Love can come back, again and again, until it's with you for ever. That's what our mum says.'

The owls shrieked above. Brendan stroked my hair.

'Do you think you'll always live in New York, Brendan?'

'Hmmm?'

'Do you always think you'll live in America?'

He leant over me. 'Oh, you're fecking cute, you know that, Halo? My sisters said you were.'

'Yeah, right.'

'They've all got crushes on your brother, you know.'

'Vince?'

'No, the kid, Fred, isn't it? How old is he anyway?'

I stared up at the moonstone plastic of the polytunnel. 'Fred's eleven.'

'Shit. Cradle-snatchers.'

'What do you mean?'

'The girls.'

'What?'

Brendan's face frowned in the moonlight. 'What's the matter, Halo?'

I sat up. 'Where are they?'

'Hey—'

'I've got to find my brother.'

Before he could grab my wrist, I was gone. I was doing the real cantering now, the cantering with my legs, the cantering to find my little brother and protect him from three Irish girls: the cantering to stop Fred doing what he'd been wanting to do for most of his life.

9

My Nana Lew's garden meant colours and smells.

Big colours.

Big smells.

Tonight they were putting me off the scent.

The moon was bright and I ran through her kitchen garden, over the lettuce and tomatoes, potato greens and brassicas, her plain-looking herbs that hid their magic. The most exotic thing Nana had in her kitchen garden was the passion flower. She told us that the passion flower was Christ. 'Cross my heart, lovies, it's Christ right there, see. The purple is his heaven and the white is his pure nature, and them five shoots there is the five wounds on the cross. Don't snatch, Vincey boy. And look, the three shoots there is the three nails. Bang. Bang. Bang. Simple. Learnt that in the capel, I did.'

The English Bastard's greenhouse stood in her walled garden. Grasshoppers chirruped, the moon shone down.

I knew they were in there.

Nana said old plants had seeded themselves in the old greenhouse: these were plants the English Bastard and the English Bastards before him had brought back in their woollen pockets from hot countries. 'Stole, that's what they did,' Nana told me, 'men like that raped it all.'

She also said there were plants in that greenhouse that could eat you alive, and I believed her, because all year round they'd press themselves up against the mildewed panes, sweaty and green. They twitched like triffids when you passed. I knew the English Bastard's elegant glasshouse was dangerous. Things happened to you in there – on account of the tropical heat, Nana said.

The panes were steamed up, hot to touch, and I heard Siobhan inside. She was yelling, 'Me next, me next, Fred!'

I'd lost Brendan in Nana's vegetable patch. He called my name from the brassicas and I could hear his jeans swiping against cabbages firm as cannonballs. 'Halo, come back!' He sounded desperate and I couldn't think why.

I wiped a pane but the condensation was on the inside. I stared at the fleshy green fronds of those tropical plants pressing up against the glass, as if they were tasting. The front door to the greenhouse stood ajar so I slipped in.

'Get on with it Aifric, you've had him ages.'

'Yeah, come on.'

I hid behind Nana's voodoo lily; the one she called Devil's Tongue and said was good for our bowels (though none of us wanted the Devil's tongue near there). A tinge of rotting meat hung around its drooped stalk. Flies buzzed. I edged away and hid behind the fleshy leaves of a Bird of Paradise plant. I saw Fred sitting in the Bastard's old bath chair; he was wrapped around Aifric, or maybe she was wrapped around him.

He was snogging her like all the air was inside her mouth and he had to get at it. I saw his tongue moving, sloppy round her lips. I thought of Brendan's kisses and was glad of them.

'Come on Fred, Aifric's had her turn,' a voice said. It was Siobhan, lost in the green. 'Fred!'

'Hmm?'

My little brother stood up and staggered across the Victorian tiles. I moved through the soft banana leaves and saw Siobhan on Nana's striped deckchair. Fred was snogging her now, his brown hand like a kitten's paw kneading her breast.

'My turn next!' Niamh shouted. She was standing against the glass, one foot against it. 'Me next!' she yelled.

Fred stopped his kneading, and stood. He shuffled over and pushed into Niamh, blind, his hands moving down to her bum.

'Kiss me then, Fred.'

He didn't look enthusiastic.

I remembered how, a few years ago, Abraham sent a choker to Fred. There was a little silver photograph of Sitting Bull that held the leather cords in place, and Fred would push it tight to his throat. There was a note that came with the necklace:

Son,
So you know your history. Don't forget Wounded Knee.
Your father,
Abraham

Nana called it 'Abraham Connor thinking he's an Indian', because it was at the time when Tequila did their shows wearing headdresses and moccasins, and talked about being Cherokee. 'About as Cherokee as Napoleon!' Nana had cried as she chucked a chop at a collie. Still, after that, Fred and I watched *Little Big Man*. We sat under Nana's eiderdown in her parlour, and we cried and laughed at Dustin Hoffman, all in the same breath, and Fred asked me, 'Am I like Dustin Hoffman, Lo-Lo?'

'What d'you mean?'

'Because I'm an Indian?'

'Dustin's not a proper Indian,' Nana chipped in. 'That Dustin's an actor playing a white man playing an Indian.' Nana liked to sit in on our afternoons; she would sit and suck on sugar mice. 'And you're not an Indian, either, young man.'

'Abraham said I'm an Indian. He said you have to say Native American now.'

'Well that Dustin there is a Jew in any case,' Nana added.

'What's a Jew?' Fred asked.

'Chosen people who can't mix the meat and milk. My Ida in Newport, her dad was one. Died badly, he did, in the war. My Ida, she don't like to talk about it. Now them Americans,' she pointed to the telly, to Custer's Last Stand, 'they're all Jews, see.'

'Abraham says we're Indian.'

'Jews.'

Fred took a moment – a blond-haired Custer was shouting at his troops, more than a little mad.

'Nana?'

'Hmmm.'

'Does that mean my mum, Jenny, was a Jew?'

'Somewhere back she was bound to be, pet.'

Fred stared harder at the telly, 'And the Indians there, are they Jews too?'

Nana smiled, the snout of a sugared mouse sticking out from her thick false teeth. 'Well, look at Dustin there, he's an Indian and a Jew, ain't he?'

Fred frowned.

'Don't listen to Nana,' I whispered. 'I'll give you a book, Fred, we're doing Anne Frank at school.'

Fred looked wide-eyed and whispered back, 'Is she an Indian, Lo-Lo?'

I rolled my eyes and pinched him under the blanket.

'Hands where I can see them!' Nana yelled and she crunched the sugar mouse until pink spittle came. Sugar made her eyes cloud; she rocked in her chair and sighed, 'Had a cousin marry a Jew, see. Win was her name. Oh, I was jealous as jealous could be. Up in London, she lived, the East End, and I'd go up on the train with my auntie Hazel. It was such a treat. I loved to stay with cousin Win.' Nana rocked back. Back and forth. Back and forth. Then she stopped. She was staring at Fred's hands as they moved beneath the eiderdown we shared.

Back and forth. Back and forth, and up and down my legs went his hands.

Plants dripped as I crouched beneath green. I watched them all: Fred and Niamh against the glass, Siobhan flat in the deck-chair, and Aifric making train noises as she moved backwards and forwards in the English Bastard's old bath chair. I was still thinking of *Little Big Man*, because it was just like the scene where Dustin Hoffman climbs from one sister to the next in the dark of his wife's tepee. Dustin's doing it as a favour for his wife, because the white man has killed all her sisters' hus-bands. And Dustin's tired, his heart's not in it, because he loves his wife.

I knew Fred wasn't enjoying himself. Fred was only doing what he was told, just like Dustin Hoffman in *Little Big Man*.

He moved his head out of Niamh's neck and took a gulp. His hand moved to her front, down her stomach, and past the band of her jeans. His head followed. Fred crouched. Niamh closed her eyes and gasped and then the greenhouse door opened wide.

For a moment I wondered if it was the ghost of Nana's English Bastard, then it swore in Irish.

'Brendan!' Aifric squeaked.

'Fucking right it's Brendan, what the hell are *you* up to, Niamh?'

Fred was all hands and a head where it shouldn't be. I crouched further down beneath the banana plant.

'What do you think you're doing to my sister, you little prick?'

Fred looked around, and smiled.

'We're only having fun,' Siobhan said from the bath chair.

Brendan turned. 'You too, Siobhan? Put your fecking blouse on. Jesus.'

'We're old enough to do what we want, Brendan.'

'Not while I'm here you're not, now get out. He's a kid, Niamh, I'd expect better from you—' But before Brendan could finish, Niamh ran out, crying.

Fred stood up, wiped his mouth and put his hands in his pockets. Siobhan and Aifric dashed past their brother, giggling, but I stayed where I was. Silence dripped. Then Brendan broke it.

'What's your game, kid?'

Fred shrugged.

'Notching up girls on your bedpost? *My* sisters? You going to say anything?'

Fred stared back.

'You love your sisters, Fred?'

'I love both of them.'

204

'Good. Sisters make the world go round. You've always got to look out for your sisters. You get me? Y'know I should knock your block off, kid.'

'Why?'

Brendan stepped round some pampas grass towards Fred. 'Listen, I don't care if you're eight or eighty, you treat my sisters with a bit of respect, right? You're not a kid in a candy store, you know. You've got to choose, you can't have them all.'

Fred's eyes widened. 'Why not?'

Brendan couldn't help himself; he laughed. 'What do you mean, "why not"? Because it's just not right.'

Fred stepped forward, as innocent and impish as Peter Pan.

'Why?' he asked. Then he smiled. It was, in all honesty, the stare of a wondering child. After all, I suppose that was what Fred was: a child caught with his fingers in the wrongest of cookie jars, but a child nonetheless.

Brendan sighed. 'I'll tell you why, kid. It's because you've got to want one person more than you want the rest. It's human. We're not animals, you know.'

Fred nodded like this was new and interesting information. 'OK.'

Brendan sighed. 'You seen your sister? Halo?'

Fred looked at the banana plant I was hiding behind; my heart thumped as he smiled and turned back to Brendan. 'Why do you want to find Halo? Do you like her?'

'Course I do, she's a beautiful girl, right?'

'If you say so,' my little brother said, and he giggled. I watched him follow Brendan to the door, and then they were gone.

✳

The thing about running is the preparation. I've always known that. Tie the laces in a double bow; jog on the spot, stretch the calves then the arms and the shoulders. You'd be surprised how much the shoulders mean to a runner. Relax them and you're speeding, pistons dancing. Tense them and you're done for before you've started. You'll crawl back tight as a balled-up spider. It's all in the shoulders.

That morning I double-bowed my good trainers. I stretched where I should. I wrapped my hair up in a ponytail because even if it did slow me down I loved the bounce of it: heavy red between my shoulder blades. I knew how our horses felt with their manes, because it was the timing of that bounce, the thrash of it that kept me going.

They were leaving today, the O'Boyles. They had cleared up their mess because they were the tidiest of friends, and it was time for them to go back home with hangovers and a tin of new songs. I ran down our narrow stairs.

I could hear the triplets outside. I could see the shadow of my family on the porch. I joined them.

'We'll write to you every day!' the triplets were saying, but I knew they were girls in the present tense. As I watched them I knew they'd have other friends, other chats, other honeys, other come-here-to-me's before the week was out. They were going back to a place where the boys tasted like strawberries, fags and bitter Guinness.

I'd already said goodbye to Brendan because he'd found me in the early hours and had made my lips sorer than they were before. He'd written his telephone number and address on a lined piece of paper. He said if he had longer, he'd fall in love with me. I knew Brendan was all words. Still, he was a beautiful kisser, with conker-coloured eyes. I'd squirrelled away that piece of lined paper in a place Fred would never find it.

'All right so, Halo! Come here to me and give us a hug.' Nuala held out her arms, and as I was swallowed I thought how much she felt like soft Siobhan. 'Now,' she told me in my ear, 'don't you break the heart of my boy – you write to him, call him. He's fallen big time, you know.'

I smiled and shrugged. I looked for Brendan, my cheeks red as berries, but he wasn't there.

We all waved as they left, me in my running gear, my belly cramping. I decided to jog after them down the track, pounding the ground; trying to find a rhythm as my insides turned.

It was only when I came back from running through the hill farms, wet with sweat, and stood under our dribble of a shower that I saw it between my legs. It was only a little blood, but it was enough. I was still a virgin, but at last I could raid Molly's supply of Tampax and Dr White's.

At last I could grow up.

10

Rockfarm bubbles with stories. They pop and spit, one step behind you. They breathe hot words down your neck, in the dark of the studio, from the pool of red light in Nana's hall. It's because stories are ghosts, Nana says, and ghosts, well, they were folk once, weren't they? So that's all stories are, see, the ghosts of folk that can't let it be.

There are stories to be found beneath my grandmother's kitchen table. It's a table I spent my afternoons under as a child, here in her Big House. It's a table I often lie under, and I'm lying here now because the O'Boyles are gone and Nana's told me I'm to live with her. 'You're a woman now, sunbeam. You can come upstairs. You can blossom down the hall from me, my flower. Better late than never.'

The trouble is, I don't want to be a normal girl. I don't want to grow up. Not yet. I've got to wait.

I've got to wait for Fred.

When I was little I'd lie here while Nana's collies paced around me like lions protecting a cub or a kill – I could never tell which – I'd lie here and gaze up at the stories that were written in the oak.

There are stories embedded in my grandmother's table because of the grim faces there.

Look.

You could call them simple knots in the wood, but I know better.

That one there, down by my left foot, is Mabel, and Mabel's just fallen in a bog and she didn't mean to die. Mabel's face is grain swirls of a scream, like that painting by Munch. Mabel is always yakking.

The face right above me, at eye level, is Percy, and Percy is big and angry and he got himself frozen in the North Pole. Peter, on the other hand, is small, he's the little wood knot in the right-hand corner by my shoulder, and Peter got lost in the woods and swallowed up by the very oak tree that this table once was. Peter looks scared, like a little boy should be, and I've tried to coax him out a million times, but he's timid: a bit of a coward, to be honest.

As a kid, I'd lie here and talk to these wood knots I called faces. I talked to them and I named them, and it was this that teased our other ghosts out.

They're everywhere, see.

My nana's ghosts, her stories, bubble from the lips of those three white-faced boys wearing uniforms in that photograph on the kitchen sideboard. The same stories sit on the wooden perch next to the stuffed green budgies, in that cage Nana stands in the corner of the kitchen. And there's too much story in the thin silver that makes up those three medals pinned into a frame on her wall.

In fact sometimes you have to put your fingers in your ears.

They are funny, the dead. They look at things sideways, from an angle you've never thought of ('a dead one', Nana Lew says). One thing the dead are obsessed with is detail. Was it a Monday, a Wednesday or a Thursday morning when you found the pin? And that varicose vein, it first hurt that second Sunday in the cold church, third pew, that's right, isn't it, lovey?

Nana Lew communed with the dead, that was part of her job, her calling. She'd shake on lilac talc, put a red bulb in the socket and draw the heavy curtains in her parlour. 'It's all about effect – believe in that and they're yours,' she told me.

My nana communed with the dead for a fiver.

'Will you appear to us, tonight? Mrs Richards? Ivy? Can you hear me, love?' she'd cry into the night. 'Will you make a sign? Will you come out of the shadows?'

I'd sit on the curling maple stairs and shudder as I listened, because I knew the dead come as they are, or rather, as they were. I knew if Ivy came out of the shadow she was in, a leg would be missing, or an eye hanging out. I knew this because of Dai, Albert and Jim Llewelyn, my very own Great-Uncles. Great with a capital *Grrrr*. These were the white-faced boys in that photograph on the kitchen sideboard. Because in Nana's house 'dead' didn't mean forgotten, and it certainly didn't mean gone.

They have always talked, my three boy-uncles. They have always told me stories: their stories. They talk like three men in a bar, their voices grown and weary, though they have the faces of children. You see, Dai, Albert and Jim are big brothers who will always be big but will never be older, not any more. Just like our Robert, they're stuck, frozen.

There's hardly a whisker between them. Dai, Albert and Jim were thirteen, fourteen and fifteen when they died. Still they wear their British Army uniforms, though these are torn and burnt, as are the Beloveds. That's what Nana calls her brothers, Dai, Albert and Jim; because they are. Nana spits rum on the slate floor and tells me that's for their spirits to fly, though I know they've never left.

She has pictures, my nana; she has an altar too. If you peek out from under this table here you'll see it in the corner by the Rayburn. It's funny, isn't it, how those Queen Anne legs rise, bulldog-bowed, to a simple top that's littered with trinkets, with jumble? Now that's not jumble, that's where you'll find the bird-cage with those three stuffed budgies. That's where you'll find three toy guns, three golden bullets, and a half-smoked cigar. There's a big black Bible and money too. Change – brown and silver – fills a demijohn, and notes – too many to count – are pinned to a drooping Boy Scout flag on the wall. Nobody touches that money. That's a death wish to do that, a death wish through and through because that is where my three boy-uncles linger. It's Nana Lew who calls it 'lingering'; like her altar is a village bus shelter, stinking of cider and fags, and her big brothers are bored teenagers, up to no good – though I suppose that's somewhere near the truth.

Nana says her big brothers are the best things in the world and they went off to a war to save jolly old England; just three Welsh boys for a place called jolly old England.

'It were a grand old time,' Albert, the eldest, tells me.

'It was hell,' says Dai, the next, while Jim, the youngest, nods.

And they tell me a story. Albert first.

'His name was Harold, see, and he didn't look old like us, still they let him in. Harold lived two doors down. Glasses, small lad, but he always tooked to us. Came with us to Llandudno Junction, to the office there, and we all lied together, didn't we lads?'

'That we did!'

'All of us round the country was lying. "Yes sir, eighteen years old, sir." Nod, nod, nod, we did. Over there, in the field like, I met one was eleven. Irish lad.'

'That Billy Jenkins from Merthyr was fifteen, same as you, Albert.'

'That's right, Dai, that's right, that is. So we all went down the junction because the scouts told us to be men, see. For King and Country they said. Gave us good grub too.'

'And it was better than hodding.'

'Oh, bloody hell yes. Better than crawling on your belly in the black pits, see.'

'You're not wrong, Albert, not wrong.'

'So we signs up with Harold. "Eighteen, eighteen, eighteen, eighteen," we all said, lying through our teeth and standing on our toes. Dai here stuffed newspaper in the bottom of Da's boots. Gave him a whole two inches, that did. Jim here just kept quiet, like. Voice hadn't broke, had it lad?'

'It bloody had!'

'Ha! But that didn't matter because we had wages and we were off to training and that was a grand old time.'

'Aye.'

'Just that.'

'Good grub.'

'And then, after training, which wasn't much, we get there.'

'Right.'

'Harold lasts the day.'

'Right, Bertie. Dead by night, he was. Thirteen. Unlucky, see.'

'The smell of that place.'

'Still on us, it is.'

'But we get put on pigeons and dogs. That's our game. We know how to talk to them, know how to have them do our bidding, look after them real well.'

'Weren't pigeons, Albert.'

'Was.'

'You got a couple of crows was all.'

'Sent the messages home, didn't they? In any case, we last ages. We're the Llewelyn brothers, famous in the pit, famous in the trench, famous out of it too, right?'

'Right, Bertie. All the lads depend on us. Men twice our age, they did.'

'Right, Jim.'

'We led them to Victory, we did.'

'Right, Dai.'

'We weren't wasted.'

'No, Jim.'

'Weren't pigeons, Albert, they weren't pigeons.'

They said they couldn't see it coming. Not even with all the fizz-pop-bangs, the yellow gas, and the squeals of the dogs. Keeper the Airedale went that morning, blown to nothing but singe. Trigger the Jack Russell went next. He flew, Dai said, small and white; the little fella flew through the gun smoke and straight to the Happy Hunting Ground – where Dai wanted to go himself – anything but this, he said, off to the Happy Hunting Ground and glad. That day none of them saw it when it came, not even with all those nests of wire and that blood-warmed mud to sleep in.

Dai was the dog man – the dog *boy*, the Sergeant pointed out, because Dai was just fourteen – and those mutts would do anything for him. It was Albert and Jim who were the bird men – they were the bird *boys* – because they billed and cooed and squawked themselves, and they could get those wings to fly anywhere. It had started with pigeons, because pigeons might have won the war, all told, but by the end – at least the end for

213

the brothers – it was the crows they worried about.

The crows were four fledglings they'd found drowning in the mud on the field: too young to go it alone, too young to do much else than hop. They were four fledglings the brothers took in their knapsacks, fed on biscuits and trained. Albert said he liked crows because they were smart. Jim said he thought they were little Charlies, little Charlie Chaplins, because they walked like that funny fella he'd seen in the new moving pictures back home at the church hall. Those crows waddled black waddles and soon they were four glossy birds, growing fat and strong on those carrion fields. They were also birds that warned the Llewelyn boys. Before any human or canine sense could pick up the whistle of a bomb, the crows' flat black ears would twitch tufts of feathers and they would lurch up, into the smoke, as the brothers went to ground. It was Jim who said he'd like to pin a medal on their shoe-shined breasts, though he couldn't think how. Crows, though, are not sentimental creatures – just listen to them retch out their song; and they didn't die before or with the brothers, faithful, no; but the crows did peck at the boys' soft bits before flying up from those whistling battlefields.

Sometimes my boy-uncles would put on a show when they appeared. Sometimes I crawled out from under the kitchen table to have a look.

'All right there, Daisy?' they'd say to me because they thought 'Halo' a fool's name.

'Yes.'

'Give me your answer, do!'

'I'm half crazy!'

214

'*All for the love of you!*'

'Say hello properly to your great-uncles then.' Dai smiled and held out a hand, and they were all laughing and I knew what was coming because if I reached out, that hand would fall off. They'd even added extra bits: a gash in the leg, a bullet hole in the eye, one through the cheek; all of Uncle Jim's teeth missing. They changed it every time, just for me. Once Jim had an *extra* leg. 'What's the matter, love?' he asked, and then he smoked through the side of his cheek and literally laughed his head off.

Nana Lew couldn't see them. 'You've got it, Halo,' she told me. 'You give them my love and tell them not to be so cheeky.'

She said I'd got something, seeing her brothers like that. She called it the third eye. So that makes a regular me and a Cyclops me, all rolled into one. A sea monster. A spider. An octopus.

There is one thing I've always wondered, and it is this: if I'm so good at seeing things, why haven't I seen Robert? When I can see these old-young uncles I never knew, why can't I see my *own* brother? Why hasn't Robert whispered into my ear in the dark of Nana's hall, *Where are my Matchbox cars, Halo, and my Ziggy Stardust LP?*

You know, the one that isn't Mum or Dad's, the one in my room hidden under my pile of Beanos because I nicked it from Vinyl Heaven, the new record shop in town, remember? It was that Tuesday afternoon with Davey Price when we was off school because we both had sprained wrists from swinging too long on the blue rope Dad tied to the oak branch in Beggars' Field back in November – the day after Bonfire Night – when I begged and begged him to string it up—

Robert has never come back. He's never come back to ask,

Halo, who the hell is Fred Connor and why is he in my bedroom?

As I lie under my nana's table, finally a grown-up, I want to ask Great Uncle Albert something: Great Uncle Albert who was always good with advice.

I want to ask him: how do I tell Fred I'm in love with him? How do I tell Fred that I've always been in love with him, since that very first evening he floated onto our farm?

I suppose Great Uncle Albert will tell me to wait: wait until the boy grows up, wait until he realizes that his oldest sort-of-sister is his best bet.

My toes point beneath the table and my heels settle into the cold slate floor, as I ready myself.

People do speak to ghosts, you know.

1-800-PSYCHIC-NOW!

They do it, so why not me?

And do my ghosts answer back?

Always.

PART THREE:

1996

1

Crazy Love ran in our family, that was a given.

Although Mum's horse had long since settled beneath the concrete Dad finally poured on him, other crazy loves had risen to the surface at Rockfarm. I suppose, no matter what point in time you stopped us and dipped your hands in to pull us apart – like fingers in the sand – there would always be a grain of crazy love. After all, there was Nana and her boy-brothers (the wool of their new army uniforms still itching through her memories), and there was Dad and Mum (and Dad could never rub away the toffee-apple taste of *her* fairground lips). Yet somehow when you're busy with the business of living, crazy love can just take a back seat. It can be quiet for a while: bone-still and trapped beneath hard concrete.

It's never forgotten of course, because love bubbles under. And if it's crazy enough it will growl, snort, snap; until one day there'll be carnage.

The truth was, the years slipped by. Fred was seventeen and Fred had girlfriends. Fred was eighteen and he had gigs. And now, Fred was nineteen and he had done what we knew he would. Fred Connor, my little brother, was almost famous. He was about to be a rock star.

And me? Not much had changed for me. Once upon a time I was a small girl in love with a boy who wasn't born yet. Soon I was a teenager, desperate for an eleven-year-old boy to notice me. And now, eight years later, I was lost in my twenties and still in love. I was in love with my nineteen-year-old brother who wasn't my brother at all.

Of course there were others to love him now; there were legions of fans. That's what the record company told us, and Nana Lew told us that *legions* sounded like the Devil's party.

I stood in my parents' hall, a pair of old trainers hanging off my rucksack. Stiff, I stretched my journey out.

I hadn't seen my mother in months.

I breathed in the smell of rose talc and yeast, her smell as the years went on. I looked across the hall at her framed photos and counted Mum's rock'n'roll dead: Freddie Mercury, Frank Zappa, Serge Gainsbourg; they'd left us a while back. Kurt Cobain was a boy gone in the dead of night, that's what Nana told me down the phone. Nana said our rock stars were dropping like flies. Sometimes I wondered if Dad still mouthed his prayer; it would take him all night now.

'Mum? We're here!' I yelled up the stairs.

I heard rummaging.

'Mu-um!'

'Oh, Halo,' she stumbled out of her bedroom onto the landing, 'your journey all right? Put your bag with ours in the back room down there.' Mum didn't trip-trop down the stairs to embrace me, silly of me to think she would: she just yawned. 'Make us a cup of tea, love.'

Mum looked tired, less girlish. Vince had decided she was at the Cleopatra-with-Antony stage, or the Elizabeth Taylor in *The Sandpiper* stage. She was still beautiful.

'Is Vince here, Halo?'

'We drove down together.'

'Lovely. Now Molly's going to meet us there, she's making her own way. You know our Molly. Cup of tea. Don't forget.' She went back into her room and the rummaging sounds started up.

'Where's Dad?' I asked.

'Cleaning out the Land Rover. The courtyard I think. I got him a little Hoover. It's amazing and you can hold it in your hand. Imagine. The studio's booked. I can't remember the band. Manchester-something? Your father will know. They do it all on computers, you know. It's very clever, but Dad'll tell you everything, baby. I just don't seem to want to cook. We've got outside caterers in.' It was the most information I'd had from my mother in months. 'Oh, you know your grandmother's coming too, right?'

'Nana Lew?'

'Well *my* mother's in Spain, love, so yes of course Nana Lew. It's a family outing after all. Fred's booked us into a lovely hotel, Halo. He sent backstage passes, the lot.' She walked back onto the landing. I noticed she had a pair of red knickers in her hand. 'Oh, I'm so excited.' Her cheeks were flushed. 'Come on, Halo, a cup of tea, please love, I'm parched. Then you must tell me what you've been up to.'

Maybe she knew I had nothing to tell (I answered phones all day for a record company, I lived with Vince in Willesden because I didn't want my own place), because Mum was gone again, back to rifling in her cupboard for things she wouldn't wear.

I sniffed at the air in our hall: the rose talc and yeast, my mother. I touched the furry wallpaper. Then I dumped my ruck-sack and walked through the living room past the old TV and into the kitchen. I was going to make my beautiful mother a cup of tea.

The last few months were the longest I'd gone without running back to Rockfarm. Twice I'd put my trainers on and I simply ran from London. I got as far as Heathrow the first time; Reading the next. I ran into the night. Dad picked me up from Newport railway station in the end and Nana rubbed her special sage sludge onto my blisters. I wanted to run back to Rockfarm because I loved it. I loved it so much I never quite knew why I left. It was just the way things were. Children had to leave. We had to leave Mum and Dad to a peace they'd wanted their whole lives, a peace they'd only really touched one summer in a tiny caravan on a patch of wasteland in Tiger Bay. It was a peace they had before the babies came.

'Oh, Vincent, my heart!' Mum cried. I heard the pitter-pat of her bare feet down the stairs and the smacking of lips. 'My Vincent!'

I swilled the pot.

'Vin-cent!'

'How are you, Mum?'

'Oh I'm fine lovie, I'm fine, come upstairs and help me choose what to wear. I want to look a million dollars for our Fred. You'll do my hair, too?'

'Course I will, Mum.'

'Halo's in there making tea.'

'Great.'

I stared out at the glitter of our grass in the sun, at the old barrels and fence posts Molly and I once used for horse jumps; rotten now. Donny –my old Shetland – was blind and deaf, but still he dug into life. Ziggy and Stardust were gone, to the

Happy Hunting Ground Nana said, within hours of each other on the same day. She called me down for the funerals and we cried in the rain as Rhysie tugged the levers on Dad's digger and the big steel jaws chomped up the red ground. We were still crying when Rhysie locked thick chains around Stardust's neck, revved the blue tractor, and dragged him into a deep, red grave. By the time Ziggy, the biggest of the Welsh cobs, slid into his, the tractor was lodged in the mud and we were soaked with wheel-spun earth. Nana said a few horsey prayers over the holes and we left Rhysie to cover up our childhood friends.

They're just outside the window now, Viking mounds already covered in our lush grass, golden lit by summer. Ziggy and Stardust have stayed where they were buried; they haven't reappeared like Crazy Love.

I gazed at the line of Nana's tight hedges – blackthorn and hawthorn – and I thought how safe home was. Nana weaved those hedgerows herself on her wedding day. She said she'd walked those fields with seed and sapling and laid them out, her young fingers stabbed by thorns, just so she could have sloe berries like black pearls in her gin, just so the cowslips and daffs and lady's purses would shoot up along the land that was hers now (because she'd seen to that). 'I was making it mine, see, planting like that. My blackthorn and my hawthorn closing my land in for me.'

Nana said planting was history and you could read a family tree by the bloody tree itself. 'It's what comes out of the land, Halo, because it'll always come back – what was buried, it'll always return, pet.'

*

223

'Dad, tea?'

His top half was in the back of the old Land Rover. His bottom half was crowded with flocking chickens and ducks, trying to catch the debris of crumbs. The mini Hoover was on the bonnet of the car.

'Dad?'

His hair shook like a rooster's crest but it was blond with age, not so fierce and red any longer.

'Da-ad?'

That last Hellmouth album had left him deaf in one ear. Dad had turned occasional producer. He had a computer in the studio now; he said some bands didn't need instruments at all. Dad was a genius with that computer. Nana called it G-O-D.

'Dad? Dad!'

'Oh, Christsakes! Oh, hello love.' He leapt at me. I just rescued the tea from a hug. 'Halo. Nutmeg. How are you? You run here?'

'Don't be silly. I drove down with Vince.'

'You ready to drive up again?'

'I suppose.'

My family's logic was written all over our journey that day. Vince and I lived in London but we had travelled down to Rockfarm in order to travel back up to London in a crowded and stinking Land Rover with our family. All because Mum wanted her hair done by Vince.

The truth was I would do anything to come home, even if it was for a few hours.

'You seen young Fred up in London?' Dad asked.

'Not really. He had some shindig at his record company. We went to that.'

'How's your job?'

I shrugged.

'Your mother wants to bring Fred back down with us, just for a few days.' Dad picked up the small hard-bristle brush; he didn't look very sure.

'That would be good.'

'Yeah, but he's on tour isn't he, nutmeg? Still, I can't tell your mother that.' He lifted his neck like he was about to crow; he looked me up and down. 'Now you're looking fine, girl, you really are, by Christ.'

'Oh, Dad—'

'Really. You're looking gorgeous.'

'Da-ad. Don't be silly.' I laughed but I hugged him again. The cracks on Dad's lips were deeper, the freckles paler. He went back to work on the car because Dad only said what was necessary.

I patted the bonnet. 'Will this old girl make it?'

'Oh sure, sure. Bit smelly, but she'll do.'

He kicked through the quacking ducks. The nameless band from Manchester wandered out of the studio. They all had the same pudding-bowl haircut, and wore trainers and kagouls. They frowned in the sunlight as they puffed on fags and waved at Dad. I breathed in and smelled my home.

We were sitting in the back, me sandwiched between the softness of Nana Lew and Vince. They felt so similar either side of me. Mum sat regally in the front and Dad, my beloved dad, winked at me in the mirror.

Nana Lew wore her backstage passes round her neck like diamonds. She tapped the laminated strips. 'These ones have all the colours,' she told us, 'I bet we can get in every room. Bet we can.'

'It's only Fred, Nana, you can see him when you want to, anyway.'

'Oh no, this is different love. This is getting everywhere. It's like the keys to the kingdom, it is,' and she rubbed her hands together. 'I wonder where they'll take me?'

'Loony bin I expect, Bubby.' Vince sniffed.

'Now, Vincey boy, why do you have to go and call me that?'

'What?'

'That bubbly word.'

'Well you are. You are my bubala.'

'I have told you before, Vincey boy, I am not your bloody bubbly-whatsits, I am your nana and that's that.'

'A bubala is a nana, Nana.'

'For some it is.'

'Does it matter?'

'No.'

'Well, Bubala Lew—'

'I told you Vincey—'

I didn't know why Vince had suddenly embraced all things Jewish and I didn't know why Nana didn't like the bubala, but I giggled all the same.

I watched cars pass us, some honking, and thought about our trip to see David Bowie as Ziggy Stardust more than twenty years ago. I thought of the smell of pear drops, of sweet white wine, and I wondered if Fred would be as memorable. I wondered if he'd make the girls and the boys scream as much as David did.

Mum touched her hair. 'His first big gig. Oh I'm so excited,' she said, and I watched her reflection in the mirror. Mum was alive, vibrant; the nub that hung down between her two front teeth would be glowing deep red now.

Gigs are strange things. They are little sensual moments: like taste, like smell. Gigs are moments that whine in your ears for days.

That night in Kentish Town, Fred's band weren't good, but Fred was a star. A star with six original songs, too many covers, and silver glitter on his eyelids.

The family sat up in the balcony sipping free champagne. We were the blessed side of a coiled red rope. We'd never sat at a gig before – Vince and I would usually rush to the front and long for the crush. Nana pulled her church hat down and all I could see was her grin.

'When's he on?' she asked.

'It'll be soon, Mam, just be patient.' Dad looked nervous.

Nana reached for the champagne and glugged, 'Oh! Bubbles!'

There was buzzing and chattering and a heat rising up from the crowd below. The air was sticky, but it didn't smell of pear drops and sweet white wine, not yet.

Mum leant over the railings. 'We're so high up, Ivan! Oh!'

'Yes, love.'

I'd come to this venue with the O'Boyles once, years ago. It was St Patrick's Day and we saw The Pogues. Niamh, Siobhan, Aifric and I stood on the stairs and sang along to 'Dirty Old Town'. When Kirsty MacColl came on we sighed to 'Fairytale of New York', but afterwards I hid in a corridor while the O'Boyles chatted backstage; I'd never taken to things like that.

'Isn't there a support band, Dad?' Molly asked. Molly was late; she'd arrived a few minutes ago with Dorian, her boyfriend. Nana called Dorian a 'straight lad who'll come to all good, more's the pity'. Vince said Dorian had eyebrows so neat he was hard to trust.

'Nope. It's just Fred, Moll. It's like a showcase.'

'A what?' She turned up her nose and I turned to my father.

'Dad, do you know what he's going to play? Is it the songs you wrote with him?'

'I expect.'

'And what's the band's name, Dad?' Vince asked.

'I don't know. Fred told me the record company put them together.'

Nana drained her glass. 'That's terrible.'

'It's what they do nowadays, Mam.' Dad shrugged at us.

Nana pointed a finger at him. 'It's still terrible. It ain't natural.' Her church hat was at an angle. Nana was drunk. 'It's like that Hearty-ficial Insemmy-nation. Like what they do with the bulls and the cows in Belgium.'

We all stared. Dorian coughed into his drink.

'What?'

'They keep those poor bloody cows and the poor bloody bulls down in labri-storeys and instead of just letting them get together as God intended, they have a whosimaflip and they draw out all their business and then they put it all together in a way God wouldn't. In a petri-fried dish.'

Dad shook his head. 'Mam, what are you talking about?'

Nana refilled her glass and hiccupped. Vince's shoulders were shaking with laughter.

'And then that makes a baby cow in a labri-storey with muscles all down its back and shoulders like it's a walking bit of steak and nothing else, and then they feed it up until it's all perfect but wrong, like, and then they keep it in the labri-storey with all the other poor baby cows with muscles all down their backs, and then they kill it and they eat it.' She emptied her glass. 'Belgiums. Wouldn't trust *them*. It's hearty-ficial, see,' she pointed her finger at the stage, 'like them.' Nana clucked her tongue. 'I don't know, putting our Fred out there with folks he don't' – hic – 'know. And for them to play his songs and such when they haven't even done their how-d'you-dos. It's just like them Belgium labri-storeys. It's hearty-ficial.'

Nana slammed down her empty glass. Her teeth were coming lose. Dorian was staring at her and forgetting to breathe.

'And another thing, he's too young for all this.' Her hand waved around the auditorium. 'He should have stayed home and worked. It's too soon. Isn't it, Ivan? What would you say? It's too soon for the lad, am I right? He should have stuck and worked with you.' Nana grabbed the neck of the champagne bottle but it was empty.

Dad said nothing. He shifted in his seat and I was suddenly afraid that my grandmother was right.

The thing was, it had happened quickly. Fred had a few songs. Fred had a record deal. Fred was a star. Fred had a tour: all in eight months.

'We'll see,' Dad said, trying to smile.

'Oh, he'll be just wonderful,' Mum said, 'won't he Vincey?' She was staring down at the heads below.

'Yes, Mum, he'll be perfect.'

Mum threaded her arm through Vincent's and they pointed at the roadies in black on the stage. The crowd were clapping below us now, impatient; my belly danced.

*

There was no denying that he looked beautiful. There's no denying that the screams almost blew the roof off.

Nana screamed along with them, so did Mum and Vince. But Dad, Molly and I, we watched. We watched very carefully.

Fred was a fine performer, he knew what to do, he billed and cooed and flirted; but the band was out of time, lost. In the end Fred saved it. He went solo. After Tequila's 'Little Girl', Fred sang the six precious songs he had written with our father: 'Dolly Mixtures', 'The Boy in the Lipstick and Polish', 'Hoodoo Voodoo Mama', 'The Summer of '77', 'My Beloveds', and 'Dead Horses'. You could tell the songs that were Fred's; they were the ones about lost mothers and prairies and making all sorts of girls and boys happy. Dad's songs were about fairgrounds and dresser drawers and candyfloss: they were about gap-toothed women and true love.

Fred sang all these songs as if they were his own.

The covers, though, were dedications to us. Fred told the crowd as much. He yelled, 'Hey! Look up there! That's my family! Drinking the free champagne!' And everybody did look.

Fred sang 'Goodbye Jenny', speeded up and spat out punk-style, for Dad. He sang 'War Pigs' for Mum, because he told the venue he wanted to wake her up for good, and she giggled and clapped her hands to that. 'Uptown Girl' was for Molly, which made us all laugh, and 'La Vie en Rose' was for Nana, though she said what with the racket that came from the stage, she couldn't tell what bloody song it was.

Fred sang 'Lady Stardust' for Vince. And he sang Patti Smith's 'Horses' and David Bowie's 'Rock 'n' Roll Suicide' for his other mother, Jenny.

We sat there blushing at Fred's dedications because, as Vince said, it was like he was telling the crowd our lives, our secrets.

'I don't like it,' Nana Lew shouted. 'It ent *real*.'

'This one's for my big brother up there. "The Prettiest Star". Because Vince, you're the prettiest star to me.' Fred said this with his hair in his face, mumbling into the microphone like a confession. I felt Vince shudder across the table, while below us, bodies at the front yelled, 'Fred, you're the prettiest!' and, 'I love you, Fred!'

I leant my forehead on the railings and let my spit drop down as Fred sang Bowie's song to Vincent.

'Lo-Lo, are you out there?' Fred spoke over the applause. 'Lo-Lo, this is for you. If only all the girls could be like you, my wild pony of a sister!'

I fidgeted, waiting. Then Fred sang the Buzzcocks' 'Ever Fallen in Love (With Someone You Shouldn't've)' and I felt my cheeks burn. I prayed for it all to stop; but before I could slip under the table and run away down the streets of Kentish Town, Fred was following it up with his own version of 'Stallion Boys', and he was telling the crowd about Jenny Connor, the mother he never knew. I felt my thighs relax as Fred's voice twanged.

We all knew – when the crowd yelled for more – that our foundling son, our cuckoo-brother, was going to be big. As we sat at our table, ears ringing, still sipping the free, flat champagne, as the roadies dismantled Fred's stage, as we watched the plastic glasses, fag butts, dropped hats and bottles being swept up below: we knew.

Nana was using her passes.

She tried every door and it was my job to stick by her. We

stood in a small room where tall, pretty people laughed out loud. Nana was sweating and rubbing her pass with greasy fingers.

'Will this get me out of here, sunbeam?'

'Well you got in, I'm sure you can get out, Nana.'

We looked around. Mum was cuddling up to Dad; Vince was standing against the wall, one hand to one elbow, looking down at his feet. Vince didn't like crowds.

'Let's go and find that boy, sunbeam,' Nana said. 'All this rabbit is too much for me. I'll just tell Ivan we're off and if he doesn't see me through the week—'

'He'll see you through the window, yeah.'

I walked through the lines of beautiful girls, down the narrow labyrinth of backstage. The black-haired girls, the blonde-haired, the dark, the pale, the red like me; they were all waiting.

They were waiting for Fred.

There was processed meat in the dressing room and Nana fingered it. She popped an olive in her mouth and flicked at a gherkin.

Dressing rooms remind me of PE changing rooms. There's even a smell of rubber and canvas daps. This one was packed with the half-undressed, too. Nana shoved past thin people and I followed. She was spitting out the olive when she found a tight huddle.

'You in there, laddie? You coming out?'

There was a muffled response.

'Come on now, we're all waiting for you in that other room. Don't let me get the stick' – we all knew Nana's stick, willow and sharp as vinegar – 'come on now, lad.'

'Nana!' Fred poked his head above someone else's shoulder. 'Lo-Lo!'

He squeezed his way out of the mess of bodies like an eager newborn. He was shirtless, and his skin was golden. Fred wasn't as big as his uncles, but his muscles seemed locked tight beneath his smooth skin. Right now his cheeks were flushed and his eyes were steel beneath the glitter. He looked strange.

'Did you like it? Did you like it, Lo-Lo? Did you like the gig, Nana?'

'Of course we did,' I said.

'Did you, did you, Nana? Did you like it? Did Mum like it? Did Vince? Did Molly? Did Dad, did Dad like it? I wanted Dad to like it. I mean I wanted Ivan to like it. I did. That's what I wanted, more than anything, I wanted Ivan to like it.' He scratched his neck and I saw the Sitting Bull necklace there against his Adam's apple.

'You OK Fred?'

'OK? Course I'm OK, I'm flying Lo-Lo, I'm flying. Where are the rest anyway? Where is everyone? You know, *everyone*. Where are they?'

Fred told us he had a thing called a rider, and what did we want? Nana considered him. 'We're all in the bar thing, out through there, Fred love. Now, you getting enough sleep? You look done in.'

'Lo-Lo, my Lo-Lo,' he said, ignoring Nana and staring down into my eyes because Fred was taller than me now. 'Lo-Lo, my sis, my Lo-Lo,' he said again and I saw the silver glitter sparkle on his eyelids as he put a hand round my straight waist and hugged me to him.

233

He smelled of everything I could ever want. He pressed his nose into the crown of my head and sniffed. I watched his Adam's apple move up then down. His hands gripped my neck, his thumbs holding my chin, and he said in my ear, 'Did you like my song for you?'

Fred had proper stubble. He had a jawline, one to die for, Vince said. I could feel his muscles against me as he moved. I let my hands rest on the bare skin of his hips. He buried his face in my neck and I felt his lips open. I shivered with his hot breath: his oranges and musk.

'Now Frederick, I asked you a question my lad and what I said was, you getting enough sleep?'

I wished Nana hadn't pinched him because he stood up straight and he giggled. 'Come on Nana, come on Lo-Lo, I want to see everyone else. I want to see Mum and I want to see Ivan. I want to see Vince and I want to see Molly. Have you seen Abraham? Because I asked him to come, I did, and my uncles, I asked them to come, but I don't know if they did. Do you know if they did? Did you see them? Do you think they're here? Nana? Halo? Oh, come on,' and Fred locked arms with us both and we pushed forward, out of the crowded room.

Strangers patted Fred on the back and Nana tut-tutted through the streams of sweat that ran beneath her church hat.

There was little after that: a few hugs. Congratulations. Then Nana had to be taken home.

Fred skipped breakfast with us at a hotel so ridiculously opulent Nana had Vince go out and buy her another suitcase. 'I ent leaving all this lovely stuff here,' she said, 'there's all sorts: robes and towels and little towel shoes and sewing kits and ear

234

cleaners and shoe sponges and hangers and laundry bags and the mini-bar and well, I'm just not *leaving* it, love.'

We didn't see Fred again.

A woman came and shook our hands for a reason we didn't understand and then Vince was driving the family back home to Rockfarm because Dad was tired. Vince and I were driving to Wales to pick up his car to drive back London, and by then, Fred would be gone: to Munich, to Paris, to Madrid. There were tour dates.

Over the next year or so we'd be waiting for the tickets and directions, Vince would be ready with the hair rollers for Mum and the patience for Nana, and Fred Connor would sing us his dedications from a foreign stage. That was simply the way it would be.

'One thing,' Nana said as cars sped past us. 'That boy has got to have more songs. You got to work on that, Ivan.' She tapped her teeth. 'And another thing, he's got to eat well and get some sleep. He's all skew-whiff. That's what he is. Isn't that right, Halo?'

'Don't, Gladys, don't spoil it,' Mum sighed from her half-sleep, 'it was such a lovely time. Don't go and spoil it now, please.'

My grandmother kept her false teeth shut, she closed her thin lips over them, but I watched her fingers tap-tapping something out in her lap. They were tap-tap-tapping something worrisome, and like crabs scuttling across glass, they wouldn't settle.

235

2

I didn't go back to London, it was forgotten. Answering phones was forgotten. Instead I planted Swiss chard and radishes for Mum. I dug in blackcurrants; for a whole year I tried to tame the blackberry hedges, but lost.

I relished every moment because my days were filled with what I loved best. I patrolled Rockfarm with a tool belt hanging from my boy-hips, checking leaks, connections, tile grout. I picked Nana's garden bare and concocted juices for Mum that made her smack her lips at the sharpness. I sawed fruit branches and moved logs and bricks; I polished Nana's brass, and hand-washed her lace curtains. I followed Dad into the studio with electric screwdrivers and snips. I watched him at the G-O-D computer and shook my head. Donny the Shetland finally left us for the Happy Hunting Ground, but I was glad to dig the grave myself; I dug it beneath Nana's cider apple trees, because they were his favourite.

For a year I brushed and tidied Rockfarm, and I let the hair grow on my legs until Vince said what with that and the tool belt, I really had gone over to the other side.

'Are you still a virgin, Halo?' he tried, one Sunday when he was visiting. We sat outside on Mum's deckchairs.

'Oh, stop it Vince. Are you?'

He blushed. I was twenty-six that year, Vince was thirty. We were late starters.

'I asked you first, Halo.'

'It's none of your bloody business, Vince, and it's hardly you to go asking questions like that. You get more like Nana Lew every day.' I glugged tea from a builder's mug.

'I'm worried about you, Halo, that's all. You shouldn't lock yourself away like this.'

'I'm not. I'm helping out.'

'I know you are. They couldn't do without you, love, but—'

'But what?'

'You shouldn't be a virgin.'

'You were at my age.'

'That's different.'

I threw the cooling tea into the grass. 'Well don't worry, Vince, I'm sure with all the horse riding I've done, technically I'm not intact.'

'Oh, Halo, that's not what I mean—'

'Take this in to Mum, will you?' I shoved a punnet of black-berries into his hands. 'Please.'

So the days passed, calm, and with a slick of sweat on my skin I didn't have to think. I didn't have to think about Fred or Mum or the fact that I was happiest here, at Rockfarm, simply treading water.

I occupied one of Nana's first-floor rooms because Mum and Dad said they wanted to be alone in the gatehouse; after all, it had been just themselves for a few years now and they'd taken to it. Dad bought Mum a glow-in-the-dark globe and whenever she couldn't sleep, he said they watched it. He spun it for her and asked her where she wanted to go. He stuck small bits of Blu-tack on the bits she chose and he told us that that was where they'd disappear to one day, because he'd promised.

The thing was, we were all waiting, and one of the things we were waiting for was Fred.

We'd been trying to get hold of him for the longest time, since June and the snap of Nana's laden plum branches. Fred was in Sweden, Fred was in Tokyo; Fred was in Nashville because apart from Rockfarm he said he liked it there best. Fred had cracked America, easy as an egg, and all we saw were the clippings that Nana dutifully cut out.

FRED CONNOR U.S. TOUR

The much-hyped Fred Connor is half way through his first U.S. tour. Interviewed in Duluth, Minnesota, birthplace of Bob Dylan, Connor spoke of his wide-ranging influences, from Leadbelly to Gram Parsons, from Patti Smith to Alice Donut, from German Electronica to Britpop. Connor also singled out his 'two fathers' – producer Ivan Llewelyn and Tequila lead singer, Abraham Connor, as central to his creativity. Fred Connor will be playing an Independence Day gig with Tequila on 4th July at Roseland, NYC.

Fred played at Sin-é in the East Village; he played CBGB. He played Berkeley Square, and 'La Vie en Rose' charted across the world. Fred had done what we knew he would, and he'd done it young and he'd done it with ease. Fred was a rock star. He was famous and he was loved.

'Can't talk, they're calling me, Mum,' he yelled down the line from an unpronounceable festival: Oklahoma, Germany, Nor-

238

way, or for all we knew somewhere in bloody Greece. 'I'll try again tomorrow,' he said, 'but I'm coming, I'm definitely coming home—'

Fred was coming because of Mum. This was the other thing we were waiting for.

Fred was coming for a reason none of us wanted to admit. And we all craved Fred because he was the salve. I think that somehow we believed Fred would make it all better. Maybe he would.

Dad shivered as Mum put down the phone. 'She'll be fine,' he whispered to us as we huddled in the kitchen, watching her move towards the sofa, an arm out.

Vince came home for long weekends now. Molly tried to, and when she did we liked to talk about Fred because it was too hard to talk about anything else. We would sit in Mum's open-plan sitting room, Mum lying on the sofa and us on the floor with toast in our hands, and we'd try to pinpoint the hows and the whats and the who-knew-firsts regarding our foundling brother. Mum would tell us, 'It was me. I knew first. As soon as I walked up your grandmother's stairs and heard him cry, I knew what a special boy he was going to be. It was in his eyes, my loves.' She glowed, warm, and we smiled.

'I thought it was his *hands*,' I told her and leant my head against the arm of the sofa.

'No, it's his voice,' Vince said, 'that's why he's so successful. Fred has a great voice.'

'Thanks Einstein,' Molly said.

'And songs, he's got great songs,' Dad told us, 'I've helped him with enough of them. And did the little bugger put me down for royalties?'

We laughed then, Mum glowed brighter and that was when Dad asked us to think about it, by Christ, and to see that with Fred it was more than these small parts – the eyes, the hands, the voice, the cheeky grin, the full lips, the feral smell, the parentage – no. With Fred Connor it was the whole package. Sure, there was his voice, his hands, his songs, his sound, his beauty, his parents, but most of all it was his Fred-ness.

'At least he's got more songs now.'

'Yeah. Well done, Dad.'

'Did you send them to him on that computer of yours, Ivan?' Mum asked, sitting up a little.

'Yes, Dolly. Magic it is, isn't it? We can work together on that machine and we don't even need to be in the same room. By Christ we don't even have to be in the same country.'

'Well that's handy,' Molly sniffed, 'because I haven't seen Fred in over a year.'

'That one, "Fairground Girl". That's beautiful, Dad,' Vince interrupted. He glared at Molly and she nibbled a crust of toast, sheepish.

Mum closed her eyes and told us she'd like a nap. Dad hugged her and just for a moment we had to look away.

3

One night in Nana Lew's house the spell broke and I couldn't settle.

We had called the doctor for Mum, and left them to it. She was sleeping now, but that wasn't enough. I sneaked down my grandmother's stairs. The black-faced miners gazed out at me in the moonlight with their teeth like diamonds and I breathed in the musty hall.

I sat on the chaise longue under the stairs, and I reached for Nana's black phone. I dialled the old-fashioned way: an index finger in the holes. I dialled a number so long my finger actually ached. There was an echo.

'Yup?' a voice croaked.

The clicks came.

Click-click.

'Fred?'

'Yup.'

'Fred?'

'Yup?'

'It's me, Halo.'

'Halo?'

'Yes, Halo for fuck's sake—'

Click-click.

'How did you get my cell?'

I twisted the material of my nightie. 'Sorry I bothered you.'

'No, Halo, I'm sorry. It's just—'

I heard a voice in the background: Fred told me to hold on and he told the voice to go back to sleep. The voice said, 'But, baby,' and I laughed, hard.

'Halo?'

'Isn't it the bloody afternoon over there?'

'What?'

'Oh, never mind, look, tell Gina Lollobrigida to bugger off and get your arse over here, Mum's really ill.'

'I know.'

'You don't seem to care.'

'Don't say that, Halo. There's just so much work to do here—'

'Oh, it sounds like it. Yeah.'

The funny little clicks continued. I slumped off the chaise longue and down on Nana's cold Victorian tiles.

'Since when do you call me "Halo" anyway?'

'What?'

'You just called me "Halo". What, now you're famous you're all grown-up?'

'Oh, Lo-Lo, don't be an arse.'

'Don't be a rock'n'roll cliché, then. And anyway, I'm not an arse. Fred, we just want you home. Mum wants you home. Is that really too much to ask? After all she's done for you, you little—'

'Don't, Halo, I know she wants me home but she also wants me to do what I'm doing. She loves it, Halo. And she's not that sick. It's not like she's going to die or anything. She's just tired, that's all.'

I heard the boy in his voice and I was quiet.

'Lo-Lo?'

'Yeah.'

'Do you miss me?'

I laughed: I couldn't help it. 'What do you think?'

'I think you do. I think you miss me so much you don't know which way is up and which way is down. I think you miss me so much you play my records.'

'I wouldn't go that far.'

'I think you miss me so much you're still a virgin.'

I hung up.

The grandmother clock tick-tocked, echoing up into the rafters of the Big House; I thought I heard the black-faced miners growl. I left the receiver on the leather table, off the hook, and I lay down on the cold tiles until they bit into my bones. As I lay there I cursed the day a band called Tequila and a girl called Jenny Connor rode a silver-shiny bus up our potholed drive and scared our chickens. I cursed the fact that Fred lived and Jenny died.

I did a proper curse too, like Nana had taught me.

Then I tried to think of other things, of other stories. I tried to remember.

Ivan Comfort Llewelyn felt love for the first time when he was fourteen and proud of his middle name.

He'd queued all day at the Dolls' Fair in Tiger Bay because Dolly Palmer's Shoot the Dictators stall was busy. The queue wasn't necessarily all men, there were women too, drawn to young Dolly's creamy face because not many were interested in pellet guns and targets. Mum had been born in a drawer *and* she was a draw, Dad said, and that was why Grandma Min sat on a high stool behind her daughter's stall, holding a willow stick.

She'd whack the stick on the counter.

Grandma Min read dime-store novels. The colourful small books that an equally small ex posted to her all the way from America.

It was another crazy night in town as Candy Dreamer pursed her red lips, ready to play, Min read.

From time to time, Grandma Min looked up from her tales of Private Dicks and their Molls and the Lives Gone Bad Down on Main Street, and she'd smile at her only daughter, her gift from Wales. And if those punters grabbed the chance to stare too long at her Dolly Halcyon Palmer, Grandma Min would slam that cane down on the counter, snap! After all, Grandma Min was an old hand on the fairground. She had been born small so she knew she had to get life to fit her, rather than the other way around. And as people slipped pellets into their guns and aimed at those painted tin faces, Grandma Min was happy because here on that high stool (a little like a baby's chair) she was on the same level with one she loved best; at last she could look her Dolly straight in the eye.

Whack-whack with her cane and a 'Move along now gents, move along' with her voice that sounded high as a muted trumpet. 'Move on now, ladies and gents, nothing to see here. Back of the queue, now.' Whack!

Ivan Comfort Llewelyn was in that queue. The boy tried to believe that the little squashed lady – the one who didn't look up from her book but slammed her cane down, barely missing fingers – didn't scare him. It was the girl who scared him: the one with her hair black as the ravens that topped his mam's oak tree.

The girl scared him so much Ivan felt the marrow in his

244

bones drain out. Ivan Comfort was just fourteen.

Ivan Comfort queued all day and that night he still hadn't talked to the girl. So he slept in the flapping mouth of a tent and listened to tigers rumble. Of course there were no tigers at the Dolls' Fair, there were no tigers in Tiger Bay, because what Ivan Comfort was listening to was the engine of his heart, revving, grumbling, as he tried to breathe in the smoky sea-air.

Ivan stayed in the throat of that tent for a week. Big gypsy men gave him cups of soup, home-made in their caravans. They told him the girl with the ravens in her hair wasn't for him. Grandma Min gave him a blanket and a pillow and a flea in his ear as her heels sank in the tigerless Tiger Bay mud.

'Go home. Go on, sling your hook, lover boy. You're too young for this caper.' Grandma Min said this because this was how she liked to speak. Grandma Min said apples and pears and teapot lids and a good kick up the 'arris.

'At least have a bleeding bath in me tub,' she said. 'You're not fit for the farmyard, son.'

Ivan stared down at the raffia matting the coconut stall man had given him to sleep on.

'I got bleeding hot water, I have.'

Ivan Comfort took her at her word; he didn't like the sound of *bleeding* hot water. 'No thanks,' he said.

'Too praad?'

'Sorry?'

'Too praad, my lad?'

'Sorry?'

'You will be, sunshine. You will be.' Grandma Min was tenacious as a Jack Russell. 'Where's your mother?'

'Sorry?'

245

'Oh, you give me the hump, you do. I said "where's your mafa?"' Min said this like she was talking to an idiot, which in truth she thought she was, and her round flat face came in closer to Ivan until he could see the heavy gold necklaces on her little tight chest. It was like her bones had a struggle keeping all of her inside.

She clicked her tongue; something was giving.

'You come home with me, sunshine,' she told him, a little gentler now because she'd finally seen how young he was.

'No.' Ivan was at least firm.

'I've a surprise for you if you do.'

'I can't.'

'Listen, son, you won't do no good sat here filthy like that. And you want to know something? Well, that gel of mine, she's taken a fancy to you, hasn't she? Taken a bleeding fancy to the young kid squatting on our pitch. So, you get yourself up and follow me and we'll scrub some sense into you.'

Grandma Min held out a very small hand and Ivan took it.

'We've an understanding then. But listen here,' Min's tiny face stepped in closer again, 'you cross her you cross me, get me? I don't care how bloody young you are, you touch a hair on my gel's head, and you will regret the day you were bleeding born, my son. You will regret the day your mother and your father first clapped eyes on each other. You will regret the day your great-great-great-great-grandmother first crawled out of her cave and gave a gent in a *facking* animal skin a wink. Get me?' Min pointed a stub-finger at Ivan's eye. 'We understand each other?'

Ivan was still. That's what Minny said later, *still bloody waters run deep, right*?

246

Ivan smiled. 'I love her,' he said.

After all, love ran in our family. It was a crazy love, Mum said, and it was the sort of love that can be worse than no love at all. It was the sort of love you could never bury.

4

It was Vince who picked up our mother's mother, Grandma Min, from Heathrow. Majorca was where she lived now, short on breath and Spanish. To Grandma Min it was Ma-jaw-kah and always would be. 'Can't get on with the lingo, just bloody can't,' she told us.

I stood stretching on our porch in my running gear as Vince drove up. I watched Grandma Min struggle as he picked her out of the Land Rover like a doll and dropped her gently on the track. I waved though I wasn't pleased to see her.

It wasn't that I didn't like or, indeed, love Grandma Min. We always saw her once a year at Easter, and she made us laugh.

It was just that Grandma Min here meant *it* was serious.

Vince carried her small red vinyl suitcase. He winked as he passed me. 'Small but a handful,' he said.

'All right there, gel?'

Grandma Min always spoke before she got to you. It was as if she couldn't wait, as if she wanted all attention on her *now*. I smiled and stared as she waddled up our concrete path. I was always surprised by how tiny my maternal grandmother was. I think she was even smaller than I remember, like the Majorcan sun had shrunk her to a raisin.

She stopped, chin out, and looked up at me. 'You still farting about round here, then, gel?' She adjusted the red and probably

Dior handbag on her little wrist. 'What sort of a get-up you call that then, gel?' She pointed at me with a stubby finger.

'I'm going for a run.'

'Going for a raan? Who are you, Sebastian bleeding Coe?' She tapped her bag and considered me. 'You're as bad as bleeding Gloria there.' She poked another stubby finger after Vince. 'You dress up like a feller and he dresses up like a gel. You two should swap, then you'd be right.'

Grandma Min looked around her, at the green fields, at the splats of cow shit just behind her on the track.

'I don't know,' she sighed, 'my Princess. My Dolly on a facking farm.'

I sighed. I heard this one every year. 'It's not really a farm, Grandma.'

'What's that then?' She pointed at the biggest of our new sugar-brown cows. 'Facking Scotch mist? And don't call me Grandma, I've told you before, me name is Minny, Minny Dolores Palmer, so use it.'

I smiled.

'You lost your bleeding tongue, gel? And him, Gloria there, does he think I need picking up in a facking combine harvester?'

Vince pushed past, almost felling her.

'Here, watch it sunshine, I may be small but I'm your bleeding grandmother and you be thankful for it!' She watched Vince stomp to the Land Rover for another red suitcase.

'He seen a quack?'

'Sorry Minny?'

'He seen a doc-tah? He needs help he does, never mind my Dolly. She'll not be getting any bloody grandkids with that one.'

It was a wonder my tiny grandmother was still alive. Years ago she'd told us she was a goner. She said she was too old for a midjet or doo-warf or whatever she was (because she hadn't seen another doctor since one had told her mother she would-n't reach sixteen). But now she was standing in front of me: brown and healthy-looking in her best Spanish frilled dress. Grandma Min had a death wish that hadn't come true.

I think it was the work that kept her going. She worked *all* the Dolls' Fairs now, from an office in Majawkah, and she was rolling in it, 'like a pig in shit, gel'. Europe was her oyster, though she didn't like what had happened to her fairs there. 'No, I don't like it one bit,' she told us. 'Thing is, they like their bleeding monkeys too much, that lot, and I won't have it. They get them poor facking monkeys smoking fags and drinking gin, and since when is a monkey meant to smoke bleeding Benson and Hedges? They got cigarette girls in the bleeding jungle? They got a tobacconist's under a facking palm tree? No.' She'd sniff, 'And have you ever seen a monkey? Eyes like my bloody auntie Nash they got, too close for bleeding comfort. Hands like an old boyfriend of mine, too. Lenny the Pink.'

My grandmother told us she was a bleeding medical miracle. She should have been dead years ago, she said, but she was here, ready to cure our mum, to do something that our other grandmother's teas and the trips to the hospital just hadn't managed.

'You going to invite me in then, gel? I ain't no bleeding vam-pire.'

'Of course, Minny.'

'Your mother still got that freckled geezer then?'

'Dad's here, yes.' I pulled the head off a pink rose.

'You still Daddy's gel, ent cha? You've got his colour. I mean, look at your red hair. You poor cow.' She held on to one porch post, helping herself up the steps in her high heels. 'Yes, gel, I'm here though I shouldn't be. I've got me helf back see, and what's back I'm giving to my Dolly, and then we'll see who's right as rain.' She heaved herself up the last step and took a sniff.

'Needs a bleeding clean this place, you got any elbow grease pumping through those skinny veins, gel?' She creased her small nose. 'Now where's my Dolly then? She's what I came for, not you lot.'

I nodded to the back door. 'She's out in the garden, Grandma.'

'For gawd sakes call me Minny, call me Min, anything but bleeding "Grandma". And you tell that Vincey-boy-lady-boy to put the kettle on, I'm parched and the tea in Ma-jaw-kah is shit. Take cases of PG back with me, I do.' She muttered to herself as she walked through our living room, into the kitchen, and to the open back door.

'Dolly? Dolly gel?' I heard, her voice suddenly gentle. 'Ah, Dolly, look at you my lovely gel. Just look at you.'

My grandma Min, for the time being, was gone.

Dad had found a task in the studio, something to take him away from his mother-in-law. Vince said he was off to play Billie Holiday records over in the Big House with Nana and Rhysie the postman.

I made tea. After all, I was the background one: the one who did small tasks silently, easily, and so I made the tea. Mum lay on the sofa in the sitting room, and Grandma Min was perched on the pouf at Mum's head. They were holding hands.

'Mummy?' my own mother said. 'Mummy, tell me about how I was born.'

'You want the whole story, my Queen?'

'Oh, yes please, Mummy.'

I picked up the dishcloth.

'You was born on the night the Dolls' Fair took Swansea.'

That wasn't exactly true; it was the German bombs that took Swansea that night.

'And you was born in a special place. You was born where only I could find you. The bottom drawer of a big mahogany dresser, smart and rich it was, and you was gurgling inside it. And there you were where only I could find my little Queen.'

'And where was that, Mummy?'

'Why, it was in my very hotel room, Room 213, The Halcyon Hotel, Angel Road.'

'Did you open the drawer, Mummy?'

'That I did, my Queen, and when I saw your beautiful face, when you reached up a hand and caught a scrag of my hair, well that's when I knew you was mine because that was when I swallowed my heart, love.'

'Did you, Mummy?'

'Yes I did, my gel.'

Grandma Min spoke softly to my mother. It was a relief.

'And that was when I tippy-toed downstairs, because the bottle that was left with you was empty and you was so hungry you was about to scream that place down. Louder than the bombs that was screaming above us you was. So I sneaks down to the lobby, and I rings the bell, just to check, and when no one comes – because it was a fleapit place, my Queen – I run into the kitchen and I steal you some milk. I warm it first mind, in a little copper pan. Had to climb up on the counter meself for that, nearly had a tumble.' Grandma Min reached out with her free hand and touched Mum's cheek. 'And I remember waiting over that milk and praying "Don't let anyone else find her. Let her be mine."'

Mum sighed and I sat down at the kitchen table to listen.

Grandma Min was telling Mum how, at breakfast in the hotel's damp dining room, she saw a waitress with red rings round her eyes and a look like a popped balloon. That, she decided, was the gel, the gel who'd left the baby and the empty bottle, because that gel may have had rings round her eyes but she had no ring on her wedding finger. So Grandma Min watched her and she wondered whether the gel was crying for the loss of her baby or for the fact that it was a midget who'd found the baby in the room. As Swansea shook, my grandma said she already loved the baby too much to let her go, and so she let the red-eyed girl cry into the red soup she was serving; she let her snot and bawl into the watery mashed potatoes. She didn't blink when the girl leant over to take the ten-shilling note my nana had left on the table, and she didn't balk when the girl whispered, 'Take care of her, missus,' down into Grandma Min's little ear.

'And are you glad, Dolly? Did I do right? Are you glad or sorry I took you?'

'Oh, I'm glad, Mummy, I'm ever so glad.'

I watched my mother's head gently fall back onto the arm of the sofa as Grandma Min whispered about walking out that night, right onto the shattered Swansea streets in her high heels, her small body carrying a large baby and a large suitcase (the largeness of both being relative to her). She whispered how she dodged falling rubble and had to climb over what, a moment before, had been standing. She said it was a long and lonely walk for a midget, or a dwarf, but Grandma Min was bringing home a baby and Mr Palmer would never expect that. It was fate, she said; it was a funny word called kismet. It was something Grandma Min called *fahmlee*. The way she told it – as I sipped my tea at the table and my mother's head nodded – it was simply a happy ending to the surprise of finding a baby in your bottom drawer.

'I was shaking, mind,' she whispered, 'sure as them buildings. And I weren't shaking for the bombs or the bleeding Jerries. It was the feeling I had, my Queen. I had never felt that before. Never.'

I suppose, as she stepped onto rubble in high heels, my Grandma Min wasn't fearful of the broken glass or unexploded bombs: she was afraid of the love rising up in her like heartburn. Perhaps she was also afraid of the ghost of a voice that might have screamed, 'Bring back my baby!' into the bombed night. As I watched her stroke my mother's black hair, then her white cheek, then her arm, and finally her long, elegant hand, I knew we were all feeling like that: afraid.

5

Because the only time Grandma Min lowered the volume was when she talked to Mum, we tried to keep them together. With my mother, Grandma Min was gentle; she rubbed Mum's shoulders with small hands, she giggled and gasped. She never said 'that bleeding freckled Norbert' to our mum.

We set her up in Nana Lew's front room because stairs weren't her thing and Mum wanted to be alone with Dad in their house, at night at least.

'Always ruled by the other, that gel,' Grandma – or as we now had to call her, 'Minny' – said. 'She was always up for a bit of how's your father. Specially with that lad. He must have something I don't know about. Can't fathom the rest.'

Nana Lew made up a camp bed with stiff, rough sheets and Vince bought Minny a carry-around stepladder and an electric fire. One morning Nana Lew went into town and splashed out on an electric kettle, a small fridge and dainty new cups and cutlery (for a doll, she said). She told us she'd do anything to give that woman her own space and keep her out of hers. So there they were: one nana with the run of her own house, and the other quite happy in her miniature world downstairs.

They were an odd pair, the two nanas, if they were a pair at all. One not quite four foot, neat and girlish, the other wide and solid as Welsh granite. I watched them as July hummed and August came.

'What's this then, Gladys?'

'What do you think it is, Minny? Cake. That's what that is.'

'Oooo, we don't want cake at our age.'

'And why's that?'

'Kill you, cake will.'

'Rubbish.'

'We've got to watch our figures, gel. Fat round the heart and we're goners.'

'Rubbish.'

'Can't have cake.'

'Yes we can.'

'Raw food, that's what I eat.'

'Raw food? I'm cooking my beef, thank you.'

'Ooooo, no, gel, not meat. I don't eat meat. Vegetables. Straight from the bleeding ground. Grated carrots. Beets. Celery.'

'Rabbit food.'

'You see a cotton tail on me, gel? I don't think so. It'll keep you alive, that stuff will.'

'Please yourself.'

Minny carried the small stepladder around with her. She was quick with stepladders. One bit of cheek and she was up them in a flash and giving you a slap in the face.

One night as August croaked, Fred was on TV.

Vince and Dad had moved Nana's fat-legged séance table, with her crystal ball, and we huddled into the parlour.

'You want the sofa here, Glad?' Rhysie rubbed his stubble, because Nana liked him like that. Rhysie was a permanent fix-ture now.

'Middle of the room is best, Rhys, and there's a little old child's chair for Minny in the downstairs lav.'

I watched my grandmothers bristle, either end of the room. Mum was the only one to move, slowly, onto the sofa. 'Is he on yet?' she asked, and the tension broke. Minny sat at my mother's side like an incredibly aggressive toy dog. Later Vince would tell me that her pose was exactly that of a Bichon Frisé.

Fred was on a studio stage, with smoke puffing. He was wearing what was now his signature pink cardigan. Fred was sent pink cardigans from all over the world. He sang a song called 'Mother and Son' and I watched my own father grin with a pride we'd never given him, because he and Fred had written this song together.

The camera loved Fred. He kept his hair in his eyes as he played guitar, ready to shake it away and open those seal-pup peepers when he got to the crescendo of: *'like a mother, a mother and a son. At last I'll see you when morning comes.'*

It *sounded* better than the words; it was a slow song and as the smoke puffed out and Fred was accosted by flashing coloured lights, the studio audience screamed and he smiled. We shuffled closer as the camera focused in. It was plain to see that our brother was perfect.

'He's so beautiful, Ivan,' Mum sighed.

'And he did it well, Dolly,' Dad said. 'Sang it perfect, by Christ. That was live, that was.'

'Have you seen the video?' Vince asked.

'I have,' Minny muttered through a mouth of nuts, 'and I was shocked I tell you. That lad has all his clothes off like a bleeding baby, though he don't look like one. Ends up in a supermarket, filling his trolley with food. I'm sure it's meant to be clever, meant to mean something, but I couldn't make head nor tail. Fred there has to put a melon over his wotsits. Dirty little—'

'Mummy!' our mum laughed.

Grandma Min sighed. 'It's all about this, you know.'

'What, Mummy?'

'This, my pearl. Fahmlee.'

Vince's head sank. We all knew what was coming as we'd had this speech at many Easter Sunday dinners. It was always family for Grandma Min because family, or 'fahmlee', was all you got. Minny said her family were thieves and crooks and fairground, but still she loved them something fierce.

Minny pinched my mother's arm and said, 'You may be bloody Welsh now, gel, but my side of the fahmlee, well, you got a bit of everything.' She splayed her tiny fingers out and counted off.

'You got Irish. That's me mother. Strict as a bleeding church she was. Slapped your knuckles with a knife if you spoke first, she was a right mad cow. Me and me dad, we couldn't stand her.' Minny picked up her tiny glass of sloe gin with a chubby though dainty hand.

'I loved me dad. It was his side as was fairground. Me mother hated it. She wanted a proper house, four walls. So Dad was off working and he left me with her, and I hated that.' Minny sipped. 'Now on me dad's side, me dad's dad, me granddad, he was a black with eyes like a Chinese. Come over from Trinidad, he did.' She snorted a laugh. 'Yeah, always thought that was a bloody marvellous word, "Trinidad", almost called you that, Dolly my love. But then I thought, sod it. I ain't never seen me dad's dad, me granddad. He left me nan in the lurch, he did.'

I heard Vince groan.

'And after me dad's dad – the Trinidad – me nan went with an Indian, a real Red Indian. He come all the way from Canada. Me

258

nan said he come in a canoe, though I doubt it. I remember him. You couldn't forget him, he was almost seven foot tall, had feathers in his hair, and he said he'd wrestled a grizzly bear and won.

'And it was this granddad as got stuck here on the fairgrounds, see, and that's how we ended up in them. He called himself Bill, poor big bugger. Hands like bleeding canoes, he had.'

I could hardly keep up with Grandma Min's family, who I suppose were mine too if you don't count the Swansea drawer.

Minny held her glass so tight I thought it might shatter. 'So,' she shook her head, 'what you've all got to remember is, it don't matter. It don't matter a jot where, or who, or why.' Minny fixed each of us with a cod-eye. 'Yes, yes, yes,' she said, pointing her prongs at each of us in turn. She clucked and smiled at Mum. 'All you need to know is fahmlee is as fahmlee does, and there's an end to it.'

'I propose a toast,' Vince said. 'How about "to family"? How about that, Min?'

We laughed.

'That's right on the money, that is, Gloria,' she told him. 'You might be a ginger beer, love, but you'll do.'

This time my Grandma Min laughed too.

I had to bend my legs but I did fit under Nana Lew's table. I could still see the grim grain faces on the underside of it, staring down at me: Mabel, Percy and Peter. A new generation of collies paced around me, suspicious, and I thought how little had changed in my nana's kitchen.

There was a CD player now, a Magimix and an electric kettle, but little else was new. It still smelled of cake and collie pee, and Johnny Cash and Elvis Presley still gazed down at me.

Maybe, just like my nana's kitchen, I hadn't changed much either. Vince said for a girl who spent most of her life running, I wasn't going anywhere. The truth was, I regretted every year I'd spent away from Rockfarm: the winter I'd missed the wild ponies when they came down off the hairy-backed hills and wandered into the control room; the spring when Dad and Fred made their songs in the studio.

A thought had been buzzing at the base of my spine for days, perhaps weeks or months, and now I let it fly.

Part of me was glad my mother was ill.

I was glad because it meant I had to stay here in the place I loved best.

I stared up at the grain faces in Nana's table and my hands came together in a prayer, and in that holy kitchen I prayed for forgiveness. I prayed quickly, in whispers, and I prayed with the old magic of my father's prayer.

'Dear Cla-rence Pine Top Smith. Dear Blind Le-mon Jefferson. Dear Robert Johnson. Charley Patton. Billie Holiday. Eddie Cochran. Patsy Cline. Sam Cooke. Jimi Hendrix. Mama Cass. Jim Morrison. Janis Joplin. Brian Jones. Buddy Holly. Otis Redding. Gene Vincent. Gram Parsons. Elvis Presley. Marc Bolan. Sid Vicious. Ian Curtis. John Lennon. Bob Marley. Phil Lynott. Chet Baker. Memphis Slim. Nico. Johnny Thunders. Marvin Gaye. Serge Gainsbourg. Freddie Mercury. Frank Zappa. Hoagy Carmichael. Conway Twitty. Kurt Cobain' – I took a gasp and, eyes closed, I breathed again – 'and Jenny Connor. Please forgive me.'

The collies had settled and I squeezed out from under the table. I reached behind one of the kitchen doors and I picked up

Nana's hard-bristle brush, and then I swept away her red-brick dust from her thresholds.

I was letting what was out there in.

The thing is, I sleep all over this place like a cat: never in the same place.

That night I chose the chaise longue under the stairs in the hall, with a sheet. I watched brick dust dance in the moonlight, and I closed my eyes. That was until a click-clack-click made me shut them even tighter. The click-clack-click echoed.

It wasn't the grandmother clock.

It got louder, as if it were coming closer, and I thought how it sounded like steel-capped boots. When I opened my eyes, it wasn't John the Baptist come to life from the stained-glass windows. *It* was wearing a pink cardigan and holding a case in the shape of a guitar. *It* smelled of oranges and musk.

'What are you doing sleeping down here, Lo-Lo?' it asked.

6

'Lo-Lo, pull it off, will you?'

I let him lift his leg up between mine and I pulled his heavy boot. This close, Fred smelled of whiskey.

'And the other one.' Fred was sitting in the grand high-backed carved chair that Nana stood against the damp marks in her hall.

'Hold on, Fred!'

'Shh! I don't want to wake anyone up.'

'Well you shut up then.' I tugged and at last the boot was off.

'Thanks.' Fred had kohl around his eyes.

'How did you get here anyway?'

'How do you mean?'

'What I said. You don't drive, so did you fly? Hitch?'

'I have a limo.'

'Very posh.'

'I'm tired, Lo-Lo, can I sleep with you?'

I turned my back to put his boots down, neat beneath the hall table. Now he smelled of dust and leather and something sweet, maybe glitter and glue.

'Where's your room, Lo?'

'It's the big orange one upstairs. I painted it.'

'Ew, I prefer Molly's old room.'

'Well sleep in there, Fred, she's not back until tomorrow.'

'No, I want to sleep with you.'

I backed into the darkness. He laid his hands out on the plush arms of the chair, a little king. 'How's Mum?'

'The same.'

'What does that mean?'

'It means she's not any better but she's not any worse. She says she's not in pain. Nana helps her.'

'I'm going to get her the best treatment. Anything.'

'Whatever you think, Fred.'

'I am.' Fred had silver rings on his fingers and he drummed them on the arms of the chair. I felt behind me for the edge of the hall table and I clung on.

'Where have you come from, Fred?'

'I don't know.'

'Where's the limo?'

'Outside.'

'You are serious then? Is the driver going to wait?'

'Yup.'

'Doesn't he want a bed? I can go and—'

'Nah. He's kipping in the seat. He's a cool guy, Terry.'

'I'll make him some tea.'

'I want to go to bed *now*, Halo.'

'Will you stop calling me that?'

'It's your name isn't it? Anyway, we've all got to grow up sometime.'

I hadn't seen Fred for a year. I considered him. 'Where were you, Fred? Where have you been?'

'What do you mean?'

'Again, what I said. Where have you been?'

'God, I don't know, Lo-Lo, everywhere.' He shrugged and I

saw the boy again. 'Please can we go to bed?' He picked up his guitar case.

I ran out of the shadows and I sprinted up the stairs, two at a time, past the fifteenth step and down Nana's long landing, light and quick.

'Lo-Lo!' Fred whispered. 'Wait up!'

I thrashed out of my clothes and yanked on my Past Times Victorian nightie, long sleeved and tied at the neck with ribbon. I jumped into my bed in my new orange bedroom, and the springs bounced. They jogged me up and down as I lay there, trying to be still, trying to steady my breath. I thought about my shoulders and the tension I knew too well.

I put the white sheet above my head.

I listened to Nana's stairs creak.

Of course he couldn't sleep.

'How do the trousers of a man with five willies fit, Lo-Lo?'

'Eh?'

'Like a glove.'

'Fred!'

We were children again, Fred with the sheet above our heads as he told me jokes and tickled me until I told my best ghost story.

'You can hear him howl some nights,' I whispered in his ear. 'I've heard him. I call him the Moonlight Dog Boy and he'll crawl up the climbing roses to my window here and then I'll see him in all his glory. He's hairy, but beautiful, with black flashing eyes, and he'll jump onto the floor there and then she'll appear.'

'Who, Lo-Lo?'

'The English Bastard's great-great-great-great-great-great-great' – I counted on my fingers – 'great-great-great grandniece. Because it was her who loved the Moonlight Dog Boy, who, before the curse that turned him into a dog was cast, was just the Welsh stable boy.'

'Who cursed him?'

'Her father's housekeeper. She was a witch, see, and in love with the master, and so when he commanded, she obeyed. And it was her who found them together, when the boy was just a beautiful lad and the niece was a shy girl. She found them up in the stables, clasped to each other, and she told the master. That's when she cursed the boy, and he turned into a great black dog right in front of the girl.'

Fred snuggled closer. 'Tell me more, Lo.'

'And the years passed and the master died, poisoned by the housekeeper who was never truly loved in return, the house-keeper fled and the daughter was left alone with the dog, as big as a wolfhound, bigger, even. And though the curse could never be lifted, each night that big dog slept at his lover's feet. The daughter never married a human, and so that line of Bastards died with her, but she led a happy life, and she's up in Nana's churchyard now, buried with her stable boy, buried deep and happy with the big black dog. And sometimes, Fred, you can hear them in this house. You can hear a girlish giggle, a howl, and then a lick.' I poked my tongue in Fred's ear.

'Ah!'

'Shh!'

'Lo-Lo! You frightened me.'

'Good. You know, they shine in the moonlight, Fred, and they stand over there. He's not a full dog, he's like a man-dog, walking on his hind legs and as handsome as anything.'

'What do they do then, Lo?'

'They kiss, she giggles and he growls.'

'That sounds lovely.' He touched my lip with a finger.

'It is. And then they're off, out the window in a flash of white and I can hear them out on the lawn scaring the peacocks and shushing the owls. They do it when the moon is yellow. Nana says that's their time.'

He moved into me, face to face. 'Tell me another.'

I talked through the strata of stories of Rockfarm: the stories he had missed. It was easy to tell Fred tales of love in the dark. Fred let his hand rest on my hip, then he put a hairy leg over me. It was heavy.

'Are your bags in the car?' I asked, frozen.

'Haven't got any.'

'You not staying?'

'I was on the way to a gig then I changed my mind. I told Terry to drive me down here. I gave him all the money I had. I suppose they'll be after me tomorrow.'

'Who's "they"?'

He moved away from me, onto his back. 'The record company. My manager. The band. Oh, everyone, Lo-Lo.'

All at once Fred sat up. He leant over me, eager. 'Lo-Lo, if they call don't tell them I'm here. Please. Terry said he wouldn't say. He said he's on my side and when your mother's ill, your mother's ill. You won't tell them, will you Lo-Lo? Don't tell anyone I'm here. We'll give Terry more money, keep him quiet. Just don't tell them. Please.' He lay back down. His head was in my armpit and his hand on my stomach. His breaths were quick.

'Shh,' I soothed.

'Promise?'

'Of course.'

'Say it then.'

'I promise.'

'Cross your heart?'

'Yes. Cross my heart and hope to die, Fred.'

'Don't say that.'

'Just cross my heart then.'

'Lo-Lo?'

'Yes.'

'I'm scared.'

'What of?'

'I'm scared about Mum.'

I listened to the tick-tock of the grandmother clock. I listened to the brick dust dancing in my grandmother's house. I listened to the growls and the giggles that pit-pattered up and down the stairs.

'Hug me, Lo-Lo,' he said.

And I did, tighter than ever, until Fred slept like a baby.

The sun came up and I turned my tired eyes on him. His mouth was open, his breath sharp with cigarettes, his double eyelashes fluttering and his strong nose flared. Fred on his back with one arm above his head and the sheet down to his boxer shorts; Fred with brown and small muscles and hair that ran in a neat line from his belly button down; Fred with that Sitting Bull necklace still fastened around his neck; Fred with the blond of the sun in his dark hair and too much of something darker beneath his eyes. I fell back and slept.

*

He was walking around my room in a small white towel, wet. He looked thinner, standing up.

'Morning, Lo-Lo.'

'Hmm?'

'You going to make me some breakfast?'

I patted down my corkscrew hair. 'Are you going across to see Mum?'

He looked up at me like he'd look at a nagging aunt. 'Vince here?'

'I think he's driving down today. He's got the floor above. Goes back to London at the weekends for work.'

'Still doing the cabaret?'

'He loves it.'

'He's great, too. I prefer it when he just plays himself. Sings himself, you know what I mean?'

I picked sleep from my eyes. 'Maybe.'

'I want to get back into the studio with Dad. We need more songs.' He stared at the full-length mirror and flicked his hair. 'Hey, Lo, do you always wear that sack to bed?'

'What?'

'That bloody chastity sheet of a nightie, you look like some crazy Pre-Raphaelite chick.'

'Fred, don't say "chick" – you sound so *nineteen-seventies*.'

He giggled and slumped his shoulders, sticking his thumbs up, 'Cool, man. Crazy chick. You blow my mind, daddy-o-baby.'

I threw a pillow at him and we both laughed. 'You're such a fucking cliché, Fred.'

'Well, Lo-Lo my love, the girls love it, the boys love it, I've got the grannies on my side too, and look, I've got a morning boner. Just for you.' He put his arms out and the towel lifted.

'Fred!'

'I can't help it, we can't *all* be celibate virgins in this family.' He let the towel drop to the floor. I squeaked. 'OK, OK, Miss Tight-Fanny Knickers.' He stepped, naked, into his leather trousers and I threw a sneaker at him as he laughed and ran into the hall.

7

Vince, Molly and I sat in a row on Vince's bed, the old mattress sagging. We were waiting in Vince's old room to see Mum, the three of us lined up like guilty children dreading punishment.

Dad had made this bedroom into a waiting room. He'd put magazines on Vince's bedside table. *Melody Makers* and our old *Beano* annuals were stacked up on the floor. Dad had nailed three flying ducks to the wall next to Vince's old posters of David Bowie and Tippi Hedren. An armchair by the window had a standard lamp perched over it like the moving eye of an alien, and that was where Dorian sat because Molly had married him and now he was one of us.

Dorian flicked sharply through a magazine. Molly had married young because she was good at making her mind up; she had done it alone at some Scottish kirk with none of us to help.

Dad had set this up because other people came to see Mum on her bad days: other friends. Their fingers would have flicked through the music papers too, through our childhood comics. They would have creaked open that wardrobe and let the light shine on Vince's old sequins, the dresses he had clumsily run up himself, the ones with the chiffon and the imitation pearls that rattled in the draught. They might have thought it was a rattling skeleton in the closet, which I suppose it was. They might have wondered what enormous girl had once lived in this room; then they might remember Vincent, the big-boned boy with the plucked eyebrows. The kiddie who had chipped red nail varnish and who knew all the words to 'La Vie en Rose' before he even did French.

I was glad that Dad set visitors up in here. It was red and warm: it was Vincent.

'How long has *he* been in there?' Molly spat.

'He's only just come back, Moll. She'll want to see him.'

'The prodigal bloody son, is that it?'

'Yeah, something like that,' Vince said and he smiled. Dorian turned a page of my *Beano* annual 1979 even sharper.

'It's ridiculous. *We've* come all this way. We were up at four in the morning to get here on time,' Molly barked.

I slunk against the wall. I was thinking how it was like *Gone with the Wind* and here we were, the loyal southern relatives, but it would be Scarlett – rosy-cheeked and chin out – who would get to see the dying Miss Melly first.

Fred Connor was our Scarlett, of course.

Molly bit the skin on the back of her hand. 'He's not even our brother.'

'Moll—'

'Well he's not.'

'Molly, please.' Vince scratched his skin as if something unseemly was in the air. 'That's like saying our Robert isn't our brother, just because—'

'*I* didn't know Robert,' Molly snapped, and then she collapsed, quite suddenly, her tight lemon cardy giving way, her chest over her legs. I was on one side and Vince was on the other so we each put an arm around her.

'Molly, don't.' I whispered. 'Mum'll hear you.'

'Moll, my darling, it's difficult for us all,' Vince said and we

271

both glanced at Dorian as we patted the back of our deflated sister. Something above his eye was twitching. When we were being polite we called Dorian 'not our cup of tea'.

'Dad won't even let me talk to the doctors' – Molly was inflating again, the lemon cardy filling up – 'and she needs the best, the best treatment, but she's just sitting there, waiting. It's cancer. We know that, but—'

'Shh, Moll—'

None of us had said that word out loud yet. It was a shock.

'I won't. It's utterly mad. They could cure her, I know they could. She could get some years at least. She needs to go to a hospital. She needs to have it cut out of her, she needs treatment, she needs—'

The shadow of Dad fell on us. He closed Vince's door behind him and walked in front of the small fire grate, hands behind his back like a Victorian father. He was staring down at Molly.

He coughed.

'Thank you, Miss Llewelyn, for your input,' his voice was steely quiet, 'but do you think that I haven't tried everything?' His foot tapped, like he'd caught us smoking in our bedrooms; like he'd found us listening to the wrong type of music.

'But, Dad—'

'No buts Miss Molly. Don't you think we went to London? Don't you think I've got those tickets to America, the ones your other brother in there sent me months ago, just to take her off to the best hospital in the world? Don't you think we considered that? Don't you think we've been dealing with this quietly, firmly, the way it should be? Don't you think, by Christ, that we've searched for the best, found the best, but got no answers? Do you really think at all, Miss Molly?'

272

Dorian looked up. He looked like he was about to say something.

'Your mother has made a choice, and it's hers. They said it's too late. They said all kinds of things I will never repeat to you children. They upset your mother and so she made her choice, and I for one stand by it. And that is all I'm going to say.'

Molly was crying, 'But I want to see her, Dad. Why can't I go and see her first, why is it always Fred?'

'Number one, your brother's back and he's in there' – Dorian made to interrupt again – 'number two don't be so bloody dramatic, you're as bad as your nana, by Christ.'

Dad's tone became gentle again; he let his hands drop to his sides. 'It's not now, Molly girl. She's fine now, just sleepy, so you don't have to wait up here like it's the last. And we're all off to the pub tonight, remember? So all of you, come downstairs with me and leave your mother be, let her have a rest after Fred and then we can all have a good night tonight, OK?' He smiled a little and I saw his teeth, you rarely saw Dad's teeth. 'So who's for toast? I'm making some for that Terry, that driver of Fred's. Do you know he used to play in the skiffle band My Mother's Washboard? Amazing. So who'll join me?' He slapped his hands together. 'Halo, you can make the tea.'

We stood under a weeping willow, each of us skimming stones across the snakeskin surface of the river. We still stood in order: Vince first, then me, then Molly, and last, Fred. Dorian had instructions and a shopping list to do in town.

Vince wore a poppy-print summer dress. Molly still hugged her yellow cardigan and Fred was bare-chested with leather trousers: trousers that stayed up by the skin of his hips,

273

trousers that let us see almost everything and Vince couldn't help staring.

Fred had beautiful skin, it was brown without the sun; and the hair around his nipples – the line that ran down from his belly button – was almost unseemly in the bright light.

A fish jumped, flashing white and silver.

'That's a salmon.'

'Fred, it's a trout,' said Vince.

'A pike,' I grinned.

'You're all wrong, it was a bloody eel.' Molly squinted in the sun, and she threw a stone that reached the opposite bank.

The cool wind from the forest blew on our backs. I heard it move on through Beggars' Wood. I glanced back at the first thick line of beech and oak. It had been years since Fred and I played in there.

'She's not that ill, you know,' Fred suddenly said.

Molly sniffed at her youngest brother.

'We can help her. I'm sure of it.'

'How, Fred?' Molly asked. 'How do we help her? Do you as ever have all the answers?' She stared off into the distance. 'You heard Dad.'

'Oh, Molly, you're so bloody straight aren't you? Think about it, we don't listen to the quacks; we get her away from this place. A clinic, fresher air. An oxygen tank. I don't know.' He shrugged, skimmed a stone.

'And how are we going to pay for that, Mr Hotshot?'

Fred looked across at us all and smiled. 'Me, of course. I can get the best treatment, I can pay for anything. I can make it right, I know I can.'

'It's not that simple, Fred.'

274

'Why, Vince?'

'Oh, sweetheart,' Vince sighed.

Fred's cheeks flushed. He stared at the water. 'You're all crazy,' he told us, 'you're crazy, we can't just sit around all day and *wait*.' Fred kicked at the pebbles. 'I've already lost one mother. I can't lose another. I'm not like you all, I can't do nothing. I'm different. She's bloody wasting away before your eyes, and—'

Molly threw her stone to the ground and turned on him. 'And we're doing nothing are we? Well thank you. Listen to me, Fred, we can deal with *our* mother *our* way and money is not the answer.'

'Never thought I'd hear you say that, sis.' Fred tried to laugh.

'Oh piss off you prodigal bastard.'

'Molly—'

'Molly—'

Vince and I stared at them, pleading.

'Well he comes back here pulling his weight around and taking Mum off to some, oh I don't know, mountain in Switzerland or something, and we're just meant to bow and say "oh, thank you Fred, Mr Rock-Star Fred". It's always been the same. He just muscles his way in—'

Fred pushed himself up against Molly; he held her shoulders and pressed his face close to hers. He smiled at her and I saw the weasel. 'My gorgeous Molly,' he said, 'you don't have to bow to me,' I saw those weasel teeth flash white as that salmon's belly in the river, 'but, you know, on your knees would be nice. I've always wanted to see my pretty Molly in front of me on her knees. Know what I mean?' He licked the tip of her nose.

Vince gasped and Molly leapt on him. 'You dirty little shit!

Shut up! She's not your mother, she's not your mother!' Molly was scratching at him, at his bare chest, his shoulders.

Fred didn't try and stop her.

She didn't stop. 'You fucking wanker. How dare you say that? How dare you! You've made our lives a misery. Why don't you just fuck off to your real father and leave me and my brother and my sister alone. They need you to be gone. They need it, you wanker—'

Vince and I grabbed Molly but it was hard to keep her still.

'She's my mother, she's my mother. She's my mother, Fred, not yours!' Molly collapsed. She was sobbing, gulping. Fred wiped away the little beads of blood from where Molly had scratched him. He wiped his cheek, his chest, and he sucked his fingers. Then he walked to Molly and for a second I froze, because if anything I knew my brother could be cruel and enjoy it. But this time Fred knelt on the dusty floor and gathered Molly up: he hugged her in a way he had never hugged any of us.

'I know she is your mother, I know she is, Moll, and I'm sorry. I really am. I'm only sorry.' He began to cry with her. I couldn't remember the last time I saw Fred cry.

Vince and I stepped away.

A swan was flying towards us, coming in to land on the river, the sound like the whine of a wind turbine. It skimmed on the water, giraffe neck out, the black spots of its eyes watching us until it reached the bend of the river and I saw the fat oak, the one I called Molly's oak.

Right then I thought of Dean Turley and a flash of white knickers, I thought of the day Fred smashed into Dean with Molly's newly felted hockey stick; *fuck off my sisters.*

Molly was gently crying in his arms, exhausted.

Vince sighed and wiped the sweat from his top lip. He turned to me. 'Even if he could help her, Halo, Mum will never leave here. She'd never leave Rockfarm, she loves it too much.'

I chucked my last stone in, heavy. 'I wouldn't be so sure of that, Vince. Everyone wants to live.'

§

It was a quiet night. Mum and Dad wanted to go to their bed-room early and turn on their glow-in-the-dark globe. They wanted to touch countries they'd never seen and then lie back with full bellies and dream about how it might be to live there.

'You think we're at it all the time, don't you Halo?' Dad had said.

'Dad!'

'Well, OK, most of the time we are, but your mother, she gets tired and nowadays we prefer to talk.'

'Daddy!'

'What?'

In his more-than-middle age my father had become honest as an idiot. Nana said it was because of Mum. 'He can only tell the absolute truth now, sunbeam. Only the absolute.' I consid-ered how frightening that was. In his more-than-middle age my father was very handsome; his red calmed by strands of blond and his brown face as lined as a cowboy's. 'He looks just like a Louis L'Amour hero now, my Ivan does, he looks just like Robert Redford as a glorious gunslinger,' said Nana.

I lay in my bed in my orange bedroom, alone. I touched the pillow next to me; there was no Fred tonight but my sheet smelled of him. Molly and Fred had been inseparable since the river. I didn't know where they were now.

Above me Vince was busy choreographing. That meant he'd

just taken delivery of a new dress. Tonight he was deciding whether to be Dusty Springfield or Bonnie Tyler. I told him there was no competition but he insisted he had to play to his roots. 'The thing is I can do Bonnie's voice, not sure if I can do Dusty's.' I listened to him banging out a routine directly over my room. I think it was 'I Just Don't Know What To Do With Myself', but it could have been 'Total Eclipse of the Heart'. Vince could go on all night, so I picked up a blanket and walked out onto Nana's vast landing.

I could hear Minny's high rasp from the front room below. She liked to sleep with the door open. At nights I often looked out for the Beloveds, but I had almost stopped believing in them. It was strange actually living in my grandmother's house; I was beginning to see it as just an old house with stairs that creaked for the fun of it, with windows that leaked, and with pictures on the walls of people who had gone before their time.

I pit-patted down the stairs as quick as Scarlett on Rhett's lethal staircase. I leapt through the stained-glass light of the hall, and I thought how Minny's pug-dog snores gave authority to the tale of the Moonlight Dog Boy.

I liked the stab of cold gravel. I had big feet and a light body so the stones didn't hurt. There was a hot wind outside.

Peacocks trailed the lawn. Terry, the driver, had parked Fred's black limo by Nana's garden wall. Nana had Terry preparing her garden beds – August was almost done with and Nana wanted her second crop in.

Maybe I slept all over this place –never in the same spot – because I didn't want to be found. Tonight the hot breeze led me across Nana's lawn, past the browning croquet hoops and towards the polytunnels, ragged in the wind.

I walked under the enormous cedar where an aqua peacock perched. It cried out with that trod-on baby wail – a warning – and I walked on, crunching brown cedar needles beneath my feet; my nightie flapping against my legs.

Nana's four polytunnels were lined up in front of me, as long and opaque as light-starved worms. I chose the one where the rhubarb pushed up towards the moon. It was so warm inside that I lay on my blanket.

I closed my eyes and I listened.

The rhubarb was moaning tonight, or maybe that was the wind spitting through the rips in Nana's plastic arches. I stretched out on the ground, my arms above my head and my legs out and apart until I felt that wind, breathy, on myself. The line of rhubarb plants nearest my head was luminous in the moonlight and I sniffed at their sharpness; I thought of sugar and custard and then I thought of something else: I thought of Brendan.

I hadn't thought about Brendan O'Boyle for years, although it was nice that he'd thought about me – he'd tried with post-cards, letters and then the phone but eventually they stopped. I suppose New York was too far away.

There was a hole in the roof of the tunnel and clouds moved quickly over clusters of stars. A big yellow moon – a harvest one, Nana would say – glowed. I wished on it for something I knew I'd never get. The sugar-brown cows lowed from Beggars' Field and I thought of their misty breath in the moonlight. I could hear their steps, the rhythm of their munching jaws.

I didn't notice him. Maybe it was on account of the cows, on account of the rhubarb moaning like the summer wind out there.

It was his breath I felt, and then his hands.

He was kneeling at my head when I finally saw the shadow. For a moment I thought it was the Moonlight Dog Boy, until he leant down and kissed me full on the lips.

'Lo-Lo,' Fred said, and then he carried on kissing me, upside down. It was funny: a nose to my chin and a chin to my nose. He moved his hands down my body, over the small breasts I was stuck with.

'Lo-Lo.'

The Sitting Bull necklace was hanging between my eyes, cold. I stared up at his Adam's apple as it moved with each swallowing kiss. His hands moved further down until he brushed me, he stroked me, and his lips left mine. His hands came back up with the hem of my nightie.

Fred was naked. Later he told me he thought he might as well come prepared. Later he told me he followed me into my grandmother's garden when he spotted me walking across the lawn like a ghost in that stupid nightdress.

He said that was when he decided.

Fred stood and then he lay down next to me. In the moonlight I picked a grass blade from his shoulder. I felt his lips on mine, the right way around now, and everything seemed to fit. Everything. Because when Fred dragged my starched nightie up and over my head, when he said I was golden red in the moonlight, when he left my lips and began to kiss me from my chin downwards, from my breasts downwards, from my belly button downwards, from the inside of my thighs downwards; when he grabbed my hip and moved on top of me, when he parted my thighs with his knee, when he began to do the thing he had done maybe a thousand times and I had never done, it didn't hurt: not exactly.

281

Maybe he bit my ear to distract me.

All I know is, the pushing crack of the rhubarb filled the air around us and I don't think the cedar falling or the ground splitting would have registered, because all I could feel was Fred moving inside me, and all I could hear was the sound of his breath and his voice telling me, 'Lo-Lo.'

After the first time, we stared up at the cloudy plastic and found our breath. My body was clammy and I enjoyed the drips of condensation that fell, moment to moment, from the plastic roof and onto my skin.

'Lo-Lo,' Fred said as he pulled me to him again, hip first. 'Lo-Lo. I want it again. Again, Lo-Lo.'

And we did.

'Lo-Lo. It's family. It's family, Lo-Lo.'

'Yes.'

'Ah, Lo-Lo, it's family.'

'Yes.'

'Lo-Lo, you're beautiful.'

'Yes.'

I searched out those parts of him I'd always wanted: the smooth skin that ran from his hip to his armpit. I licked each rib, along the bone. I swallowed the oranges, the musk, while my skin sucked in more scent. Fred bit the tight strings of my Achilles tendons; he gnawed on my sharp shoulder blades, and told me my other parts tasted of honey and bitter sweat. I pressed my fingers into his collarbone; my hands pushed between his strong bristled legs as he sniffed behind my knees and grabbed at the jut of my hips. He licked and sucked and cried out, marking his place, while I thought about silver buses and prairies; I thought about pregnant bellies and freckled yee-haw faces; I thought about the straw of the barn and I thought about strawberries and stars until I was back on a wide, flat beach, running like a horse, nostrils flared, with a heart so big it could burst.

'Ah, Lo-Lo.'

'Yes.'

'I love you, Lo-Lo.'

'Yes.'

Fred moved, slow at first, then faster than I could ever have imagined, and we did it again, and again.

We did the thing that brother and sister shouldn't. We did the thing that Cathy and Heathcliff never managed (unless you count all those forgotten days out on the moors).

We did it until our lips cracked and our throats were dry. We did it until everything else felt like it didn't belong to us.

And then we did it some more.

We did it until the baby tawny owls above us shrieked and fell from their perches; until the vixen lay down in the nettles and ate them up. We did it until we shook with something more than pain. We did it until every touch made us flinch.

'More, Lo-Lo, more. Please,' Fred gasped.

We did it until my running stamina was spent. We did it until Fred snored on top of me and inside me; and as soon as I heard that I closed my eyes too.

9

There was a blanket around me when I woke. My nightdress lay over the delicate rhubarb and stalks had snapped.

I was alone.

As I stared into the rhubarb I saw something pierced onto a snapped stalk. It was a note. I lay there until the heat in the tunnel made sweat run down my parched body. I lay there until I heard Nana Lew call my name from the Big House porch. Nana was used to gathering me up after a night's sleep.

It took a long time for me to reach out and pull the note away. It took me even longer to read it.

Sorry. (it said)

I shouldn't have. You are my sister.

Fred Conner x

Right there and then in the hot light of the day I laughed. As I moved my thighs and the soreness made me cry out; as the condensation drip-dropped onto the scorching rhubarb and my scorching skin, I laughed. I laughed because of the way Fred had signed the note. It was just like he'd sign his bloody autograph.

Fred Conner x

Nana's cries made me stand up and slip the nightdress over my head. Her 'Hay-law!' across the lawn made me poke my head out of the polytunnel, wipe the sweat from my face and wince as I walked under the cedar towards the house. I stopped to let a breeze blow against me and cool my sore body, and that was when I saw that the long black limo had gone.

I stood in its tyre tracks. I ran the soles of my feet along them: they were warm. I was too exhausted to spit, sprint, or shout 'coward!' down the drive. In any case, there was someone else shouting, and it was Nana Lew.

I turned my head, sharp, at her new words because they were, 'Hay-law come in! Hay-law, love, she's dead!'

It wasn't my mother. It was Princess Diana.

A car crash like Marc Bolan, but we couldn't add her to the prayer. As Dad said, Princess Diana was in a different category to Blind Lemon Jefferson and Clarence Pine Top Smith.

Nana and Grandma Min spent the morning crying, baking cakes, and juicing. Nana clicked the dusty CB radio on, she wanted her own service up at the capel, but the line fizzed: no one was listening to FoxyRed any more. Vince cried a little and played the piano in the parlour, and Molly and Dorian drove into town for papers and Sky News. I stayed upstairs in the Big House, happy for the space. I could put a chair against the bathroom door and run a bath.

I winced again as I sat in the hot, salted water, but with my arms wrapped around my eczema knees I felt a moment of gushing relief. I felt like Nana must, whenever she pissed like a horse by the side of the road, the pickup door open.

Then I laughed one of those crazy-people laughs because I

knew, sure as the hot stab in my belly, that if Fred hadn't slunk off like the weasel he was, we would still be at it now. In the hot daylight: while our grandmothers wailed and mourned. Fred and I would do it until we died. We'd do it and we'd do it until we gasped and our bodies gave out.

We'd do it because I could never get enough of my brother and now I finally knew that he could never get enough of me.

We were inexhaustible.

I went under the water and opened my eyes. When they stung with the salt, I clearly saw that this would kill us.

The ceiling was peeling, white paint flaking, and I wondered what I looked like from above: a sore girl with her thighs apart, her long freckled legs sticking out either side of the roll-top bath. A girl underwater, red hair rising to the surface like that Pre-Raphaelite Ophelia, and just like that silly cow I was going to die for love: like her I didn't know how to grasp hold of the grassy bank, the reeds, and stop that current taking me.

I *wanted* it to.

I sat up, grabbed the soap bar, and turned it in my hands until it broke. I scrubbed my legs until they were as sore as the rest of me. I could at least try and get Fred's oranges and musk from under my skin. I could try and disentangle his hair from my own hair. I could scrub his prairie DNA out of me once and for all. I used Nana's nail brush until the skin on my thighs pin-pricked with blood.

Nana Lew was talking in the hall below. 'Those poor boys,' she said as the lighter pit-patter of my other grandmother caught her up.

'Bleeding motherless now,' Grandma Min echoed, 'and what was she anyway, a Lady Di or a Princess Diana?'

'They're all calling her the Queen of Hearts now.'

'Like in that *Alice in Wonderland*?'

'No, Minny, like "she touched our hearts", see, like she said she wanted to be remembered. She never wanted to chop off anyone's head. Oh, it's still such a shock, isn't it?'

I put a flannel over my face, bit my lip and I let myself cry.

'Has anyone seen that Terry?' Nana Lew cried back into the hall. 'Has anyone seen him or his limosi-thingamabob? Because he's not touched his breakfast, he hasn't made his bed, and he's got my best spade!'

10

Fred had been gone a month. They had found him, he was back on tour, so the manager, the press and the record company had stopped calling. In fact the phone stopped altogether; the studio was a mess, we had no bookings. While the rest of the country mourned loudly for a princess, we were quiet. Vince said it was natural, he said we had gone in on ourselves and it would take a different sort of shock to get ourselves out now.

'Mum?'

'Yes darling.' She smiled and lay back in the hammock, her face in the last of the sun.

'How did you know it was only Dad? I mean how did you know he was the one?'

'Only him, Hitler and Mussolini, you mean?'

'Yeah.'

'I don't know, Halo.' Mum took a deep breath. She needed to do that now. She said the pain wasn't so much but none of us believed her. 'Maybe I wasn't sure. Maybe it was because he chose me. Because he chose me absolutely, you know. Ab-sol-ute-ly.' She sighed. 'Your father *waited*.' Mum pulled her blanket up to her chin. 'You're like me, Halo baby, though you think you're not. But you're the most like me, and *you* need someone to choose you. Maybe they'll have to wait too.'

I watched Nana's fat sheep in the meadow. I thought about the fairground and my dad at fourteen, making his forever-choice, and I knew Mum was wrong, I was nothing like her: I had chosen and no one had chosen me.

I watched her in the weak September sun: it was as weak as her, it was like she was fading with the last of the summer. I hadn't told her about my night with Fred. I'd told no one. I had kept the note though, the one Fred speared on the rhubarb, and it was that note that kept my head above water; it made me sniff my nose, up, up into the air like Molly. At nights, when I couldn't find a safe place to curl up and sleep, and the phone called out to me, I'd take that note out of my copy of *Wuthering Heights*, I'd stare at it and I'd sniff Molly's sniff. That note made me itchier than my eczema.

Tonight Fred was playing the Aragon Ballroom in Chicago. Dad said our Fred was back in the machine and we should all pray it didn't eat him up and spit him out.

Mum swung gently in the hammock while across the track I heard Rhysie mow up the peacock shit and clover on Nana's lawn. I smelled sharp, sweet grass and ammonia.

'Mum, do you want me to drive you to the beach this weekend?'

She sighed. 'Oh, yes love. I do so want to see blue. That sea blue. That's what I want to see, because really, it's never blue, is it?'

Mum had gone mad on colours.

Dad said she wanted to drink them in and never forget them: the colour of the Gower sand, the pink of rosebay willowherb on the fairground wasteland. When Fred was here in August, she'd tried to fathom the exact colour of his eyes. After an entire afternoon she told him it was impossible. 'You've got as many colours in those peepers of yours as the Lord God puts in what you see. You reflect back, my boy, that's what you do.' Fred laughed and told her she was a better riddler than Nana.

Mum had been chasing blue this week. I wished it was spring and I could give her a cornflower, a forget-me-not.

'Yes, the beach, Halo baby, but let's go in the caravan,' and she pointed.

It wasn't really a caravan and it had arrived after Fred left. Fred had had a ridiculous red bow tied around the whole thing, and it was a ribbon as wide and as red as Nana Lew.

The caravan was parked in Mum and Dad's garden now and Grandma Min had whistled through her teeth when Vince lifted her up and carried her into its living room. Mum, on Dad's arm, had gasped. She'd reached up and touched the embossed wallpaper, already there; she'd crowed over the flushing loo and the shiny hobs in the more-than-fully equipped kitchen. Fred's caravan was silver on the outside, and inside it had *everything*, down to a fish tank, filled. There were two bedrooms and a red double bed fit for any queen. Mum lay on the bed and told us all she wouldn't move for seven days. She didn't. On the eighth day Dad cleaned out the loo and stocked up the fridge, and they drove off in it for another week.

'It's actually a motorhome, Halo,' Mum had cried from the tall passenger seat window, 'a motorhome, not a caravan with an engine. And it's all the way from America!' When they came back, they had the kiss of the sun on their skin and a tiredness that made them both go to bed for another week.

Now I watched Mum's bottom lip shiver.

'Which beach do you want to go to, Mum?'

'Oh, anywhere will do.'

'Horton. The Sands?'

'Oh, that would be lovely.'

I pushed her hammock, gently.

Because it was the very last of the summer, Nana Lew and Grandma Min were down on the road picking blackberries – they made a good picking team, one for the lower and one for the upper branches. I didn't like the summer leaving us. It was too cold for Mum in the afternoons and we'd have to put her to bed. Dad was in charge of injections and the district nurse.

That afternoon he came for her a little early.

'Come on Dolly darling,' he whispered as the hammock creaked, 'I'm upstairs and you're coming with me.'

'Right you are, Ivan,' she said without opening her eyes, and my dad, with arms of oak, slipped his hands under her and lifted her up, sure as he'd lifted any child. Her blanket trailed across the grass.

I cleaned up my mother's morning: the tea things, the cookbooks she loved to pore over, her notebook and sketchpad, her Walkman with Fred's songs, and the photograph album she loved to open now.

This was where we were then: us in our own small world.

We were like that, the Llewelyns, we could close ourselves off, tight as clams, fierce as sows. That September we hadn't cuddled round the TV or saved for a ticket to London to share in any nation's grief – English or Welsh.

That September we had our own.

It was the middle of the night and I woke with a start to a jangling tinkle and thud. It was Dad's old Land Rover, driving off with the trailer attached.

I was surprised to open my eyes and find myself in Mum's

291

motorhome. I was in the red bed with my own blanket.

I lay in the dark and listened to metal rattle as Dad drove the trailer and Land Rover away. Fred would be playing now, live in Chicago: girls and boys would be screaming in the Aragon Ballroom. Fred had described that place to me, he said it was crazy-special, and now he'd be looking up at the hacienda balconies, at the big ballroom, and he'd be thinking of nothing but the song he sang. That's what our dad taught him: to sing the song, you have to be the song. To be the song, it has to speak inside you. 'It's the need, Fred, the obsession. It's the passion, by Christ,' Dad told him. It was a riddle to the rest of us, but that was my quiet dad all over.

Fred would be watching the red balloons with his face on now, the black confetti, the silver glitter, because Fred liked a gimmick or two at his gigs. Fred would be spraying the sweat of a hard job over the crush at the front of the stage, and as he sang 'Red-Headed Girl With Love on Her Mind' he'd think of nothing but the song. When that was done he would yell out, 'This one's for my beautiful Welsh mother!' and the boys and the girls would scream and the balloons they held, the balloons with his face on, would rise to the ballroom's ceiling. 'Do you all love your beautiful mothers?' Fred would yell out and they'd yell back, 'Yes!' Then he would sing 'Dolly Mixtures' for them, the song he wrote with the hand of my father. The crowd would join in on the chorus—

> 'She cooks love up in a bowl,
> I drink down slow.
> My beautiful gap-toothed mama—'

Fred would slide his hands up and down his electric Ricken-backer, because that was what he had taken to lately. And later, when the sweat and glitter were wiped away and his brain would be a fuzz of things he liked to swallow, Fred would be with as many women as he could, as many as he could manage in the whiteness of another hotel room. That was, as long as they didn't have red hair and freckled skin, because Fred Connor couldn't look at anything, at least in the flesh, that reminded him of his sister.

I got up from the caravan's red bed and made tea.

11

It took Dad weeks to wrench the summer back with heat lamps. By then we were picking red apples, hollowing pumpkins, and thinking of mushrooms. By then leaves had turned gold while rain slicked them to a mush on the lichen ground.

That didn't put off my dad because Dad had built a see-through plastic extension over the front of Fred's motorhome. He'd built Mum a conservatory at last, and he'd bought heat lamps. Nana said he was making time stand still and sweaty.

Dad had also laid the back garden with sand, the proper sand he'd gathered those nights and brought back in his trailer. Nana said a builders' yard would have done but Dad said no, it had to be sand from the Gower; it had to be the right smell and touch, the right alabaster-white, the right talc-white (he said he couldn't find the exact word for the colour), it simply had to be right for his Dolly. So from the Gower it was. It took him ten night trips with the Land Rover and the trailer to get the sand he wanted, and it gave him an ache he couldn't cure. But finally we could sit beneath the plastic and the wood extension just outside the motorhome door, and root our toes through Dad's stolen sand. The grains were often warm as I watched a misty drizzle spit outside. I found a crab that was now in a black bucket by our front door. Grandma Min had found an empty tin with NIGERIA stamped on it, and she wore shoes after that.

Mum lay on her sofa in the sand because Dad was bringing

the furniture from the house in here. There was the standard lamp, the leather pouf, and her Kenwood Chef, too. I sat leaning against the arm of her sofa, sweat dripping beneath my jumper because of the heat lamps, as rain dripped down the cloudy panes of Dad's plastic lean-to. I was reading to her and I was reading about Fred because Vince cut out all the interviews and the pictures and sent them to us.

'"Fred Connor wants to be an enigma"' – I coughed – '"His mix of country and early American punk brings to mind the bastard son of Johnny Ramone and Gram Parsons, though Fred Connor works on being as pretty as the last. But maybe there's more. Maybe Fred Connor really is making something new and maybe, once he stops singing his mother's songs, he'll know exactly what that is."'

'What do they mean, love?' Mum laid a pale arm behind her head.

I looked at the magazine picture of Fred. It was only his face, glossy in black and white. They'd slicked back his hair; they'd done him up in black lipstick and black eye shadow. He was scowling, drips of wet on his face.

'It means they don't know what to call him, Mum. It means they don't know what he is. They don't trust him.'

'How do you mean, love?'

'I mean they don't trust that he's real. That he isn't just all made up.' I touched the picture.

'Oh, that's silly that is. Silly people do go on.' She was staring over her blanket, at something I couldn't make out. 'I want to see the field, love,' she told me, 'tell Ivan that I want to see green today. The field.' She hummed for a while without open-ing her mouth. 'There's peas in the freezer, Halo. Dark green, too. There's your Nana's cabbages. A lime maybe. I want to see that, and I want to touch it, baby. It's green today. Do you think you can get me a dock leaf?'

And so I passed the days with my mother, giving her bits of colour, reading Fred to her, as my stomach turned with sickness and my fingers itched and my dad rubbed suncream on her white shoulders, just in case the heat lamps hurt.

'I've sent them all letters,' Mum told me. It was a bright day and the fireworks were a few weeks away, but we were still in Dad's extension. 'I've also written some I won't send. You'll all have to open them when the envelope tells you.'

I shifted in the sand. I was reading American *Vogue* because Fred was in it wearing Jean-Paul Gaultier, and as Molly said on the phone, he was looking a bit of a dick.

'What, Mum?

'Letters.'

'What letters?'

'The ones Ivan posted for me. Let's see.' She brought her fingers out from under the blanket. They were shrivelled. She spent some time counting. 'A few days ago. I don't know. He's got the other letters under our bed.'

Her IV tube hit against the arm of the sofa as she reached out for a handful of the red rowan berries we'd picked for her. She held them, stared down at them with big eyes, and poked. 'Though none of you can open those ones under the bed. Not until I'm gone.' She crushed a small berry between finger and thumb. 'So they'll be coming soon, Halo baby, and you've got to make the place nice.'

I nodded.

'And you've got to make the drinks and the food and the tea.'

'Yes.'

'And then you've got to look after your father. He'll need looking after' – she squished another berry – 'he'll need all the help. Without me.'

My fingers shot into the sand and my leg muscles twitched; I thought about my next run. I'd go up and down Beggars' Hill until I couldn't even think of breath.

'When they all come, Halo, you've got a lot of things to sort out. Afterwards, I mean. What I've been thinking is' – she took a deep breath – 'I've been thinking that you've got to get on with your life.' She hummed again. She said humming and morphine and Nana's tonics helped. 'As my own mum says, "it's not a rehearsal". No. It isn't. It's for real. So you remember, love. You've got to try. Do it all. Just try.' She let the berries drop in the sand. I thought of the strawberries Dad had bought; they were in the fridge and all the way from Africa.

'Hand us that switch of red, Halo baby. And tidy up those magazines.'

I passed her a crimson square of red corduroy. I'd been to the haberdasher's to find Mum as many colours as I could. She'd been keeping to red for days now. She snatched the material like a greedy child.

'He's not a bad boy and he's not a particularly good boy either, you see.' She stared down at the lines of red. 'He's just a boy, see. And boys, well. They will be boys. And they *will* shatter you until you can never put yourself back together. Yes.' She sniffed the soft red; she gasped, catching at her breath. 'Boys'll go off and take stupid risks. Boys play in graveyards. Boys travel the world, and never call again. They make you love them, boys do. But you see, that's just their nature, Halo baby.' I felt her look at me. Maybe I was as red as the corduroy. 'That's just them being boys. You can't change them. It's like all that rock that's under us now right now, baby. Beneath your daddy's sand, beneath the grass. It is what it is, and it will always be, and that's the end of it.'

Mum had her eyes closed. Her forehead was clammy. She was concentrating.

'Thing is, I want you all to be happy. As happy as I am. As happy as I've been. And it's difficult, I know that. But you, Halo. You've got to wait. I know you have to wait. I've told you that before. You've got to wait for someone to choose *you*.' She gasped a little more, her voice drowsy as the morphine worked. 'You're like me, love. It's a pity you never took up the drums. I suppose you never took to much really. Nothing but him and those books. Running. Though you always come back, don't you? But you've got to wait, baby. That's all there is to it. Then you'll know. Then you'll be happy. You'll see.'

I tried to get the words out. 'I'm happy here, Mum.' My voice broke.

'I know, pet. I know.' She breathed, deeper than before, conserving energy, concentration; keeping what crouched in her at bay. 'But there's more. Not a different place, mind, but there's always more, love. You can't just run out in the hills all day and then come back up our drive.' She sighed, eyes still tight shut, and spoke slow. 'But you're a funny creature. You may look just like your daddy but it's me, love, it's me who you really are. And sweetheart, one day you'll play the drums. Because you're my Halo. My Diamond Star of a Halo. And you're the best of me, baby, you know that don't you?' She took a deeper breath.

'Thing was, you just didn't need me to love you best. That was all. The others did. But my Halo girl, the one that nearly killed me, you're special. You always have been.' She opened her eyes and they were big, clear and clean. 'But don't you go and tell anyone. You promise? Do you promise, Halo? Do you?'

'Yes, Mum.'

'Oh, my mouth's so dry. Give me my glass.'

I passed her her Elvis glass. There was The King transferred around it, young and pretty and in black and white. I dipped the stick in, the lolly stick with the blue mouth-sponge at the end. I placed it outside her mouth and let my mother's lips find it, like a suckling baby on a teat; first outside to soften the dry lip-skin, then inside. She bit and sucked, impatient. I wiped her chin.

'And you know,' she took a long breath, 'you know you will get over him, baby. You have to. He's a good boy. Keeps sending me plane tickets. Though your father knows I'll never go. But you. You've got so much else to offer, lovely. You'll see.' She looked back down at her square of red. 'I expect my Vincey will be first to come. He's a good boy he is. Our Molly will take her time. Our Molly has her own mind, and a will strong as your Nana's granite. Our Molly will do it all, you know.'

Sudden rain spat and a draught gasped on the hot sand. The blue day was gone. I crawled over to my mother and laid my head by her hand. She patted my crazy hair for a moment.

'Now, before Vincey gets here, go and get your father's tea will you?'

His thick arms hugged me from behind and he buried a smooth chin in my neck. Electrolysis. Vincent had spent a fortune. 'Hello darling.'

'Vince.' I turned and hugged him back.

It's funny when at last you do cry. It comes in snot and gasps and unintelligible words. I was thankful for Vince's thick black jumper. He made me drink the tea, all to myself.

'Minny still here?'

'Course' – I hiccupped from Mum's kitchen table.

'How's Dad?'

'He's out there now, with her. He's setting up the telly and video. The nurse has been, though Mum's got direct stuff now, it goes right into her. The spine I think. And there's Nana's teas.'

Vince covered his mouth. He was white.

'She's OK really, Vince. As OK as she can be and they're just living out there now. She can't really do the wheelchair any more. But it does worry me. There's a terrible draught and what if the pain get worse? They've got one of those other nurses coming, the special ones, and Nana gives her that tea that helps, but it's crazy, it's crazy, Vince.' I broke down again, a little calmer this time. 'She can't go. She's fit and healthy. She talks to me all day. She's not dying, Vince, she's telling me stuff. About cooking, about how to make a cheese sauce because she says she's starting off easy with me—'

'Shh, darling—'

'—and she calls me on the intercom and she tells me to hurry up and make the tea and how she's got a special recipe planned and she wants me to read all these books to her. Then I get there and she's asleep. She's made a list, you know. Then there's the stuff about Fred, the stuff you send, she loves that. I read it to her. And then there's the colours and—'

'Slow down, Halo.'

'—there's the things, you know? All the things she wants telling about, again and again, as if she's hanging on to them, as if she's grabbing them and it's them that aren't letting her go. I mean, last week we spent a whole afternoon on the colour of a corn on the cob and her Kenwood Chef. She had me bring it to her, she caressed it for hours. It was the touch of it, she said. Then there's the photograph albums, and the stories she makes me tell and re-tell her. The stories she has Minny tell her, Nana Lew too. And the songs. I have to play her the songs and show her the colours and tell her the stories and try and make her recipes—'

'Shhh—'

'—and, remember her blankness? There's just none of that now, she's bright and awake and she never switches off. Even with the morphine. Have you seen her eyes? Wide eyes. Clear eyes. That's what it is. She can't go, Vince. She's just too alive.'

'I know.'

'You don't.' I was trying to breathe again.

'I'm going to put you to bed now, Halo.'

'I'm not a kid, Vince.'

'You'll always be my little sis. Come on. My room? Drink your tea, then.' Vince stood over me like a prefect. 'Halo? Can I ask something?'

'What?'

'Is he coming?'

'You mean Fred?'

'Yeah.'

'No. I don't think so. I don't know, I hardly answer the phone.'

Vince looked blank for a moment. 'Come on, let's get you to bed,' he said.

I woke, cold, on Vince's satin eiderdown. The door was open and I heard Molly shouting orders from the kitchen beneath. I wanted to run down and kiss her, but Molly wouldn't like that.

'It's a mess,' I heard her say, 'it needs to be sorted. Dorian, you clean this out. I'm calling the nurse. I need answers.'

'Molly—'

'Don't "Molly" me. I need to understand what's going on, Dorian. Simple as that.' I heard a cupboard bang.

Molly made me laugh.

I remembered that impulse: the need to understand, and the anger that came before it. It was a little like Mum and her grasping hold of colour. I used to need to grasp hold of THE FACTS. Now I knew they couldn't make her better. They didn't make any difference: the facts made it worse. I turned in Vince's bed; it smelled of smoky bacon crisps.

'Go over to my nana's and make my father a hot chocolate, Dorian, he needs his sugar.' The door slammed.

I'd missed Molly. Our Molly who was fun before Fred came along. Our Molly who had had to become the sensible one: the one to protect us all. Molly was holding on as tight as Mum was to her red corduroy. They were holding on together.

I sat up and rubbed the cold condensation from the window. Bulbs gazed blue inside Mum's motorhome extension because Dad kept the day running twenty-four hours in there. It looked cosy. I could just make out the plastic blurs of Vince and Molly moving things around inside; fussing. It looked like Dad and Mum were on the sofa. I closed my eyes again.

It was the sounds of Grandma Min and Nana Lew in the kitchen below that woke me again.

'Just a sprinkle of that, love, not too much.'

'You sure, Gladys?'

'Oh, it don't need much. We'll give her the red drinking straw today. She's on her red. And the hotty. You got the kettle on?'

'Oh yes, Glad, I can't—'

'Minny, now then, don't my love—'

I heard the little squeaking spurts of my Grandma Min's crying and the soothing hum of Nana Lew. *'Go to sleep my baby, my curly headed baby,'* Nana Lew crooned.

I wiped drool from my chin and I pressed my forehead against the cold windowpane. My family looked warm beneath plastic as I listened to my small grandmother sob downstairs. Then there was the sound of a guitar because there always had to be a guitar. There was music coming from Mum's extension and it was Patti Smith, Mum's favourite. Patti Smith was singing 'Horses' from the motorhome as Minny sobbed her little squeaking sobs, like a toy dog winding down. I listened to the two sounds together. Then I heard another noise: a strange noise.

It was a thud-thud-thud, a jugga-jugga-jugga. There was no band here to record a thud-thud-thud or a jugga-jugga-jugga, and anyway it wasn't coming from our courtyard. The volume rose. It was an electric knife carving at Christmas; it was a Kenwood Chef mixing; it was a pneumatic drill coming closer and closer, and that was when I saw the lights in the sky. For a moment I wondered what Vince had put in my tea. For a moment I believed in aliens' love of farms and crop circles. The beam of light was getting lower, lower, and finally it landed in Beggars' Field. I could make out the trees at the end of our garden shaking in the blasts of wind.

I rubbed the pane again. Vince ran out of the motorhome.

I saw a helicopter.

I was downstairs and out of the kitchen door before either of my grandmothers could blink from the kitchen table.

'Mum, is it Mum?' I yelled into the night.

'What?' Wind blew at Vince's hair.

'Is it Mum? Is it taking her to the hospital?' I shouted. I didn't want this moment but I knew it would come. I ran after my brother, down towards the field. 'Why is there a bloody helicopter in our garden?' I screamed.

Vince walked on, bold and straight, and I hung back until the machine took off again, blowing leaves, branches in its wake. I waited until I saw *two* brothers walk up from the line of poplar trees, arm in arm.

Fred was thin and he'd grown his hair. It touched his shoulders. He had a beard. His black silk shirt shook in the helicopter wind and I shivered. Vince was holding Fred close: a bear with his cub.

'Look who it is, look who it is everybody,' Nana Lew cried from the kitchen door, 'it's Fred!'

My brothers were laughing. Molly came running out from Mum's oasis. We stood together and watched him walk closer.

'Hey, Molly,' said Fred.

'Hello. I thought it would be you. Only you could dis-bloody-rupt us like this.' She hugged him anyway.

He hadn't looked at me yet.

'Come in, lad!' Grandma Min yelled from the kitchen. 'You'll catch your bleeding death out there!' Then she stepped back, caught in a sob.

'How is Mum?' I heard Fred ask.

'Still here,' said Molly.

'She called me, told me to come.'

'You'll get a letter, too,' I said and he finally saw me. The wind shook him.

'Will I?'

'Yes. A letter that tells you everything.' I crossed my arms over my tight chest and I went into the kitchen to tend to my grandmothers.

Once it was light, Dad brought straw bales down from the barn
with his tractor. We sat on them in a circle round Mum while
Fred played the guitar, because today she had given up speaking.

'She wants songs about horses,' Dad told him, so Fred tried
'Wild Horses'. He played it with a country twang and his voice
was as pure and cracked as Gram Parsons'. He didn't sound like
him exactly, and he didn't sound like Mick Jagger, either. As I
sat on sharp straw and watched I decided that at last Fred
sounded like Fred.

Mum smiled from the sofa and we thought of more horse
songs: 'Crazy Horses' by the Osmonds, 'Horses' by Patti Smith.
'Stallion Boys' by Jenny Connor. Finally Mum shook her head.
After that Vince tried Edith Piaf, and he and Fred sang 'La Vie
en Rose' together. We laughed. Then Fred tried his own songs.
He tried the songs that he and Dad had written. He sang an
acoustic 'Dolly Mixtures', and Mum joined in with her hands,
moving them up and down above her blanket, her lips not quite
able to move over the words. He sang 'Candy Floss Girl' for her
too. In fact Fred wouldn't stop. I think he wanted the songs to
fill the gaps, to fill the gaps where we had to listen to Mum
gasping for breath. He sang 'Boy in the Lipstick and Polish' for
Vince, 'Girl in a Rush' for Molly. He sang a new one, 'I Am
Elvis', and we laughed again. He sang 'Pray for the Singers in
Heaven' for Dad, and another new one, 'If You Want Me You'll

Have To Find Me 'Cos You Don't Know Where I'm Gone'. As Fred sang, as he pounded Dad's old Gibson, sweat flying, we fed Mum what she wanted.

It didn't matter.

Vince let her baby-sip a perfect Martini; Dad stuck his finger in a chocolate éclair and she slowly sucked at the cream. Nana made her take those sips of her crazy tea and Molly rolled a perfect joint and held it up to Mum's lips.

Dorian had driven home.

In the end we had to smoke the joint for her; we had to blow it on her and let her sniff. Fred sang 'Goodbye Jenny', and as soon as he did we wished he hadn't. *'Good-bye, Jenny, goodbye little child of time. My little blackbird Jenny girl, hope I see you on the other side,'* he sang and we moved out of the way as Fred stood, holding the guitar. He walked closer to Mum. He sat right next to her and crooned, soft as butter.

'My little blackbird Jenny girl, I'll see you on the other side.'

Dad wiped a tuft of cream from Mum's lips and Nana and Vince had to take Grandma Min out; Minny had crumpled days ago.

At the other end of the sofa, I held my mother's foot and I rubbed. I rubbed in Body Shop peppermint-something and though her foot was cold and clammy, it was strong. I felt the small muscles, the firm bones, the tendons all move under the skin. I thought how alive my weak-as-a-kitten mother felt to touch. I rubbed, gently, as she breathed, quick and shallow; her eyes bigger than ever today.

'Here, give her this, Dad.' I held out the switch of red corduroy. It was worn down in the middle now by her constant rub. Mum took it for a moment, but it dropped in the sand.

307

'Squeeze my hand, pet,' Dad whispered to her, 'just a little squeeze.'

Fred put down the guitar. He turned away from Mum, just for a moment, and I saw he was crying like the rest of us. He wiped his face and the door opened and a bit of the cold morning came in.

'I've got more tea for her,' Nana told us as she walked in, 'stronger this time, Ivan, and just warm. Do you think she can take it?'

Dad shook his head.

'You hold her hand there, then, boy, and don't let go,' Nana told him firmly. She shooed Fred out of the way, sat on the closest bale and spoke to my mother. 'Dolly love? Dolly? Come on, it's Glad here. I want to ask you now, can you manage this for me, Dolly? See this here cup. Can you manage just a little for me? You know what it is. You asked for it, darling. If you don't want it no more then don't take it. But if you want it all now, here it is. You'll sleep, Dolly. You'll just sleep my darling.' Nana held up the cup. I saw my mother take a huge gasp of breath and lift up a white hand. The IV tube wobbled above her. She touched the edge of the cup and then she touched her lips.

'You want it, Dolly?'

Mum's eyes became wider. She smiled half a smile, just one side of face and her dry lips. I wondered if she could swallow.

'We're going to have to lift you up a little for this, Dolly love.' Nana motioned to Dad and Fred. Dad pulled Mum up and she groaned. Fred lifted her head, and Nana placed the delicate teacup at her lips. Wide-eyed, Mum took a little. I heard the birds outside. Another day. Moving on. Sure and lethal as the jaws of a plough chewing through our red earth.

I rubbed my mother's feet.

'Remember how we picked these together, Dolly? When you first came back from the hospital? You and me out in the Bastard's garden, picking the poppy heads and the pennyroyal and the nightshade in the sunshine and you remember what you asked me then? Yes, take a little more, there you go, my darling.' Dad and Fred were staring at the ground; their faces looked like they were screaming but no sound came out. 'Now,' Nana continued, 'Dolly, what you said to me was, "I'm picking it now, Glad, because I'm in control of this, and when the time comes I want you to add a little extra of your special stuff and give it to me. You do one of your special teas with this and you give it to me and it will all be easier. Not Ivan, he couldn't. Not the kids, I wouldn't. Not my mother, her heart's too small. You, Glad, you're the only one who'd do it right." That's what you said to me so here I am, my beautiful, perfect Dolly Llewelyn. Bottoms up.'

The morning after young Ivan Comfort Llewelyn had at last discovered more than he should of Dolly Halcyon Palmer on that fairground wasteland of Tiger Bay, he opened the caravan door and the world was a little different. In truth he was expecting her small mother with a shotgun, but when Ivan Comfort Llewelyn opened that door, he saw nothing. At least it was almost nothing because after all, what does nothing look like? No, what he saw was the wasteland, their wasteland. What he saw was their beautiful wasteland because the fair had gone. There was no Hitler, no Mussolini, no cap guns and shooting, no stall to get a dictator right in the puss! There was only the wasteland of Tiger Bay and the rosebay willowherb that sent puffs of white-haired and silken seeds off into the next current of air. From the caravan steps, Ivan Comfort Llewelyn watched those white seeds dance in the breeze and then he caught one between his fingers because he was quick as a bat. Ivan Comfort Llewelyn turned the seed between finger and thumb and he let it go. The pretty silk hairs caught the warm wind and it was lost again. Ivan turned then; he turned back into the caravan. He smiled at his Dolly – perched so pretty on the end of her little bed – and he closed the caravan door and he locked it. Ivan Comfort locked it from the inside.

TRACK LISTING FOR DOLLY HALCYON PALMER-LLEWELYN
FROM IVAN COMFORT LLEWELYN

Horses – Patti Smith

Stallion Boys – Tequila

Sad-Eyed Lady of the Lowlands – Bob Dylan

War Pigs – Black Sabbath

Wuthering Heights – Kate Bush

Wild Horses – The Flying Burrito Brothers

Get It On – Marc Bolan and T.Rex

Oh! You Pretty Things – David Bowie

Bohemian Rhapsody – Queen

Candy Floss Girl – Fred Connor/Ivan Comfort Llewelyn

Don't – Elvis Presley

Magnolia – J.J. Cale

After the Goldrush – Neil Young

After the Goldrush – Prelude

Oh My Love – John Lennon

$1000 Wedding – Gram Parsons

Lady Grinning Soul – David Bowie

Dolly Mixtures – Fred Connor/Ivan Comfort Llewelyn

While My Guitar Gently Weeps – George Harrison

In My Hour of Darkness – Gram Parsons

Blue – Joni Mitchell

Simple Twist of Fate – Bob Dylan

Where Have All The Flowers Gone? – The Searchers

Black Girl – The Four Pennies

I'll Wait For My Love – The O'Boyles

Be-Bop-A-Lula – Gene Vincent and His Blue Caps

When Will I See You Again? – The Three Degrees

The Needle and the Damage Done – Neil Young

She – Gram Parsons

Hoodoo Voodoo Mama – Fred Connor/Ivan Comfort Llewelyn

Angie – The Rolling Stones

Sweet Thing – Van Morrison

Trouble of the World – Mahalia Jackson

Sarah – Thin Lizzy

Sunday Morning – The Velvet Underground

You've Got to Hide Your Love Away – The Beatles

Sweet Marie – Hothouse Flowers

Take Another Little Piece of My Heart – Janis Joplin and Big

Brother and the Holding Company

Fool to Cry – The Rolling Stones

Sign on the Window – Bob Dylan

Dream a Little Dream of Me – Cass Elliot

Where Do You Go To (My Lovely)? – Peter Sarstedt

13

By end of the week Nana Lew said they were coming from far and wide, but Vince said it was mostly Wales. The press had invaded because of Fred, so we hid him in one of Nana's bedrooms while she brick-dusted and booby-trapped her Big House.

Dad insisted on doing everything alone. He went to the undertakers. He went to the priest and he yelled. He went to the vicar and he yelled. Vince said if there'd been a rabbi close by, or an imam, Dad would have yelled at them too.

Dad and I argued.

While Mum was laid out and beautiful in Nana's parlour, we stood in the cold hall and we had words. I closed the parlour door on the two nanas, Vince, Molly and Fred, while Dad stared up at the stained-glass John the Baptist.

'We all need to go tomorrow, Dad. All of us need to go to the crematorium. As a family,' I whispered.

'It's just her and me, Halo.'

'What about us, Dad?'

'You have each other.'

'You have us, too.'

'You have the rest of your lives and whoever you chose to spend it with. I don't have Dolly.'

'Neither do we.'

'It was me and Dolly and that was it.' He kept his eyes on the colours in the window.

'So why in the blazes did you have us at all, Dad? Answer me that.'

'I loved her best, Halo. I loved her best.'

I banged my fist on Nana's telephone table and I thought of swearing at him. Nana's black-faced miners gazed down at me, stern fathers, and the coal dust settled. 'Well you won't stop Grandma Min going, Dad, that's for sure. You can bully us but you can't bully her. Mum was her world.'

'I have to do it alone.'

'Well you tell Min that. I'm not.'

The next day Grandma Min didn't go; she couldn't go. Her heart was dead, she told us, and Nana Lew carried her up the stairs to a fresh new bed.

The four of us, Vince, me, Molly and Fred – the Rockfarm kids – were sitting on Vince's bed again, in Mum and Dad's house. We were squeezed together, for space and warmth; we were wearing black and we were waiting for our father to come back from the crematorium. I stared at the flying ducks he'd nailed up; I stared at David Bowie as Major Tom above the fire grate, and I wondered if my parents' love was a selfish thing.

'She looked beautiful yesterday,' Fred said.

'She always did,' Vince smiled.

'Yes,' Molly agreed, and from the very end of the bed, she flicked her hair.

It was Nana who had insisted on an open coffin and we didn't mind. We wanted to see Mum's beauty one more time, in the flesh, even if it was flesh that no longer worked. The night before, we'd stood around the coffin in the parlour, rubbing bits of her – hands, feet, cheeks – and it wasn't so bad: she was still

she. Dad had cut a thick strand of her black hair, his own rooster crest shaking along with his hands and the stainless-steel
scissors.

'What time is everyone here, Halo?' Molly asked.

'Nana told them six.'

'Is Grandma Min still in bed?' Molly had taken to Grandma
Min in the last week.

'Yes, the doctor's with her. Poor Min,' I sighed, though I was
glad she was out of the picture, sleeping with sweet dreams of
her Dolly. Min had hardly spoken a word and that scared me
more than her foghorning about the place.

'Dorian and Rhysie are up in the courtyard setting everything up,' Molly added, 'the food, the beds, the drink. It's all
under control, Halo.'

I shrugged.

Fred had his arm round me on one side, and I had Vince on
the other; they sort of met round the back. Fred was a silent
crier: he looked prettier with wet cheeks and blurred black eyeliner. He gasped and suddenly leant over his knees; he curled
his feet up on Molly, his head in my lap. 'I'm so tired, Lo-Lo.'

I stroked his hair.

'I want it to be just us and I want to sleep.'

'Shh—'

'I don't want anyone else.'

'Well tough,' Molly told him, 'Mum's friends are coming.
She'd want you to make an effort. You're going to have to put on
a brave face and mingle. Do you think the rest of us want to?'

Fred looked up at her and put his fingers in his ears. Vince
smiled.

I heard the car first and I felt Vince freeze next to me. The front door slammed in the wind and we bolted off the bed like excited kids; excited kids expecting holiday gifts. Fred rumbled down the stairs first and we pushed and bounded into the front room, arms grabbing, wanting to be in front. We stopped in front of our father: adult again.

'She's hot,' Dad said. 'I had to put her down there. Feel.' He pointed at the kitchen table where a black thing sat. Dad unzipped the carrying case and there was our mother. The urn looked like a 1970s ice bucket. Molly burst into tears and grasped hold of Fred. Vince and I held out our hands like foolish children walking towards a hot grate. We touched our mum, fingertips first. It wasn't truly hot, it was warm; it was comfort. I shivered as the cold rain blew on our windowpanes, and I was glad that my beautiful mother took the chill from my hands.

'We're going upstairs,' Dad told us, 'we've got packing to do,' and he picked our mother up, pressed her under one arm and slipped out of the room, easy as a gust of wind.

'Where are you going, Dad?' Vince tried, wary. We looked at one another.

'Everywhere! Nowhere! None of your business!' Dad shouted down at us. He slammed their bedroom door shut.

It was a spread to make my mother proud, Molly and I had seen to that. We'd cleaned and dusted the studios and chalets. We'd copied out every recipe in Dolly Halcyon Palmer-Llewelyn's *Book of Dishes*. This was the book she'd kept safe behind a grille above her cooker; the book she wrote her recipes in, a book where she matched taste with sound for the musicians who had come to depend on her.

I was proud of my barbecued spare ribs (that weren't barbecued at all). Molly sucked her lemon syllabub fingers and smiled. We'd set it all up in the long rehearsal room and we'd had to clean out the summer cobwebs, because it had been months since a band was here. Still, the beds in the chalets were made up for those who'd need them, and the ducks quacked quietly on the courtyard pond. The chickens stood in a miserable huddle by the stables, as if they knew.

Dad was still down at the house packing when the first guests arrived. There were so many faces I simply nodded at the studio door and handed them a glass. I suppose some were famous. Some were certainly rock stars.

'We'll miss her.'

'She'll be cooking in the sky.'

'She's in a better place.'

'Maybe it was easier this way.'

'She'll always be with us.'

'Beautiful Dolly.'

'Oh, man.'

I let the platitudes and the tears wash over me. Someone told me Mum was only in the other room, waiting for us. I tried not to spit.

I watched Dorian in his rented suit as he goshed and gasped at the famous faces. I watched some of these faces sit in the corners of the vast room and sob like children: my mother had nurtured these musicians and they seemed thankful. Nana circulated with plates of cake; sugar for the shock. Vince sat in the centre of the room, playing his Wurlitzer keyboard: he played Gram Parsons' 'She' and wore a calf-length black dress, very Katharine Hepburn in the shoulders and the pleats.

I listened to the song and melted a little.

'Halo. Oh, Halo, come here to me pet, I'm so, so sorry.' I turned to see Nuala O'Boyle. She was almost the same, a little wider, a little less red on top, but she was Nuala. 'It wasn't long ago your parents came over to see us. We had such a blast. I'm so sorry, love. We had prayers said but sometimes—'

I cut her off with another hug: I knew if I heard one more death platitude I'd have to put my trainers on and run.

'Halo!'

'Halo!'

'Halo!'

The triplets disengaged themselves from Molly and ran to me. Molly said watching us was like watching a nest of red snakes twist and turn: me, Niamh, Siobhan and Aifric.

'Halo.'

'Come here to me.'

'Halo.'

I gasped for breath at their frenzied hugs.

Siobhan's breasts seemed bigger, her hips too: Aifric was skinnier, and Niamh, my Niamh, was blooming.

'Yeah, I know, I'm due in three weeks, can you believe it?'

'Niamh—'

'I'm not married either. Daddy won't talk to me. It's not like I'm not with the father, we're crazy about each other, just don't want be married.' She looked into the crowded room. 'Shit, is that really Hellmouth there?'

'Yes.'

'And that's—?'

'Yup.'

'Wow. Is Fred here?'

'Yes.'

318

'He came all the way from America?'

'Yup.'

'He still as crazy as he ever was?'

'I guess.'

'It's not turned his head, all the fame stuff?'

'Nope.' I creased my nose. 'And he's not *that* famous, Niamh.'

'Ah come on, there's kids in Tokyo know who Fred Connor is. You still protecting him, Halo?'

I shook my head. 'Not any more.'

Niamh coughed, she looked down at the floor. 'I'm so sorry, Halo.' Her lip shook, 'I just don't know what to say.'

'That's OK.'

'No it's not—'

'Honestly.'

'You're my friend, I should make it better.'

'No one can, sweetheart, but bless you for trying.'

Niamh took my hand and smiled. Then she tugged and she led me outside to the flagstone patio and the November night. There were fireworks banging in the distance and for a moment the sky lit up.

'Halo,' she said slowly, 'I've someone to show you.'

For an odd moment I thought it might be another Mum, all new and put back together again. Niamh pulled me to her and whispered in my ear as we walked, 'Now he's come all this way, Halo, so be nice, OK?'

I looked into her too-blue eyes and frowned, I looked down at the tight ridge of her dress where a new baby sat, and then I heard a voice I still knew.

'Hello,' it said, and by the time I turned and saw her brother Brendan, Niamh was gone. Brendan flicked a cigarette into the

319

night, it curved like a firework and he walked towards me. Brendan's hair was longer, conker-coloured and in his face. I tried to count up the years since we last met: nine thereabouts.

'I won't ask you how you are,' he said.

I was glad. He kept coming though, as if he was going to walk right through me, and then his arms were round me, squeezing. I felt his face in my neck as he leant over. I felt his heartbeat and sniffed his scent of mint chocolates and smoke. He came up for air, stepped back, his hands on my shoulders. 'You're looking lovely.'

'Oh, yeah, right.'

'You are.'

I smoothed down my black jumper, my black jeans. I touched my tight stomach and I sat down on the edge of the wet flag walkway. The ducks were quacking and from inside I heard the whine of a National guitar.

'Fred,' I said.

'Hmm?'

'That'll be Fred playing that.'

'Yeah. He's everywhere. The boy's done well.' Brendan sat down next to me and, quietly, he put an arm around me. I heard the tight denim on his arm creak and I put my head on his shoulder.

'My dad's not here yet,' I told him.

'That's not surprising.'

'Why?'

'He probably wants to be alone. I remember how your parents were. The way they were with each other. That was some kind of love. I think—' He stopped for a moment as a red firework exploded in the sky. '—I think when you love that much you just

320

have to take your time.' A mass of white sparks fizzed and popped above us. 'Crazy,' Brendan said, 'you lot and fecking Bonfire Night. Guy Fawkes on the fire. That is so *harsh*—'

He was trying to make me laugh, so I did. It didn't last long. 'They're not my lot, Brendan.' I tapped a sneaker into the mud. 'I don't know who my lot is any more.' I let my body move against his as I heard Fred sing 'Dolly Mixtures' from inside. I let Brendan play with my ringlets.

'You're still the most beautiful girl I've ever seen,' Brendan said.

'And you're still mental.'

'Halo, I mean it.'

'Don't be silly. You don't know me.'

'I'd like to.'

'You don't know what a mess I am, what—'

Brendan leant forward, and almost a decade after the first time, he kissed me. It was like dark wood. He tasted of Golden Virginia and honey; his stubble itched.

'You're older than me,' I told him.

'That doesn't matter any more.'

'I'm in love with somebody else.'

'You'll get over it,' he whispered.

Brendan kissed me and this time I kissed him back. I kissed him to get the touch of Fred from my mind and my skin. I kissed him to forget about my mother. I sniffed his neck, his earlobes, the backs of his hands; I licked him to fill myself up with singed hair and tobacco and to rub out every thought of oranges and musk.

'Slow down, Halo. Slow down,' he tried to say.

I wouldn't.

'Halo, please, I can't—'

'Don't you want me to?'

'God yes. Oh God, yes. But not now, not tonight. It's—'

I stopped. 'It's my mother's funeral.'

'Yes.' He held my head in his hands, keeping me still. 'Yes,' he said, and it echoed through the courtyard.

The studio door opened and the party inside blasted out: just for a moment. The door slammed.

'Lo-Lo?'

Fred was standing over us.

'Who's that, Lo-Lo?'

I looked up. 'It's Brendan. You remember, Fred. Niamh's brother? Siobhan's brother? Aifric's brother? One of the O'Boyles?'

Fred was silent. He was so big now: tall and bearded, but he had the same look as the day he held Molly's hockey stick and swiped at Dean Turley's delicate parts. 'Can I have a word, Lo-Lo?'

'What is it?'

'In private.'

Fred and I hadn't had much in private since the night in Nana's polytunnel, over two months ago. We hadn't had much in private since the night he came back in that ridiculous helicopter. Since then, Fred had stuck to Vince like Velcro, he and Vince slept in Vince's old room in the gatehouse; like sentinels keeping an eye on Dad.

'Why now, Fred?'

He bit his lip. 'Because I'm leaving. Please, Lo-Lo.'

I stared out at the chickens by the stables. I shrugged. 'All right.'

Brendan's grip got tighter.

'Brendan, you're staying, right?'

'Yes.'

'I'll see you later then,' and I stood up.

Dad hadn't done much to the barn and the corrugated-iron roof rattled in the wind: rust flaked away easy as old paint. The farm machinery piled up by the bales was generations old, and rats lived in the guts, building homes and fat-bellied generations. I sat down on a straw bale, my arms crossed tight. Fred sat next to me and we were quiet. Fireworks exploded over the hill and in the town, and every now and then I started at the noise.

Fred pulled my hand from under my arm. I resisted and he pulled again. Once he had it he brought it to his own lap. My muscles tensed, hard. Fred brought my hand to his soft lips and kissed it.

'Don't, Fred—'

'Why?'

'One time is enough.'

The fizz-bangs of fireworks popped green and blue, lighting up the tall hills. Fred kissed my hand again, palm up. I felt his hot breath between the creases. My back arched and my stomach twinged. 'Fred,' I said. 'Fred, listen.'

'I want to make love to you, Lo-Lo. Now.' He kissed between my thumb and forefinger. I heard him sigh.

It took strength I didn't have, but I put a hand either side of his face and I lifted it to mine. He was so fucking beautiful, even with the beard.

'Fred,' I told him, 'Fred. I love you. I'll always love you. Too much.' I smiled. 'But sweetheart, you *are* my brother. You are.

323

You're as much my brother as Vince is. And I *want* you to be my brother, Fred.'

I'd never said so many words to him in one go. Not even when I was drunk. I felt a little dizzy, a little not-myself.

'You fancy Brendan, don't you?'

I let go of his face. 'Don't be childish. It's got nothing to do with Brendan.' I kicked a shoe against the bale of hay. 'It's us. You know that. It's always been us. Listen, you don't know, you were too little, but I've been – I've been like this for *years*, Fred, for almost all my life and I need to stop.'

'You think I don't know that, Lo-Lo?'

'No, I don't think you do. I don't think you put yourself in anyone else's shoes, Fred. They're just your shoes. Always your shoes. Nice shoes, but—'

'Don't joke, Lo-Lo.'

There was a white fizz-bang in the black sky and I thought how Mum would like that.

'I remember too, Lo-Lo. You think that I don't see everything you see. But when I was little do you really think I didn't see every fucking ghost in Nana's house? Just like you? Do you think I didn't recognize you as soon as I could open my eyes and focus? Do you think I didn't stick to you like glue because of that?'

'Oh, Fred, it's not one of your songs. It's not fiction. This is real. Don't talk in riddles like bloody Nana please.'

'You don't believe me.'

'If I did believe you, would it help?' I watched more white sparks reflect in the black puddles.

'Come with me, Lo-Lo.'

'Where?'

'I don't know.'

'Oh, that's helpful.'

'Lo-Lo, please. We fit, you know we do. We're the same person, we—'

'Exactly. It's not healthy.'

'Who says?'

'Me, that's who, Fred. Me.' I pulled out a long straw stalk and chewed; it tasted of sweet muck, it tasted of home. 'Fred, you know I'd never leave here,' I turned to him and his eyes flashed, 'and I know that's why you're asking me this. Don't get me wrong, I don't mind. I love you so much. But Fred, we'd kill each other. You'd grind me down to bone, to ash, just like Nana's monks, like her capel. Just like—'

I was done.

Fred was quiet. He stabbed a heel into the ground. 'Lo-Lo, do you really think I haven't fought all this time, I haven't searched for different ways of loving you?' He put his arm around me and I leant into his brown neck. I sniffed. I let my arms hug around him and we listened to the rats, making homes, making mischief.

'Come with me, Lo.'

'I can't.'

'Make love to me then, right now. Just one more time.'

I laughed. 'I can't, Fred.'

'Why not?'

'It won't be enough. It will never be enough. You know that.'

'I'm going away,' he whispered.

'Where?'

'I don't know, somewhere really cold. I'd like to live somewhere cold.'

'Scotland's cold. Alaska's cold.'

'Maybe.' Fred kissed the crown of my head. 'You know Mum was right, Dolly I mean.'

'You can call her "Mum", Fred.'

'Well Mum once told me you were hard as nails. She said you were contrary, you know? How some people are soft under a hard surface, how it's all show, like Nana. But Mum said you were the other way round. Soft on the outside and hard as flint underneath. And you are, Lo-Lo.' He put his hand under my chin and lifted my face to his. He kissed my lips, gentle but full. 'I can't break you, can I?'

'No.'

He smiled. 'Not even with my good looks and my money?'

I pinched his side. 'No.'

A barn owl swooped down and the rats were quiet. 'Fred?' I said against his cheek. 'Be careful, won't you?'

'Hmmm?'

'I don't want you in Dad's prayers. Not ever. Be careful. No prayers, Fred, no rock'n'roll dead.'

I felt him laugh. 'I am careful, Lo-Lo. Jenny Connor wasn't, but Fred Connor is.'

The party was spilling out into the courtyard below us. I heard men yell 'Dolly!' into the night. None of us had seen Dad. 'In My Hour of Darkness' played, Gram Parsons and Emmylou Harris singing sweet and brittle harmonies on Dad's old CD; it was followed by them singing 'Love Hurts'.

I wanted to tell Gram and Emmylou that *everything* hurt.

'I'm going down to check on Dad and Grandma Min,' I said.

'Are you going to find that Brendan bloke, too?'

I shrugged against him and Fred was silent. Fred was sulk-

326

ing because Fred was used to getting his own way.

'Is there nothing I can say, Lo?'

'No.'

'Nothing I can do?' He hugged me tighter.

'No, sweetheart.'

Of course on the night of my mother's funeral I didn't realize it, but Fred Connor had done quite enough to me already.

My father left with the glow-in-the-dark globe of the world in the early hours of the morning. He was off to find things, the note said. It also said 'don't let me down, Halo'. Dad took a little sprinkle of Mum in a vial around his neck. The rest of her he left here on this mantelpiece.

In the mornings I make Nana's tea to settle my sick stomach, I mix my muesli and I talk to Mum. After all, we are Welsh and I like to look at her up on that mantelpiece in Nana's parlour. I look at her and I feel a little jealous of the way she was loved. I chew tasteless oats and sticky seeds, alone. I splash my face with cold water in the kitchen, and I stretch for my morning run.

14

After Dad left we closed up their house. Nana turned the water off with a spanner but we kept the cracks of the windows open. Nana said it was so the spirits and the air could move about.

We closed up the motorhome, too.

We left the sand and the sofa outside under Dad's plastic and wood extension; we left Mum's records and her turntable there too. Over the following months I'd watch the extension turn green; a pleasant green. It was a sea-moss green that Mum would have loved.

Grandma Min was back in Spain, but not even her young husband Carlos could cure her. Molly had left, and just like he said, Fred was gone.

As December crackled on, I worked on the chalets. We had no bookings so I changed the colour of our walls. A good base magnolia was what it needed. Nana brought me tea and I sniffed it before sipping, still sick. She stepped over the dust-sheets, dipped her fingers in the Dulux and said I was doing a grand job. At nights I went through Dad's past studio bookings. I wrote letter after letter, because I was old-fashioned. I composed ads for Rockfarm at Nana's kitchen table and by the time my first booking came, Vince was gone, and Nana, Rhysie and I were alone at Rockfarm.

When the phone rang for the second time in one day, I thought I'd struck gold, but the American voice on the other end of the line seemed to be asking me if I'd seen Fred. I was used to this. It would be a fan or the press. I hung up and unplugged the phone. The next night when I walked back into Nana's hall – after a day trying to fathom Dad's G-O-D computer – I plugged the phone back in and it rang, almost immediately. The same voice asked me the same question.

'Is he with you? Don't hang up.'

'Who is this?'

'Tommy.'

'Tommy who?'

'Tommy Geolla, your goddamn brother's manager. Now I'm asking you, lady, you seen him?'

'No.'

'For real?'

'Of course. Why?'

'He's disappeared.'

'What do you mean, "disappeared"?'

'I ain't heard from him for a month.'

'He'll be somewhere. He's probably with his dad in America.'

'Abraham hasn't seen him. Fred Connor flew back to the States on the fourteenth, and nothing since.'

I sat down on the chaise in the hall and pulled my trainers off; I held the phone between my shoulder and neck. 'Mr Geolla, I really shouldn't worry. Fred always turns up.' I pulled off my socks: my feet were sweet with sweat, and swollen. 'But if he comes here I'll make sure he gives you a ring, thank you so much, goodbye.'

The thing was, Nana and me, we didn't watch the TV. We rarely read a newspaper and anyway, if anything needed to be passed on, Vince or Molly would tell us. I knew Fred was OK. I knew Fred was somewhere. And if he had escaped, well, so much the better for him. I was getting fat, I was living at Rockfarm, and mostly, I was happy.

'They say he's disappeared, gone for good. Like Elvis,' Nana said as she topped and tailed a swede.

'Elvis died on the loo, Nana.'

'Shh!' She jabbed a knife at a picture of Elvis.

'Well he did.'

She motioned at Elvis above her jukebox and put her fingers to her lips. I laid out the two cabbages I'd just dug from the garden.

'Fred's just buggered off somewhere, Nana. He'll turn up. In a limo or a helicopter or a bloody ship. It'll carve its way up our drive, don't worry.' I sniffed and pushed on the knife.

'He's got style, that lad. The helicopter was good.'

'Don't Nana, I can't talk about that' – I stood back from the soil and the newspaper and the green of the cabbage leaf – 'not yet.'

'Minny called this morning.'

'That's nice.'

'She's said I should visit her in Spain. She said she'd keep an eye out for Ivan.' Nana sighed.

'He'll be back by Christmas, Nana Lew. Dad would never miss Christmas. Don't worry.'

'Christmas is on Monday, sunbeam.'

We'd had a postcard from Las Vegas. Dad wrote,

Dear Family,
We are fine. There are so many colours here for

330

your mother, especially at night. It sparkles.
We'll be home presently.
Your loving Dolly and Ivan.

'He will be here, Nana, you'll see.'

She looked up at me, and her flat face glistened. 'To be honest, sunbeam, I don't mind if he don't come. I love him rotten but he's got to find his own way. Just like your Fred.'

'Fred's not "my Fred", Nana.'

'Yes he is, love.' She sniffed and cut off another swede top. 'Especially now.'

'Especially now what?'

'Does he know about that?'

It was just a little point, a gesture across the table. My grandmother flicked the blade of her knife downwards and towards my belly.

I cut into the cabbage.

'I said, does he know about that, sunbeam?'

'About what?' I focused on the ribbons of green, the way they turned from dark to almost white in the centre.

'About your condition?'

'What condition?' I didn't take my eyes from the cabbage. 'Stop bloody talking in riddles, Nana.'

'All right, sunbeam, if that's what you want I'll speak plain. Does Fred know about you being pregnant?'

The green tops of the swede in the scraps bowl were frilly, soft to touch. I felt sicker than I had for the last few months. 'Nana. Don't be silly.'

'I'm not the one being silly, love.'

I decided to look up at her. 'You're talking nonsense.'

'Am I?' Nana put down the knife. She stood up and held my shoulders. She leant over and whispered in my ear, 'Sunbeam, let me tell you. You are blooming and you never bloom. You're bigger round the middle. To me you look about three months' gone, maybe more. You got colour in your cheeks, you throw up in the mornings, you cry a lot—'

'My mother died, Nana.'

'—and that packet of tampons hasn't been used in the upstairs bathroom since Molly left.'

'I don't use tampons.'

'Are you pregnant, Halo?'

I put my knife down. I stared at our reflections in the early-dark window. I felt the tears rise. I felt like a child. I whined. 'How am I meant to know, Nana?'

'Oh, sunbeam. Your curse stopped?'

My grandmother was nothing if not direct. I took a deep breath. 'Nana, I don't have regular periods. I never have. Running I suppose.'

'Then we'll have to get you to the doctor's, do this properly.'

I shrugged against her strong hands. I'd do whatever she asked. It was easier. She sat back at her station. 'You sure it's Fred's?'

'Nana!'

'What?'

'I've only done it once.'

'Once is enough.'

'Don't.'

'When was it then?'

'August, end of August.'

'So that's—' Nana counted on her fingers, her tongue

332

between her teeth. It took some time. 'I thought there was a chance, you and that Irish boy?'

'No.'

'He liked you.'

'Nana, please stop it. Let's just do this.' I nodded at the vegetables. 'Put some music on, will you?'

Nana pressed a remote control; she hardly touched her jukebox now. Before I could cut the top off an onion, Elvis was singing 'Wooden Heart'.

'Do you feel different, sunbeam?'

'Nana, please—'

I cleared up the newspaper that covered the table, I thought about vegetable soup, vegetable tagine, because that was all we had right now. I tried to think about cabbage and swede, but all that came into my mind was an answer to my nana's question.

Did I feel different? Yes.

I put the newspaper in the scraps bin. 'Nana, please don't tell anyone.'

'Tell them what, sunbeam?' And she looked up and she winked.

My father did miss Christmas. He missed New Year, while I missed the sharp smell of him and the golden toast that wasn't made. Molly stayed with us until Boxing Day, alone. She told me it was good I was putting on weight at last, and that I should cut my hair.

'Are you a lesbian, Halo?'

'What?'

'I don't mind. I don't care if I'm the only heterosexual sibling.'

'Oh Molly, no. I'm not a lesbian. Though I've never tried it, so maybe I could be one day.'

'What's the matter with you then?' Molly wasn't as good at guessing as my Nana Lew.

Vince didn't come for Christmas or New Year. He said he was too sad and all he wanted was a bottle of Malibu and his old vinyl. Before December was through he did call me, he called me to say there was a rumour that Fred really had disappeared for good.

'Who told you that?'

'It's in the papers.'

'Well what does that mean, Vince?'

'I don't know.'

'"Disappeared for good"? Does it mean abducted by aliens? Does it mean the police are looking for him? Does it mean he's dead?'

'I've had a call from Dad.'

I looked up at the tick-tocking grandmother clock. 'Why did he call you?' I listened to the old clicks of Nana's phone.

'He called me and he said he was going to find him.'

'Who?'

'Oh keep up, Halo. Fred. Dad said he was going to find Fred. What he actually said was he and Mum were going to find Fred.'

'Christ.'

'Aren't you just a little bit worried?'

'No.'

'I mean none of us have heard from him. Neither has Abraham. You know Dad went to see him?'

'Abraham?'

334

'Yes.'

'We just got a postcard from Las Vegas. We don't get phone calls here.'

'Don't be like that, Halo.'

'Sorry.'

'Well Dad's been all around. He says he's got some sort of American sky pass.'

'Oh.'

'Anyway, he went to see Abraham and Fred hasn't contacted anyone. I mean, Halo, he could be dead in a ditch somewhere. He could have got himself beaten up. He could have—'

'It's OK, Vince.'

'What do you mean "it's OK"?'

'It's OK. He's just off somewhere. He's fine. He's taking a rest.'

'Have you heard from him?'

'No.'

Vince sighed. 'It's Halo and her psychic powers, is it?'

'I just know that Fred is fine.'

'They'll have a detective after him by now, the manager will—'

'Oh Vince, do try *not* to be dramatic.'

He breathed heavily. I slapped my bare feet on the tiles, waiting.

'Halo?'

'Yes?'

'Is it true?'

I looked up at one of Nana's grinning miners. 'She told you, didn't she?' I sighed. 'Did she tell Molly?'

'I doubt it. Molly thinks you're a lesbian. So is it true?'

335

'That I'm a lesbian?'

'No, that you're—'

'Yes it's true, Vince.' It was almost four months' true; I'd done the maths. 'Nana and I did a test. I'm having a bloody baby.'

He screamed and I had to hold out the phone. 'Oh, Halo! You don't do things by halves do you? Oh, I'm going to be an uncle! And have you told him? Oh, you have to tell him. You are keeping it aren't you, Halo?'

'I don't see why not.'

'And you'll ring him?'

'How?'

'On the phone. I know you've gone feral down there, Halo, but—'

'He's disappeared, remember?'

Somehow the clicks were louder. I heard Vince breathe: slowly, deeply. 'Sorry?'

'Vince?'

'I—'

'What?'

'I was talking about Brendan, Halo. I thought it was Brendan.'

I looked up at the same miner and his grin twinkled now. 'No, Vince. I thought Nana told you? It wasn't. It wasn't Brendan at all.'

I could hear his breath.

'Fred?'

'Who else?'

'Shit. Halo.'

15

The Llewelyn family are at heart engineers. Not musicians, not managers, not producers or roadies, and certainly not rock stars. We are engineers and we like to fiddle with things behind the scenes, get down and dirty with a toolbox: get things right, if we can.

By Valentine's Day I was more than pot-bellied: I was a skinny-legged but broody-bodied chicken, though I still ran. In fact I was better at running – suddenly I had ballast and I could leap along ridges. The old hill farmers yelled at me; they said if their sheep jumped about like that, there'd be no lambs come the spring.

At last I was the only one in my family who had changed: everyone else was the same. Nana and Rhysie made love long into the night, even if Nana was holding onto her eighties by the skin of her teeth. Dad was still out in the world with Dolly and his glow-in-the-dark globe. Fred was still missing, and Molly and Dorian visited when they could, which wasn't often; then Molly visited when Dorian couldn't, which was best. Vince – my lovely Vince – was quiet. He faded. At first he wouldn't talk to me. Then he took to singing songs down the phone, more melancholy than he could manage. Finally he talked about moving.

'I want to live in New York, Halo.'
'Why New York?'

'I don't know.'

'What is it, Vince?'

'Where is he, Halo? Don't you care? Don't you care at all?'

'Fred's fine, Vince.'

'So you know something I don't, is that it? He's calling you but he's not calling me. It's the usual is it, Halo?'

'Shh. Vince.'

Dad had no luck either. His postcards came from Reno, from Cape Cod, from North Dakota, South Dakota, San Francisco, all signed 'Dolly and Ivan'.

We're going North, Seattle then Alaska maybe.
Dolly has always wanted to see a bear.

Then one day other letters came, addressed to each one of us and from a lawyer called Pilgrim Deedes. That name made my Nana laugh, though the letters didn't.

'Silly boy,' she said from the head of her kitchen table, 'he had no need to do that.'

'At least Vince will stop worrying now, Nana. We know Fred's alive.'

'Hmm.'

What I wanted to say was, at least we know for certain Fred wasn't hanging from a barbed-wire fence getting pecked to death by birds. He wasn't slumped over himself, purple and gone for ever in some studio. No, Fred was most definitely out there because Fred had instructed Pilgrim Deedes (and Nana still laughed) to sign over the rights to his songs to us. They were carefully divided. There had been thought.

'Girl in a Rush' was for Molly.

'Hoodoo Voodoo Mama', 'My Beloveds' and 'I am Elvis' were for Nana.

'Candy Floss Girl', 'Dead Horses', 'Dolly Mixtures' and 'Pray for All the Singers in Heaven' were for Dad.

'Boy in the Lipstick and Polish' was Vince's.

'If You Want Me You'll Have to Find Me 'Cos You Don't Know Where I'm Gone', 'Red-Headed Girl With Love on her Mind' and 'Summer of '77' were for me.

There were more of course, because Fred and Pilgrim signed over the lot, and almost immediately the cheques arrived.

We needed an accountant. For a while having money made my family unhappy. That was, until we forgot about it and went back to how we were. I ran the hills and as I saw the spring flourish, I tried to think of no one.

It was when Nana had hushed phone calls that I began to suspect: it was when Molly would suddenly arrive at the weekend and ask me about the future of 'my child', because I couldn't hide anything now. The only thing was, I didn't know what to suspect.

One day there was a phone call and it was from Dad.

'Oh, my Ivan!' Nana cried and I ran to the hall. I waited, impatient as a child in a lavatory queue: I wanted Dad back, I wanted his shrugs, his bouncing hair, his freckled hands that built this place. It wasn't just the golden toast I missed.

I held the receiver. 'When are you coming home, Dad?'

'One day, pet. Don't fret.'

'But, Dad—'

'Don't fuss, Dolly and I, we need a little more time, a little more time together, nutmeg.'

'Dad, please—'

But he wouldn't let me finish and in the end I sat on Nana's chaise longue and I let Dad speak.

'—and there, Halo, was this huge grizzly, no word of a lie. Up on his hind legs he was, coming to your mother and me, and that's when this Indian bloke as big as the bloody bear itself leaps out and shoots a gun above its head. By Christ, that was a moment. Marshall's his name, the Indian fella, and over a drink Marshall told us about the salmon, because that's his tribe, see. That's why he has the gun because the bears aren't in his blood and he's in the wrong place and he wants to be further up north where the salmon are, so him and me, we're off. We're off together in his truck, me and him and Dolly and the gun. I'm doing the petrol and he's driving and he's happy as anything—'

I held the receiver to my hot ear and wondered whether my father had gone mad. Then I realized he was just being his mother's son with these stories: at last he was Gladys Llewelyn's conker-eyed only one.

'OK, Dad. When you get there, you'll call, right? You can't leave it so long next time.'

'Oh, sure, nutmeg.'

'Don't just call Vince, call us too.'

'Of course.'

'And where are you going exactly?'

'Where the salmon are.'

'Yeah, OK, but where is that?'

'North.'

'Just look after yourself, Dad. OK?'

'You know I will, nutmeg.'

'And you'll come home soon?'

'We both will, nutmeg, me and your mum, we'll both come home soon.'

He hung up and I sat in the dark of the hall for a long time after that.

That weekend I told Molly that we needed to get Dad back; that it was Dad we needed.

'No, Halo, *a* dad, that's what you need. For that.' She pointed at my belly.

'Oh, shut up.'

'Well it's true.' She tickled me then, she sat on me and tried to make me fart because Molly had taken to spending most of her weekends here at Rockfarm.

The day the new band arrived I decided to clean my parents' house. It had been closed up since December: waterless and draughty. Molly was here and in charge of the greeting. Vince was down too – thumbs through the sleeves of his jumper – and he was cooking because he'd taken to that. The band was called The Black and that was all I knew. Nana had taken the booking.

I stood in Dad's garden. The winter had been kind to his motorhome extension; only the plastic roof fluttered because it had come away at the join. The plastic windows were green with weather, but I couldn't go in there, not yet.

The kitchen smelled of Mum. Nana and I had cleared out the perishables, turned off the fridge, but in this still, dark house, the smell of my mother – rose talc, turmeric and cinnamon – had grown like mushrooms in a cave. I switched the fuse box on, and light flickered as the March afternoon blew on the windowpanes.

I started downstairs. Books went into neat piles; worktops and tables were dusted. I started easy. Upstairs and my mother's unmade bed: the crease of her on the old sheets, that would have to be another day. I filled the kettle and found my bleach. As my tea brewed I pushed and wiped and I forgot to think.

I didn't hear the knocking. I didn't hear the polite cough. By the time a voice spoke I was down on my knees, sorting through album covers, uniting sleeves with vinyl left dust-caked on the floor.

'Halo?'

Of course I jumped, if you can jump when you're almost seven months' pregnant.

'Halo?'

I sat up slowly; I turned round and he smiled a creased smile and stepped into the kitchen.

'What are *you* doing here?' I asked.

'I'm with the band.'

'What do you mean?'

'I'm the producer. That's what I do now. Look, let me help you—'

'No, no, it's OK. Just let me grab hold of—' I reached for a chair leg, trying to help myself up.

'No. Here.' Brendan knelt down in front of me. He put his hands under my hot armpits and lifted me. We were face to face. He was stronger than I imagined.

'I'm cleaning,' I whispered.

'I can see that.'

I looked down at the floor. I felt like a kitten, carried by its mother: limp and foolish. 'I haven't been back in here since. Since she died.'

'I'm sorry.' His hands were still gripping tight; I felt his thumb on my collarbone: firm. I tried to shrug.

'How are you, Halo?' He wouldn't let go.

'I'm fat.'

'You're not *fat*, Halo.'

All this time Brendan was staring at me, and it was one of those stares that gets you right in the eyes; it was one of those stares that makes you fretful and sweaty. I worried my armpits would give me away.

'I waited for you,' he said.

'Pardon?'

'I waited for you. In the chalet. When the fireworks went off. At Dolly's funeral, her party, last November. I waited.'

'I'm sorry. I—'

'That's OK. I don't mind waiting.'

I listened to his breath: it was loud.

'So it's not mine, then,' he said.

I laughed. 'No. No, it's not yours, Brendan.'

'Pity.'

The wind spat. I was thinking of my tea, brewing to a sludge on the counter. I was thinking I quite liked the feeling of Brendan taking just a bit of my weight.

'You can let me go, you know. I'm quite able.'

He frowned.

'I'm not going to go anywhere, Brendan. I'm cleaning.'

Over tea and soft, stale biscuits, Brendan told me about his band. He said they were young, foolish and pretty, and that nowadays, that seemed to do. He told me there was one kid, the lead guitarist, who had it. He said this kid wrote the songs and he was a genius. He said the problem was, the kid wasn't the pretty one. When Brendan laughed a vein came up on his forehead, a vein like a divining rod; he ran one hand through his auburn hair, it was to his shoulders now, and he looked down. I liked it when Brendan laughed. That afternoon we drank four pots of tea and as dark came too early, I lit up my mother's house.

'Do you know where he is, Halo? Fred I mean?'

'Not exactly.'

'The world's been worried about him for a long time now.'

'I'd know if there was anything to worry about.'

'Right. Won't he come back once you tell him?' This time Brendan didn't laugh. That divining vein on his forehead didn't appear.

'Tell him what?' I took a gulp of thick tea.

'That he's going to be a daddy.'

The house hummed; the timer on the cooker ticked. I was staring into my builder's mug, at the surface of the golden tea, almost cold now. I let the seconds go, and then I let them go some more. I tried to speak, but it didn't work. I looked up at Brendan; the oaky man on the other side of my parents' kitchen table.

He shrugged. 'It was a good guess, I suppose. My sisters said you were always sweet on him, then I saw for myself last November.' He looked away at something on the carpet: maybe a maggot or a crazy swirl. 'You think you guys'll get together in the end?'

'Don't be silly, Brendan, he's my brother.'

He did laugh this time. He laughed and the divining vein came up. He laughed and his hand ran through his hair. He laughed and he called me and the whole lot of us Llewelyns crazy.

344

'Well you can talk, the O'Boyles aren't exactly normal.'

'Ah, we are, we are.'

'Niamh, Siobhan and Aifric looked up our arses with torches when we were kids.'

'They didn't!'

'They bloody well did. And they practically raped Fred every summer.'

'Now that I can believe. I was there, remember?'

'Oh, yeah.' I nibbled a soft biscuit. 'Brendan?'

He smiled. 'What?'

'When you were a kid—'

'Yeah.'

'Did they look up your arse with a torch, too?'

'What?'

'Did they?'

This time we laughed together.

It wasn't as simple as that: not at all. Brendan had work to do and I was busy spring-cleaning. I toothbrushed between chalet tiles; I used bicarbonate of soda on the silver. Nana said I should look to the doctor, to childbirth classes, so I put on my trainers and I ran. I'd had my scans and that was enough.

Brendan came clean at last. He told me it was Molly who'd traced him, Molly who'd engineered the whole thing: him coming down with his band, though, as he pointed out, the rest of the family had helped.

I sat at the top of Beggars' Hill, exhausted. The climb really did floor me now. Molly fretted. 'What if something happens and you're halfway up?' she said. 'You are ridiculous, Halo.' I sat up there on the plastic squares Nana had given me for the piles I didn't have. I sat up there and stared through her old binoculars, I stared down at Rockfarm, at my land. I saw the budding bloom of the fruit trees. I tried to find the mounds of Crazy Love finally captured beneath concrete, and Ziggy and Stardust in the emerging green of Beggars' Field.

I came up here to read the letters Dad sometimes wrote. He had written to say he was with the salmon people, somewhere outside of Seattle. He spoke about going further north.

—Alaska and then maybe across the sea to Russia or wherever that is, nutmeg. I just have a feeling. I have a feeling your mother and I will find Fred up here, in the snow and the ice. My salmon friends, Don and Marshall (Marshall's the big Indian bloke and Don's his brother), well they tell me to listen to my dreams and follow the salmon. They're teaching me basketball too, but I think I'm too old. I'm dreaming a lot about our Robert, you know. Dolly says it's natural. Sometimes I don't know what's natural any more, by Christ. Sometimes I forget I'm dreaming. Is the studio doing well? Are you getting by? I know you won't let me down, nutmeg. Write back c/o Marshall here in Wellpinit. I might be gone by then, though.

I spread out another of Nana's plastic squares and lay back on Beggars' Hill. Speckled buzzards circled above me like I was fair game. The binoculars were heavy on the breasts I finally had, and the baby kicked. I thought of Jenny Connor riding

Stardust in the fields below me. I thought of how big she had seemed to me as a child, and I wondered if I was the same.

I'd heard from Fred. One day G-O-D the computer flashed at me in the studio, and there he was. Rhysie had to show me how to open the message because Rhysie was good with all sorts of mail. Fred was Prairieboy, so I clicked and I pressed and I read.

lo-lo. I'm sending this to ivan's email address. maybe both of you will get it. where i am is really cold but don't think I'm not thinking about you. i miss you all.

lo-lo. i heard about dad leaving. where is he? are we both lost?

tell my dear family that I'm good. I'm more than good. Keep it quiet because I like this new life. don't worry about me, I'm fine. I'm happy. first time in a long time. I've found a girl and I might settle down. even marry, like Cat Stevens says. what's the Cat's name now?

I didn't reply. I didn't tell Fred a thing.

But it was strange to think of Fred *and* my dad both out there in the cold North. I couldn't understand why anyone would want to leave Rockfarm. I reached out to each side of me and grabbed at the grass of my nana's hill; I thought of bones and skulls, of catacombs and history. I thought of oaks and wood gods: rock stars and mud.

'Je-sus—'

I rolled to one side and I saw Brendan's head below me.

'How the feck do you do it, Halo? It's nearly killed me.'

347

I smiled and he crawled the last part, one hand grabbing at couch grass. In the other hand he had a small wicker basket.

'How do you live in the country? It's dangerous.' He threw himself on the ground next to me.

'Oh, don't make a fuss.'

He took a deep breath then looked over at me. 'You having trouble there?'

I was on my side, trying to push myself up with one arm. 'I can't sit up, Bren.'

'Your sister's right, what if you rolled down this hill, Halo?'

'Don't be silly.'

'It's not being silly if you hurt yourself and it's not being silly if you hurt the baby either.'

'Don't fuss.'

'Let me get behind you.'

'I'm fine.'

Not for the first time, Brendan heaved me up into a sitting position. He stood behind me, his familiar hands gripping beneath my armpits: it seemed the only place to get a firm hold.

'Halo, you shouldn't be allowed out. You can't look after yourself.'

'Oh, shut up.'

'I will not and you have to be nice to me because I brought you lunch.' He pointed at the basket. It had a gingham cloth on top. I wanted to laugh. Brendan laid out the cloth first, then the picnic. There were small Scotch eggs. Little sandwiches with the crusts cut off. Real lemonade and red apples. He was looking at me. 'Do you mind? Can I?' He reached his hand out, palm up.

'Can you what?'

'Touch you there.' His head nodded at my belly.

348

'If you want.'

Brendan sat behind me, his stomach against my back, his legs stretched out and against my legs. Maybe he thought I was safer this way; he could catch me if I started to roll. His legs were so much longer than mine. He pulled my hair out of the way to rest his chin on my shoulder. Then he curled his arms round my side and placed his palms flat on my belly. I closed my eyes. 'There,' he whispered. 'There.'

We both felt it kick.

'It's a boy, isn't it Halo? Hmm?'

'I didn't ask.'

'I think it is.'

I listened to the buzzards keen in the wind and I looked down at Brendan's golden hands on my belly.

'Why do you like me, Brendan?' I asked.

I felt his chest tickle against me with a laugh. 'You asked me that once before, remember?'

'But why do you?'

'Because—' He cut off; it seemed like he was thinking, weighing it all up. '—because I'm a man who doesn't mind the wait.'

I leant back against him. 'But Brendan—'

'Yes?'

'It's not just me. It's me and whoever this is.' I touched my belly too, hands over his.

'I know.'

'That's weird, isn't it?'

'Is it? Your family didn't seem to mind. Your mammy didn't, did she? Your daddy didn't either.'

For a moment I had no idea what he was talking about. Then I remembered. Fred. It was Fred, our cuckoo, our foundling-pet who Brendan was thinking about. Maybe it was Dolly and her drawer too, because maybe my family had told him everything.

'But why in the hell would you want to come near *me*, Brendan?'

'You can't help who you fall in love with, Halo.'

I shivered. Brendan took one of his long pauses. My feet itched.

'Are you still in love with *him*, Halo?'

'Some days.'

'If he came back tomorrow would you want to be with him?'

'No.'

'What if he wants to come back and be a daddy and all?'

'He can be a daddy, Brendan, but he'd make *me* miserable.' My certainty shocked me. I watched the line of poplar trees near Dad's house glint and shake.

'I won't,' Brendan whispered.

'Won't what?'

'Make you miserable. I'd make you happy. It could be what I do.'

I laughed, just a little. 'That's very gallant of you, Bren.'

'I'm a gallant sort of a guy.'

I tried to turn, then thought better of it. 'I'm tired,' I told him.

A grey cloud eclipsed the buzzards and Brendan rubbed my arms. 'Halo?'

'Yes?'

'I've got to go.'

'OK.'

'No, I mean really go. We're all done here and I've got to get back home.'

I watched a car drive down our track and turn left at the

gateposts. I lifted up Brendan's hand and started to pick out the silk threads of thistle barbs from his fingertips.

Wet sand had stuck to the soles of my feet and the red bed was sprinkled with grains. Though the air in my mother's motorhome was damp, it still smelled of new. There was little of her smell in the bed because she'd hardly used it. She'd spent her time on the sofa in Dad's extension. No, this bed had just a few of her hairs, one or two flakes of her skin, and I lay there on my side holding my belly as it wriggled. I listened to the fierce March winds that made Dad's extension groan.

There was another creak: a weighty creak on the plastic steps. The motorhome door opened. I stopped breathing. I didn't breathe because I couldn't choose: did I want those gentle footsteps to be my father come home? Did I want them to be Fred's, or to be someone else's altogether? I watched the door to the bedroom open. I waited for the light behind the figure to fall on me.

It wasn't Dad because the shadow kissed me, and he kissed me in a way a father never should, though a brother might. But it wasn't Fred, and as Brendan pulled off his shirt and dragged my big nightie over my head, I was glad. Brendan slipped beneath the red sheet and he was soft. His leg hairs didn't itch and his chest was smooth. He kissed me with an open mouth, like he couldn't wait, like he was just twenty and he was hungry again.

I did most of the work. It was nice and it was impossible and it was funny. We lay there and laughed. Then Brendan switched, he was quiet, and he touched me again.

He ran a finger down my spine, he ran it further, further,

351

until he'd turned me round, lifted me up, and he was back to where he started. Brendan was serious. 'Oh fuck,' he said.

'Shh!'

'Oh fuck.'

'Shh!'

'Fucking hell. Oh—'

'Brendan—'

For a gentle man Brendan liked to swear a lot when he made love. He still does. He swore with affection and his swear words were thrills.

'Oh—'

'Shh!'

'Jesus fuck!'

'Brendan, shut up!'

'Oh, Jesus Christ. Oh, Halo. Oh, fuck.'

'Brendan, please.'

I stroked his forehead.

'You love me, don't you?' he panted, more of a command than a question. 'You do, don't you?'

I let the wind gulp and spit at us and then I told him that if he could just be quiet, then I could try.

16

If Ivan Comfort Llewelyn felt love for the first time when he was fourteen and proud of his middle name, Dolly Halcyon Palmer felt it fluttering at sixteen because she'd been pretty blank so far.

And the night Dolly felt it she was ready.

She was bathing the dirty boy in her mother's tin tub by her own caravan's gas stove, the caravan that came as a sixteenth-birthday present; a small and white home she loved more than the nameless dogs that flocked the fairground after dark.

Dolly plunged her hand into the brown water. 'What's your name?' she said because she realized she'd forgotten her manners and asked this boy to strip before the niceties.

There was something about him, there was no denying that: he made her do things back to front, in the wrong order. There were also his eyes: conker-coloured, a rich brown you might drown in.

She plunged her hand in again, squeezed out the sponge, and the boy blushed. He didn't blush because he was naked; he blushed because he was finding it hard to speak in front of this girl.

'It's Ivan,' he coughed.

'Ivan.' She tried it out on her tongue, like she would a new shoe on her neat foot. 'Is that all?' she asked, because Dolly Halcyon Palmer didn't like dull names.

'No.'

Dolly lifted up the boy's arm and scrubbed with the sponge. She was surprised to find hair there: soft red hair that made her blush.

'My whole name is Ivan Comfort Llewelyn,' he said and Dolly shivered. 'That's what my mam calls me.'

'And your father?' she asked, hiding her face in his soapy armpit.

'I don't know. I don't have one of those. Not one I can remember anyway.' Ivan stopped his mouth: suddenly it was too easy to talk to this girl. Dolly lifted his other arm and scrubbed.

It was terribly soft, that sponge, and the girl's weight leaning in on him was thrilling. That was when Ivan thanked God and Mary and little Jesus and the whole bloody troupe of spirits his mam kept hidden in her house, he thanked them for the heavy frothing bubbles that foamed on the surface of the water: the bubbles that were covering him now.

Ivan closed his eyes. 'What's your name?' he whispered into her hair, though he knew already, he just wanted to hear her say it.

'Dolly. Dolly Halcyon Palmer. Under now.'

'What?'

'Under the water.'

Ivan did what he was told, though he made sure to try and cover his secret parts with his hands; the parts not even his mam had seen (at least not recently). Under that water he felt Dolly push his chest down and that print of her hand was as hot as a pan of coals.

He blew bubbles underwater and wished on every popping one. He let her hold him under as her other hand moved through the hair on his head, his thick, dark red hair he could never keep still, not even with Brylcreem.

Ivan came up. Baptized.

He came up a man, he thought, and he opened his eyes to hers. Hers were black eyes, and as this girl knelt, he saw something in them. He couldn't say what it was, like he couldn't say why he'd been sleeping in the open mouth of a tent at a fair run by a midget woman.

At that moment Ivan stood up. The sound of water rushing off his skin and into the tin tub woke Dolly a little, and she reached for the big white towel. But something stopped her. She looked. She looked up at this boy-who-clearly-wasn't-a-boy: she looked at this red-headed lad who had done with blushing and stammering and who now stood before her tall and handsome and a little crazy in the eyes. He was so much more than the boys and the men she skipped away from on the wasteland; he was so much more than the fellas she sometimes dreamt of.

She finally stood and wrapped the white towel around his hips, and their skin touched. And the moment the front of Dolly's blouse pressed into the boy's wet and flat stomach, the gas rings of her gas oven blasted on, sure and strong.

Ivan started.

'Oh, it's always doing that,' Dolly lied. 'Don't worry.' She took another towel, asked him to step out, and began to dry him, feet first.

Ivan found a spot on the ceiling. He gazed up and his eyes didn't move from that tiny damp mark until he found himself being doused with talcum powder that smelled of roses.

'All done,' she said, and, exhausted, Dolly Halcyon Palmer crawled over to her small single bed, lay down, and fell asleep.

So the first night that Ivan Comfort Llewelyn stayed in Dolly Halcyon Palmer's caravan at the Dolls' Fair in Tiger Bay, he couldn't believe his luck. He was warm. He was clean. He literally smelled of roses. He closed his eyes between the cool sheets on the camp bed that Dolly had made up, and he touched his new body.

Her name was Dolly. Dolly Halcyon Palmer. He'd found out that much as he slept beneath the flaps of the tent. Tonight he had found out so much more.

Dolly Halcyon Palmer's favourite novel was *Wuthering Heights*.

She first read it at the only school she stayed at long enough to finish a book. A school in a place she couldn't remember now, but she would always remember the teacher. A Miss Grey who had told Dolly, 'Read this. I think you'll like it,' and every week after that Miss Grey had given Dolly a list, a list for the library, and Dolly consumed it. By the time the Dolls' Fair left that nameless town, Dolly had decided never to go back to school, but to always, always, have a library card.

Dolly was a romantic, but she liked to look at things skewed, so she preferred Heathcliff to Mr Darcy. She even preferred him to Edward Fairfax Rochester because Rochester only got Dolly going when he sounded like Heathcliff, when he raged and talked in riddles. Dolly thought Rochester was a bit soft, and in the end, tamed.

Ivan Comfort wasn't Heathcliff, though. Ivan was red for a start, not black-eyed and devilish. Ivan was kind and almost a boy and sometimes Dolly thought he was as gentle as Edgar Linton. But it was because of Ivan that Dolly understood it was best to keep men like Heathcliff on the page. Keep them on the page or at the back of the queue, keep them in your dreams, or at least don't let them grow up.

Boy-Heathcliffs and girl-Cathys are manageable, she thought, but if you let them grow they'll kill you.

At the very beginning, though, in the days and the months and the few years after that first tin-tub bath in her caravan, she and Ivan Comfort *were* Cathy and Heathcliff as girl and boy. They didn't have a Penistone Crag or an endless heathered moor, but they were young enough to chase each other on the fairground wasteland. They were game enough to throw stones at seagulls down at the Cardiff docks and get chased by the Somali sailors. They were impish enough to nick lipsticks and throat lozenges from Boots the Chemist in whatever town they'd pitched up in. They were frustrated enough to pinch each other's flesh and tug each other's hair, like only a Heathcliff and a Cathy would: like they *really* meant it. And so most nights they'd come back to the pitch bruised, strands of red or black hair caught on their fingernails, and their pockets filled with make-up and sour sweets they'd throw in the council bins.

Of course Dolly didn't think like this exactly, she just knew she wanted to touch the boy as much as he wanted to touch her, and so they waited and while they waited they pulled each other's hair out.

Dolly kept *Wuthering Heights* by her small bedside table in her very own caravan (she'd slipped the hardback copy into her knickers at a WH Smith in another nameless town). She read and re-read it and made Ivan swear he'd never run off. She also vowed never to title-tattle, never to criticize him, even when her own mother did.

'Red-headed bugger, hanging about the place. When's he

going to sling his hook and get off home, gel?' Minny would ask.

Home. Ivan Comfort had almost forgotten about home. The spell of Dolly and the fairground was too strong. He'd just left. After a month he'd written his mam a postcard. After three months he called her. After a year his postcards started to come back to him with 'no longer at this address' in Gladys Llewelyn's writing. Still he moved only with the fair, with Dolly, because Ivan Comfort was waiting.

He was waiting for this brother-and-sister malarkey to be well and truly over. Ivan Comfort was a romantic too, but he was a practical boy who was becoming a man.

Of course when it happened, once Dolly got past eighteen and Ivan clawed at sixteen, it all seemed much easier.

It happened one night when Ivan couldn't play any more. It happened the night after he'd pinned Dolly down in the wasteland and just stared at her, until she could no longer breathe. It happened when he'd taken that bloody book *Wuthering Heights* from her bedside table and burnt it in a brazier with the rest of the day's rubbish.

That night he knocked on her caravan door with a bunch of dog daisies he'd picked, and an apology on his lips; but that never came out. She let him in, and then she let her thin dress drop on the caravan's shagpile. Ivan retched. He retched because the desire that had turned his belly over and over for two whole years – since that first day in the queue, since that first night under the Tiger Bay stars in the gaping mouth of that tent – that crazy, burning desire was now thrashing and tumbling out with the beauty he saw in front him: quite simply, it made him sick.

He found making love to Dolly was easier than looking.

It was easier than the nausea. It was also easier than pulling her hair and pinching her perfect skin (though there were purple bruises still, but these weren't the same; Ivan gave these in a different way). And as he moved inside Dolly it was so much easier than anything that had gone before: it was easier than his mother's squares of cake, easier than the first time he heard the blues, it was easier than leaving the farm and trying not to think of it again.

Making love to Dolly Halcyon Palmer – that night and every night since – was easier just because it was right.

When Dolly's periods stopped, that was easier too. As her belly grew, the fair huddled in to comfort her as much as the boy she'd sworn herself to: as much as that real Comfort, Ivan Llewelyn.

'Robert. We'll call him Robert if it's a boy,' he said one night, as they shared her single bed, 'after Robert Johnson.'

'Who's he?' Dolly asked.

'The greatest guitar player in the world.'

And that was all Ivan told her.

Of course much later Dolly would spend a good few years blaming her Ivan for this name. Blaming him for not filling her in completely, for not telling her all about her first son's namesake: about that ambitious, gifted Delta boy at the crossroads, about that guitar-picking genius who simply disappeared. And for reasons Dolly couldn't bear to hear.

PART FOUR:

2006

1

Telegrams are strange things: blank brief tellings in type. A death. A marriage. An announcement on a tissue-thin strip. Ours was no different.

'How can you be one hundred years old, Nana?'

'Easy, Halo. Stay alive.'

I looked across the kitchen table at her and she wasn't a bag of skin, in fact my nana was as fit and portly as ever, her face lined but firm. I wondered what she'd been taking to preserve her like that: bat's liver perhaps, or voodoo lily on toast.

'But Nana, why didn't you say?'

'Why should I?'

'Well, I thought it was just a normal party.'

'It will be, sunbeam.'

Evan reached up and snatched a Welsh cake. 'Big Nana, you're a hundred. That's *so* old. You're a hundred and you're having a party.' Currants and crumbs filled his mouth.

I touched my youngest son's auburn hair; Evan was a conker-eyed lad like his father, and his grandfather. 'Evan, close your mouth.'

He smiled, lips closed, and Nana laughed.

'Well the boy's right, Halo. Come here, sunshine.' She held out her soft, sagging arms and Evan walked into them, willingly. They were each other's favourites, a woman a hundred years old and her great-grandson. She rubbed his back, patted his small bum and said, 'Now Evan, you know how your Nana stays so young, don't you?'

I saw a shake of auburn hair in the mass of Nana's skin.

'It's because your Nana's only as old as the man she feels,' and she slapped his bum again.

He giggled. 'Gerroff, Nana!'

'And I've got me some pixie dust – I'll be younger before the day's out, you know.'

Evan wriggled, kissed her and ran out into the back garden; he ran to his older brother and little sister who were kicking balls about on the shimmering grass.

Nana shook her jaw, her dentures loose. 'You got everything together for tomorrow, sunbeam?'

'Yes Nana, you know I have.'

'They're all coming, aren't they?'

'Course they are, Nana.'

'Tell me.'

I stood up and grabbed a knife. 'Here, take this. You chop, I'll tell.' I kept an eye on her chopping hand, just in case. 'So there's me and Brendan and Tigue and Evan and Bella.'

'You lot live here, sunbeam. I'm not daft.'

'All right. There's Molly and Jamie—'

'I said I wasn't daft, they live here too.'

'We don't know that.'

'They *will*.'

My ancient grandmother would be right, she usually was. Molly and her only son Jamie moved in with us soon after Nana's party. Molly and Jamie came; Dorian didn't.

'And Dad's here already. He says he's staying with us for the whole month.'

'Good.'

'The rest of the O'Boyles are coming tomorrow.'

'Yes.'

'All your friends from round here have replied to Rhysie.'

'Yes.'

'Vince and Lieb are flying in from New York tomorrow.'

'Yes.'

'And that's all I know about, but you did the invites Nana, there's bound to be millions more.'

'Not millions, lovely, but the few. And the few will be here, sunbeam, you can count on that.' She winked.

'A few we can do.'

'And there's Fred.'

I glanced up at my nana's walls; the Johnny and the Elvis pictures were greasy, yellow in fact. She wouldn't let me take them down. I cut through a garlic head and saw the Beloveds' altar, crowded now because so many others had joined them. There was a beautiful photograph of Dolly there, caught mid-laugh. There was one of Grandma Min too, dressed up in a Stars and Stripes outfit, neat and prim and standing next to her Carlos, who was sitting. Grandma Min died a year after Tigue was born. There was also a photograph of Princess Diana on the Beloveds' altar; there was one of June Carter and a big bright one of Johnny Cash, too.

'Yes, there's Fred,' I said.

'You did invite him, didn't you, sunbeam?'

'Of course I did, Nana. But you know Fred.'

'I do.' Her big teeth dropped for a moment: my nana's mouth was shrinking. 'Think I'll pop back home, just for a rest, lovely.'

'Need any help?'

'I do not.'

Nana stood and a new generation of collies stood with her: her black-and-white humbug pack. Nana leant on her stick but she walked rod-straight and out through the hall. 'You get it all done tonight, sunbeam, then it won't seem like such a task tomorrow!' she yelled.

'OK, Nana.' I put my knife down.

'And remember, if I don't see you through the week—'

'Yeah, I know, you'll see me through the window!'

When my grandmother left this Big House, it became mine. When she walked out across the lawn, past the self-seeding peacocks and the rotted stumps of a long-forgotten croquet game, this kitchen table became my own.

I'd taken down the black-faced miners from her hall. I'd wrapped her crystal ball in cotton wool and put it in the attic along with her jars of special teas and poisons and more besides. Nana had moved over to Dad's house, to my childhood home, the gatehouse, because she got smaller and we got bigger. She didn't mind. She said it was simple logic.

I sat at what was now my kitchen table – the big oak-grained table – while the white Rayburn bulged like a bloated whale from one end of the kitchen and my mother's old stainless-steel cooker glinted from the other. I watched the heads of my three children, as they rose and fell above the sill of the window. Their black, auburn, and blonde heads bounced and their hair stuck up in the air, electric. They yelped like puppies, my children, and I saw Brendan climb up and join them: their daddy jumping and squawking with them on the big trampoline.

*

I lie in my bed most nights and hear only the crickets and the grass-rustle of Nana's sheep. I hear the trailing tails of the peacocks on the lawn, and the thuds of the baby owls as they fall from the cedar. These are the sounds of Rockfarm because Brendan's soundproofing of the studio works better than Dad's did.

I listen to my children sleep; I like to keep their doors open. I listen to the grandmother clock tick-tock in the hall below, and sometimes I hear the Moonlight Dog Boy pad-pad and whimper up my stairs. Nana took her brick dust and her dried-up cat foetuses with her when she left; anyone can walk in and up the stairs of the Big House now. Tonight, I'm listening out, just in case. We know the sound of those footsteps. Brendan has an ear for them, as does Tigue. The new tawny owls screech and click from the cedar and the peacocks blast their mournful cry, but I keep an ear to the hallway, alert as any farm cat.

'Is he coming, Mum?'

I tightened my dressing gown and flicked on the kettle. I looked down at Tigue, my eldest and the copy of his seal-eyed father.

'I don't know, sweetheart.'

He shrugged and stabbed the butter with a bread knife. 'It doesn't matter, Mum. Fred's like that, isn't he?'

'Yes, he is.' I smiled at Tigue. I mushed his black hair and he frowned with eyes that sometimes, in a certain light, were violet.

'Don't Mum, my hair!'

'Sorry.'

'It's my hair.'

367

'OK.'

'You seen Dad?'

'He's up in the studio.'

Tigue bit into his buttery toast. 'Mum, the new band are so cool. They mash. Like me.'

'What's that love?'

'Oh, Mum, you're such a fuddy-duddy. I'm going up to see Dad. See you later' – and he ran out through the hall with too much toast in his hands.

'Don't bother them, Tigue! Remember, they are musicians!'

'Don't fuss, Mum!' he yelled back.

Tigue's sprints were faster than mine, and he'd always sprint to Brendan. His sneakers squeaked on the Victorian tiles and I knew he'd be up in the courtyard in less than a minute, toast and butter down his T-shirt.

Vince and Lieb were upstairs, showering and whatever-ing. Vince had lived in New York for years now, and he was almost famous: almost famous around 15th Street at least. He played the piano and crooned in the way that only Vince could, and I visited him in between babies, resident bands, and Brendan, because I missed my eldest brother the most. In New York, I ran in Central Park. I ran around the reservoir like Dustin Hoffman did in *Marathon Man*. I slept like a baby in my brother's crisp, white Martha Stewart sheets. Vince would always be fascinated by New York. He was like a kid with a stick poking at an ants' nest. Over the years, I had come to love the city, too, and Vince was pleased; he said it was a wonder to get me to leave Rockfarm at all.

Before Lieb, when Vince lived alone and Tigue was walking and talking (so I could leave him with Brendan and Nana Lew),

I boarded an aeroplane for the first time in my life, and I visited my older brother. That was when Vince told me the best secret, the one he'd been keeping until last.

We were lying in his bed, me listening to the squeals of the Chicano transvestites on the street below. We were both staring up at the golden blades of Vince's ceiling fan, watching as our faces blurred and merged. It was late and we were drunk and a little high. Vince turned onto his side, the bed shook, and he nestled his chin into my neck and whispered, 'Have you found him yet, Halo?'

I waited for two turns of the fan above us. 'Have you?'

'Don't be like that. I just want to know.'

'He writes sometimes on the email thing. He's still here in America, I think.'

Vince sighed. It was one of those sighs that could leave a small man half there. 'I miss him, Halo.'

'Me too.'

'But I love him, Halo.'

'Yeah, I know, Vince. Me too.'

'No you don't. You've got Brendan now.'

The blades of the fan cut the air up above us, and a fire engine blasted out a confused song from somewhere across town.

Vince's hand moved to find my hand. 'I can't live without him, I can't, Halo,' he told me, and I watched my reflection on the blade as it was dragged out, contorted, next to the big lump of my brother. That was when I knew. I watched the fan turn, once more, twice more.

'When was it, Vince?'

'Only once, after Mum died.'

369

I tried to picture it: Fred and Vince together. Vince and Fred in the rhubarb tunnels. I wondered if Vince had been a virgin too, like me. I didn't have to wonder who made the first move.

'Have you spoken to him since?'

'No. Not really.'

'He—'

'Don't, Halo, don't say it.'

'What? That he screwed us both? But he did Vince, didn't he?' I watched the blades, suddenly angry. 'I mean, do you think it was only us? What about Molly? What about Nana, Mum, Dad—'

'Halo!'

I laughed, because I couldn't sigh like Vince. Not any more. I couldn't sigh like my big brother who had been cut in two by Fred's loving arms sure as the air was being cut by the fan above us. Vince's breath smelled of milk and his tears stung my neck, but I let him cry because Fred had forgotten to slide those two cut halves of my big brother together again. Fred's fingers had worked magic, but they were lethal. Butchers' fingers: pianist fingers, playing at cutting us all up.

That night in New York I reached out to the wall and I turned off the fan. I listened to Vince's gulps and the cockerel laughs of the girl-boys down on the street. I watched city shadows morph on the apartment's walls. They were the kind of shadows that could have been anything; they could have been anything at all.

I line the chairs up first. Nana wants them in front of the Big House's pillars. She wants us neat and sitting, the wisteria heady behind us.

'Here?' Brendan asks. He's holding a stack of heavy oak chairs. His strong arms are golden in the sunlight. He puts the chairs down and I turn around and I kiss him.

'Hey—'

'What?'

'Nothing, just surprised me, that's—'

I kiss him again, little soft kisses until his mouth opens and his golden arm is down my back. My husband still swears blue murder in our bed. He swears wherever we find ourselves, because I still like to sleep around the place like a cat. Brendan swears, he curses, and I've grown to like it. I've grown to depend upon it.

'Oh get a room,' Vince tells us. 'Is this where we all are?'

I wipe my mouth and nod.

'Just because your husband's so bloody handsome, Halo.'

'Oh and yours isn't?'

Vince smiles. 'He is sort of cute, isn't he?'

'Oh, don't be so American, Vince. You and Bren put the banner up, will you?'

'Yes, ma'am!' Brendan salutes.

'Come on Brendan, before she thinks of something else.'

'Hang it between the pillars!' I yell after them.

Vince is right. Lieb is cute. Very cute. The photographer has put him on the end of the row, but Nana moves him next to her. She likes Lieb. Vince stands behind him, hands on his shoulders, and Lieb has a hand on one of his. The children are lined up, legs crossed, on cushions on the gravel. They frown, stones stabbing their ankles. It's Tigue who has the troop under control.

371

'Stop fidgeting, Bella!'

'I'm not—'

'Evan, sit still!'

Tigue, the older brother: Tigue, who'll look after us all.

The banner says 'NANA LEW IS A 100!' It's simple, right to the point, and Nana loves it because the children made it. We stencilled the letters and they spent the afternoon painting them in with bright red, Bella's favourite colour. The rope that holds one end of the banner up has slipped a little down the left pillar, so it's at an angle, but that doesn't matter.

Molly has Brendan behind her because I asked him. A few of the O'Boyles are here and Niamh and Nuala are sitting next to Molly. Niamh's two girls are sitting down next to their cousins. We've roped in the resident band, Snow Children, to make up the numbers, and as Nana said, they're handsome lads so they'll make a pretty picture. Dad and Rhysie are sitting next to each other though there are three empty seats between Nana and Dad, and further on, an empty seat at the very end of the row, next to Fred.

Fred came up the drive in a black cab two hours ago. We paid the fare and he had a nap. Tigue is cross-legged at Fred's feet and it is uncanny: even their hair is the same length, just to the shoulder and perfect. The one difference, I think, is the weasel look. Tigue doesn't have it; Fred still does, but I'm a mother and I would say that. Fred has his hands on Tigue's shoulders and he's smiling, like a fisherman showing off the biggest catch. Fred will stay a week, maybe two. He will stay and Brendan will bristle, but it's OK. In a family where Crazy Love has to be buried again and again, where red capes hold the most precious of things, a little bristling is good.

The empty seat the other side of Fred is not because he's unpopular, it's not because all those years wandering have got him out of the habit of a good soapy wash. In fact there are empty seats all about the place in our family portrait, and these are the few my nana was talking about.

She knew they'd come. I wasn't so sure.

The photographer keeps crouching and looking through his camera: he's not keen on the empty chairs; he says there are enough people to fill them all, what about all those standing at the back? Why can't they just sit down?

I can't tell him the empty seats are taken, so I shrug and say that's the way my grandmother wants it, and after all she is one hundred years old. I let him click his camera, but I take my own pictures, too. I don't want to be in the frame, at least not yet.

'Are you done, sunbeam?' Nana yells. 'You've got to come and sit down.' Her church hat shifts down her forehead.

'I'm not sitting, Nana! I'm going to stand next to Bren. I'm tall enough.'

'Just hurry up, Halo!'

But I can't, because I want to take more photographs. I want to click my camera again and again over what I see, because for the first time in many years I can see them. I can see them as I press the viewfinder to my face and look.

There they are.

By Lieb at one end, there are the three Beloveds, my Great-Uncles with a capital *Grrrr*: Dai, Jim and Albert Llewelyn in their uniforms, but with the buttons shiny in the sun and their puttees clean and newly wrapped. There's not a mark on them, all limbs and eyes and noses are present and correct. They wink at me.

Between Nana Lew and Dad are Grandma Min, my mother, and my big brother Robert. Grandma Min has a hand on my mother's arm, and Mum is holding Robert's hand. I can see Mum is trying to reach over and touch Dad too, but it's hard. She frowns, and Min – small, her legs dangling mid-air from the chair – taps her fingers on my Bella's head. Bella looks up and giggles, but it's Robert I can't take my eyes off.

Robert who is just a little older than Tigue; Robert my brother who I hardly remember; Robert in a brown Humble Pie T-shirt; Robert who is so young, that at last he breaks my heart.

I click.

But there's the other empty seat, the one at the very end of the row, next to Fred, the empty seat that isn't empty at all. I'm clicking away so fast, trying to grab at what I see. I know I have saved the best until last, because Jenny Connor is laughing and she's waving at me. She's gazing at Fred, too, and then down at Tigue at his feet. I hear a prairie giggle, a whisper of a yee-haw. I hold the camera to one eye, because it's easier this way. It's just what I see: it's what I see now. They are all waving, and once again, I click.

'Come on, Mum, you've got to be in the picture. Come on!' Tigue shouts.

An emerald peacock strides across the gravel in front of my family, and once again, I click.

All the boys are bouncing on the trampoline and all of them are full of Nana's cake. Even Brendan, even Fred; even Uncle Vincent is jumping, though he makes the small ones bounce too high when he lands. Lieb's on the trampoline too, delicate Uncle Lieb who looks more like a son to Vince than a husband.

From the kitchen window I watch the hair on their heads fly up, electric, as I wait for Bella.

Bella my youngest: Bella with strange blonde hair who is nothing like me or Brendan and somehow that makes her special.

'I'm ready, Mummy.'

'OK, coming.'

'Ready Mummy!'

I go down on all fours like a collie and I crawl beneath my grandmother's kitchen table. That's where Bella is. We lay head to head and she tells me the stories of the grim grain faces in the thick oak above us. She knows them all.

'That one's Percy and he was caught in the river, and he couldn't swim, not like us, so he was in the water and he drownded and then he was frozen in the pole.'

'Did Nana tell you this?'

'No, she can't get under here, Mummy, don't be silly. She's one hundred now. It was Percy who told me that.'

'Oh.'

'Granny was talking to me last night.'

'And what did Nana say?'

'No Mummy, not Big Nana, Granny Dolly.'

I stared up at the frozen Percy. 'And what did Granny Dolly say?'

'She told me about her fair and how lovely it was and she told me about how when she was very little she was born in a drawer.'

'She didn't.'

'She did. And she was a beautiful lady, Mummy. Not like you.'

'Oh, thanks, darling.'

'But she was *really* beautiful, like a princess, and I wished I looked like her.'

'You, Bella, look like yourself and that's good enough. Anyway you know you're gorgeous.'

She giggled. 'You're funny, Mummy.'

'We're all funny, darling. We're all hysterical.'

She giggled some more. 'And the boys, I saw the boys yesterday and they came out for the picture.'

'What boys, darling?'

'You know, Nana's beluff-ids. Those boys. They wear uniforms, they're all brothers and they call me Daisy.'

'Oh.'

'Yeah and they're better than *my* brothers because they talk to me.'

'That's nice.'

'Mummy?'

'Yes.'

'When you were little, did *you* talk to them?'

'Yes. I did, Bella, I did.'

The collies are circling and a child is crying outside. It's Evan, my conker-eyed middle child, and Vincent's saying, 'Sorry, oh I'm so sorry.' I can hear Fred laugh his high-pitched laugh as Tigue says, 'Don't laugh at him, Fred, you wouldn't like it if Uncle Vincent fell on you.'

Nana is walking up to the studio with the band, Snow Children. The rest of her guests have arrived. She will party all night with them, into her one-hundred-and-first year. Rhysie and Fred and Brendan are holding Nana up as they move up the track. Lieb and Vince are putting the children to bed in the Big House.

376

I walk along the lawn, past the peacocks: the children love to put the tail feathers in their buttonholes, their hair. I pass the English Bastard's big gateposts with no gate, and I stare across the track at my parents' old house. The upstairs windows are dark, but it's all on downstairs. Nana likes her electric, she says it's because she went so long without, so she'll always leave a light on and never mind the bloody planet. I start to walk up to the studio, but I stop and I turn. I see my father in our old back garden and he's sitting on the front steps of the motorhome. The extension he built with so much love has long rotted away, though there is sand still – in the grass – if you run your fingers through it, if you know what you're looking for. Dad throws what's left of his tea into the nearby nettles and he stands, stretches, and shakes his rooster crest like age hasn't touched him. Dad will be sixty-four next birthday. He just stands there, still for a while, and then he smiles; it's such a huge smile that I look for someone in the garden. He's smiling at something he recognizes, then he steps out of the way, as if he's letting someone by. My father opens the motorhome door, but again, as if he's letting someone in first. Even from this distance I hear him sigh, and then he goes in himself. But before he closes the door, he pops his head out and he sees me. My father laughs and he waves, and then he slams the plastic door on his little patch of wasteland.

On my way up to the courtyard and the crash of electric guitar, I think of how I came into the world to music: to black Marshall amps, the crash of golden cymbals, and goose grease. As I walk under the brick arch, past the duck pond and the scratching chickens, I listen to the children's horses whinny and I stop, put my hands together, and I pray.

'Dear God and Robert Johnson and Charley Patton and Otis Redding, and John Lennon and Elvis Presley and Sam Cooke and Marvin Gaye, and Janis and Gram and Jimi and Dear Jenny Connor and our Dolly Halcyon Palmer-Llewelyn, please. Please keep us safe tonight. Keep us all in this place for this one night.

'Keep us all safe here at Rockfarm.'

STALLION BOYS

(Jenny Connor)

They come from the prairie,
Oh them colts they sure are wired,
While the whining tall grass sings wild licks,
Like a steel guitar on fire.

Stallion boys kick like whiskey,
They'll squeal like a woman, too,
Them boys need it a-all so bad
They can't see for blue.

Driving through the night, they cried
Driving all night wo-oh all night
They need it all so bad
Those boys can't see for blue

Stallion boys are in town tonight
Stallion boys are gonna drink and fight
Put up your bucks on the barrelhead son
Five card stud, bet yourself some fun
There's a pretty girl looking out for you
Stallion boy, see what you can do
You stallion boy, see what you can do

Acknowledgements

Thanks go to Philip Gwyn Jones, Aidan O'Neill, and everyone at Portobello Books for a great year. Huge thanks to my agent, Veronique Baxter at David Higham Associates. Thanks also to Markus Naegele at Heyne in Germany, and in Holland, thank you to Manon Miltenburg at Nijgh & Van Ditmar, Vivian de Gier and Rene van Veen. In Australia, thank you to Miranda Van Asch and Kelly Fagin at Allen and Unwin.

Thanks to the families and friends out there, big thanks to Laurence McGovern and Joan Graham.

And Fritz, the book, the songs wouldn't be possible without you. We miss you. If I don't see you through the week, I'll see you through the window.

www.tiffanymurray.com
www.myspace.com/fredconnor
www.writebythesea.com